DREAMING OF TOMORROW

Daisy Buckland has returned to her native Swansea and awaits the birth of her child while Josie Jenkins, parted from her adored husband Stan, aims to create a respectable home. When her twin sister Francie confesses she is pregnant by an unnamed man, Josie has to sort out the mess and find a home when their bullying father, Reuben, puts them out on the street. The deep and sustaining friendship between Daisy and Josie is a great support to both of them in the dark days of World War Two and the difficult years beyond.

DREAMING OF TOMORROW

DREAMING OF TOMORROW

by
Doreen Edwards

Magna Large Print Books
Long Preston, North Yorkshire,
England.

British Library Cataloguing in Publication Data.

Edwards, Doreen
   Dreaming of tomorrow.

   A catalogue record for this book is
   available from the British Library

   ISBN 0-7505-1312-8

First published in Great Britain by Judy Piatkus (Publishers)
Ltd., 1997

Copyright © 1997 by Doreen Edwards

Cover illustration © David Browne by arrangement with Artist
Partners

The moral right of the author has been asserted

Published in Large Print 1999 by arrangement with Piatkus
Books Ltd.

Magna Large Print is an imprint of
Library Magna Books Ltd.
Printed and bound in Great Britain by
T.J. International Ltd., Cornwall, PL28 8RW.

To my mother Mabel Govier
whose love, faith and encouragement
have sustained me throughout.

Prologue

Mumbles, Swansea June 1945

Being madly in love, Daisy Buckland decided, was the most rejuvenating thing in the world. She felt she'd lost ten of her twenty-seven years. She was like a young girl again, intoxicated with excitement, bursting with energy. There was a sense of walking on air. She even suspected that if she tried, she'd fly like a bird.

She felt excitement, bubbling up in her throat like laughter, at the memory of sitting in church with Rhodri earlier that morning, holding hands tightly while the banns for their wedding were called. She'd felt him trembling and had such a rush of tenderness towards him. He was the best of men, her Rhodri, and in three weeks' time she'd be his wife at last. Her heartbeat skipped at the thought of being Rhodri's wife for ever and ever.

Still up there on cloud nine, Daisy opened the back door and breezed into the big kitchen of *Tŷ Heulwen,* her stepmother's guest house overlooking the wide sweep of Swansea Bay, with its magnificent views across the stretch of open sea to the faint mauve hills of Devon.

'Hello, Mam. I'm back at last, see. Rhodri wanted to talk after church, and plan. You know what he's like, don't you? There's good of you to look after Valerie for me, but I wish you could've been there to hear my banns called.'

Teapot in hand, Edie Philpots turned from the stove.

'Sit down a minute, Daisy lovey. There's something I have to tell you.'

Daisy felt her elation abruptly checked by the strangeness of her stepmother's tone, and the strained look on her face. Her heart lurched in panic, and her first thought was for her little daughter, Valerie, two years old yesterday.

'Valerie! Oh, God, Mam!' Daisy clapped her hands over her mouth. 'Has something happened to Valerie? Don't tell me there's been an accident?'

'No, no, lovey. Nothing like that. Valerie's safe in the gardens with the children. No, there's been a telegram from the Admiralty.'

Daisy's panicky thoughts skipped immediately to Gareth, her stepbrother, the apple of Edie's eye. Daisy knew her stepmother had lived in daily dread since he'd gone off to fight in 1942. Now the War in Europe was over it would be a bitter tragedy indeed if something had happened to him just when the fighting might be over soon.

Daisy quickly stretched out a hand to her stepmother.

'Mam, don't tell me it's Gareth?'

A tremor passed across Edie's face before she shook her head.

'No, the telegram is for you, Daisy. Mam-gu saw the telegraph boy knocking at your door earlier this morning. She brought it to me. I opened it, lovey. I thought it best.'

Daisy felt nonplussed. There had to be some mistake.

'The Admiralty? I wonder why that is, then, Mam? I mean, Gerald's been dead two years now. Why would they get in touch with me again after all this time?'

Two years, but it seemed a life time ago since she'd received the telegram telling her her sailor husband had been lost at sea. That was a painful, unhappy time for her, a time of grief and uncertainty, when all she'd had to sustain her, her only symbol of hope, was the promise of the child she was carrying.

But that was all ancient history, wasn't it? Now there was Rhodri and the love they shared, the love that made her feel warm and cherished and safe; the love that made her pulses race and her head spin with happiness. She didn't know now what she'd do without it.

Edie sat down at the table, taking Daisy's hand in hers. Her eyes were glistening with tears and her lips were trembling.

Daisy looked at her stepmother, suddenly frightened again, seeing the look of deep compassion on her face.

'Daisy lovey, Gerald is alive. The Russians found him in a prisoner-of-war camp in Poland. He's been there since 1943.'

Daisy could only stare speechlessly, hardly able to take in Edie's words. Her husband was alive? How could he be? They'd told her he was dead. She had grieved for him. She'd been lonely, lost, until Rhodri came into her life.

11

'Gerald was handed over to the British last month. He was demobbed three days ago,' Edie went on. 'He's been sent home to Yorkshire.'

As the truth began to sink in Daisy gripped the edge of the table and held on, feeling suddenly dizzy and confused. Her husband was alive! He couldn't be. She was going to marry her darling Rhodri in three weeks' time!

An icy coldness rose up from her feet, numbing her legs, freezing her belly. It rose up and up, touching her heart like the cold hand of death.

'Oh, God, Mam.'

'Now Daisy lovey, this is a shock for you, I know, but you mustn't give way.'

Daisy could only stare at her stepmother in dismay. How could this mistake have happened? But what did that matter now? It was the consequences of that mistake which were truly appalling. She'd thought herself a widow for two years. She'd let herself fall in love again, really in love, a kind of love she'd never known before, not even with Gerald; the kind of love she'd never believed she'd find.

And Rhodri! Daisy felt her heart turn over with anguish. He loved her so very much; she had no doubt about his feelings for both of them, Valerie and herself. And the child adored him, too. They were so wonderful together, like father and daughter. Now he would be cut off from them, and Valerie wouldn't understand why she couldn't be with him. They were no longer his family, as he liked to call the two of them. This would be a terrible blow for him;

he'd be devastated, heartbroken. Daisy let out a whimper of despair at the thought of the pain she must inflict on him. He didn't deserve it. Neither did she.

Overwhelmed, she burst into tears. Edie rose immediately and put her arms around her, holding her tight. Daisy clung to her stepmother, desperate for that comforting embrace.

Her happiness was disintegrating before her eyes, her world turning upside down. In the space of a few minutes her picture of the future was completely changed. Instead of the longed-for happiness as Rhodri's wife, she faced bitter disappointment, heartache and uncertainty. It was frightening, to realise she didn't know what lay ahead now, for her or her child.

What she'd felt for Gerald in those crazy years in London, with every minute having to be lived to the full in case it was your last, was now so vague in her mind it wasn't even a memory. Had they really loved each other or had they merely been swept along by the urgency of living in a war-torn city, carried away by the danger, the close proximity of death that haunted every fighting man and his loved ones? How could it have been real love when she couldn't even remember how she'd felt?

And why hadn't Gerald written to her after he'd been released? What was the meaning of his silence? If it weren't for the Admiralty telegram, she'd have gone on believing herself a widow.

It was like a bad dream. Her breath almost stopped for a moment as Edie's words echoed in her mind once more. *Gerald is alive.* She couldn't believe it. She didn't want to believe it.

Daisy was appalled at her own thoughts. Surely, even in the anguish of her loss of a life with Rhodri, she wouldn't wish Gerald dead? She felt deep shame at the thought, and the tears flowed faster. Of course she was glad he had survived, but his living put an end to her happiness. It was cruel—cruel for all of them. Perhaps even more terrible for Gerald. He was coming home to a wife who no longer loved him. That was a bitter fate after all he must have suffered.

She felt a sob choke her.

'Look at me, Mam. I'm crying not because my poor husband isn't dead but because he's alive. Oh there's awful, isn't it, Mam? What kind of woman am I?'

Daisy felt the gentle touch of Edie's hand on her face.

'You're a warm, loving woman,' her step-mother said, and Daisy could hear the tears in Edie's voice. 'With so much love to offer any man. Fate and the war have played a cruel trick on you, but then life *is* cruel. We've just got to find the courage to live through it.'

Daisy gulped down her tears, trying to pull herself together. She must think clearly, decide what to do next. Try to find the words to tell the man she loved with all her body, heart and mind that she could not marry him.

'I'm thinking of Rhodri. Us getting married, that's all he talks about. There isn't a truer man than him, Mam. I thought myself so lucky to have found him, and now he'll hate me for what I've done to him.'

'Now that's absurd, Daisy!' Edie patted her shoulder, her tone sharpening. 'Rhodri will know you're not responsible for what's happened. No one is. He'll find the strength to cope. It's *you* I'm worried about.'

Daisy pressed her lips together, struggling not to cry again. It was doing no good. She had to face up to things.

'Perhaps I *am* responsible, Mam? Life was so uncertain in London when I met Gerald in 1941. People all around us were falling in love, getting married, as though the world would end tomorrow. Gerald and I ..., we rushed into it, too. Our married life consisted of just odd weeks snatched now and then when he was on leave. When I knew I was going to have Valerie I was so happy. Thought it would be all right, after all. But when that first telegram came I knew, Mam. I knew we'd been foolish and hasty.'

Edie shook her head sadly, placing a hand over her heart as though it hurt her to say the words.

'Always afraid of that, I was, Daisy, but I never said anything to you, lovey. Wouldn't interfere, see. Your life after all, isn't it?'

Daisy nodded miserably.

'It was a mistake getting married on the hop as we did, hardly knowing each other really.'

15

She closed her eyes tightly in an effort to stem the threatening tears. 'Yes, it was a mistake, all right, and now Rhodri and I are paying for it.'

Edie kissed her cheek gently, and Daisy could feel her stepmother's tears of sympathy.

'It's no good looking back, lovey,' Edie said firmly. 'It's the future that matters now. I don't know what you'll do, but one thing you should bear in mind, though. Gerald is Valerie's father.'

Daisy nodded again. Edie was right. Gerald had never seen his child, didn't even know she existed. Valerie and her father had the right to know one other. One indisputable fact remained: she was Gerald's wife, and whether or not their marriage had been a mistake, she had taken sacred marriage vows. These could not be shrugged aside because her love now belonged to another man.

She and Rhodri had been so close, and now all at once this insurmountable barrier was between them. She was suddenly a married woman. She could never touch him or kiss him again. Never again would she lose herself in his arms.

Daisy felt a great pain in her heart. Could she live without Rhodri, live without his love? She would never survive, she knew she wouldn't. Her very soul cried out in anguish at her cruel loss. Again she put her arms out to her stepmother for loving comfort as she had as a child.

'Oh Mam. What am I going to do?'

Chapter One

London, January 1943

'You all packed for the off, ducks?'

Daisy glanced up, smiling at the young woman standing in the bedroom doorway adjusting her nurse's cap to a rakish angle. She and Patsy had been flatmates, colleagues and such good friends for nearly three years now, and Daisy was going to miss her very much. She'd miss the camaraderie, the companionship, the support of all the nursing fraternity, but especially Patsy. They'd seen the worst of the London blitz together, helped nurse the victims, comforted the bereaved, and somehow they'd survived themselves. Now out of the blue had come the parting of the ways. Daisy felt a lump in her throat at the thought of saying goodbye, but bravely held her smile.

'Just about, Patsy love.'

Patsy came further into the room.

'Shall I make you a cuppa before I go on duty? For old times' sake.'

Flopping down on the bed, Daisy let out a sound that was half a laugh and half a sob.

'Don't! You'll have me in tears again in a minute.'

Patsy came and put an arm around her shoulders, looking down into her face.

'I'm going to miss you, Daisy, old girl. Where am I going to find another pal like you, eh?'

'Oh, you won't have to look far, not with the mad parties you throw.'

Patsy looked comically glum.

'Got to amuse myself somehow. Keeps my mind off the prospect of my Wilf ending up in Davy Jones's Locker ...' She paused, aghast, collapsing on the bed beside Daisy. 'Oh, me and my big mouth! I'm sorry, Daisy, I didn't mean ...'

She patted her friend's hand.

'It's all right, Patsy. I don't expect people to avoid the subject. Gerald's gone. I'm slowly coming to terms with it.'

She didn't know if that were true or not, really. Coming to terms meant accepting and that she couldn't do yet. At odd moments she caught herself half believing Gerald would breeze into the flat unexpectedly, looking devastating in his petty officer's uniform, swing her off her feet exuberantly and suggest they crash some all-night party. It was at one of Patsy's mad parties that they'd met and been instantly attracted. Gerald was so exciting to be with, always on the go, always in the thick of it. Daisy hadn't really lived, she often told herself, until she met Gerald Buckland.

It always amused her that though he'd be at sea for months on end, he instantly knew where the action was in Town: the best place to have a good time and forget the bombs, the death and destruction, for a few hours.

He seemed to have endless friends and

18

acquaintances, and if one of them 'bought it', as he termed it, he'd be in deep depression for an hour or so then suddenly burst into feverish life again as though defiant of death. Live now, that was Gerald's motto. That was why they'd married, really. 'We have to live hard in this war,' he used to say 'so let's play hard, too.' Gerald was so alive, so buoyant, so full of crazy ways to snatch a few hours of pleasure in this cruel world. Live now ... She couldn't believe life was over for him.

No, she hadn't yet accepted Gerald's death and knew it would be some time before she did. But she had their baby to think about now.

'You know, Patsy, I wouldn't be leaving my work and going home to Wales, see, if it wasn't for the baby. Owe it to Gerald, I do, to make sure our child is safe. I wrote to him straight away, to tell him about the baby. Hope he got the letter before ...' She gulped, but pulled herself together again quickly. 'Do you think he was pleased to be a father?'

''Course he was,' Patsy said, patting her hand. 'Tickled pink, knowing Gerald.'

'Wrote to his father, too,' Daisy said. 'But I never got a reply. I often wonder if his family didn't approve of me, you know, some girl they'd never met. I can understand that, mind.'

Patsy tossed her head.

'Why wouldn't they?'

Daisy shrugged. 'The way Gerald talked about his family, I got the impression they were next to landed gentry. Maybe they think he married beneath him.'

19

'Well, Gerald was never stuck up, was he? But never you mind them, Daisy.' Patsy sniffed. 'You're going home to your own family. I bet they can't wait to see you. By the way, ducks, will you be all right on the journey? It's a long way.'

'Fine I'll be, thanks.'

Daisy grasped Patsy's hand tightly, suddenly overwhelmed to be leaving her old life, and the people who had been close to her over the last three years—people who amid constant daily danger had grown as close as family. She felt a little guilty, too, going home to the comparative safety of Wales and leaving them to face it all.

'Patsy, thank you for being such a good friend to me. I'll never forget you. Write to me, won't you? You've got my address.'

Patsy squeezed her hand in return.

'And you let me know about the baby, ducks. And if it's a girl ...' Patsy's voice caught as though trying to swallow a sob. 'Will you call her Valerie in memory of my little sister?'

Daisy planted a quick kiss on her cheek.

'It's a promise, Patsy. Now you'd better scoot on duty or Sister Trumble will have your scalp.'

'Crumbs!' Patsy jumped up quickly, pulling her cap to a more respectable angle. 'I'd forgotten Hatchet-lady.'

She bent and gave Daisy a kiss in return.

'Look after yourself, Daisy, my dear ducks. And have a good life.'

The flat was curiously silent, empty and forlorn

as Daisy let herself out for the last time. It was a cold wait on Paddington Station, crowded with civilians and service people in varied uniforms, so typical of London these days. Looking around her, Daisy knew she'd miss the excitement of meeting people of so many nationalities, making new friends, opening her mind to new ideas.

But she was going to be a mother, so perhaps it was fitting that she should leave all that behind and live a steadier life. Yes, she'd worked hard at the profession she loved, and had had a lot of fun too, a wild freedom. She'd been responsible only to her patients and herself. Now she would have a new kind of responsibility. She was looking forward to it.

On boarding the train for Swansea, she was thankful to find an empty compartment, and took a seat next to the window. It wasn't long, though, before her compartment was packed full. Kit-laden service men and women were crammed into the corridor, too. She'd been afraid to lift her heavy suitcase up on to the rack, and was thankful when a cheerful soldier did it for her.

A young man in a petty officer's uniform sat opposite, arms folded across his chest, eyes closed, perhaps trying to catch a catnap. He reminded her of Gerald and she felt a wave of grief strike her. She turned her head quickly to gaze out of the window, conscious of the hot tears that were clouding her vision.

It wasn't fair, was it? They'd had so little time together, really. There were so many things she didn't know about him; hadn't had time to learn, and now it was too late. She couldn't help wondering about the silence from Gerald's family, and their strange lack of interest in their grandchild. What would have happened, she wondered, if Gerald had survived the war? In all honesty she couldn't even imagine him in peacetime, doing an ordinary job, leading a humdrum life. What would her own life have been like if he'd taken her home to his people in Yorkshire? Would she have been unhappy there? Would the marriage have survived?

Daisy sighed. It was no good speculating on what might have been. The reality was that she was left a young widow with a child on the way. As Patsy pointed out, she had a family who loved and supported her, but suppose she'd been alone in the world? Being a widow with a child to support must be the worst thing. She thought back to her childhood, remembering how Edie, her young widowed stepmother, had struggled valiantly against hardship to provide for Daisy and her stepbrother.

Had they been hasty, she and Gerald, getting married on the hop? It frightened her to think that they had. Perhaps they'd been irresponsible? Live now, he used to say. But what about tomorrow?

Daisy gazed out at the passing landscape without really seeing anything. With Gerald gone, tomorrow was harsh reality for her. She had a loving family but couldn't impose on them for ever. She'd have to find her own place to live. There was her war widow's pension, but that wouldn't go far. It went without saying that she'd carry on with her midwifery career, and she was thankful she had that to fall back on. Life wasn't going to be easy, far from it. One thing she was sure of, though—whatever was to come, for the remainder of the war and in the peace after, she'd get through it somehow. She had to. She had a child to think of.

Daisy felt warmed by a new excitement. A child of her own! Deep in her heart she knew one of the reasons she'd agreed to marry Gerald was the prospect of a family of her own. It was sad that he would never know his offspring, but she and the child were alive now. Life went on, and one had to make the best of things. That's what her stepmother would say anyway. That was what Gerald would probably have said. There was a future before her and Daisy was determined to do the very best she could for her child. She'd make a good life for them both, come what may, and she'd find happiness again somehow.

Chapter Two

Swansea, February 1943

Despite protests from Edie, her stepmother, Daisy was determined to practise midwifery in the town, at least until her baby was born. She wasted no time in finding herself two comfortable rooms in St Helen's Road, near

Hospital Square, put up her little brass plate and prepared herself to engage her patients.

Edie came up from the Mumbles the day she moved in to make sure she was comfortable and that everything was clean.

'I've scrubbed the linoleum in the bedroom,' she said, carrying in another bucket of hot water. 'I'll do your living-room now. I hope there aren't any bugs here, Daisy?'

'Now, Mam, the place is as clean as a whistle. Made sure of that, I did.'

'Can't abide bugs.' Edie got down on her knees, scrubbing brush in hand. 'They're the very devil to get rid of.'

Daisy felt agitated, seeing her stepmother on her knees like that. She knew Edie had only her best interests at heart, but she wanted to start out on this venture independently, start the way she meant to go on. She was a widow and had to fend for herself. It was no good relying on others, no matter how devoted they were.

'Mam, I wish you'd let me do that.'

'In your condition? Talk sense, Daisy, will you? You want to take care of yourself, my girl. If you must go on working, I don't see why you can't carry on your practice down the Mumbles, near your family, like.'

'I'd love to practise in the village, Mam, but there's no scope for another midwife down there,' Daisy said. 'Not until Nurse Ellis retires in August, anyway. I'll have had my baby by then. Might be able to take over her practice. We'll see.'

'Worried sick, I'll be,' Edie said, scrubbing vigorously. 'You're too close to the town centre by here, and February's always been an unlucky month for air raids in Swansea. Look at the awful blitz.'

'Mam, that was two years ago. You told me yourself there hasn't been a raid on Swansea for the last seven months.'

She'd been home three weeks and despite the long lull in nightly raids she still couldn't adjust to the tranquillity of Edie's guest house in the Mumbles. She'd not been able to switch off that inner alertness she'd developed living in London. One small part of her brain was always listening for the dreaded sound of enemy aircraft, even as she slept.

Edie paused in her scrubbing to look up at her. Daisy could see concern in her stepmother's eyes and felt a wave of deep affection for this woman who had always been a wonderful, loving mother to her. Edie was God's special gift to her, Daisy had always thought, even as a small child.

She smiled down at her stepmother.

'Jerry's already flattened everything in sight, Mam,' she said, picturing in her mind the town centre as it was now, the very heart of it no more than a sea of rubble, a shocking sight to one returning home after a long absence. 'What else is left to bomb?'

Daisy was to recall with chagrin the flippancy of her words one Tuesday night a fortnight later. She'd already gone to bed and was just

25

drifting off to sleep when loud hammering on the front door had her sitting bolt upright in bed, confused for a moment, wondering where on earth she was and what was happening.

The hammering continued. The rooms above her were occupied by a woman and her three children, the husband being away in the army. A dentist had the downstairs front rooms for his practice.

It must be someone needing her. Daisy scrambled out of bed, pulling on a dressing gown. Careful not to switch on the light, she made her way gingerly along the still unfamiliar passage to the front door and opened it to see the shadowy figure of a young woman on the step.

'Who is it?' Daisy asked, peering at her.

'Oh, Nurse Buckland, thank God you're here.' The young woman sounded breathless, as though she'd been running. 'My mother, it is, see. Can you come straight away and see her? She's awful bad. Soaked in blood, she is. She's lost it, I think.'

'Come in a minute while I get dressed,' Daisy said promptly, turning and hurrying along the passage. 'What's the name? Have I seen your mother before?'

'Sophia Randall, my mother is. From Victor Street.'

'Oh, yes, I remember her,' Daisy said over her shoulder.

The young woman followed her along the passage and into her living-room. Daisy went into the bedroom and began to dress in her

26

uniform as quickly as she could. It sounded like a miscarriage.

'Have you fetched the doctor yet?' she called from the bedroom.

'My father won't have the doctor, see.' The young woman's tone turned noticeably bitter. 'Said the midwife would do. I'm awful worried, Nurse.'

Daisy jammed her swelling feet into her shoes and hurried into the living-room. The young woman standing nervously in the centre of the room looked to be five or six years younger than herself. She was startlingly pretty even with the frightened expression on her face. Thick ebony-coloured hair fell about her shoulders as though she herself had just tumbled out of bed. Daisy remembered then where she had last seen her.

'Yes, I remember your mother. Saw her at the clinic last week, didn't I? You were with her. It's Josie, isn't it?'

Josie nodded, her dark eyes large and glistening, brimming with tears.

'Yes, that's right. Josie Jenkins, I am.'

Daisy remembered Sophia Randall very well. Josie followed her mother's looks. Sophia had obviously been an olive-skinned Italian beauty in her youth. Now she was worn out with work and care and child-bearing. At forty-five she was too old to have another child, and Daisy had told her so at the visit to the prenatal clinic. Sophia had said nothing, eyes downcast, face shuttered, and Daisy had realised her advice was useless as well as unwelcome.

'You'll have to call the doctor, Josie,' she

27

warned, as she gathered up her bag and prepared to leave. 'You should've done it straight away. Sounds like your mother's had a miscarriage. She'll need expert medical help.'

'It's my father, isn't it?' Josie said, scowling, her lips tightening as pent-up anger replaced the tears. 'Keeps Mama short while he spends like a sailor himself on the drink and that ...' She paused for a moment then went on, 'Can't reason with him when he's been on the booze, see.'

Remembering the bruises on Sophia's arms, Daisy understood perfectly Josie's obvious resentment of her father. So many women were like Sophia, in the terrible trap of being under the domination of a brutal, uncaring husband. It was frustrating that they couldn't or wouldn't accept help. But, Daisy reflected, she'd never been in their position, so she shouldn't judge.

They hurried along the blacked-out streets with the aid of a masked torch. There was a sharp frostiness in the air, but the night was clear with even a little moonlight to see their way towards the Sandfields. Bomber's moon, Daisy reflected, and felt chilled at the thought.

They walked past the gates of Swansea Hospital, windows painted black to prevent the escape of any light, and across Hospital Square.

Daisy was remembering who the Randall family were. Josie's father, Reuben, was distantly related to Edie by marriage; Reuben's sister had married Edie's brother. They were a family of beachcombers and rag-and-bone men, who'd never done an honest day's work in their lives according to Edie's mother, but then Mam-gu had never been entirely happy about her son marrying into that family.

Daisy knew most of the Randall clan lived in the Sandfields, an area of intersecting narrow streets of two-up, two-down terraced houses, separated from the foreshore of Swansea Bay by the Oystermouth Road. Reuben Randall rented a corner house in Victor Street with a yard at the side which he used for his rag-and-bone trade.

Josie let them in through the gates of the yard, which was cluttered with all kinds of refuse and junk, most of it rusting or rotting by the look of it. As they passed through the back door into a cramped lean-to scullery, Daisy could hear a man's voice raised loudly in rage and slurred with drink.

'Knock your bloody head off, I will, if you answer me back again.'

Daisy saw Josie glance at her, face scarlet with a mixture of anger and embarrassment. Daisy smiled reassuringly. There was nothing she hadn't heard before, but she was sorry for Josie's obvious humiliation. It must be very hard on her, having to cope with a father like Reuben Randall.

'Upstairs, your mother is, is she?' Daisy asked in a matter-of-fact tone.

Josie nodded. Daisy could see she had her hands tightly clasped together, her knuckles white, and knew the girl was under an awful strain.

'Get the doctor now,' she said firmly. 'I'll go

29

up and see what I can do for her.'

Josie hesitated, her expression showing uncertainty. 'My father ...'

Daisy set her jaw decisively.

'I'll deal with him. Go on, get the doctor. Every minute counts.'

Josie turned and hurried out of the door, and Daisy made her way through to the living room. Three children were huddled together on a horse-hair sofa, all of them crying. The eldest, a boy of about twelve, was holding the side of his face, and Daisy could see bright red marks on his cheek, as though he'd just been slapped with a heavy hand.

Her lips tightened as she went out into the passage and climbed the narrow stairs, devoid of any linoleum or carpeting.

A tall, heavily built man in a grubby singlet came on to the landing from the front bedroom, leaning on the banister for support. He smelled so strongly of stale liquor that Daisy had to steel herself not to recoil. Looking up at him, she was instantly reminded of the way Sarah, Edie's sister-in-law, had looked. Reuben had the typical Randall colouring: pale skin, and hair so light in colour it was almost white.

He stared down at her belligerently.

'Took your bloody time, didn't you?'

Daisy climbed steadily towards him, her face set in determination. She could see the kind of man Reuben Randall was. A bully, and probably a coward, too. He'd have a hard time bullying her, though. One thing living in London in the blitz had done for her—it had made her

30

tough. She'd seen too much death and horror on the streets of the city to be frightened by a mere bully.

'Came as soon as I was called. Sent for the doctor, I have.'

'Doctor!' Reuben swayed backwards with the force of his own exclamation. 'Won't have no bloody doctor by here, I won't!'

'Well, he'll be here soon, see, so you'd better pull yourself together, Mr Randall.'

He leaned towards her threateningly.

'You got no bloody right, woman. Who the hell do you think you are, ordering the doctor? You going to pay him then?'

Daisy's patience snapped.

'Want your wife to die, then, is it?' she cried back angrily. 'That suit you, would it, Mr Randall?'

Though he barely made way for her on the narrow landing, Daisy lifted her chin defiantly and pushed her way roughly past. She had no intention of wasting precious time on him. He'd made her angry and that was unprofessional of her, letting his ignorance and stupidity get under her skin.

Ignoring him, she hurried into the front bedroom where Reuben's long-suffering wife Sophia lay in agony.

'The doctor will be here soon, Mrs Randall,' Daisy said gently, hoping to sound reassuring. 'I'll try and make you comfortable in the meantime.'

Sophia Randall's lips moved but there was no sound, and her eyes remained closed. The woman was dangerously weak and Daisy's examination confirmed what she already suspected: Sophia's pregnancy was over, and judging by her condition, she'd be lucky to survive herself. Daisy prayed the doctor would arrive in time.

Reuben continued to stand on the landing, ranting throughout her examination, but finally, with one last shouted oath, he clattered downstairs, his booted feet heavy on the uncovered stairs.

Daisy was relieved to hear him go and felt some of the tension leave her body. But it wasn't to last. While she was bending over the woman in the bed, her sharp hearing caught the first faint dreaded sound and the old familiar fear gripped her heart. Enemy bombers! She knew that ominous, menacing engine throb so well. The sirens hadn't yet sounded, but she knew she wasn't mistaken. Her first thought was for the children downstairs. Their drunken father was probably already asleep somewhere.

Sophia opened her eyes, staring up at Daisy in terror as though she too could hear the distant bombers.

'My children ...'

'Lie still now, Mrs Randall,' Daisy said softly, smoothing back Sophia's hair from her damp forehead with a gentle hand. 'I'll see to the children. You save your strength.'

Reluctant to leave her patient even for a moment, she nevertheless hurried downstairs. The children were still in the living-room; the smallest, a boy of about five, was clinging to his older sister, sobbing his heart out. They looked at her fearfully when she came into the room.

'Get your coats, hats and scarves on quickly,' she said to them, gently but firmly. 'There's going to be an air raid. You must go out to the shelter.'

The eldest boy wiped a hand across his eyes, jumping up from the sofa and pulling his brother and sister with him.

'Haven't got one,' he said. 'Dada's got junk in it.'

'Where do you go when there's a raid, then?'

The boy gestured towards the narrow passage.

'Cupboard under the stairs.'

'What's your name?'

'They call me Johnno.'

'Well, come along then, Johnno,' Daisy said briskly. 'Put your coat on anyway. Help the other children with theirs.'

At that moment the sirens started up, wailing out their warning message. It was a sound that never ceased to make Daisy's blood run cold, no matter how many times she heard it. The children moved towards her as though for protection, and she could see the fear in their young faces.

'What about my mama?' the little girl asked tearfully. 'And Josie and Francie?'

'Your mama must stay upstairs,' Daisy said as calmly as she could. 'She's poorly. Josie's gone for the doctor. She'll be back soon.'

The sound of aircraft was threateningly loud now and already there were distant explosions to be heard. Anxious to get back to her patient, Daisy quickly ushered the children out into the passage and opened the cupboard door. An old mattress lay on the stone floor of the cupboard with some blankets lying higgeldy-piggeldy over it. In a corner at the back was an old china chamber pot. The cupboard looked bleak enough with its grimy walls, but it was better then nothing.

'In you go, kids. Don't worry, I'll be upstairs with your mama. Where's your father?'

'Gone out,' Johnno said. Daisy could hear a tone of relief in his voice, and her heart went out to the child, to all of them.

'Stay here until the All Clear sounds. I'll come and look at you from time to time, right?'

'What about my sister Francie, then?' the girl persisted. 'In bed, she is. She never hears the sirens.'

'Don't worry. I'll call her.'

Daisy was more than curious about Francie Randall. With her mama desperately ill, it would seem she'd gone to bed unconcerned. It was an attitude that seemed unnatural to Daisy. She'd wake her and insist she took care of her brothers and sister. They must be very frightened alone and not knowing what was happening to their mother or Josie.

It was Josie she was most worried about. With the constant threat of red hot shrapnel falling, the open street was a dangerous place to be in an air raid. Daisy prayed the young woman would keep safe.

Her curiosity was further roused on reaching the landing when a young woman in a nightie came out of the back bedroom. Seeing Daisy she leaned nonchalantly against the door-post, folding her arms. So *this* was Francie Randall.

The sounds of bombs exploding were nearer, the explosions coming in rapid succession. The very framework of the small house seemed to quiver from the impacts. Daisy could hear the whistling sound the bombs made as they hurtled towards their targets, or at least thought she could. It was a sound that would be in her head for ever, a sound that filled her with terror. She'd never be used to it.

Her mouth going dry, she trembled despite herself as several more deafening explosions came in rapid succession. She clutched at the banister, and couldn't suppress a gasp.

Francie regarded her with a faintly amused sneer.

'You never hear the one with your name on it, so they say,' she said.

She looked to be a little older than Josie, Daisy judged.

'How's Mama, then? All over, is it?' Francie asked, but there was no real concern in her voice.

'It's far from over, I'm afraid. She's lost the baby, and she's very ill,' said Daisy tightly. 'Josie's gone for the doctor. The children are in the passage cupboard. Will you get dressed and look after them, please? I'm waiting for the doctor.'

Francie yawned. 'They'll be all right, mun.

35

Going back to bed, I am. On early shift at the Ajax, see.'

'I think you might be a little more concerned,' Daisy said tartly, annoyed at Francie's indifference. 'Sophia's your mother, too. You shouldn't leave it all to Josie. I expect she's younger than you.'

Francie's mouth tightened. 'She isn't! Josie's older than me by three minutes. Twins, we are, see.' Her lips stretched into a humourless smile on seeing Daisy's look of surprise. 'Yes, remarkable, isn't it?'

With one last disparaging glance at her, Francie turned back into her bedroom and closed the door firmly.

Daisy went into the front bedroom to offer comfort to her patient, trying not to tremble at the sounds of destruction around them that disturbed the night.

By the yellow light from the naked low-wattage bulb hanging from the ceiling, Daisy saw that Sophia's eyes were open and she still looked very frightened. She wasn't afraid for herself, Daisy sensed, but for her children.

'My children? They are safe, yes?'

Daisy put out a hand to touch Sophia's cold fingers, feeling a renewed surge of pity for this downtrodden woman, and her children trembling in the cupboard under the stairs.

'You mustn't worry. The air raid will be over soon. Are you in pain now?'

Sophia's eyes closed wearily.

'I am so tired ...'

Her voice trailed away, and Daisy realised

she had lost consciousness again. Please let the doctor come soon, she prayed silently.

To take her mind off the sounds of destruction, she turned her thoughts to Francie sleeping in the next room, apparently indifferent, in such contrast to Josie's desperate concern for their mother. She wondered at the difference in the two young women, in attitude as well as looks. It was difficult to believe they were sisters, let alone twins.

In looks Francie was the absolute opposite of her sister. She had plenty of the pale Randall hair and skin like fine, white china. She was as striking as Josie in her own way, but there was a certain hardness about her eyes and mouth that made Daisy feel she could never like her, not the way she had taken to Josie.

Daisy had already guessed both Josie and Francie were munitions workers by the discolouration of their hands. She realised that they had a hard and often dangerous job, but that didn't excuse Francie's letting her sister take on all the responsibility. Twins! Daisy couldn't get over it. Did they have *anything* in common apart from the day they were born? she wondered.

Her thoughts were interrupted by the sound of brisk feet on the stairs and the familiar bluff tones of Dr McClusky. At the same time, miraculously it seemed to Daisy, the All Clear sounded. She almost sobbed in relief, and as the big Scotsman came into the room, said a little prayer of thankfulness that they had once again been spared in the air raid and that help for poor Sophia was here at last.

'Ah! Nurse Buckland,' Dr McClusky boomed out on seeing her. 'Good! Good! What've we got here, my girl?'

'She's miscarried, I'm afraid, Doctor,' Daisy said. 'She's slipping in and out of consciousness, and she's very weak.'

Dr McClusky came quickly to the bedside, bent over his patient and gently took her wrist between finger and thumb. At that moment Sophia opened her eyes and stared up at him.

'How are you feeling, Mrs Randall?'

Sophia tried to speak but it seemed an effort. Dr McClusky pulled back the blood-stained bedclothes and began his examination.

'Miscarriage, yes, and she's lost a lot of blood, too, but the crisis is over, I believe,' he said when he had finished. 'She's going to be all right, but she'll need careful nursing.' He glanced up at Daisy, smiling. 'You've done well, Nurse, as usual.'

Daisy smiled and gave a brief nod of acknowledgement, pleased at his appreciation of her skills. It made her feel proud of her profession.

'Thank you, Doctor.'

She glanced down at the woman on the bed. Sophia seemed to be resting more easily now. She would pull through this time. But for how long would she be safe? Until the next time she became pregnant?

An ashen-faced Josie came to the bedroom door as Dr McClusky was wiping his hands. Her lips were trembling as she gazed apprehensively at Sophia's pale face on the pillow.

'How's Mama, Doctor?'

Dr McClusky slipped into his coat and went to the door, motioning Josie out on to the landing, out of earshot of the patient.

'She's been lucky this time,' Daisy heard him say quietly. 'I want a word with your father. Is he about?'

Daisy quickly joined them on the narrow landing. She knew the answer to that one.

'Mr Randall went out some time ago,' she told the doctor.

'He won't be back tonight, Doctor.' Josie averted her eyes, looking shamed-faced. 'And if he is, he'll be too boozed up to listen.'

Dr McClusky looked grim. 'Well, tell him to come up to the surgery tomorrow to see me, will you?'

Josie bit her lip, glancing from the doctor to Daisy and back again. She shook her head helplessly.

'He won't come, Doctor. It's no good.'

'Pop in here tomorrow, I will, Doctor,' Daisy volunteered quickly, more to save Josie's feelings than anything else. 'I'll have a word with him. I believe I know what you want to say to him.'

The big Scotsman's expression showed concern as he stood at the top of the stairs, ready to leave.

'No more pregnancies. It'll probably kill her next time. Impress that on him, will you, Nurse?'

When the doctor was gone Daisy drew Josie into the bedroom to see Sophia. In whispers, she explained to the girl about her mother's condition and reassured her that the worst was over.

Daisy could see Josie was almost in tears as she gazed down on Sophia, lying so still in the bed.

'Is she unconscious, Nurse?'

'No, she's sleeping now,' Daisy whispered. 'We won't disturb her to change the sheets. That can wait until tomorrow. What she needs now is rest.'

'Can't thank you enough, can I, Nurse Buckland?' Josie said, as they stood in the living-room while Daisy put on her coat and hat. 'You saved her.'

She was looking relieved now that she realised her mother really was out of danger, but she was also looking very tired.

'Call me Daisy,' she said, smiling. 'Are the children all right?'

'Put them to bed, I have, poor kids.' Josie put a hand to her mouth to stifle a yawn. Daisy could see she was near to exhaustion and felt sorry for her. 'Frightened for Mama they were, more than anything else.'

'Your mother will be fine now,' Daisy assured her, patting Josie's hand. 'Don't worry. I'll call in over the next couple of days just to keep an eye on her.'

'Got to go into work tomorrow, see,' Josie said, 'but I'm going to ask for some compassionate leave to look after her. I don't know if they'll give it, like.'

'That would be ideal,' Daisy agreed. 'What's the best time to see your father, by the way?'

Josie hesitated for a moment, looking dubious.

'I wish you wouldn't, Daisy. Leave it to the doctor, mun. Nasty at times my father can get, mind, and I don't want him to upset you. You know, in your condition, like.'

Daisy lifted her chin.

'When you know me better, Josie, you'll understand I never shirk my duty. And besides, I've dealt with tougher customers then him in my time.'

Josie shrugged, obviously too tired to argue any longer.

'Takes the horse and cart out to go on his rounds about eight o'clock, he does. You'll catch him before then.'

Daisy took her leave and started on her walk home to St Helen's Road. It was the early hours of the morning already and it seemed a lot darker now than when she'd arrived. The blackout was total. But she had her masked torch, and knew the way like the back of her hand. She'd spent a happy childhood in her step-grandmother's rented house in Brynmill nearby, and she'd had many friends in the Sandfields.

She walked carefully but as briskly as she dared. She was longing to get to her bed. Not only her back but every bone in her body was aching, and she knew her ankles were swollen up like balloons.

Perhaps Edie was right. Perhaps she was foolish in persisting with her work while she was pregnant. In not taking shelter in that air raid she had risked not only her own life, but the life of her unborn child. What right had she to do that? Was it pride that made her go on or was it that working with people who needed her kept her from dwelling on Gerald's death and feeling sorry for herself? It would be all too easy to slip into self-pity because, although she was loath to admit it even to herself, she was lonely.

Daisy's mind went immediately to Josie Jenkins. She'd felt drawn to the girl straight away. She'd been impressed by the defiant tilt of Josie's chin, the compassion in her eyes as she'd looked at her mother. Josie reminded her strongly of Edie. They had nothing in common in looks, but Daisy recognised instinctively that they had the same fighting spirit, the same courage. Edie had always been strong and determined, blessed with ready sympathy, and not easily daunted by life. Josie had those same qualities, ones that Daisy had always admired in her stepmother.

Josie would make a good friend, Daisy decided, and thought she'd like to get to know her better. Since coming home to Swansea she'd missed the friendship of another young woman of similar interests. Someone to go to the pictures with, chat to, confide in perhaps. She'd had so many companionable friends in London and really missed the continuous whirl of duty and play.

Family only went so far. She longed for some company of her own age. All her friends from the old days were either in the Forces or away working as Land Girls or scattered over the country in munitions factories. She'd taken to Josie instantly and hoped that somehow they might become friends.

Daisy thought back again to Francie's revelation that she and Josie were twins. They were so utterly different, she could still hardly believe it. Daisy sensed warmth and deep feeling in Josie, in keeping with the Italian looks inherited from her mother, while Francie seemed cold and distant. Was that only on the surface, perhaps? There was no need to speculate about Josie's feelings. She wore her heart on her sleeve, thought Daisy, and she could sympathise with that, being outgoing herself.

She'd never seen or even heard of twins so dissimilar. Francie's coldness, her curious detachment even during the air raid, was something Daisy found very disturbing—though perhaps it wasn't all that surprising, having met Reuben Randall. With a father like that, Francie might very well have grown a shell of detachment around herself as a defence.

Even so, Daisy suspected that Josie and Francie were not as close as many twin sisters. Daisy had immediately spotted the wedding ring on Josie's finger when they'd first met at the clinic. There was no ring on Francie's hand. Maybe she'd already lost some young man in the war? Daisy reflected. That might account for the bitter expression she imagined she'd seen in Francie's bold stare.

Deep in thought, Daisy struck the toe of her shoe on a cracked paving stone and almost stumbled. She must keep her wits about her

43

in the blackout. But she was tired, and the air raid, the plight of Sophia Randall and her children, were playing on her mind, depressing her. She'd be able to think more clearly in the morning.

Daisy walked carefully on through the blacked-out streets, finding her way more by instinct than anything else. She had just turned out of a side street and on to the main road, intending to make her way towards Hospital Square, when the shadowy figure of a man stepped out of a darkened doorway and flashed a masked torch in her face.

'Halt! You can't proceed any further. Unexploded bomb.' The torch-light ran over her uniform. 'Oh, sorry I startled you, Nurse. Been on a call, have you?'

With relief Daisy recognised the faint outline of an ARP Warden's helmet.

'Yes. I want to get to my rooms on St Helen's Road, opposite Argyll Chapel.'

'Sorry, love. A high-explosive bomb has dropped right outside the hospital gates. Bomb squad's working on the perisher now.'

Daisy was alarmed. 'The patients ...'

'It's all right, love. Been evacuated, they have.'

Daisy felt her shoulders sag with weariness, yet at the same time was thankful the bomb hadn't exploded on impact.

'Suppose I'll have to go all the way round, then?'

''Fraid so, love. Mind how you go, now. And good night to you, love—or what's left of it.'

Nothing left to bomb! Daisy remembered her own words ruefully as she retraced her steps and began to trudge gingerly along Lower Oxford Street, saying a quick prayer for the men risking their lives to disarm the unexploded bomb.

No, there wasn't much left of the night; not much sleeping time left, and she had to face the wrath of Reuben Randall in a few hours' time.

Never mind. Worse things happen at sea, Daisy reflected, then felt like weeping at the thought. She wanted to weep for Gerald and all the young men like him whom the sea had claimed as its own. And she wanted to weep for all the women like herself who were left to mourn, alone and lonely.

Chapter Three

Josie always looked forward to the weeks when she was working afternoons at the Ajax munitions factory. She tried to get an extra hour in bed then, if she could. Often she'd have exciting dreams about her husband Stanley; lovely dreams about his coming home safe and sound, holding her, kissing her, loving her ...

Everyone said she'd been lucky so far, with Stanley stationed in Iceland, away from any fighting. But Josie was fearful their luck wouldn't last. The tide of the war was turning now; everyone said that, too. Rommel was cornered in

Tunisia, and she couldn't help worrying Stanley would be posted out there.

It would be the end of her if anything happened to him, she knew it would. She often cried for him at night in secret. Yet she wouldn't let herself think even for a second that her Stanley wouldn't return to her. She loved him so much, missed him so much. She could hardly wait for them to be together in a place of their own. Despite her fears, she was always looking out for good rooms to rent after the war; saving every penny so they could have a nice home, a different kind of home from the one she'd grown up in.

It didn't look as if she'd catch any dreams this morning, though. She'd wakened, startled, when Francie had noisily got up at four-thirty for the early shift. The Ajax was in Landore on the eastern side of Swansea, and the morning shift meant early rising to catch the special bus laid on by the factory. It was a fair old walk from the Sandfields to Landore if you missed it.

Josie longed to get that extra hour this morning. It had been a terrible night, what with Mama taken so ill and losing the baby, chasing around for the midwife and doctor until all hours, and then the blooming air raid on top of it. She felt like an old rag doll left out in the rain.

Francie hadn't been much help again, as usual. Josie sighed with resignation. Life could be so much easier if Francie would co-operate with her like any other sister, instead of being an Annie Awkward all the time. It was as much as she could do to keep her temper in check with Francie at times.

She felt sometimes it would be better to clear the air with a good straight talk to her sister, even a row if necessary, because that was the best way, she always believed. Still, there was enough unhappiness and ill-feeling in the house already without adding to it by quarrelling with her sister.

Josie did her best to battle against Reuben, stand between him and Mama and the younger children when he got violent. So far Francie remained neutral in those bad times, choosing to ignore the fact that things were getting worse; Dada was getting worse.

Josie had been ashamed on hearing talk in the street that Dada was seen too often in the company of some woman from Port Tennant, seen drinking with her in The Archers in Quay Parade, a rough, disreputable pub down by the docks. Some big, fat piece, Tom Kiley from next door had leeringly told her; a beauty without paint, as he'd described her. Josie had been outraged and mortified.

She hadn't mentioned it to her mother, but she had confided in Francie, then wished she hadn't. Her sister was scornful and abrasive. Sometimes she felt she and Francie were more like sworn enemies than twin sisters. As much as she wanted to have things out with her sister, she didn't want to push Francie over to Dada's side. It was bad enough the way things were.

Mama said it was jealousy on Francie's part, her being antagonistic towards Josie, but Josie

47

couldn't believe it. Why would Francie be jealous of her? Her sister was pretty and clever, and could get any bloke she wanted.

With a groan of weariness, Josie pushed back the bedclothes and swung her legs off the bed. Apart from having to see to Mama and the kids, another worry was pulling her out of bed this morning. Nurse Buckland ... Daisy ... was coming round to speak to her father in place of Dr McClusky. She knew what had to be said. Mama mustn't get in the family way again, that's what Dr McClusky wanted to impress on him. Josie wished the doctor would speak to Dada himself instead of leaving it to Daisy. She was dreading Dada's reaction. Reuben would be insulted that a stranger, and a mere woman at that, was trying to dictate to him, and on such a private matter. He'd fly off the handle again and wouldn't need any drink in him this time.

Josie was worried for Daisy. She'd taken an instant liking to the midwife; a capable, sympathetic, no-nonsense kind of young woman, not afraid to carry on with her work even though it was obvious she herself was expecting. Josie admired her already for her calm, professional manner. She particularly admired the fearless way Daisy had stood up to Dada the night before, but was more than worried really: she was afraid for Daisy. Dada sober and outraged was perhaps even more unpredictable and dangerous than Dada the worse for drink.

Josie was glad to see her mother looked much better, and was delighted when she agreed to have tea and a little toast. She made breakfast for her brothers and sister, but couldn't face any food herself.

She particularly dreaded facing her father that morning and knew it would be a strain being halfway civil to him. She hated him, she was ashamed to acknowledge. It was sinful to hate one's father, she knew it was, but she couldn't help it. He treated her mother abominably, and Mama was the gentlest of women. That was the trouble. He'd knocked the spirit out of her. Josie knew *she* wouldn't put up with it. There'd be murder done if she were tied to a man like her father. She thanked God her Stanley was a different sort of man.

Josie felt her back go rigid with tension as Reuben came in from feeding the horse. She wasn't surprised to see a deep scowl on his face. He was always morose the morning after a night of heavy drinking. She wondered where he'd spent the night, because he hadn't come home until well after daylight when she'd heard him clumping upstairs. He'd probably been with that woman. She felt her blood begin to boil at the thought of it.

Josie regarded him with deep resentment and distaste. He looked rough, needing a shave. She knew he hadn't bothered to wash, not even his face. She'd have put on a kettle for boiling water if he'd asked her, but she wouldn't offer. Reuben would be suspicious of any kindness like that, thinking she was after something.

Why did he always have to look like that, as though he had no pride in himself? That was the way alcoholics were, Stanley had told her; illogical, violent, with no pride left. She'd been ashamed to acknowledge her father was an alcoholic. Stanley said she shouldn't be. It wasn't her fault.

Josie eyed him warily as she placed in front of him his breakfast of bacon, eggs and fried bread.

'What's this rubbish, then?' His scowl deepened. 'Wouldn't feed this to the pigs, would I?'

Josie's lips tightened at the unwarranted criticism, feeling the nerves in her midriff tighten with strain. It was more than just the drink making him unreasonable. He was spoiling for an argument, she could see that. He hadn't struck her since she'd married Stanley, even though they'd had several barneys over his treatment of her mother. She knew the only reason he held back was that, in his eyes, being married, she now belonged to another man like some piece of furniture. But that had made her bolder lately, given her courage to challenge him more often.

This morning, though, she could see he was looking for an excuse to use the back of his hand, if not on her, then one of the kids. She had to protect them.

'What you always have, Dada, isn't it?' she said tightly but controlling her tone, determined not to be drawn into losing her temper.

Mama was always warning her about her quick temper, and Josie tried hard to keep it in check. Playing into his hands otherwise, Mama said. But she had no spirit left to fight anyway.

'Bleeding pig swill, this is.'

'There's almost a week's rations on that plate, Dada. Not going to waste it, are you?'

Not that he cared about rationing, or people going hungry. Reuben ignored all that. He was well in with the black market in the town, which meant none of the family went short, not of food anyway. Dada liked his food and Mama was a good cook, like all Italian women.

Josie didn't know whether she approved of the black market or not. Everyone was dabbling, though, weren't they? You couldn't see the kids go short of anything if it wasn't necessary. Dada wouldn't part with any money if he could help it, so she didn't know what he gave in exchange for the supplies, and didn't want to.

Reuben waved a hand dismissively.

'Go on! Throw it in the bin. Useless! No bloody good to anybody, you're not, Josie. God help Stan, if ever he comes home, with you for a wife.'

Josie ground her teeth as a wave of hot anger threatened to sweep over her.

'Good cook, I am, almost as good as Mama,' she said through clenched teeth. 'Stanley's always praising me for my cooking.'

'Poor bugger! Don't know no better with the mother he's got, does he?'

Reuben pushed the plate away from him, taking out of his pocket a tin of tobacco and some cigarette papers and starting to roll a cigarette.

'Where's your mother, anyway? Down by here

she should be, seeing to my wants, instead of lolling about in bed.'

Josie clutched the bread knife tightly in her fist, her hand shaking. Thinking about her mother, pale and exhausted upstairs, and how ill she'd been the night before, her resentment and anger against him flared up like lighted paraffin, searing her throat. If things went on like this much longer she'd do him an injury one of these days, she knew she would. He'd go too far and she wouldn't be able to stop herself.

Yet she was ashamed of such feelings towards her own father. It wasn't right. It was sinful. She should be stronger. She shouldn't let his goading get to her. She must try to ride it out without quarrelling with him, especially this morning.

Swallowing down her anger with difficulty, she relaxed her fingers around the knife, putting it safely on the bread board.

'Mama's too weak yet.'

'Weak, my backside! Your mother's like a blumming horse, mun. What you want to go calling the doctor for? Listening to that bloody nurse. No need of it.'

Josie clasped her hands together tightly, repelled by his callousness.

'Mama lost the baby, didn't she? She's ill, Dada, very ill. Too drunk last night, were you, to remember that little detail? Too busy with that fat fancy piece of yours, right?'

Reuben stood up, lifting a hand threateningly.

'Watch your lip, my girl! Not too old to feel

the back of my hand, are you? Married woman
or no.'

Josie felt a great welling in her chest, of raw,
bitter anger at his threat. Lips drawing back
from her teeth, she snatched up the bread
knife again, lifting her chin defiantly, hurling
a challenge into his face.

'Go on then, Dada. Go on, give me an
excuse, then.'

Reuben lowered his hand slowly, his glance
flicking from the knife to her face. She knew
all her hatred was exposed for him to see.
Perhaps he was shocked by it. It gave her a
bitter satisfaction to see momentary uncertainty
in his eyes.

He turned away, reaching for his old donkey
jacket and cloth cap hanging behind the kitchen
door.

'Silly bitch!'

With that parting shot he opened the back
door and went out, heading across the yard to
the lean-to where he kept the horse.

Shaking with reaction and relief, Josie flopped
on to a chair, choking on her own terror. She'd
come that close! She wanted to cry but held her
tears in check. She mustn't give way. It wasn't
over yet. There was still Daisy's visit to get
through.

She hoped he'd be off with the horse and cart
before Daisy arrived. There would be ructions
again and he'd show her up, humiliate her
as he had done all her life. It was awful to
hate one's father, but it was just as bad to
be ashamed of him. Apart from his drinking,

Josie was deeply ashamed that her father was nothing more than a tatty rag-and-bone-man, a scavenger of other people's rubbish. If he were in scrap metal, like Uncle Sam, it would be another matter. Collecting scrap seemed more respectable somehow, and it helped the war effort.

Reuben ignored the war, as he ignored shortages. Josie knew many people were afraid of Reuben Randall, afraid of his unpredictable temper and uncouth ways. She was all too well aware that those same people looked down on the Randalls for the way her father scavenged a living, and the rough and ready way they lived. She hated being looked down on, being thought inferior and common. From a young girl she'd taken pride in herself, no matter how others had treated her. She was determined she'd rise above it all, make something of herself.

When she and Stanley first started to court she'd been afraid for him to meet her family. She'd known him since they were teenagers, running with the same gang of pals. Stanley knew what her father did for a living, but knowing that and meeting Reuben in the flesh, seeing how they lived, was a different matter. But her darling Stan had taken it all in his stride. He'd looked Reuben right in the eye, with a broad, fearless, even defiant grin on his face. She'd loved him all the more for that fearlessness. She suspected Reuben secretly respected Stanley for it too. He'd never, ever said a bad word against him anyway.

Josie felt her shoulders sag with despair.

If only Stanley were here. He was the very opposite of her father. Stanley was always laughing, always cracking a joke. And he was so loving, warm and good-natured. He liked closeness, to touch and be touched. That was one of the things she loved about him. They couldn't stand together unless he had a hand on her shoulder, or an arm around her waist. She'd known, perhaps long before Stanley had himself, that they were meant for each other. He was the only man for her, the only one. She'd never want anyone else. And he would never want anyone but her, would he?

Josie roused herself from her reverie. It was no good sitting here dreaming. With a sigh of reluctance, she followed Reuben out to the yard, anxious to see him gone. He'd just finished putting the horse between the shafts of the cart when Daisy appeared at the yard gate.

Josie's heart sank again at the sight of her. She admired Daisy and wished they could be friends, but how would she be able to look the midwife in the eye if Dada cut up rough and shamed them all?

She hurried over to Daisy at the gate and whispered urgently to her.

'Dada's in a bad mood this morning. Let the doctor talk to him, mun.'

Daisy pushed at the gate, her smile bright and determined.

'There's no time like the present, Josie. Don't worry. I'll be tactful.'

Reuben glanced briefly at the midwife as she came into the yard then got on with harnessing the horse. It was obvious Daisy was dead set on speaking to her father on the delicate subject of Mama's pregnancies. With a sense of helplessness, Josie moved away a little out of earshot, so's not to add to his fury, but not too far, in case Daisy needed her intervention.

Josie was filled with renewed admiration as she watched Daisy's tall, straight-backed figure fearlessly confront Reuben. After the first brief exchange which Josie could not hear, Reuben turned his back, tending to the horse, showing total disregard for the young midwife, but Daisy persisted, talking earnestly.

'Bloody hell!' Reuben swung round on her with a shout, wagging a long finger in her face. 'Keep your nose out of my business or else, see? Don't want you round by here no more, interfering between husband and wife.' He waved an arm threateningly. 'Go on! Bugger off!'

'Dada!' Hot with shame and apprehensive at the fury in his voice, Josie hurried forward to intervene. 'Don't speak to Nurse Buckland like that, Dada. Only trying to help Mama, she is. Listen to her, mun.'

'Josie's right,' Daisy said.

Through her voice was steady enough, Josie could see the young midwife's face had whitened with alarm and felt concerned for her. Despite her obvious dismay at Reuben's reaction, Daisy stood her ground firmly, and Josie could only admire her the more.

'Your wife almost died last night, Mr Randall,' she said bravely. 'It mustn't happen again. She's too old for child-bearing. All I'm asking is that you take precautions or exercise a little restraint.'

'Restraint?' He gave a harsh laugh, his mouth twisting in a sneer. 'Take your own advice, you ought to, isn't it?' He glanced meaningfully at her abdomen swelling under the belt of her navy blue serge raincoat. 'Not much restraint you had, did you, when you let somebody put *you* up the spout?'

'Dada!'

Mortified, Josie looked at Daisy's shocked expression and wished the ground would open up and swallow her. And with the hot blood of humiliation burning her neck and face, she also wished a thunderbolt would dart out of the blue and strike Dada, strike him dead. What must Daisy think of them all? What must she think of Josie for belonging to such a family?

The young midwife turned away abruptly and hurried from the yard. After directing a glance of contempt and hatred at her father, Josie ran out on to the pavement after her. Daisy was walking rapidly along Victor Street, back straight, shoulders stiff, obviously deeply offended.

Josie ran after her. 'Nurse Buckland, wait, please!'

When Josie called again, Daisy slowed, then stopped and turned. Josie ran up to her, putting a hand on her arm.

'There's sorry I am, Nurse Buckland, about my father insulting you like that. You must think we're awful people.' Josie gulped back

57

choking shame, trying to find words of apology. 'But we're not all like Dada, honestly. I'm so sorry he upset you. Please don't hold it against us ... me.'

Daisy's smile was a little hesitant at first, then she seemed to relax and her features softened.

'It's all right, Josie. Not one to hold a grudge, I'm not. Life's too short, isn't it? Especially these days.' She put a gloved hand over Josie's in a companionable way. 'Don't know why his silly insult affected me so much. I'm still not over losing my husband, you see. Still a bit sensitive.'

'A widow, are you, Nurse Buckland?' Josie put a hand to her mouth in consternation. Now she felt even worse. 'I didn't know that. Oh there's awful I feel now, mun.'

'Of course you didn't know. How could you? Don't worry about it. And my name's Daisy, remember? Listen, I'll come back with you now to see your mother as I intended. I'm ashamed I let your father put me off my duty.'

Josie bit her lip. She knew her mother needed the midwife's help until she was stronger, but didn't like the idea of Daisy's coming back to the house with Dada still there. She wasn't sure she could get compassionate leave, and didn't like the idea of the midwife coming round while she was in work, when she wouldn't be there to keep an eye on her father. She didn't know what would happen if Daisy and Dada came face to face again.

'Perhaps you'd better not,' she said. 'Once he's taken a grudge my father can get very nasty.' She grinned at Daisy, shame-faced. 'Even worse than today.' She looked serious again. 'Wouldn't want anything more to happen. You in your condition, like.'

Daisy started to retrace her steps towards the entrance to the yard.

'Sophia's my patient,' she said firmly. 'Hitler's bombs never stopped me doing my job. Neither will Reuben Randall. I'll be ready for him next time, don't you worry.'

Josie fell in step beside her. Her gaze was on the open yard gates, and her heart was in her mouth. Please let Dada leave now, she prayed silently.

Her prayer was answered immediately. As they reached the gates the old horse plodded out, Reuben sitting high on the cart seat. He didn't even look in their direction but went off down Victor Street at a sharp clip, his whip cracking above his head.

Josie felt weak with relief. She glanced at Daisy, meeting her answering look, and simultaneously they both burst out laughing.

Mama was showing a lot of improvement, and Josie was relieved that Daisy seemed pleased with her patient's progress.

'You're looking much better, Mrs Randall,' she said.

'*Si*. I think I get up soon. My children, they need their Mama.'

Josie glanced apprehensively towards Daisy, who laughed and shook her head. Her tone was firm when she replied: 'Can't have that,

Mrs Randall, indeed no. You must rest for two or three weeks, maybe more. We'll have to see. The children will survive. They have Josie here.'

'What are you thinking of, Mama?' she said quickly, to back up the nurse's advice. 'You've been very ill.'

Her mother looked doubtful and anxious and Josie felt a surge of love and tenderness for her. She was determined Mama would make a full recovery before resuming responsibility for the family. It wouldn't suit Dada to have his wife laid up for weeks, but he'd have to lump it. Mama had been through a dreadful ordeal and it was all his fault.

She reached over and gently stroked her mother's hair.

'Rest up like Daisy says, Mama, and leave everything to me.'

'I'll pop in again day after tomorrow,' Daisy said, when they were standing at the bottom of the stairs some time later.

Josie watched the young midwife put on her coat and hat. Daisy had such a lovely face, she thought, open and honest and compassionate. Despite her bereavement she seemed serene and composed, truly professional. No one would guess she was grieving inside. Josie felt suddenly very sad for her loss, and wanted to comfort her.

'There's sorry I am about your husband, Daisy,' she said, and squeezed her arm in sympathy as she helped her into her blue serge coat.

'Don't know how I'd feel if I lost my Stanley. Can't wait for him to come home, see. There's glad I'll be when this blooming war is over, isn't it?'

'Won't we all?' Daisy said, shrugging into her coat and buttoning it up. She was looking keenly at Josie, then suddenly seemed to make up her mind about something.

'Come round to my rooms this evening for a cup of tea and a chat, right, Josie? If you haven't something better to do, of course, and if your mother can spare you for an hour?'

Josie felt her face glow with pleasure.

'Oh, there's good of you to ask me, Daisy, especially after my father's rudeness to you.' Then with deep disappointment she remembered the Ajax. 'But working this afternoon, I am, see.'

She felt like wringing her hands with frustration. Daisy did like her and was offering a chance to be friends. It was more than she'd hoped for. Daisy might think she was being funny by refusing. She felt opportunity slipping through her fingers.

'One evening next week, then,' Daisy said, pressing her hand. 'Say you will, Josie I'm longing for a bit of company. With my family living down the Mumbles, I'm on my own a lot in the evenings, and I'm not used to it after sharing a flat in London. We could chat, or perhaps you like listening to the wireless? Some good programmes on now, aren't there? I love listening to *ITMA*, don't you? That Tommy Handly's a real scream, isn't he?'

'We haven't got a wireless here,' Josie admitted glumly. She couldn't imagine what it was like to sit with her family around the fire of an evening, say, laughing together. That seemed like another existence.

'Well, you can listen to mine,' Daisy said. 'My stepmother got it for me for company, but it's not like having someone to talk to. Say you'll come over?'

'Oh, there's lovely that'd be, mun. Love to come, I would.' Josie was delighted to realise Daisy sounded as eager as herself, and felt her cheeks flush with excitement. 'I'll bring some photos of my Stan.'

Josie felt apprehensive as she picked her way carefully through the blackout to the tall house on St Helen's Road where Daisy had her two rooms. A week had gone by and now she began to wonder if Daisy really meant her invitation. The midwife had called several times to see her mother during the week, and although Josie was there each time, having managed to get a few weeks' compassionate leave, Daisy hadn't repeated her invitation. She wondered now if the nurse had had second thoughts and was avoiding the subject.

Daisy came from a nice, respectable family. Mama had told her Daisy's stepmother, Edie, who kept a posh guest house in the Mumbles, was related by marriage to the Randalls. Edie Philpots had worked her fingers to the bone before the war to make something of her life and now Daisy's family were quite well-off,

Mama said, but not stuck up as far as she could remember, despite what Dada said. Josie liked the sound of Edie Philpots; she admired guts like that, and was longing to meet Daisy's family. A real family.

Yes, Daisy could hold her head up where family was concerned. Would she really want to be friends with a rag-and-bone man's daughter?

Josie's step faltered for a moment as she realised the enormous gulf between them. Perhaps Daisy's impulsive invitation had been prompted by nothing more than kindness, realising how badly Josie had been humiliated by her father's offensive behaviour. She hoped that wasn't the case because she would really like a friend.

Daisy's outlook and manner were so very different from the young women Josie usually met up with. Like Edie Philpots, she had made something of her life already. She was independent and respected, and Josie longed to be the same.

And she would be, too. As soon as she'd begun to work she'd started saving every penny to enrol in the Haslem System of Dress-making. When shift-work allowed she'd gone religiously to the classes held in the YMCA. She had quite a flair for dress- and pattern-making the tutor told her, and had been thrilled to complete the course with distinction. The next thing to save up for was a decent sewing-machine. She'd make clothes and sell them after the war. She and Stanley would have a good future, she was determined on that.

As soon as he came home for good she'd get away from Victor Street and her father. For years Josie had longed to leave the rag-and-bone yard and all it stood for. Beachcombing and scavenging weren't respectable. She'd hated the way some of the other kids had looked down on her at school. Francie didn't seem to mind the taunts and the snubs, but Josie had been pierced to her very heart.

But if she left Victor Street, who would stand up for Mama and the kids against her father?

Josie felt a twinge of guilt and struggled with it. Perhaps she'd help her mother to get away, too. She knew Sophia would take some persuading, but felt she must try for everyone's sake. She'd promised herself a better life and was determined to have it. Stanley was fighting for his country and he deserved something better, too. She and Stan would have children, a family of their own.

Josie glowed inwardly at the thought. She loved children, and was thrilled at the prospect of bearing Stan's. He'd make a smashing father, he was so loving.

She lifted her chin defiantly, mouth setting in a determined line. No one was going to take that dream away from her. If she couldn't persuade Mama to leave then Francie would have to start taking responsibility at home. She'd have to take care of Mama and the kids instead. Josie made up her mind to tackle her sister about it in no uncertain terms.

Josie knocked at the door of the house on St Helen's Road, her heart skipping a little with excitement as she listened for Daisy's footsteps in the passage, wondering what sort of welcome she'd get. Daisy spoke so nicely; had gone to the High School and all. Josie could learn many things from her but, she wondered, would Daisy be glad to see her?

Daisy's warm smile of greeting, by the masked light of a torch, set Josie's mind at rest. She was welcome. She felt a warm glow as she followed Daisy along the passage to her two rooms at the back of the house.

'Watch your ankles,' she said cheerfully. 'The eldest kid upstairs will leave his delivery bike in the passage. Nearly broken my neck a couple of times.'

When they were in Daisy's neat little sitting-room, Josie produced her offering from a string bag.

'Brought you half a dozen eggs, like,' she said and had to smile at Daisy's round eyes as she looked at the tempting eggs, and then the expressions that crossed her face: eagerness, doubt, guilt, hopefulness.

'Where on earth did you get these? They're not black market, are they?'

Josie tapped the side of her nose.

'Ask no questions, isn't it? I never do.'

Daisy put a hand to her throat. She reminded Josie of a child offered a bag of sweets by a stranger; longing to accept but wary of the consequences.

'Oh, they're so tempting, but black market ... My stepmother is dead set against black market stuff,' she said. 'She's convinced if we

65

eat anything black market, it'll bring bad luck to our boys over there, particularly to Gareth. She wouldn't half give me what-for if she knew I'd eaten so much as one black market egg.'

Josie couldn't help raising one brow. She considered that was putting superstition and patriotism before family, but didn't say so, not wanting to be critical of Daisy's stepmother, especially on such short acquaintance.

'Well, they're here now, aren't they? She'll never know, mun. And think of the baby, Daisy. After all, a gift from a friend, they are, and we are friends, Daisy, aren't we?'

'Of course, we are.' Daisy smiled broadly, accepting the eggs. 'I think we'll get along famously. Sit down by there then, Josie. Make yourself at home. Have some tea and a Welsh cake and tell me all about your Stanley.'

Josie stayed at Daisy's fireside longer than she'd intended. It was peaceful and cosy here. Josie knew she wouldn't rest until she and Stanley had a place of their own just like it.

The quiet, companionable atmosphere made her talkative, even more so than usual. She felt she could tell Daisy anything. She talked about her family, things she'd never told anyone else. Her father's tyrannical rule over the household; his suspected infidelity. The heartbreak she'd felt at losing her eldest brother at Dunkirk. The unaccountable animosity of her twin sister. And the great love in her heart for Stanley.

Daisy seemed at ease too, and talked a lot about her own husband, Gerald, tragically lost at sea. Yes, Josie decided, they could be great friends, given the opportunity. But Daisy would be going down the Mumbles to have her baby, due in the summer. Josie knew already she'd miss her. Daisy reassured her with promises that they would keep in regular touch.

'Besides, June is a long way off,' she said, as they stood in the darkened doorway. 'We'll have some outings in between, right? Like to come to the Plaza one evening later this week? There's a lovely film on with Clark Gable and Irene Bayliss.'

'Oh, Irene Bayliss!' Josie enthused. 'She's my favourite film star. Really glamorous, she is, mun. I see all her films if I can. She's supposed to come from Swansea, so they say.'

'That's right. My auntie, she is, as a matter of fact,' said Daisy.

'*What? Never!*' Josie was round-eyed with astonishment and extremely impressed. 'Really?'

'Well, my stepauntie, anyway,' Daisy said. 'She's my stepmother's younger sister. Ran away to London when she was only twenty, mind, and now she's a big star in Hollywood.'

Josie hurried across a blacked-out and deserted Hospital Square, faintly lit by a frosty moon. She'd never known anyone related to a real film star before, and to think Irene Bayliss was Daisy's auntie, and Daisy was *her* friend! It was a bit of excitement to share with Mama.

She turned into Victor Street, and her steps slowed. Her evening with Daisy had been so enjoyable but now that euphoria was fading. She dreaded going back to the cramped terraced

67

house; to the overcrowding and the violent rows. Dada was probably drunk already and looking for trouble, with everyone, especially the kids, trying to keep out of his way. It was no life for them and no life for her, either. She'd find her own rooms right away if it weren't for Mama and the kids, but they needed her, and she had no good excuse to leave.

Oh, Stan love, come back to me soon, she silently pleaded.

Chapter Four

Over the next few months Josie made the most of her new friendship with Daisy. She felt it was the start of something much better for her. They were a good bunch of girls at the factory, quite friendly really, but they were mostly Francie's pals. For some reason Josie always felt the odd one out. She wasn't stand-offish or prudish, but sometimes she thought their exuberance and jokes went too far, especially towards the men who worked there.

She enjoyed being in Daisy's company. They went to the pictures once a week, sometimes twice. There hadn't been an air raid since the night her mother had the miscarriage in February, and while the blackout was still a nuisance they felt they could sit in the cinema and watch a good film without having to keep one ear primed for sirens.

To show her appreciation of their friendship Josie made a coat for Daisy out of some wool blankets her father had scrounged from somewhere, dying them a lovely dark olive green. Reuben had driven a hard bargain, but her mind was set on having them. Grumbling, she'd paid him ten bob for them, but secretly knew they were well worth it. She'd got a great deal of pleasure from fitting and stitching and creating something worthwhile for her friend, and Daisy was delighted with the coat.

'I must pay you, mind, for materials and workmanship,' she said as she smoothed a hand over the warm wool material. 'There's beautifully made it is. You're so clever, Josie. I do envy your flair.'

'Listen, I don't want anything,' she said firmly. 'We're friends, right? Just thanks it is, mun, for your kindness to my mother and for the good times we've had over the last few months.'

In May a miracle happened. Or it seemed like a miracle to Josie anyway. Coming back from the pictures one night, she found her mother beaming for once, and her brothers and younger sister in a state of high excitement, practically clambering over a young man in soldier's uniform sitting on their horse-hair sofa. He jumped to his feet when she came in, and Josie almost fainted at the sight of him.

'Stanley!'

He was home. With a little screech of utter joy, she flung herself at him.

'Stan, oh Stan! Oh, my God! Is it really you, love?'

'It's me all right, kiddo.' He gathered her up in his arms, laughing. 'Better be, too. Don't want no other bloke cuddling my little wife.'

Josie couldn't believe she was in his arms again. She buried her face in the roughness of his khaki battledress. Her head was spinning with happiness and she could hardly breathe with the sheer ecstasy of seeing him, touching him, drawing into her nostrils the familiar and longed-for scent of him.

She lifted her face up to his and he kissed her in front of everyone: a good, solid, hungry kiss that made her knees feel weak and her heart start to pound. Tonight they'd be together. They'd spend the night loving each other. Josie's heart was thumping wildly in anticipation.

Abruptly conscious of their audience she pulled away, a little breathless and shy. She'd dreamed about Stanley coming home and how she would greet him, show him how much she loved and missed him. But she hadn't banked on an audience. Why hadn't he warned her?

'Why didn't you let me know, Stan? How long have you got?'

He held her close to him, grinning down into her face.

'Not saying you'll be glad to see the back of me, are you, kid? Haven't got another bloke in the wardrobe, have you?'

'Oh, Stan, don't be daft, will you?' Josie pouted. 'Making silly jokes like that.'

But even as she gently scolded him she could

70

feel him trembling as he held her and knew his flippancy was due to his pent-up feelings. They desperately needed to be alone to greet each other properly. They needed to go to bed somewhere soon. But where? Certainly not here. Oh, if only they had their own little place.

'Have you seen your mother yet, Stan love?'

'Straight here from the station, I came, mun,' he said. 'Couldn't wait to see you, love.' He lowered his voice, whispering so that she alone could hear. *'Duw annwyl!* I've missed you, lover. I want you, Josie love. Need you, mun.'

She leaned against him, her lips close to his cheek.

'I know, love. Me too. But not here.'

Josie pulled away again, turning to her mother.

'Mama, Stan and I are going over his mother's now. Gwennie don't even know he's home yet.'

Sophia's face fell.

'But, Josephina, your Stan's supper. I gotta ready, look.'

'Sorry, Mama,' Josie said. She glanced regretfully at the range where various pots were steaming deliciously. It would have been a meal for Stanley to remember, she knew. But it couldn't be helped.

'Gwennie wants to see her boy. You know how it is, Mama?'

Sophia sighed, smiling knowingly.

'Sure, I know. You go. God blessa you both. Go before your dada come home, eh?'

'Here you are, kid, have another sandwich, mun.'

Gwennie Jerkin's nicotine-stained fingers held out the roughly cut slices of bread to Josie as the three of them sat in Gwennie's small, cluttered living-room in St Helen's Avenue.

Smiling, Josie shook her head, watching the cigarette ash on the Woodbine hanging from her mother-in-law's lower lip grow longer and more precarious with every second. Knowing Gwennie, ash had probably been falling when she made the sandwiches and she hadn't noticed.

'Oh, Gwennie, you shouldn't have used up all your cheese ration on us. Never mind, I'll get you something from our house to make up for it.'

'Don't be *twp*, will you, kid?' Gwennie said, grinning. 'Nice one, I'd be, wouldn't I, if I didn't make an effort when my boy comes home?'

The length of ash fell on to the front of her jumper, stretched to its limit over ample bosoms. Gwennie brushed at it idly, leaving a dark grey stain in the faded wool.

'Oh, Stanley boy.' She put her head on one side, gazing in adoration at her son, tears brimming in her eyes. 'There's lovely to see you sitting by there, mun. How long have you got then, son?'

Stanley put his tea cup on the floor under the sofa, and stretching out his legs luxuriously, put an arm around Josie's shoulders, drawing her close to him.

'Seven days, Mam. Seven glorious days.' He

72

squeezed Josie even closer. 'Me and my lovely bit of stuff by here are going to spend every minute together, aren't we, kiddo?'

Josie looked up lovingly into his face, inches from hers. As he grinned down at her his eyes were shining with a light that made her heart take a sudden jump and a skip, setting her pulses throbbing.

Her husband was a handsome devil, she decided, not for the first time, with his strong nose and jaw, and grey eyes that could beguile and tease. She loved him beyond all reason. She prayed he felt the same about her, because if he ever left her, it would be the end of her.

'You'd better spend it with me,' she said, teasing. 'Or I'll go back to my fancy-man in the wardrobe.'

'Oh, aye!'

'What's it like in Iceland, then?' Gwennie asked, biting into the remaining sandwich.

'Blooming cold, Mam. Won't be going back there no more, though.'

Caught in the warmth of Stanley's arm around her, Josie nestled against him, not really hearing what he was saying. She leaned her head on his shoulder, closing her eyes for a moment of pure rapture. She felt she wanted to pinch herself every other minute to make sure she wasn't dreaming. Seven whole days and nights. She felt breathless in anticipation, and her heart gave a little flutter at the thought that perhaps within the next seven days she might fall for a baby. That would be perfect. Stanley's baby. Their baby. Their first.

Gwennie finished her sandwich then put out her cigarette by dropping the stub into the dregs of tea in her cup.

'Well, listen, kids. It's getting late.'

'It's only half-nine, Mam.'

Gwennie gave a chuckle, deep and rich and ripe with meaning.

'Hey, listen, half-nine is *very* late when a man hasn't seen his wife for a month of Sundays.'

Josie felt her face grow warm at the sound of Gwennie's suggestive chuckle. But perhaps they had been making it obvious. It was as though they couldn't keep their hands off each other. Josie knew how Stanley was feeling because she felt the same. It was like some terrible yet wonderful hunger and thirst that had to be satiated and quenched.

Gwennie pushed herself up from her armchair.

'Listen, I want you two to stay by here for the rest of Stan's leave, starting tonight. Make yourselves at home, like. Nobody'll disturb you.'

Josie sat up, concerned.

'Oh, we can't let you give up your home, Gwennie,' she said. But a new excitement shot through her like an electric shock at the prospect of having a place to themselves. 'It isn't fair, putting you out like that.'

Gwennie sniffed.

'Well, kid, you won't have any privacy down Victor Street, will you? Especially not with that bleeding father of yours, Josie.'

'But where will you go, Mam?' Stanley asked.

'Me and Josie could kip down on the floor by

here, couldn't we, love?'

'Don't be *twp*, mun,' Gwennie said. 'You're going to have my bed. Over my friend Doris Pugh's, I'll be. Asked Doris ages ago, didn't I, 'cos I knew you'd get leave sometime, see, Stan. Hey, and listen, you.' She wagged a stained index finger at Stanley. 'It's about time I had a grandson, isn't it, so get cracking, will you?'

Josie came drowsily out of sleep, feeling comfortable and warm. She'd been having one of her lovely dreams again, that Stanley was home. She opened her eyes with a sudden realisation. It was true. Last night was no dream. Last night had been paradise.

Josie sat bolt upright in bed, and turned to look at the place next to her, but the bed was empty. Stanley!

At that moment the bedroom door opened and he came in carrying two mugs of steaming tea. She felt a flood of warm relief wash through her.

'Morning, lover. Here you are, then. Get that down you.'

'Oh, Stanley, you're spoiling me, love. It's me that should be waiting on you.'

'What! After the treat you gave me last night?' Grinning, he climbed into bed beside her, cuddling up close, the warmth of his skin against hers sending sparks of desire through her body.

'Lovely, wasn't it?' he murmured against her ear.

Josie dipped her head, blushing. Self-consciously, she sipped her tea, recalling every moment of their night together, a night she'd remember all her life. It had been much more than lovely for her: it had been magnificent. Her Stanley was magnificent. She'd live on those memories for a long time. They'd keep her warm in bed in the lonely months ahead. But she wouldn't think of him going away just now. He was here beside her, and she would live for the minute.

'*Duw!* Josie girl, you're a smasher in bed, and gorgeous with it. Best time I've ever had.'

'Oh, yes?' Josie tossed her head in mock indignation. 'And who are you comparing me with then, I'd like to know?'

'Had every girl in Iceland, didn't I? None as good as you, though, lover.'

Josie dug a sharp elbow into his ribs. 'I'll brain you, you Casanova.' She turned her face to his, trying not to laugh. 'Do you know what I'll do to you if ever I catch you with another woman?'

'What?'

'I'll ... I'll spiflicate you.'

'Ooh! That sounds painful.'

Grinning, he put his mug on a side table and took hers from her hand.

'That's enough tea now, love. More important things to do, see. Want to make sure last night wasn't a fluke, like, so let's do it all over again, right?'

Kissing her eagerly, he pressed her down into the pillows, his hand already caressing her breast.

Josie, overcome with love for him, twined

her arms around his neck. She felt like crying with joy and happiness that they were together at last.

'Oh, Stan, I love you so much. This is like a beautiful dream to me.'

'I love you, too, kid.' Stanley nuzzled her neck gently, lovingly. 'And wherever I am, whatever I have to do, whatever is happening to me, always remember these days with you, I will. Always, lover.'

With a little cry of pleasure, she gave herself over to the fires of desire that were engulfing her.

Later, while they were resting in each other's arms, Josie allowed the real world to come into her mind for a moment. Outside their little heaven of peace and love the world was getting on with the business of war and work. While she wanted to spend as much time with Stan as possible over the following days, she couldn't get the time off. Any compassionate leave she might be entitled to had been used up earlier in the year on her mother.

She had long service at the factory and could pick and choose her holiday time, but she let the women with children take preference, and had agreed to take her week's holiday later in the year. She could mitch time off, of course, but that would be risking her job if she was found out, and she couldn't afford that.

Josie stirred, making a half-hearted attempt to get out of bed. Stanley's arms tightened around her.

'Where you going, lover?'

'Breakfast you want, don't you?'

'You're all I want, kid. Stay by here now.'

Josie sighed, giving in.

'Afternoons at the Ajax, I am, Stan love. Two till ten.'

He lifted his head to look at her, his expression almost comically sulky.

'Not thinking of going into work, are you, kid, leaving me by here on my own?'

Josie laughed, stroking his face gently, touching a fingertip to his lips. It was a generous mouth, and humorous too. It was one of the things she loved about him, his good humour. Now, he looked like a little boy whose mother says he can't have a toffee apple.

''Course I'm not going in today, silly. Gwennie can tell them I'm bad. One day won't matter. But the rest of the week I've got to go in. I can't help it, Stan.'

Frowning, he pushed himself up on an elbow.

'But I'm home on leave, mun, Josie. By here with me you ought to be, see, not gallivanting off to the factory. What'll I do by myself all day, then?'

She ran a hand caressingly across his chest, revelling in the warmth of his skin. She always felt a little heady when he was close by her, and she knew she always would.

'Can't afford to lose my job, Stan love,' she said coaxingly, longing to kiss him, feel his arms tight around her again. 'I'm on good money now, I know, but we need every penny.'

78

'You get most of my army pay as well, Josie. Isn't that enough?'

'No, it's not enough, Stan,' she declared, getting stern control of herself and struggling to sit up. 'I'm saving up, aren't I? I want us to have a nice place after the war. Might even *buy* a house, isn't it, for when we have a family.'

'Oh, flip!' Stanley swung his legs off the bed. 'Listen to you, then, talking like Lady Muck now. I don't want no responsibility of a house, Josie. Don't even know if I'll have a job when I come out. My Uncle Bill said it was a shambles after the last war. Don't want no blooming mortgage round my neck as well, do I?'

Josie bit her lip in disappointment. She'd thought he'd be as enthusiastic as she was. If Stan had a fault it was a slight shrinking from responsibility. She knew it scared him a bit, and could understand his point of view, too. Life was uncertain enough for them now. She didn't want to worry him or put pressure on him, not with the way things were. Josie had courage and confidence enough for both of them.

She'd love to own a house, but it wasn't as important to her as Stanley's happiness. She wouldn't let them argue, not on his leave.

'Well, perhaps buying a house is a bit ambitious, love,' she agreed, to placate him. 'But I'm determined to have a nice place for us. Not around here, either. I'll stay in the Ajax as long as I can. After the war I'll be taking up dressmaking as a business, like. I'm good at it, Stan love. I can make it work for us.'

He turned back to her, smiling.

'Why don't you start at it full-time now then, lover? Give up the old factory, mun. Never mind about the money. It's dangerous there. Tommy Wilkin's sister had half her hand sliced off by a machine I heard. I worry about you, Josie.'

She swallowed hard. She'd been in work the afternoon that accident had happened. It had been horrifying, terrifying, and she'd been frightened and upset for weeks after. But you had to go on, didn't you, no matter what?

Josie shook her head. 'I can make the odd dress or coat for friends, like, but I couldn't do dress-making full-time in Victor Street, Stan. There's no room for a start, and my father would interfere. He'd say I was making money off his back and want a share. He'll get nothing from me, though. I'll see Mama all right, but Dada can take a running jump off Mumbles Pier.'

Stanley's expression became serious and concerned. He touched her cheek gently.

'There's awful bitter you sound, love. Get away from there, you should. Rent a place now, mun. We wouldn't need to use my mam's rooms when I'm home, then.'

Josie sighed, feeling a lump rise in her throat. If only she could, but an overwhelming sense of duty anchored her to Victor Street.

'Got to stay, I have, see, Stan, to take care of Mama and the kids. Dada's getting worse. Drinking more than ever and gone awful violent. Don't know why.'

She couldn't bring herself to tell him about

Dada's fat fancy woman from Port Tennant. Too ashamed.

Stanley's mouth tightened.

'He's not knocking you about, is he, Josie?' He gripped her arm, looking quite fierce for a moment. 'I'll swing for him if he is.'

She shook her head, reluctant to say too much about her father's increasing animosity towards her. She could take care of herself. Hatred of Reuben Randell kept her from fearing him.

'How's your mother managing with you by here with me, then?' Stanley asked.

'Francie's keeping an eye on things.'

She hoped that was true anyway. She felt a strong duty towards Mama and the kids, but Stanley was the most important person in the world to her. She just had to have this time with him. Her sister must take her share of responsibility.

'Francie's on early shift this week. Dada's out all day totting with the horse and cart, so she'll be there later when he's had a skinful.'

Stanley sighed, settling back under the covers again.

'Of course you're right, Josie love. Got to look after your job. We don't know what's going to happen, see. You need the security of a job. If you should be left without ...'

Something in his voice made Josie look at him sharply. She leaned her elbow on the pillow beside him, looking down into his face.

'Stan, what is it?'

'Well, love, this is embarkation leave. Iceland

won't see me no more. Got an idea it's going to be pretty hot where I'm going. I'll be wishing I was back in the cold.'

Josie swallowed hard. What was to happen to him when this leave was over? It was the one thing she'd avoided thinking about. Now she had to face it.

'Not the Middle East, Stan?'

'It's just rumours, love, but I wouldn't mind betting I'll be kicking up sand before long.'

Deep in her heart she'd known their luck had finally run out. Stanley was to be sent to fight in North Africa. A sudden coldness clutched at her heart and her throat tightened in dread. She put out a hand to stroke his face.

'Oh, Stan, I'm frightened for you. My friend Daisy lost her husband earlier on this year. There's sorry for her, I am. I'll go mad if I lose you, Stan love. Stark, staring mad.'

His arms slipped around her and he drew her down to him.

'You won't lose me, lover, not if I can help it anyway. Like I said it's rumour, but we'll have to face it. Thousands of other couples are suffering the same way. Come on, let's forget it for now. Make the most of my leave.'

Josie went off to work each afternoon, but it was hard keeping her mind on what she was doing. She thought of nothing else but Stanley, longing to be with him.

'Josie!' Islwyn Davies, the foreman, shouted

in her ear above the din of the works. 'What the bloody hell do you think you're doing, woman? Put the bloody safety guard down, mun. Want to lose a hand, do you?'

She couldn't get back to Gwennie's fast enough in the evenings. Stanley would have a cup of tea waiting for her and something to eat. It wasn't long before they were in each other's arms, in a world of their own. Josie lived for those hours when Stanley's love-making wiped out all her fears—until the light of a new day came anyway.

On Friday evening she came home and immediately noticed a change in him. Usually while she ate the meal he'd prepared, he'd be full of chatter about the people he'd bumped into during the afternoon. This evening he seemed to have little to say. He sat at the table with her, making patterns on the table-cloth with the handle of a spoon.

'What's the matter, Stan?'

He looked up, obviously startled by her question.

'How do you mean, lover?'

'You look upset about something. Worried about going back, like? Is that it, Stan?'

He reached across and caught at her hand, squeezing it tight.

'Josie, you know I love you, don't you, kid? You mean everything to me, mun. Don't want anything or anyone to come between us, like.'

She gave a little laugh.

'Don't be soft, Stan, will you? Nothing will

come between us. I won't let it. And if you're thinking I might be tempted to go with someone else when you're away, put it right out of your head, love. You're the only one I want.'

A spasm of emotion passed across his face for a moment.

Puzzled but touched by it, Josie put down her cup, rose quickly from her chair and went to him, sitting on his lap, putting her arms around his neck.

She kissed him and his arms tightened around her fiercely. He was trembling slightly. He was afraid, she could tell, and her heart went out to him.

He drew back a little, looking into her face, though it puzzled her to see that he didn't look her directly in the eye as he usually did. She wanted to tell him that there was nothing shameful in being afraid, but hesitated, not wanting to embarrass him.

'Listen, Josie love. If I'd done something thoughtless, something wrong ...' He hesitated as though unsure of how he should go on. 'If somebody said something against me, you wouldn't stop loving me, would you, kid?'

'What are you on about, Stan?'

'Sometimes a man does stupid things, you know, on the spur of the moment, like, without thinking too much about it. Later, he's sorry to hell and back. If I did something like that, you wouldn't hate me, would you, kid?'

Josie put her hands on his shoulders and looked deep into his eyes.

'Is this some kind of a test of my love, Stan?

Because if it is, I'm a bit hurt.'

'*Duw annwyl!*' He pulled her fiercely to his chest, holding her tight against him. 'I wouldn't hurt you on purpose, love, you know that, don't you?'

His voice sounded despairing, Josie thought, with a quiver of her heart. She couldn't remember ever seeing him like this before, but then, she'd never before seen him prepare, steel himself for the prospect of killing or being killed. Violence wasn't in his nature, unlike her father. Of course he was frightened of what was in front of him, any man would be, and most would be ashamed of that fear and try to hide it from their loved ones.

'Stan love, nothing you could ever do would make me stop loving you. Nothing. Now put it out of your head, will you?'

Josie stood up and pulled him to his feet.

'Come on! Only got a couple of days left together, haven't we? Let's make the most of them. I've managed to get tomorrow off. We'll have most of Sunday, too, before you have to leave.'

Stanley shook his head.

'But there's something I have to tell you, Josie. Something you should know ...'

'Don't want to hear it, Stan love.'

She thought she knew what it was. She was frightened for him, too, and didn't want to face up to that fear yet. The time to face up to her numbing dread would be when he'd gone away and she was alone. Not now. They must be happy while they were together. For all they knew it could be the last time.

'Write to me, Stan, and tell me all about it then.'

His shoulders sagged.

'All right, kid. Perhaps it's best. This is our special time and I won't spoil it for you.'

Josie knew she'd remember the following two days, their last two days, all her life. Stanley was more loving, more attentive, than she'd ever known before. It was just the two of them alone in their own world, spending their hours making love or just clasped in each other's arms in companionable silence.

While Stanley's love-making was as passionate as ever, Josie sensed that his earlier despair had not completely evaporated. It was during these silences that she was aware of it most. If anything, Stanley was normally a chatterer; teasing, cracking silly jokes, rarely silent. She'd never seen him so serious before, and wasn't sure she liked it.

Even Gwennie noticed his strange mood on Sunday evening when she came over to see him before they left for High Street Station.

'You two had a tiff or something?' she asked in the kitchen downstairs as Josie prepared him some sandwiches. 'There's quiet he is, mun, isn't he?'

'No, Gwennie,' Josie said. 'Nerves, I think it is, like.'

'Our Stan nervous?' Gwennie was scornful. 'Remember the first day he went away? Like a blooming schoolboy, he was, going on a day trip to the sands.'

'This is different, Gwennie,' Josie said quietly. 'It's probably North Africa this time. He's afraid, poor love.'

Gwennie looked dubious.

'Know him of old, I do. He's got something else on his mind, he has. What's he been up to, then?'

Gwennie wouldn't come to the station, but said her goodbyes in her rooms. She was weepy and sorry to see her son go away again, but underneath, too, Josie sensed Gwennie was glad to be back in her own place. Who could blame her? Didn't she herself long for a place of her own?

Josie looked around the untidy living-room before she and Stanley left for the station. Gwennie was glad to be back, and she herself was sorry to be leaving this little haven, too. The last seven days had been heaven, sheer heaven. But she'd have her memories of this leave to keep her going; memories that no one could take away, no matter what happened.

They waited for a bus up by the hospital. It was a lovely evening, and people were coming out of church. Josie hoped they'd spot Daisy. She wanted to introduce Stanley to her friend. She was so proud of him.

At the station there were many people saying goodbye, service people and their loved ones. The train was already standing at the platform, engine grumbling and growling as though gathering its strength for the effort of separating loved one from loved one.

In the sky above the open railway line seagulls were flying, their raucous calls reminding Josie of the wails of despairing people. She felt something like despair in the pit of her stomach, but fought it off. She wouldn't let herself despair. Stanley would come home to her, safe and sound. She just knew it in her heart. She would ache for him, yearn for him, but her memories would remind her of his love. They'd keep her warm and comforted, no matter how long they were parted.

'Write to me as soon as you can, will you, Stan love? And wherever they send you, keep writing.'

He put his kit into a compartment near the open door, then they stood on the platform, arms around each other. Josie could see the station clock; the big hand seemed to be racing round to the moment of parting. She wanted to scream at it to stop. Stop time, stop everything.

Stanley put his lips against her cheek.

''Course I'll write, love. You mustn't worry, now. Promise me you won't?'

Josie knew she couldn't promise that. He would be in her mind every waking minute, and in her dreams, too. Her lovely dreams.

'I'll write to you every day, Stan, every day. Look after yourself, my darling.'

She put up a hand to stroke his face. Even in the balmy May evening air, his cheek felt cold.

Unable to suppress a little cry of fear for him, Josie clung to him.

'Oh, God! Stan love, this is tearing me apart.'

Stanley held her tight, swaying a little as though comforting a child.

'Love you, sweetheart, I do. Always remember that. I'll be back. Don't doubt it for a minute, will you?'

The sound of the engine seemed to become louder, more demanding. Steam began to gush from its enormous sides as though warning that it would not wait for them much longer. Suddenly it screamed and roared as though in fury and people began to move reluctantly on board.

Josie didn't want to let go of Stanley. He kissed her long and passionately, pressing her even closer.

'Got to go now, lover,' he said against her ear. His voice was husky and raw with feeling, and Josie suspected he was close to tears himself. 'Won't say goodbye, though, mun. Just I'll be seeing you, kid.'

He jumped on board and let down the window to lean out. Josie held up her hands to be clasped. The lump of misery in her throat was choking her, making it hard to speak. She wanted to say so much to him, things she'd forgotten to ask, things she'd forgotten to tell him. Now it was too late.

She thought of Daisy for a moment. She must have stood like this saying goodbye to her husband, never to see him again.

'Stan, I love you. Come back to me, please. Die without you, I will.'

'Chin up, kiddo.' He tried to grin, but it was a pale imitation of his usual cheeky, carefree expression, and it tore at Josie's heart like a claw. 'And thank you, Josie sweetheart. Thank you for everything. You've made me so happy, kid, and I've been such a stupid fool. I don't deserve you, Josie. Only wish I'd treated you better, love ...'

A whistle blew and with one enormous burst of steam the engine began to move and gather speed. She ran by the side of the train, still clutching at Stanley's hand.

Something in his voice, in his eyes, made her apprehension sharpen. What was he trying to say? She had to know. It was important, she knew it was, but there was no time left for them.

'Stan? I don't understand, Stan. What do you mean?'

He released her hand, but Josie kept running, eyes fixed on his face, pale now and sad.

'So long, my lovely girl,' He waved. 'Love you. Love you, Josie. And God Bless.'

He was moving away from her, out of her reach. He leaned further out of the carriage window, waving, waving.

'Stan!'

The cry of despair was torn out of her as she stumbled to a stop. It felt like the end of the world had suddenly come upon her. How could she live with this awful fear? How would she live without him?

Chapter Five

Outside High Street station Josie boarded a double-decker bus which would take her as far as the Guildhall, the closest stop to Victor Street. Dreamtime was over. It was back to the real world, stark reality, a world at war, a world without Stanley. Already she was missing him bitterly.

Downstairs was full so she climbed the narrow metal steps to the top deck. She felt washed out, listless. She felt like having a good cry, and just in case she couldn't help herself, took a seat at the back. She didn't want the other passengers seeing her weakness.

With brimming eyes she looked idly out of the window. It still gave her a strange, eerie feeling to ride a bus across town, or rather the space where the town centre had once been, a stark no-man's-land of rubble now where once familiar buildings had stood.

The bus stopped in Oxford Street to drop passengers. It was still called the Market stop, though there was no familiar red-brick market there now, just more rubble, overgrown with bright pink and purple weeds, and tufts of hardy, spindly grass, the kind usually seen growing on old ruins.

Viewing the desolation of the town centre was always depressing, Josie found, but today

91

it was even worse. It echoed the desolation in her heart. How long before she and Stanley were together? Would she even see him again? In her mind's eye he wore the sad expression of those last moments together. She didn't want to remember him like that. She wanted to remember her own Stanley, his cheery grin, his silly jokes, his laughing eyes. What had he been trying to tell her? She wished with all her heart she'd listened while there'd still been time.

She got off the bus by the Guildhall and walked back along the main road towards the Sandfields. She dreaded going back to Victor Street more than ever. She hoped her father had been behaving himself. But Francie was there looking after things. She'd have sent word if there'd been any trouble.

The yard gates were padlocked, as was usual on a Sunday, though what Reuben had to protect Josie couldn't guess. The front door was standing open as usual, too. She went into the narrow passage in time to see Francie sauntering down the stairs.

She paused at the bottom with one hand on her hip, gazing mockingly at Josie.

'Well, look what the cat's dragged in. Honeymoon over, is it?'

'Stan's gone back, if that's what you mean,' she said, tossing her head in annoyance. 'Probably end up in North Africa.'

If she'd hoped for some sympathy and understanding from her own sister, obviously she'd hoped in vain. But then Francie had no one to miss and worry about. How could her

92

sister possibly understand the dread of watching a loved one leave, knowing they might never be seen again; the terror of realising that soon he could drop and die in some unknown foreign place? But she mustn't torture herself with such thoughts. Stanley would come back. He must.

'And as far as I'm concerned,' Josie went on defiantly, taking off her coat and headscarf, 'the honeymoon will never be over.'

Francie's lip curled and she gave a short laugh.

'Remains to be seen, isn't it? Plenty of easy pieces out there, mind, so I've heard. He might come back with the clap yet.'

'Don't be disgusting, will you?' Josie was furious, face contorted in deep disgust. She felt like slapping her sister's grinning face. 'Stan's no pushover for a bit of skirt. Not like some of the bright sparks *you* go out with. You ought to find yourself somebody decent, like I did.'

Mama was right. Francie was jealous of her happiness with Stanley. Eaten up with jealousy. She'd like to spoil it if she could. But nothing could shake her love for Stan, Josie knew. Their love was meant to go on for ever. She trusted him and he trusted her. That's what love was all about. It was something Francie obviously couldn't understand, perhaps never would understand. She was a cold fish, self-centred and envious. Josie wondered why she hadn't understood this better before.

'Oh, get you!'

Francie pushed past her. She looked as though she were about to go out. Her pale hair was pinned up in soft rolls at the sides and in front, while at the back it fell to her shoulders in a smooth pageboy style, one Josie favoured herself.

Francie had been liberal with the lipstick and rouge, Josie noticed—then she noticed something else. Francie was wearing a cream sprigged cotton dress with a sweetheart neckline. *Josie's* best dress, one she'd made herself out of a piece of material she'd bought from her father. She'd meant to wear it for Stanley on this leave, but in the excitement of his being home, had forgotten to take it with her to Gwennie's. Then she hadn't needed it because Stan hadn't wanted to go out. He'd just wanted them to be alone, loving each other.

Seeing Francie wearing it now was a painful reminder, and Josie was furious.

'Hey! That's my dress. I've only worn it once. Where do you think you're going in that?'

'Out.'

Josie was even more furious. She wouldn't dream of borrowing anything of Francie's without asking.

'Not in my dress you're not.'

She stood with legs slightly apart, hands on hips, head thrust forward aggressively, ready to make a fight of it. Pent-up despair at Stanley's leaving, a feeling she must keep under control if she were to go on functioning, was building up inside despite her resolve. Maybe she was spoiling for a fight just to relieve that pressure somehow. Maybe she was overreacting, but she couldn't help herself.

'Go on!' She jerked her head towards the stairs. 'Take it off now. And stay out of my wardrobe or else.'

Francie looked disdainful and unimpressed at Josie's very Italianate gesturing. She was suddenly very much aware of the great gulf between them. How could they possibly be twins? How could they even be sisters?

Despite their unhappy home, Mama had always tried to instill a sense of family in them. The Randalls might have nothing to be proud of but at least they could show a united front to the outside world, Mama had said. Josie had learned this lesson but Francie stubbornly held herself apart. She didn't care about family. She didn't care about any of them, not even Mama, it seemed. She was selfish to the core.

'Well!' Josie asked angrily. 'Are you going to take if off?'

Francie flicked her hair back from her shoulders contemptuously and made no attempt to do as she was told. She picked up her coat and slipped into it.

'Francie!' It was a warning.

'Oh, don't talk tripe, will you?' she snapped impatiently. 'Share the same wardrobe, don't we?'

'You know what I mean,' Josie said lips tight with anger and frustration.

Despite all her threats there was no way she could physically make Francie take the dress off, and her sister knew it.

'And where are you going anyway, all tarted up like that?'

'If you must know, Billy Parsons is taking me out. None of your business, though, is it?'

Josie's face fell in consternation, the fight going out of her.

'Oh, not him, Fran! He's a proper little crook, he is. I'd be ashamed to be seen with him if I were you.'

'Well, you're not me, are you?' Francie snapped. 'Billy's all right. Don't mind spending a bit on a girl, either.'

Josie gave a short laugh of derision.

'Yes, and where does he get the money to splash about in wartime, that's what I'd like to know? Because he hasn't got a job, has he? How he's managed to dodge the call-up, I don't know.'

'He's got a bad heart,' Francie said casually, tying a pale pink chiffon headscarf under her chin.

'Bad heart, my bum!' Josie exclaimed with some heat. 'He's no more got a bad heart than our cat. He's a right little spiv! What do you want to get mixed up with him for? You'll be getting a bad name, you will,' she said seriously. When it came down to it there were worse things than being a rag-and-bone man's daughter. 'Billy Parsons will end up in clink, mark my words.'

Francie tossed her head.

'Well, if he does so will Dada, because they're thick as thieves now.' She grinned suddenly. 'Oops! Slip of the tongue.'

Josie felt the muscles of her face tighten in apprehension.

'What do you mean?'

Francie moved towards the front door. Josie glanced enviously at her sister's legs, and the perfectly straight seams running up her calves. Looked as though she was wearing new stockings. Now where did she get those? Josie hadn't had new stockings in a month of Sundays, and was tired of darning and re-darning her old ones.

'Billy was round here yesterday,' Francie said over her shoulder as she paused on the doorstep. 'He and Dada were chewing the rag over something for ages. That's when he asked me out. He's not bad-looking, really.'

'Oh, aye,' Josie smirked. 'If you don't look too close.'

Francie tilted her nose in the air.

'He's got a motor-bike and sidecar now as well, so there. He's taking me for a run down the Gower.'

'Francie, you're a silly little fool, going anywhere with him.'

She glared at Josie angrily, eyes flashing with ill-concealed spite.

'Mind your own business, will you? You worry about that husband of yours, right? He's no angel, either. He gets up to plenty behind your back.'

'Oh, push off! Go on,' Josie said, her own anger returning. 'You make me sick, you do. Go on then. Get yourself into trouble. See if I care.'

Mama was in the lean-to kitchenette, standing at the stove, her back turned, when Josie came in.

'Hello, Mama. Cup of tea going, is there?' She perched herself on a stool near the big square china sink. 'I'm fed up to the back teeth, what with Stan going away to God knows where and that Francie pinching my things. I hope she's been sticking up for you while I was with Stan?'

'*Si*, sometimes, *cara mia*. But she don't stay in much,' Sophia said quietly, and didn't turn to face her daughter or move away from the stove.

Something in her subdued tone made Josie get up off the stool and go to her. She had the distinct feeling Sophia was avoiding catching her eye. That was unlike her mother.

'Mama, what's wrong?'

Josie took hold of Sophia's arm and turned her round to see her face—and then drew in her breath sharply, staring in horror. The skin around Sophia's right eye had already turned black, and there were black and blue bruises on her cheekbone, too.

'Mama! *He* did this to you, didn't he?'

Josie felt a tremendous surge of rage and resentment against her father rise up in her chest and then her throat, making her spittle taste bitter. The force of it made her head feel tight, as though it were spinning crazily, and for a moment she found she couldn't breathe properly.

'I'll kill him! I will!' Josie was beside herself.

She raised her fists in the air, clenching her hands so tightly in her rage that her nails were digging into her palms. 'I'll swing for him, the brute! Where is he, the swine?'

Sophia clutched at her arm, her eyes frightened.

'No! No, Josephina. You do nothing. You promise, eh? He beat my poor Johnno, too. My boy, he try to help me.'

Josie stared wildly into her mother's eyes for a moment, then with a sob threw her arms around Sophia, hugging her tight, realising that even now her mother was trembling. And Francie had let this happen! She hadn't even warned Josie about it. Her rage compassed both sister and her father then.

'Oh, Mama, I'm so sorry. Never should've left you, should I? My fault, it is.'

'No, no *cara mia.*' Sophia clung to her lovingly. 'You want to be with your Stan. You love him. It is wonderful. You could do nothing, nothing. He beat you too. I do not want this, *cara.*'

Maybe that was why Francie hadn't intervened, afraid of getting beaten? But why didn't she come and warn Josie what was going on? She couldn't make excuses for her sister. Francie was acting irresponsibly, selfishly. Thinking more of herself than of Mama and the kids. She was a lot like Dada in many ways, Josie reflected. If only she could get her mother away from here. It was the only way. She must try to persuade her.

Josie swallowed hard, holding her mother away from her, looking deeply into her eyes.

'Mama, you can't go on like this. Leave him. You've got to, for the sake of the kids as well as yourself. I'll find us a place. Saved up, I have.' She hesitated then added reluctantly, 'Francie can come with us, too, if she wants to.'

'Leave my husband!' Sophia looked deeply shocked at the suggestion and shook her head vehemently. 'It is not possible. It is not respectable, Josephina. *Santo madre!* People, they would call me bad names. I could never go to Mass again. The shame ...'

'Mama, people know what Dada's like, don't you worry,' Josie said, her lips tight. 'They wouldn't blame you. You don't deserve this, Mama.' Josie hesitated for only a moment. Her mother needed to know the worst. 'He's got another woman, too. I'm sorry, Mama.'

Sophia lowered her eyes.

'*Si*, I know. He tell me. He say he bring her here, maybe.'

'What?' Josie was speechless for a moment. 'Over my dead body!' she burst out at last. 'Oh, Mama. How can you stay with him? How can you put up with it? If it were my Stan, I'd kill him.'

Sophia smiled sadly, lifting a hand to Josie's face to stroke it gently.

'Reuben, he is not a good man, I know this. But he is my husband. To leave one's husband is sinful. I stay. It is God's will, God's law, *cara mia*. Now we talk of this no more.'

With a little cry of despair, Josie hugged her mother close to her again. How could it be God's will that gentle Mama should be

100

beaten, should have such a wretched life? Poor defenceless Mama.

Josie's heart ached with despair and anger, an impotent anger now as she realised she was as trapped as her mother. How could she ever leave Mama alone now? Even when Stan came home for good, how could she go off to a place of their own and leave Mama to her fate?

Stan would come home expecting them to be alone together in their own rooms. Would he understand why that was impossible? And there was the bright future she had planned for them, starting her own dress-making business. Reuben Randall had a lot to answer for. He stood between Josie and all future happiness. Every one of them would be better off without him.

If ever Josie had wished her father dead, she wished it then. She knew it was wicked to have such thoughts but couldn't help it. How much happier they'd all be if Reuben Randell were dead!

Chapter Six

The Mumbles, July 1943

Daisy's stepmother had opened all the windows first thing in the morning before they started their marathon clean-up. Now they were almost finished. Every square inch of paintwork had been washed down, and every piece of linoleum and floorboard in the house had been scrubbed to the very grain.

As she busied herself on hands and knees scrubbing the red quarry tiles in the narrow kitchenette, Daisy could hear the raucous call of seagulls, ever hungry, and thought she could smell the ozone, which wasn't surprising since the sea front was just a five-minute walk away from Woodville Road.

'Here, my girl! You shouldn't be doing that in your state.'

Daisy looked up to see her step-grandmother standing in the doorway, mop and bucket in hand.

'Now, Mam-gu,' Daisy said, sitting back on her haunches to wring out the floor-cloth. 'It's over a month since Valerie was born. I'm fit as a fiddle. Never better. But with your bad leg, you shouldn't be standing about mopping, should you? You'll be in agony later. Now go and sit down.'

'Sit down! I've never sat down in my life when there was a bit of work to do.' Mam-gu was indignant. 'Brought up four children, I have, on next to nothing, and kept my place spotless. Spotless!'

'I know, Mam-gu,' Daisy said patiently. 'But sixty-five you are now, mind, not thirty-five, and it's time to rest. Gramps will be wanting his tea, and Mam and me, we've nearly finished here now.'

Without a word Mam-gu put the mop and bucket down with a clatter and turned to go. Suddenly filled with tenderness for the older woman Daisy jumped to her feet. Whereas Edie and Mam-gu had always had an edgy relationship, Daisy got on very well with her prickly step-grandmother, understanding that her vinegary nature was only on the surface.

'Mam-gu, wait a minute, will you?'

Daisy put her arms around the older woman, giving her an affectionate hug. She was extremely fond of her, and of Gramps, too. She'd been only eight years old when her father, Michael, had married Edie Bayliss, who was seventeen years his junior. She'd loved her warm-hearted stepmother straight away, and when her father died so suddenly after only two years of marriage, Daisy had thanked God for giving Edie to her as a mother. And Edie's family became hers.

'Thanks so much for helping me get the place ready, Mam-gu. You know I'm grateful, don't you? I couldn't do without you.'

Daisy kissed her step-grandmother's cheek. She didn't expect any great show of affection back. She'd realised from an early age that Mam-gu. found it very difficult to show her true feelings—a knowledge Edie had never fully grasped, being naturally demonstrative herself.

There was a brief pat on the back from Mam-gu before she wriggled free from Daisy's embrace.

'I'll be over first thing tomorrow, then,' she said, mollified but obviously trying not to show it as Daisy helped her into her cardigan over her wrap-around pinny. 'To help with your bit of furniture, like. There's lucky, isn't it, I'm only two doors down?'

She was the lucky one, Daisy decided as she emptied the dirty water down the drain in the small backyard. In spite of everything she was fortunate. She had a beautiful little baby daughter and now a house all to herself.

Daisy knew Edie had been hoping she and the baby would settle down and live at *Tŷ Heulwen.* It would have been safe and comfortable and easy to do that, but in her heart Daisy knew she wanted her independence more. She needed her own place in which to bring up her daughter her own way. When Edie had offered her the tenancy of one of her terraced houses in Woodville Road, Daisy had been delighted and so grateful.

She'd been dismayed at the thought that she hadn't one stick of furniture of her own, but William, her step-father, came up trumps there. He had a pal, he said, who would fix her up with some good second-hand stuff and at a bargain price as well. William was always delighted to fix someone up with a bargain.

Tomorrow she'd be moving in with her bits and pieces. It was the beginning of a new phase in her life. It frightened her sometimes to think that she was a young widow who must struggle through life on her own. All the time Gerald had been away at sea she hadn't felt lonely, nor had she felt lonely since coming home. Now she had gained her independence, and independence had its own price. But it was one she was prepared to pay.

She was lucky, though, she reflected, because

at her back she had the security of a family who cared.

Two weeks after Daisy moved into Woodville Road, the midwife, Nurse Menna Ellis, called to see how mother and baby were getting on. Menna was short of stature and solidly built, with sturdy legs that seemed too short for her body, Daisy always thought. Her round apple-cheeked face looked shiny, as though it had just been scrubbed, a reminder of her farm upbringing in Carmarthen.

Menna was always a bit of a chatter-box, but now that she was nearing the end of her career, her tongue seemed to wag even more readily, as if she were trying to get in as much chat as she could before she retired.

For all that, Daisy was glad to see her today. Next month she would take Menna's place as the local midwife in the Mumbles, and felt greatly excited at the prospect. Even though she was a relative newcomer she loved the unique character of the area, which had changed comparatively little from the quaint Victorian fishing village it had once been.

Thankfully, it had largely escaped the blitz in 1941 which had destroyed the very heart of Swansea. Mumbles, with its assortment of little shops along the Dunns and beyond Oystermouth Square, the more recent and prestigious ones straggling up Newton Road, was a constant source of interest to her and to the many day-trippers who still, even in wartime, flocked there to enjoy the serene beauty of the surrounding bays and beaches. On a day trip to the Mumbles, for an hour or two, one could forget there was a war on.

She was very lucky to be living here, Daisy decided. She'd had her baby, a beautiful baby, and had found a home for them. Now she needed to get back to work. That was the one thing that would keep her going for the rest of her life, she decided. There'd be no time for loneliness now.

''Morning, Menna. There's a hot one, isn't it? Have a cuppa then?'

'Lovely, *bach*. But Baby first, isn't it?'

Daisy had tucked baby Valerie into the corner of the big hide armchair at the side of the fireplace, the chair that had been her father's favourite in those happy years of her childhood in the Gower. Daisy wasn't given to being fanciful but couldn't help feeling that Michael Evans's spirit wasn't far away, watching over her and his granddaughter.

'Well! There's a picture for you, isn't it?' Menna said, lifting Valerie up into her arms. 'Oh, and there's a lump she's getting, as well.'

'She's not fat,' Daisy said defensively.

'No, no, just nicely covered. Like to see chubby legs on Baby myself. And look at those eyes, will you? Knowing little madam already, isn't she?'

Valerie's large grey eyes, so like Gerald's, were regarding the midwife solemnly without the hint of a welcoming smile. When Daisy picked her up Valerie usually greeted her mother with a wide gummy grin and a couple of happy gurgles.

106

Edie said it was only wind, but Daisy knew better.

'Hey! Smile then, for Aunty Menna,' Menna coaxed, a finger on the baby's chin persuasively. Instead Valerie screwed up her little face and sneezed.

'Oh, dear me, what's this, then?'

It was Valerie's reaction to the strong smell of carbolic soap, Daisy suspected, hiding a smile.

'Any problems with her?' Menna asked. 'And how are you, kid? You're looking well, mind.'

'We're both fine,' Daisy assured her. 'Think I'm putting on a bit of weight, though. I'll be glad to get back to work. So, when are you finishing then, Menna?'

'End of the month. Looking forward to a bit of a break, I am. Going up to Colwyn Bay for a couple of weeks to my sister's place.'

'Oh, there's nice.'

Menna nodded, placing Valerie back in the nook of the armchair then looked meaningfully towards the kitchenette.

'I'll get the tea going,' Daisy said hastily. 'Scone with it?'

'Oh, go on, then,' Menna said immediately.

When they were seated comfortably with a cup of tea each and a plate of scones on the table between them, Menna seemed to feel she must give Daisy a detailed run-down on almost every patient she had until Daisy felt her head was spinning. She'd never retain it all without the records and decided she wouldn't even try.

'Then there's that Mrs Hopkins, lives opposite

107

the Tivoli. You know her. Husband's a policeman. Expecting her eighth in September.' Menna lifted her eyes to Heaven. 'Oh, and there's a fuss she makes, mun. You'd think she'd have got the hang of it by now.'

'My goodness, I'm going to be busy, then,' Daisy said quickly in an effort to stem the flow.

'Oh, aye. Hey! By the way, have you seen the new doctor yet?'

Daisy shook her head, sipping her tea, glad the subject was changed at last.

'Well, you're in for a surprise, kid,' Menna went on, rolling her eyes. 'Bit of a ladies' man our Dr Lewis, sure to be. Breaking a couple of hearts already, I wouldn't be surprised.'

Daisy had to smile at Menna's almost eager expression. The new doctor had certainly made an impression on her it would seem. There were two doctors currently practising in the Mumbles, neither under sixty, the younger ones having been called up. Daisy couldn't imagine why this new arrival was causing so much interest in Menna and at her age, too.

'What's so special about him, then, Menna?'

'Well, he's young for a start,' the midwife said. 'A good-looking bloke, mind you. From the Rhondda he is, see. Father was a miner. Played rugby for Wales before the war. Got a cap and all.'

Menna gave a ragged little sigh, and Daisy regarded her with some surprise.

'Got a way with him, he has, you know,' she said. 'Dilys Davies the Surgery told me

108

that flighty Mrs Price-Pugh from up the top of Newton called him out three times last week, and in the night as well.' Menna gave Daisy a sideways look, drawing in her plump chin. 'And her husband overseas fighting for his country. Say no more, isn't it?'

'Shouldn't jump to conclusions, should we?' Daisy warned.

She wasn't surprised that Menna knew all the tittle-tattle about everyone, but was surprised at the midwife talking like this. Her chatter was usually quite harmless. Daisy didn't approve of this kind of gossip, especially about a doctor. It could easily ruin a man's professional reputation. Nevertheless, despite herself, she had become curious.

'If he's young, why isn't he called up, then?'

'Oh, done his bit he has, mind, give him his due,' Menna added. 'Oh, aye. Wounded in the leg he was at Benghazi. Yes, lost part of his foot. Don't seem to slow him much, though, if you know what I mean, like.'

Daisy nibbled on another scone, viewing Menna's knowing little smile thoughtfully. She didn't believe the story about Mrs Price-Pugh for one minute. It was obvious though that the new doctor had made a big impression, perhaps making his presence felt too obviously. She was suspicious of that. Mumbles was a relatively small village and adverse gossip could run through its streets like a tidal wave; fatal for any professional man, but especially a doctor. It would be a pity if his introduction to the village were to be soured by unfounded gossip. There had to be a reason, though.

'You don't like him, then, Menna?' she said.

Menna looked confused for a moment.

'Oh, yes, I do. Charmer he is, a real charmer. Charm the birds off the trees. That's what I'm saying. Everybody's talking about him—all the women anyway. And him not being married, and friendly with it, like a magnet, isn't he?'

Menna reached for another scone.

'You watch yourself with him, mind,' she said, giving Daisy a sideways glance. 'You being a young widow, and all.'

'A very recent widow,' Daisy reminded her quickly, and perhaps too sharply. 'And you're talking a lot of nonsense, Menna.'

Daisy thought no more of Menna's chatter until the following Tuesday when she was pushing Valerie's pram along the Dunns on her way to Taylor's the Grocers to get her week's rations. She paused on Taylor's Corner. Early as it was a queue had already formed from the shop doorway on to the pavement. It was all queues nowadays. Still, she had to be better off here than in London, Daisy reflected, as she rummaged in her handbag to get her ration book ready before joining the queue.

As she was about to lift Valerie out of the pram, she glanced past the Methodist Chapel on the opposite corner and noticed a tall, well-built man striding out of one of the shops, probably the post office. He came towards her past the chapel entrance, walking briskly yet with a noticeable limp.

Daisy knew immediately that this must be the Dr Lewis Menna Ellis was so taken with. Grudgingly, she had to admit he was a striking-looking man, every inch a rugby player, with heavy, powerful shoulders beneath a good-quality suit. While most of the men around the village wore cloth caps with the occasional trilby on Sundays, Dr Lewis wore a smart black Homburg, and wore it with some style.

As he came past he seemed to single her out from the rest of those standing at the shop's entrance. Why her? she wondered, with a fleeting sense of panic.

He lifted the Homburg and smiled broadly at her, blue eyes vivid under well-defined eyebrows.

'*Bore da.*'

'Good morning.' Daisy nodded a return greeting, conscious of her colour rising and irritated by it. She was aware, too, of the faces around them turned curiously in their direction.

The muscles of her mouth twitched, instinc-tively wanting to return his smile but deliberately holding back, recalling Menna's gossip about him and not wanting to seem part of it.

She wasn't going to let herself be charmed by him, and wasn't going to let herself become an object of gossip, either, not when she was about to set up her midwifery practice here shortly. No it wouldn't do, especially since they might be working together from time to time. Daisy felt that in her chosen career professionalism was everything.

He paused for a moment on the pavement, hat resting against his chest. His hair was very dark and thick, and when he'd removed his hat a lock of hair had fallen over his forehead, giving him an almost rakish appearance.

Feeling a bit flustered under his steady gaze, Daisy busied herself with lifting Valerie out of the pram and holding her in the crook of her arm. He smiled at Valerie as the child stared up at him. To Daisy's amazement her baby daughter offered him a smile in return, wide and gummy. Daisy was shaken.

'Lovely little baby,' he said. His voice had the deep, musical lilt of the Valleys. 'Beautiful they make them here, mind. Must be the sea air. Wish I could bottle it and send it back home.'

Daisy allowed a brief smile at the compliment to her daughter. A charmer, yes, Menna was right there.

'Sea air is good for the rest of us too,' he went on. 'Only been here three weeks, see. Feel as fit as a fiddle now.' he smiled at her again, strong white teeth in a wide generous mouth. 'Dr Lewis, I am, in case you're wondering. Rhodri Lewis.'

Daisy gave a quick non-committal nod, unwilling to tell him her name. He was too pushy by half. She fingered her ration book in her free hand, letting her thumb riffle the pages. He glanced down at it.

'Oh, I'm keeping you from getting on, isn't it?'

'I'm about to join the queue,' she said. 'Good morning, Doctor.'

Daisy pushed the pram up against the shop front and then took her place at the back of the queue which had grown longer whilst she'd been standing. He drew level with her again and tipped his head in her direction.

'Good morning to you, then.' He touched Valerie's little hand. *'A'ch, Baban.'*

Smiling, he put on his hat and strode off with his limping gait. For some reason Daisy longed to turn and watch him go, but resolutely kept her gaze on the hat of the woman in front of her. She was beginning to understand Menna better.

Josie came out of the Albert Hall Cinema in Craddock Street into the warm air of early evening. It had been a good film, a real weepie, but it wasn't the same without Daisy. Josie missed her friend very much. They'd promised each other that they'd keep in touch and had meant it, Josie was sure, but it wasn't so easy now with Daisy living all the way down at the Mumbles.

Josie sighed. She'd have to make the effort. Perhaps they could visit the Tivoli Cinema in the village one afternoon. She would write and suggest it. She was longing to see Daisy's new baby anyway, and her new home. When would it be her turn for these things? she wondered, not for the first time.

When she got back to Victor Street the small house seemed strangely quiet. Reuben hadn't returned from his morning round. Sophia said he might be down at the foreshore looking for

113

anything saleable the tide might wash up, but Josie knew her mother really had no idea where he was. He was probably with his fancy woman, Josie thought, and found she didn't care any more. She'd be happy if he never came home. She wouldn't shed a tear if he were dead.

'Where are the kids, then, Mama?'

'Francesca, she gave them money for the pictures,' Sophia said, sipping a well-earned cup of tea while pushing the tea pot towards Josie. 'They scoot off. I don't see them since.'

'Francie parting with her money?' Josie said, gratefully pouring the steaming brew into her cup. She could hardly believe it. 'She must be sickening for something, Mama, or has she suddenly got religion?'

'You don't joke about that,' Sophia rebuked sharply. 'You miss Mass this morning, you bad girl.'

'Sorry, Mama. I was tired when I came off the afternoon shift yesterday, and I didn't get a good night's sleep. Francie was restless. She kept waking me up. I could've cheerfully smothered her. Where is she anyway?'

'Upstairs. She go out, I think.'

Josie banged her cup down on the saucer as she jumped up.

'If she's picking through my things again, I'll brain her. I will!'

Josie hurried up to the small bedroom she shared with her sister. She hated having no privacy, having to share a room, but it couldn't be helped at present. She refused to believe the situation would go on for any length of time, and kept telling herself that after the war, when Stanley came home, everything would be right for her, for them. Somehow, she'd make Mama's life more comfortable, and the kids too.

She went straight into the bedroom expecting to catch Francie rummaging in the wardrobe, but instead her sister was lying on the bed, face down. For a moment Josie thought she was asleep until Francie raised her head and then Josie saw she'd been crying.

She felt flummoxed. She hadn't seen her sister cry since she was a small child. She'd watched Francie become hardened over the years and blamed her father's neglect and brutal ways. Francie usually dealt with the vicissitudes of life with a sharp and bitter retort, and careless shrug of the shoulders, as though to show any weakness would only leave her open to hurt and disappointment. Josie saw that the hardness with which Francie faced life often made her heedless of the feelings of others. She wasn't sure, for instance, if Francie felt as strongly about their mother as she did. She suspected her sister was too wrapped up in herself. But now something had happened which had pierced her shell. Josie's heart contracted. To reduce Francie to tears it must be something serious.

'What's up, kid?'

Francie pushed herself up and sat on the edge of the bed, dabbing at her reddened eyes with a handkerchief. She gave a miserable sniff and glanced up at Josie.

'What do you care?'

Josie sat down beside her.

'Don't be so daft, will you? You're my sister, although you drive me up the wall sometimes. Now what's the matter, Fran? The sooner you tell me, the sooner we can sort it.'

To Josie's astonishment, Francie gave a loud choking sob and covered her face with her hands.

'What is it? A bloke, or what? Is it Dada?'

Abruptly Francie sat up straight and tossed back her hair as though to shrug off the problem, whatever it was. Josie wasn't impressed. Although her sister was holding up her head defiantly, her lips were quivering and large tears were welling in the corners of her eyes.

'Don't need your help, do I?' Francie said sullenly, pulling at the sodden handkerchief as though looking for a dry patch to dab at her eyes again. 'I can sort this out myself. And it's none of your business anyway.'

'It's my business when you're soaking my half of the bed with tears,' Josie said.

She tried to make her tone jocular but wasn't very successful.

Even in distress Francie was prickly and difficult. Josie wondered why she was bothering at all. Probably some chap had given her sister the elbow. It wouldn't be the first time, either, and Francie always got stroppy when that happened. Josie looked at her closely. She wasn't acting stroppy now, though. She looked really miserable and, yes, even a little frightened.

'Francie, listen, kid,' Josie said coaxingly. 'I

know you think you're as tough as old boots, but we all need help sometimes. Look! We haven't been the best of pals for a while, I know, but we are sisters. We should be able to talk to each other, especially when it's important.'

Francie's head was down as though avoiding Josie's eyes. She looked up from under her lashes, then, giving her nose an impatient wipe with the handkerchief.

'How can I talk to you, Josie, when you're always screaming at me? Like you did the time Dada gave Mama a black eye, when you were off having a high old time with your Stan.'

'I should bloody well think I did!' Josie said hotly, feeling a momentary return of the scalding rage she'd known then. 'Mama's got no one but us. You didn't even *try* to protect her. No, you pushed off out. Selfish to the core, you are, Francie.'

'You didn't have to slap me so hard, did you?' she complained bitterly. 'Too free with your hands. Just like Dada, you are.'

Josie was appalled. She jumped up from the bed.

'Don't you dare say that!' She was breathing hard, her face flushed with anger as she stared down at her sister. 'I'm not like him at all. He's a brute, he is. A swine. I'll swing for him one day.'

Francie's lip curled.

'Look at you now, all steamed up. Got it in for me, you have, and then expect me to tell you what's wrong. I only ever get criticism from you, Josie.'

She swallowed hard, trying to control her anger. Whenever she thought of the way her father mistreated her mother it set her blood boiling; she felt as though her head would explode with rage. It was dangerous, she knew it was, letting her fiery temper get the upper hand. Sometimes she did things she regretted later. Maybe Francie was right for once.

With reluctance Josie sat down on the bed again, taking deep breaths to slow her racing pulses.

'All right, that's in the past,' she said unsteadily. 'Not saying you didn't deserve it, Francie, because you did. But perhaps I did go a bit far. This is different, though, isn't it? Now tell me why you're crying?'

Francie lowered her head again. Josie could see a little pulse beating rapidly in her sister's throat, and realised Francie was frightened of something.

Josie caught her breath on a sudden thought.

'It's not Billy Parsons and Dada, is it? Has he talked Dada into doing something stupid? He's not going to get arrested, is he?'

Would that be such a bad thing though? she asked herself. If Dada were arrested, at least Mama would be safe from him. They could weather the shame of it, just to have a bit of peace. She looked at Francie hopefully, but her sister's expression was unchanged. No, Dada getting himself arrested wouldn't worry her enough to frighten her.

'Well, what is it, then?' Josie cried impatiently.

118

Francie gulped before opening her mouth to answer.

'I'm in trouble.'

'Trouble?'

'Trouble. You know—trouble!' She tossed her head defiantly. 'Now, don't say "I told you so", Josie. I don't want any preaching from you. I don't want any criticism. I'm only telling you because you're pestering me. I'm going to do something about it myself. Billy will help me.'

Josie's jaw dropped open.

'Oh, God, no! You haven't gone and got yourself up the spout?' She clutched at her head with both hands, staring at Francie in horror. 'You stupid little fool, Fran! I warned you and warned you, didn't I? It's that Billy Parsons, isn't it? I told you not to get mixed up with him, didn't I? Scum, he is. Wait until I get my hands on him, the little rat!'

'Oh, you're going to swing for him as well, are you, Josie?' Francie sneered. 'Well, it wasn't Billy, see. And I'm not saying who it was because ...'

Francie stopped short, eyes wide and round as she stared at her sister.

Josie's eyes narrowed.

'Because the man's married, that's what you were going to say, isn't it? Oh, Francie, how could you? Another woman's man.'

Francie looked into space, her features suddenly hard as granite. She hugged herself as though for comfort and affirmation of what she was saying.

'He's married, but it's me he loves,' she said.

119

'I know he does. And when the time's right, he'll come to me. When the war's over, we'll be together, him and me.'

'I wouldn't count on it, Fran. He's had his fun, whoever he is. Oh, I don't know what Dada will do when he finds out!'

Josie stared at Francie, her sister's impossible position now very clear to her. Reuben would go mad, she was certain. In his man's world he could behave any way he wanted without thought or regret, but let any one of his family fall from grace and all hell would be let loose.

And then there was Mama to consider too. She'd break her heart over this. Be too ashamed to hold up her head in church, Josie thought, angry once more with her sister for her irresponsibility and selfishness. As if they didn't have enough to put up with already.

What was going on in Francie's mind, though? She couldn't be naive enough to believe this married man would really leave his wife and possibly kids for her. In fact, Josie was certain the father, whoever he was, would wash his hands of her once he learned the truth.

And what were her intentions towards the baby? If she were willing to keep the child, it would be something positive at least. But did Francie have the courage for that? Josie couldn't help but doubt it. It would take a strong, determined and selfless woman to face up to the shame, the humiliation, the gossip, and then afterwards the hardship of bringing up a child alone. It pained her to admit it but her sister was not that kind of a woman.

But what had she meant about Billy helping?

'Why would Billy Parsons help you if he isn't the father, then?' Josie asked, wondering if Francie had been lying to her after all.

'Because he's sweet on me, see.' Francie turned her face to Josie, eyes triumphant. 'He'll do anything for me. He's willing to marry me, isn't he?'

Josie clutched at her sister's arm.

'You can't marry that little crook, Fran!'

The situation was desperate, but not that desperate. Billy Parsons would end up in prison, sure to, she told herself. Francie would be heading for a life of misery and unhappiness if she married him.

She shook off her sister's hand impatiently.

'I'm not stupid, Josie. I don't want Billy. I'm telling you, me and the baby's father will be getting together soon.' She brushed her hair back from her shoulders with a confident gesture. 'I don't want this baby anyway. I'm too young yet. I want some fun first. I'll make Billy give me some money. Eileen at work told me about a woman up by Baptist Well Street who got Eileen's sister out of trouble last year. It cost a bit, but it's worth it.'

Josie's heart gave a sickening lurch at the thought of it.

'That's awful. You can't do it, Fran. It isn't right.'

Francie rounded on her angrily.

'Don't be so sanctimonious, will you, Josie? It's not your life that's going to be messed up, is it? I'll do as I like and you can't stop me.'

'But it's dangerous, Fran. Anything could go wrong. These people aren't qualified. They don't know what they're doing half the time. They're only interested in getting their hands on your money. You could die, have you thought of that?'

Josie paused as an image of Daisy's smiling face came to mind.

'Listen, my friend Daisy is a midwife. She might help you if I ask her. Please don't do anything drastic until I see her. Promise, Fran?'

Chapter Seven

Daisy sipped her tea, watching her friend. Josie was in the big hide armchair with Valerie in the crook of her arm. Valerie's eyes were large and round, excited at seeing a new face.

Josie had eagerly lifted the baby into her arms when she'd first arrived after the midday meal, and Daisy could see that her friend was totally enraptured by her baby daughter. She knew Josie longed for a baby of her own. They'd talked about it often enough.

Josie looked up, her pretty face flushed with pleasure, her big dark eyes soft with emotion.

'There's lovely little girls are, aren't they?'

Daisy nodded, smiling. She could see the longing in Josie's eyes, and her heart went out to her.

122

'It'll be your turn soon, mark my words. Stanley won't be away for ever. There's plenty of time for you.'

Josie's answering smile wavered a little.

'Thought I might've fallen for a baby when he was home on leave in May, but no such luck. Never mind. Maybe it's just as well, considering ...'

Josie averted her gaze in a way that made Daisy wonder if something was amiss. It wasn't like her friend to be evasive. But then, Josie had a difficult life with a subdued and dependent mother, and a brute of a father. Daisy realised Josie's upbringing had been very different from her own. Edie's standards were high, drilled into her by her own strong-willed mother and passed on to Daisy. She'd no idea how other people lived until she'd entered nursing.

Daisy had sensed a high moral code in Josie, a basic integrity, despite her father's influence. But, Daisy wondered, how powerful *was* family influence? She thought she knew Josie, but did she really?

'Things bad at home, are they?'

Daisy was certain Josie's lips quivered for a moment as though she were going to break down, and thought she saw desperation in the glance that was flicked her way. That wasn't like Josie either. She was usually so defiant about her difficulties. She got over excited sometimes over things she felt strongly about. She was upset when her mother was ill, but Daisy had never seen her so near to despair as she seemed today.

'Yes.' Josie nodded. 'And likely to get worse. There's going to be one heck of a showdown with my father soon. I don't know what will happen but nothing good, I can tell you.'

'Your mother's not ill again, is she?' Daisy asked quickly.

'No, not ill, but likely to be very upset.' Josie bit her lip. 'The fact is, my sister Francie is in trouble. Usual kind of trouble, you know.'

'Oh, no. Tsk! There's awful!'

Daisy was sympathetic but not very surprised. Francie Randall struck her as a wilful sort of young woman, too sure of herself by half. Daisy felt sorry for the girl nevertheless, but even more sorry for Josie. It was the very deepest of ironies that she, married and longing to start a family, was denied while Francie, probably not cut out for motherhood was cursing her fate.

'No chance of marriage, then?'

'No.' Josie shook her head, gaze sliding away again as though the shame was her own. 'The father's married, see. My father'll kill her when he finds out. Don't know what will become of her, unless ...'

Josie hesitated, compressing her lips. There was something in those eyes as she turned her face to Daisy again that made her very uneasy.

'Oh, not thinking of doing something risky, is she?' Daisy asked, alarm growing. She put down her tea cup to lean forward earnestly. 'She mustn't do that, Josie. It's madness.'

'Told her and told her, haven't I?' Josie said. 'She could die, I told her. Stubborn and headstrong, she is. May not be able to stop her, see. She's got this friend, a bloke, who's willing to give her the money.'

Daisy shook her head emphatically. 'You must stop her, Josie. These people are butchers. You don't know the horror stories I've heard.'

Josie shrugged.

'She's practically made up her mind to do it, despite the risks. I think she's more afraid of Dada than she is of dying.'

Josie paused, compressing her mouth tightly, obviously overwhelmed. Her arm was tightly around Valerie on her lap, but now she seemed to have forgotten the baby was there. Daisy could see there was something more on her mind, something she was bursting to say though she was hesitating just the same.

'Wondering, I was, Daisy,' Josie said at last, 'you being a midwife and all, well up in the medical line, like. Could you help our Francie?'

'*What?*'

'Could you help her get rid of it safely? You could, couldn't you?' Josie persisted eagerly.

She had a pinched, anxious look around her mouth but Daisy hardly noticed it. She could only stare at her friend aghast, her own mouth dropping open.

'What are you saying, Josie? What are you asking me?'

'I wouldn't ask, Daisy, only we're desperate, me and Francie. A lot of people look down on us Randalls because my father's nothing more than a rag-and-bone man, and a drunk as well, but an illegitimate child is too much, even for us. And it's not only the shame of it, either. My father will go mad. He'll kill her, he will.'

Daisy stood up slowly, legs feeling stiff and awkward. A wave of nausea was rising from her stomach; the sensation of wanting to retch was almost overwhelming. How could Josie ask her to do this awful thing?

Looking at Josie, whom she'd thought of as a sympathetic friend, she could hardly believe they were having this conversation, that her so-called friend believed her capable of such barbarism.

She took quick steps to the armchair and snatched Valerie out of Josie's arms. She held the baby protectively against her breast.

'You'd better go now, Josie,' she said, tightly. 'We haven't anything more to say to each other.'

'But, Daisy!' Josie looked startled. 'I wanted to talk this over with you, see. Get your advice, like. You're the only friend I can turn to.'

'Friend!' Daisy almost spat the word. 'I don't know how you can ask me to do such a terrible thing. The idea revolts me. Sickens me. And to think you believed *I* could do it! Some friend you are. You'd better go now, Josie, this minute, before I say something I'll regret.'

'Well, I was only asking. Don't have to be so nasty about it, Daisy, do you?' Josie jumped to her feet, snatching up her handbag and gloves from a nearby table, her face suddenly darkly flushed. 'Never expected to see this side of you I didn't.'

'Nasty?' Daisy cried. 'Nasty!'

126

She knew her voice was rising steadily in shock and anger, and Valerie was looking up into her face, not understanding the sudden change in the atmosphere, and not knowing whether she should cry or not.

'It's more than nasty, I am, Josie.' Daisy was almost shouting now, and couldn't stop herself. 'Livid is what I am. Appalled that you could come to my home, sit with my baby on your lap, and suggest I do this awful thing. Not only is it barbaric, it's against the law as well.'

Josie slipped her cardigan over her shoulders and pulled on her gloves, her lips set tight. Her dark eyes flashed disdain as they looked at Daisy.

'Of course I know it's against the law, Daisy. Not *twp*, am I, even though I'm just a rag-and-bone man's daughter. Thought you were really my friend, I did, and you'd be glad to help me.'

'Help you break the law?' cried Daisy.

She felt a hot ball of anger rise from somewhere in her midriff to her throat, to burn there like a hot coal.

'I'm supposed to jeopardise my whole nursing career, my only living for me and my child, just so that your stupid sister can get off scot-free? Not likely! You and your family may take the law very lightly, but I don't.'

Josie's face was like thunder then, eyes sparking fire at Daisy.

'What do you mean by that remark?'

Daisy glared back. What *did* she mean? She was remembering all the things Mam-gu had told

127

her about Reuben Randall. Suddenly it seemed so typically a Randall trait that Josie could so lightly ask her to break the law, to be party to a back-street abortion, a diabolical practice about which she felt particularly strongly. Josie had certainly fooled her. How could she ever have thought they had anything in common? How could they ever be friends when Josie could so easily gloss over the difference between right and wrong?

'Well, let's face it.' Daisy tossed her head angrily. 'Your father's not exactly a pillar of society, is he? He's up to his neck in the black market for one thing, and God knows what else as well.'

She hadn't meant to bring that up, but felt outraged with Josie and now she wanted to hit back.

'You hypocrite, Daisy Buckland!' Josie's face turned pale and her lips thinned with new fury. 'You ate the eggs I brought quick enough, didn't you? Oh, yes! And what about that bit of silverside I got you for your mother's birthday? Didn't hear no refusals from you or her.' Josie's eyes narrowed. 'And what about that coat I made you? Oh, no, Daisy.' She shook her head. 'Don't you get on your high horse with me.'

'I ... I ...' Daisy was flustered for a moment. It was true. She *had* profited, for all her high-mindedness. But those things had seemed so small a the time. She'd no idea there would be such a high price to pay later.

'Oh, so I have to sacrifice my career in

128

payment now, do I?' she cried when she'd collected her thoughts.

'Payment?' Josie shook her head impatiently, and her shoulders drooped as though she was suddenly weary of their quarrel. 'Don't be so stupid, will you? We're supposed to be friends. Friends help each other, don't they? All I want is help for my sister.'

'She won't get that kind of help from me.' Daisy lifted her chin, adamant.

Her face felt stiff and taut with indignation, but at the same time she was beginning to tremble, and Valerie had started to cry, sensing the anger between them.

'Please go now, Josie. We won't be meeting again.'

They stared at each other for a few moments while Josie's expression changed from anger to despair then finally resignation. Pushing her handbag under her arm, she stalked out.

Standing there with Valerie still grizzling in her arms, Daisy waited, half expecting to hear the door being slammed in Josie's wake, but there was nothing but silence.

A lovely sun had long set though it wasn't yet dark. The sky still had streaks of mauve and pink and gold in the west, and the air was balmy as Josie stood outside the gates of the Ajax munitions factory in Landore, waiting for Francie to come off the two-till-ten shift. She sat on a low wall oblivious to the dust and dirt staining her precious cotton dress, the one that Francie was always pinching.

129

It had been a blow, a bitter blow, that quarrel with Daisy. She wished with all her heart it hadn't happened. She wished she hadn't asked for Daisy's help. Then they'd still be friends now.

But what kind of friends? Josie thought miserably. The only time she'd ever asked for a favour, Daisy got so nasty about it. She needn't have worried about her precious career because no one would have found out. What was all the fuss about?

What hurt most of all was Daisy's disparaging words about her family, as though she secretly despised the Randalls. Josie thought back to the previous months and all the outings they'd had together. Had it all been false? Had she been kidding herself all along? Daisy had never been her friend, not really. She had no real friends. She had only Stanley.

She felt a tear prickle at the corner of her eye. Her darling Stanley, God bless and protect him. He was all she had, all she ever wanted.

Josie wiped away the tear impatiently. There was no time to think of that now. She had to concentrate on Francie. One thing Daisy and she did agree on: no back-street butcher could be allowed to endanger Francie's life. She wouldn't let that happen. Francie must have the baby, like it or not, and she must get away from Victor Street somehow before Dada found out.

Josie thought about the money she'd put away for a home for Stanley and herself after the war. Some of it would have to be sacrificed. He would understand.

The hooter sounded and almost at once people, mostly women, began to pour out of the factory gates. Josie stood up and walked slowly forward amongst them, nodding to one or two women she knew, her gaze searching through the gathering dusk for Francie's familiar figure.

Her sister came out at last, and Josie was momentarily annoyed to see her walking and chatting with Molly Morgan. At least, Molly was doing the chattering. What was that nosy parker up to now? Molly knew everyone's business. Somehow or other she wormed things out of people.

Josie ground her teeth, wondering if Francie had been foolish enough to let Molly get a hint of her trouble. It would be all over the town within hours if so. No hope of hiding the truth from Dada then. Her mouth tightening at the thought of him, Josie joined her sister and Molly and saw Francie looked surprised to see her but also relieved.

Josie stared unsmilingly at Molly, trying to convey that her company wasn't wanted by the sisters. But Molly's skin was too thick.

'The Mayhill bus is almost full, Molly,' Josie said pointedly. 'You'd better hurry or you'll miss it.'

Obviously untouched by her unfriendliness Molly took a step closer to them, her copper-coloured head thrust forward, spectacles already halfway down the bridge of her sharp nose. Like a hound on the scent of a fox, Josie thought bitterly.

'I was saying to Francie, here,' Molly said, her eyes eager. 'I was saying, she ought to have an early night, take the day off tomorrow. Fainting like that. She gave us all a fright. What's wrong then, kid?'

'Food-poisoning,' Josie said, on the spur of the moment. 'Food-poisoning, it is. I've got it myself.' She placed a hand on her stomach and grimaced. 'Oh, *Duw*, agony it is. That black market pork ... I knew it was off. I said, didn't I, Fran?'

'Oh, is it?' Molly looked from one to the other, disappointed. She glanced up the road where the workers' buses were parked, waiting in the crowding dusk, eerily shadowed inside in compliance with the blackout. 'Better go, isn't it? See you tomorrow, Francie, perhaps. Hope you'll be better, girls.'

When Molly had gone, Francie gave a sigh of relief.

'Passed out cold on the shop floor, didn't I?' She said, shaking her head. 'She's been hanging around me ever since. I swear she knows something.'

'Haven't been gabbing to her, have you?' Josie asked sharply. 'Letting on about your trouble, like? Things are difficult enough without that, Fran.'

'Not said a word, I haven't,' Francie snapped. 'I might be in the club, but I haven't gone soft in the head as well, mind. I'm telling you, Molly's like a blooming ferret. Ought to drop her behind enemy lines, they did. Hitler wouldn't stand a chance. The war would be over in no time.'

132

'Well, never mind her now, then,' Josie said briskly, relieved that Francie was at least trying to be discreet. 'We've got more important things to worry about.'

'We'd better get a move on for our bus, too,' Francie said, starting forward.

'No, let it go, Fran.' Josie caught at her sister's arm to hold her back. 'We'll walk into town, get a bus from there. It's a nice night, and we've got to talk. Talk seriously, mind.'

It was still not dark. There was enough reflected light in the sky to see them on their way. A typical bombers' night, but there hadn't been an air raid on Swansea in months. The tide of the war was turning at last, and Jerry now had bigger things on his mind than bombing an already razed coastal town.

'No luck with your friend, then?' Francie asked as they walked towards the main road into town.

Josie shook her head and Francie gave a hollow laugh.

'Could've told you that, mun. You won't get nothing out of the likes of her or her family, them Baylisses. Always were a stuck-up lot.'

'You're only listening to what Dada said,' Josie snapped 'He's prejudiced because Albert Bayliss took Dada's sister, Sarah, to Canada years before the war and she died there of pneumonia.'

Why was she defending Daisy's family? Josie wondered. What did she owe Daisy? Nothing at all. Now, when her twin sister was in the deepest of trouble, her only friend had refused

133

to help, flatly and with some bitterness. It was as though Josie's friendship had been thrown back in her face.

Suddenly she felt lonely and tired. Responsibility for everything that was happening to the Randalls seemed to rest on her shoulders. If only Stanley were here to support her, love her.

'Mama will have to be told about your trouble tonight, Francie. You'll have to leave Victor Street before Dada finds out.'

'Easy said.' Francie sounded as though she would argue. 'But where could I go? No. See that woman in Baptist Well Street, I will. Billy'll pay.'

Josie stopped in her tracks, gripping Francie's arm tightly. Suddenly she was furious with her sister for bringing this unlooked for misery on them.

'Stop being such a bloody little fool, will you, Francie? This isn't a game. You were stupid, selfish and irresponsible, now you've got to pay. You're going to have this baby, Fran. First you've got to get away from Dada.'

Francie wrenched her arm angrily from Josie's grasp.

'Who do you think you are, telling me my business? I don't want this baby, see, and I don't have to have it either. Why should I lumber myself with a kid at my age?'

For all the sharpness of Francie's tone, Josie thought she could hear an underlying tremor of fear. It was so unlike Francie. She'd always thought her sister had more intelligence, was too hard-headed even, to be caught out like

134

this. Who was this married man, anyway? She wished Francie would confide in her. One thing she was certain about: he was no good, just like Dada.

'Thought you said you and the father were going to make a go of it?' Josie said. 'He's going to leave his wife after the war, according to you, so hadn't you better ask him first before you get rid of his child? It might be important to him.'

'It's me he wants, not the kid.'

Francie's response was much too quick, too defensive. Did she really believe what she was saying? Suddenly touched by compassion for her, Josie put an arm around her sister's shoulders.

'Look, kid, you're living in a pipe-dream, mun,' she said gently. 'This man, whoever he is, he's no damn' good. Not to you, his child or his poor wife. If he can't be faithful to her, what makes you think he'll treat you different?'

Francie bit her lip and pulled away from Josie's embrace to continue the walk into town. Josie hurried to catch her up, disappointed at her sister's rejection, anger returning.

'Fran, don't be stubborn, will you?'

'He doesn't want the kid, I'm telling you.'

'You asked him, then?'

'Yes.'

Francie was lying, Josie could always tell. But all at once she wasn't interested in any plans her sister had made with this man. She was only interested in seeing that Francie didn't take needless risks with her life.

Josie glanced at her as they walked. She knew

the anger she was feeling towards her wasn't just due to the mess she had got them into. It was also due to envy.

Josie swallowed hard, admitting to herself for the first time that she was jealous that Francie was having a baby when she so desperately longed for a child herself; almost consumed by envy. She hadn't really wanted to ask Daisy for that special help. All her instincts as a woman had been against it. It had simply been a way to prevent Francie taking a terrible chance with some back-street butcher. If only she could change places with her ...

'I wish I could have this baby for you, Fran.'

Surprisingly, Francie turned to her and laughed, real amusement dancing in her eyes. It was something Josie hadn't seen in her sister's face for a long time, not since they were children together.

'You and me both, kid.'

A car slowed down at the curb just in front of them and a young man put his head out of the window.

'Want a lift, girls?'

It was Billy Parsons.

Josie stopped, her mouth tightening. She couldn't stand the sight of the little crook. If Francie thought Billy was not bad-looking she needed her eyes tested. He was short, small and weedy, and with that titchy moustache under his nose, reminded her of Hitler.

She disliked him not only because of the way he hung around Francie, but also because she was sure Billy was encouraging her father to get deeper into shady dealings. For all his big talk, which seemed to impress Reuben Randall, Josie had Billy pegged as a loser who was bound to get his comeuppance one day, and drag Dada down with him. She didn't care what happened to Dada. He could rot in prison. She did care what became of her family, though, and that included Francie, for all her difficult ways.

'Tell him to push off, Fran.'

'Don't be so soft, will you, Josie?' she said impatiently, moving forward. 'He'll take us all the way home. Save getting the bus, isn't it?' She waved. 'Hello, Billy.'

Josie was still protesting when they clambered into Billy's Austin Seven, Josie in the back and Francie next to the driver.

'Haven't seen this before, Billy,' she said, looking around in the car. 'Where'd you get this, then?'

'Mate of mine knows this chap up the Uplands, see,' Billy said, noisily engaging the clutch. 'Had his legs blown off by a mine so he got no further use for it now, has he? Bought it off him for a song.' He sounded particularly pleased with himself. 'Good, isn't it, kid?'

Josie felt like choking at his total lack of sensitivity. Like a scrawny little vulture, he profited by others' misfortunes. She stared at the back of his Brylcreemed head, despising him. It looked as though Billy Parsons, at least, was having a lovely war. Billy was supposed to have a bad heart but Josie wasn't so sure. It galled her to think of her Stanley out there fighting while the likes of Billy Parsons lived the life of Riley back home.

'Where do you get the petrol coupons, that's what I'd like to know?' she said tartly, hoping to put him on the spot.

Keeping his eyes on the road, Billy lifted one hand from the steering wheel to tap a forefinger against the side of his snub nose.

'Don't want to ask no questions like that, Mrs Jenkins, see?' he said. 'Best not to know, isn't it?'

Josie ground her teeth at his patronising tone. Who did he think he was? Al Capone?

With heavy politeness, he always called her by her married name whenever they came into contact, which mercifully wasn't often. Josie preferred it that way. She wouldn't want to be on first name terms with the likes of him.

'Billy,' Francie said. 'Remember what I was telling you ... about my bit of bother, like? Wondering, I was, if you would give me the money now to ... to get rid it, like you said.'

Billy didn't answer, and a wave of relief swept over Josie. He'd never meant it. He'd been bragging as usual. Now Francie would see what a lying little creep he really was. Without Billy's money there was no possibility of her finding any back-street butcher to help her into an early grave.

'Billy?'

'Look, Fran, fact is I haven't got it, see? Bought the car, didn't I?'

'Billy, you promised!'

He steered the car into the side of the road

and pulled on the handbrake.

'I know, Fran, but you won't need the money now, see,' he said to her. 'Got a better idea, haven't I? We'll tell your father the kid's mine and we're getting married.'

Josie stared open-mouthed. Francie was staring too. There was silence for a moment while they took in his words.

'My father'll kill you,' Josie said, when she'd got over her astonishment. 'Pal or no pal, he'll chew you up and spit you out.'

Billy twisted round in his seat to face her.

'Willing to take that chance, I am, Mrs Jenkins.'

It was dark inside the car so she couldn't see his face to judge his expression. She had only his voice to go on. Was that sincerity she could hear in his tone? She couldn't believe it. His kind weren't capable of sincerity. She only had to think of her father to know that. What was Billy up to?

'Why?' Josie asked flatly. 'What's in it for you, then, boyo?'

'I'll risk it for Francie's sake. I love her, Mrs Jenkins, honest. Asked her to marry me before, I did, but she wouldn't then. Now she'll have to, won't she? Reuben will kick up at first, but I can handle him, mun.'

'You're still willing to marry me, Billy, knowing I'm carrying another bloke's kid?' Francie said. There was a curious wonder in her voice and Josie could tell she believed Billy was sincere.

'Don't care about that, Fran love. No angel

myself, I'm not. I love you, and I don't want nobody else.'

It was simply said, and despite her hostility towards him, Josie found herself momentarily touched.

Francie turned her head towards her.

'What do you think, Josie? Best thing, perhaps?'

She felt trapped for a moment. Francie was more desperate than she'd been letting on, Josie knew. Now she was actually asking her sister's advice, something she'd never do as a rule. She was probably desperate enough to take that advice, too. One word of encouragement from her and Francie would marry him.

What was the best thing to do? Josie really didn't know. Billy's solution seemed ideal to get them out of their immediate predicament. It would be so simple. Francie and Billy could announce their plans to wed first. The fact that Francie was in the family way could be mentioned by-the-way later. Perhaps Dada's fury wouldn't be so great, knowing that his daughter would be safely married before the event.

But what about Francie? What about the future? She didn't love Billy, that was certain. Probably didn't even like him, Josie reflected. But Francie was desperate now, would grasp at any straw, and Billy Parsons was certainly a man of straw as far as Josie could see. Desperation was no basis for marriage. What would Francie's future be like? Maybe Billy was sincere about loving her, but that made no difference to the kind he was, or the sort of life he led. He was a wide-boy, a spiv. She'd read about them in the papers. Petty criminals, every one. Billy wouldn't be any different after the war. He wasn't even clever. He'd be in and out of prison all his life. Francie would be left with a child, maybe more than one. And how would she live? Scratching to find a spare penny all her life. Francie could do better, given the chance. She'd made a mistake but it needn't ruin her life, not if she were sensible. There had to be some other way.

'No,' Josie said loudly. 'It won't work.'

'What?' Billy sounded astonished.

'Francie doesn't love you ... Mr Parsons,' Josie said. She couldn't bring herself to use his first name. 'Otherwise she'd have married you when you asked her before. You said it yourself. You think she'll have to marry you, whether she wants to or not. Trying to take advantage of her, you are, because she's in a fix.'

'You couldn't be more wrong, Mrs Jenkins, honest,' Billy said, evenly. Give him his due, he didn't sound angry.

Josie leaned forward and put a hand on Francie's shoulder.

'You marry him, Fran, and you'll regret it. You'll probably both regret it. Marriage isn't a convenience. And that's all it'd be. For you, anyway.'

'Fran should make up her own mind, Mrs Jenkins,' said Billy.

Francie was silent. Josie held her breath for a moment, then decided she'd had enough.

Let them make a mess of their lives if they wanted to.

'I want to get out of the car, Francie. Get the bus the rest of the way home, I will. You two must do as you like, make up your own minds.'

'Stay where you are, will you, Josie, and stop being so awkward,' Francie said to her, an edge of irritation to her voice.

To Billy she spoke in a softer tone, one so unusual in her that it made Josie wonder if there were depths to Francie she knew nothing about.

'There's good of you, Billy, to offer. Grateful I am, see. But Josie's right, and I'm not ready to settle down yet. Come on, let's get home. It's nearly chucking out time for the pubs. Want to be in bed when Dada comes in, don't I?'

Chapter Eight

Sophia was going up the stairs when they got in, having just put the children to bed in the cramped parlour which served as their bedroom. Although Josie was determined to let their mother in on Francie's secret this very night, she let her go up, knowing the moment wasn't right.

Francie refused a cup of tea, wanting to go straight to bed. She said she was tired but Josie guessed she didn't have the nerve to face Sophia.

142

Josie lingered a while, sipping the hot tea, letting the warmth of it ease her nerves.

Despite Francie's hurry to get to bed before their father came in, Josie knew that would be some time yet, if at all tonight. He was drinking with that woman and their cronies, she'd bet her life on it. He'd probably go back to that woman's place when the pub turned them out.

She thought of her mother for a moment, considering how she must feel knowing her husband was continually unfaithful to her. She couldn't still love Dada, could she? Not after the way he treated them all. Perhaps she just didn't care any more. And maybe that was just as well.

Mama just gave in to everything, Josie thought. She didn't have any fight in her. Josie paused for a moment, hands around the hot cup. Thank goodness she had more spirit than Mama. It was easy to talk, though. What would she do herself if she found Stanley had betrayed her?

Josie felt a surge of emotion at the thought. It would be something drastic, something she'd probably live to regret. She wriggled uneasily in her chair, trying to throw off the powerful feeling. It would never happen. Not her Stanley. He was as faithful as the day was long.

When she finally went upstairs, she turned immediately to the front bedroom. Sophia was standing plaiting her hair in front of a small mirror on the tallboy. Even though it was summertime Josie could not suppress a shiver, seeing her mother's bare feet on the linoleum.

'Josephina, *cara mia,* you look tired. Do you forget you're on early shift tomorrow? You should be in bed.'

'Mama, sit down a minute. Got to talk to you, I have.'

Josie steered her mother to the iron bedstead with its mattress which sagged uncomfortably in the centre. Sophia sat down next to her, looking at her expectantly.

Josie studied her mother's face for a moment. She looked worn and tired, yet Josie knew Sophia wasn't all that old. She'd married Dada young, probably too young. Despite the careworn features, beauty was still visible in her mother's face; in the curve of an eyebrow, in the turn of a high cheekbone. It made Josie's heart ache to think of that beauty faded and destroyed by brutality. It made her heart ache, too, to realise she was about to bring more pain and sorrow with what she had to reveal.

And there was no easy way to tell Mama. It was best to say it straight out, get it over. Then they could talk about what they should do.

'Mama, it's Francie. She's ... she's in trouble.'

Sophia's eyes widened and her mouth dropped open in shock. Josie grasped her mother's hand and squeezed hard, trying to pass on some of her own spirit and courage.

'She's not a bad girl, Mama, just foolish. And she's not the only one, is she? There was Betty Pritchard from number twelve last year, remember? And her father works for the Corporation.'

Sophia stared at her, clutching Josie's hand

144

tightly. She let out a long low moan of misery, her eyes becoming even wider, and Josie saw the fear in them. She had the same sense of fear herself.

'Francie must get away before Dada finds out, Mama. She thinks it'll be next February.'

Josie felt a sudden pang of envy. Why couldn't it be she who was expecting next February? Why had Francie been chosen and not herself? Josie swallowed hard against the wave of resentment that washed through her. Her happiness would have been complete, knowing Stanley's child was growing inside her, while Francie probably hated the thought of this child who was spoiling her life. She'd blame anyone but herself.

'Going to try to help her with a bit of money, I am, Mama. But she needs somewhere to go. Haven't you got a cousin still living up the Valleys?'

Sophia nodded slowly, swallowing. Tears were glistening in her big dark eyes and Josie wanted to hug her and sympathise and comfort her, but there wasn't time. She and Mama had to settle things tonight.

'*Si*, but she's a widow woman now.' She shook her head doubtfully.

'Then she could probably do with a lodger,' Josie said firmly.

'I'll tell Dada the authorities are relocating Francie to the munitions factory at Bridgend, and your cousin is putting her up for the duration. He won't know any different. But she'll have to leave soon, before she begins to show. You must write to your cousin tomorrow,

Mama. Don't be ashamed. It could happen to anyone.'

That wasn't strictly true, but she had to try and comfort her mother somehow. Francie had been irresponsible, and now they were all paying. Josie didn't mind so much for herself, but she resented the anguish Mama was going through. She'd be living in terror of Reuben finding out from now on, Josie knew.

Sophia began to sob.

'He'll find out. There'll be terrible trouble for us, Josephina. Your father, he go wild. My children, they are so innocent, but he hurt them. He don't care about us no more.'

'Oh, Mama!'

Josie threw her arms around her mother, holding her tight, struggling to hold back the tears that were stinging her eyes.

It was wicked to wish harm to one's own father, she knew, but she couldn't help it. She could never remember a time when he'd been close to them, but now he was no more than a stranger, a feared stranger who despised them. Without him things would be very tight for her mother and brothers and sister, but at least they wouldn't be living in constant dread, and they'd manage somehow, Josie would see to that. But Reuben was *not* out of their lives, and he was a threat to them all.

Josie stroked her mother's head, then tugged playfully at her plait.

'Cheer up, Mama,' she said, trying to sound jovial but blinking back her own tears. 'It may never happen, see. You write that letter

146

tomorrow. Everything's going to be all right, believe me.'

Josie closed her mother's bedroom door then stood a moment outside on the landing, listening. Sophia was still crying quietly for all Josie's reassurance that they could get away with it.

She was about to go inside again, but hesitated. Perhaps Mama would fall asleep soon and would be in more command of herself in the morning.

As Josie undressed a new thought made her blood run cold. Suppose her mother was still crying when her father came in? Had she made a mistake in telling her? If Reuben suspected there was anything amiss he would soon get the truth out of her; beat it out of her if need be.

Josie laid her head on the pillow, listening to Francie's even breathing as she lay asleep next to her. She felt so weary herself and there wasn't much sleeping time left before the alarm would wake her for the early shift. Had she made a wrong move? It might have been better if she and Francie had kept the secret to themselves. But she was too tired to worry about that now, far too tired.

The bedroom door slamming open against the chest of drawers some time later woke her instantly, and she sat bolt upright in bed, suddenly alert. Francie didn't wake, and Josie wondered afterwards if she herself had been subconsciously waiting for this to happen.

Reuben lurched into the room, his tall outline

bulky and threatening against the landing light. He lunged towards the bed, grasping the bed sheets and pulling them off.

'You dirty little slut!'

Josie struggled to get off the bed as her father took hold of Francie's hair and pulled her upright. Francie woke up screaming, staring, totally confused. She screamed again as Reuben pulled her off the bed, but her screams were suddenly silenced as the back of his hand cracked across her face.

Josie threw herself at him, tearing at his arm, feeling the pain herself as Francie was dragged towards the door by her hair. She could smell the stale liquor on his breath and felt sick.

'Let her go! Stop it, you brute. Stop it or I'll kill you!'

'Keep out of this, you,' Reuben snarled. 'Or you'll get the same.'

He gave Josie a push in the chest which sent her sprawling sideways, knocking her elbow on the corner of the chest of drawers. She felt tears prickle in her eyes as, panting in fright and pain she scrambled to her feet again and ran out on to the narrow landing.

Sophia was standing in the doorway of the front bedroom. There was blood trickling from a cut above one eyebrow, and the side of her face was reddened as though it had received a blow. Her hands were clamped over her mouth as she stared at Reuben in helpless terror.

At the sight of her mother's suffering, Josie felt a new wave of rage surge up into her throat. Glancing at her, Sophia gave a shrug of misery as though to explain that she couldn't help betraying their secret.

Shouting oaths, Reuben was holding Francie, hovering at the top of the stairs, his hand gripping the back of her neck as though she were a stray kitten. Francie seemed to sway forward under his hand and Josie's stomach lurched, rage turning to terror. She screamed at him: 'Dada! What are you doing?'

Reuben drew back, the madness of the moment past, and turned to stare at her, rage turning his face a blotchy red.

'Not going to have this slut under my roof, see? Beat the dirtiness out of her, I will.'

Before Josie could move, Reuben was forcing Francie down the stairs, the girl whimpering in terror. Josie raced down the stairs after them, her heart in her mouth. Dada was in a terrible rage, the worst she'd ever seen him in. For a moment there, she'd thought he was about to push Francie down the stairs.

'Don't you lay another finger on her, Dada, do you hear me? Call a bobby, I will. You don't want the police nosing around by here, do you?'

'If you don't shut your mouth,' Reuben roared at her, 'I'll give *you* a pasting as well.'

Temporarily distracted, his hand loosened its grip on Francie's neck and she twisted away, rushing through the living-room towards the kitchenette, probably making for the back door, Josie guessed. But Reuben was after her in a flash, drunk though he was. He caught her, grabbing hold of her pale hair and yanking it hard and cruelly. The back of his hand cracked across her face again and again and Francie screamed in terror. Josie felt that terror, like blackness, closing in on her from all sides.

'Stop it! You're hurting her, Dada. Please, stop it!'

'She's a filthy little whore,' Reuben shouted. 'Won't have no dirty tart in my house. No daughter of mine, she isn't. Teach her a lesson, I will, though.'

His hand found its mark again, and with a moan Francie buckled at the knees and would have sunk to the floor if Reuben hadn't been holding her up by her hair.

Josie rushed to Francie's aid, putting an arm around her waist to take her weight, using all her strength to hold her up.

'You've nearly killed her, you drunken old bugger,' she screamed at him, almost hysterical.

Tears were flowing down her cheeks now, but rage at her father was holding the sobs at bay. She mustn't give way now, she thought desperately. She must stop him from hurting Francie further, hurting her baby.

'She deserves it. Hit her black and blue, I will,' Reuben growled, but paused for a moment, uncertain, swaying on his feet.

'You bloody old hypocrite,' Josie shouted at him, struggling to quell her own hysteria. 'I know where you've been all night. Been with that big, fat piece from Port Tennant. If anyone's a dirty old tart, *she* is.'

Reuben's eyes widened for a moment as though astounded at her audacity in even

150

mentioning it, then narrowed as he glared at her. But he seemed temporarily silenced, and Josie, sensing her advantage, plunged on.

'You've been seen down The Arches with her, and we all know what sort of woman hangs around down by there, don't we, waiting for sailors to come in off the ships. Everybody around here is talking about you, they are, and laughing at you, you drunken old fool!'

Reuben raised a hand threateningly, taking a swaying step forward.

'Shut your mouth, you little bitch!'

'I won't shut up,' Josie shouted furiously.

Francie was coming to, moaning. Dragging her weight, Josie began to edge towards the living-room door. She didn't know quite where she was going. She just wanted to get out of arm's reach of her father.

'I wish you were dead, you old bugger,' she cried out, passionately. 'You're no good to anyone, you're not. Mama knows all about your goings-on, mind. You ought to be ashamed of yourself.'

Reuben's face turned even darker red, swelling up in rage. He took several steps towards them.

'Get out of my house,' he bellowed. 'Go on, get out! One as bad as the other, you are. Sluts, both of you. Don't want to see either of your faces round here again. Done with the pair of you, I have.'

'We're going, don't you worry,' Josie said, panting.

She hurriedly pushed an unsteady Francie

151

through the door towards the passage. They were both in their nightdresses. She wanted to get them safely upstairs to pack a few things ready to leave first thing in the morning.

They reached the bottom of the stairs as Reuben lurched into the passage.

'Where the hell do you think you're going? I told you to get out. Get out now. Go on.'

'It's the early hours of the morning, Dada,' Josie said. 'We'll get dressed and packed. We'll be off at first light.'

'You bloody well won't,' he roared. 'You go now, and as you are as well. Not taking nothing from this house, you're not.'

'But our clothes ...'

'Out!' He flung the front door open. Light streamed from the passage across the pavement.

'Put that light out!' a voice shouted from across the street. In the doorway Reuben shook his fist at the invisible watcher.

'Put your bloody lights out, I will, in a minute.'

There was silence from across the street, and with a grunt of satisfaction he turned to Josie and Francie as they stood huddled together.

'Bugger off, the pair of you! Now.' He reached for Francie's arm and shoved her towards the door. 'And you as well,' he said to Josie, lifting a hand threateningly when she hesitated. 'Go on. Clear off.'

'But we're not dressed, Dada,' Josie said desperately, bare feet on the pavement. 'You can't send us out on the street like this. Let us have our coats and shoes at least.'

Reuben's answer was to slam the front door shut in their faces and they were left in darkness.

Josie stood staring blindly in the darkness of the blackout. She felt stunned with the shock of it all, her mind numbed. She just couldn't think. She couldn't believe what had happened to them. Less than fifteen minutes ago they'd both been snug in bed. Now they were turned out like a couple of stray cats. And in their nightdresses.

Humiliation and disbelief made her cheeks burn. If her Stanley were here this would never have happened. Without him she had no one to stand by her, protect her, and felt very much alone. All she had was Francie, and her sister was the one who needed protection the most now.

Francie clung to her, whimpering.

'Josie, what are we going to do?'

'I dunno, kid.'

What could they do? Where could they go at this time of the morning? How could their father do this to them? Suddenly disbelief turned to anger at the thought of the way he had treated them. Suddenly she didn't care if anyone were watching them, observing their humiliation. She wouldn't be treated like this. It wasn't right that their own father could throw them out on the streets in the middle of the night.

Josie hammered on the front door.

'Dada, let us in! Mama, help us! Mama ...'

She heard the sash of a window being opened upstairs and felt a quick burst of hope, but it was her father's voice that answered her.

'If you don't stop that bloody racket, you'll get what's in the chamber-pot down on you. Now bugger off, like I told you.'

Josie grabbed at Francie's arm and moved swiftly away. He'd do it, too, she didn't doubt it. Gingerly, they moved along the pavement to the gates of the yard. Maybe they could get back into the house from there. Josie shook the gates hopefully, but they were firmly locked. She leaned against them for a moment in sheer weariness, then Francie was clinging to her arm, crying.

'What are we going to do, Josie?'

She pushed herself away from the gates and put an arm around her sister, trying to comfort her, though she longed for some comfort herself. For the moment she had no idea what they would do. She was completely out of her depth. But she tried to put some confidence into her voice when she answered.

'Well, we won't go to pieces, for a start,' she said firmly. 'So stop crying. He didn't kill us, did he? That's something.'

He hadn't killed them, Josie reflected, but it'd been a close thing. She wouldn't want to face that again.

'My face is hurting. I can feel it swelling up,' Francie said, tearfully. 'He's blacked my eye, I think, and my jaw aches as well.'

Josie ground her teeth. The old swine! Why was it that so many good men were being killed and maimed in the war, and someone like her father, no damned good to anyone, lived on and

154

did so much harm? There just didn't seem any justice to it.

'I know what we'll do,' she said, making up her mind suddenly. 'We'll go to Gwennie Jenkins. She'll take us in.'

'All the way down to St Helen's Avenue in bare feet?' Francie sounded dismayed. 'And in our nightdresses, as well. I'm mortified!'

It was on the tip of Josie's tongue to tell her sister she should have thought of that before getting herself in the club, but she bit back the words. They mustn't quarrel or disagree. They needed each other now whether they liked it or not. At least Francie needed her, and Josie had always had a strong sense of duty.

She was about to suggest that they'd better get started for Gwennie's when there were sounds of scuffling and scratching on the other side of the yard gates, as though someone were trying to climb up, and the next moment Josie heard her name whispered from overhead.

'Josie! Up by here, mun.'

It was Johnno's voice.

'Oh, Johnno love!' She was so glad to see her young brother yet at the same time frightened for him. 'Watch Dada doesn't catch you or you'll get a good hiding.'

'He's asleep already. Got your coats, I have, and shoes,' he whispered. 'I'll throw the bundle over. There's half a crown in the toe of one of the shoes. Pinched it out of Dada's trousers. Couldn't get any more, like. 'Fraid he'd wake up and catch me.'

'Oh, there's a good boy you are,' Josie said

155

softly. She felt like crying in thankfulness for his bravery. As brave as any fighting soldier.

The bundle fell at her feet, and Francie dived for it, hastily pulling out the clothes and shoes and slipping them on.

As she wriggled into her own coat Josie could hear Johnno's feet scrabbling on the back of the gates as though to get a better purchase as he tried to keep his balance. Although she and Francie were in a terrible predicament, she hated leaving him and Mama and the other children there at Dada's mercy. Yet what could she do?

'Thanks, Johnno love,' she said, swallowing hard against a sob. 'There's grateful we are. Now get back to bed before you're missed.'

'Where you going?' he asked.

It was better he didn't know for the moment, she considered. After all, Gwennie might not be able to help.

'We'll be all right, don't you worry,' Josie said with more conviction than she felt. 'I'll see you tomorrow some time, Johnno, and I'll tell you then what you can do for us. Now keep an eye on things for me, but don't get in Dada's way, right?'

With a whispered goodbye, he slipped silently from the gates.

Josie took Francie's arm.

'Come on, kid. Let's get down to Gwennie's before the sun comes up.'

At the corner of the street Josie glanced back. She couldn't see much in the darkness, but could picture the street in her mind's eye.

She could guarantee Dada wouldn't see hide nor hair of them again, but she hadn't finished with the house on Victor Street. There was her precious post office savings book carefully hidden away. They'd need that. She wanted Mama's old sewing machine as well. It was on its last legs but it was all she had to make her dreams come true until she could afford another one. And there were other cherished possessions, things Stanley had given her. If Dada thought he could make a bob or two out of them, he could think again.

They'd both get all their belongings back, Josie knew without a doubt, because one thing was certain: Dada couldn't be in two places at once.

Chapter Nine

A week later they'd recovered most of their belongings from Victor Street. Josie had her precious post office savings book, most of their clothes, and the old sewing machine. She felt it was a real triumph over Dada, getting their stuff out of the house without his even realising it. She couldn't have done it without Johnno, though, and was grateful. She saw how frightened her brother was now she and Francie had been forced out of the family home; frightened because there was no one left to challenge Reuben.

'If Dada brings that woman to the house,' Josie told her brother through clenched teeth, 'you come round and tell me straight away, mind.'

She wouldn't have her mother humiliated like that. What she could actually do about it, she wasn't sure, but she was willing to have a go even if it meant coming to blows, because next time she and her father clashed she was determined not to be defenceless.

She'd slept very badly during this last week and it wasn't entirely due to the wayward springs in Gwennie's sofa. She grieved for her mother, wondering how she was coping at Reuben's mercy. She could only feel hatred for him, deep-seated and bitter, and was determined to keep any eye on things via Johnno.

Her hatred and thirst for revenge on her father reached fever pitch after a few nights at Gwennie's when Johnno, came round to say that although Reuben hadn't brought the woman to the house, they'd been seen drinking together in a local pub, a stone's throw from home.

It was the thin end of the wedge, Josie thought furiously, and made up her mind there and then that she'd give her father up to the police. She knew plenty about his blackmarket activities. Once the police started probing they'd probably find a lot more besides, and he'd go to prison. Then they'd be free of him. She and Francie could move back to Victor Street in safety. She knew she ought to feel guilty about betraying her own father, but she didn't. He deserved everything he got.

Before she did anything, though, it was only right she should tell Francie of her plans.

Her sister was appalled. 'You can't do it, Josie. It wouldn't be fair, mun.'

Josie stared at her in astonishment.

'You're not sticking up for Dada after what he did to you, surely? He'd have pushed you down the stairs in another minute if I hadn't stopped him. You'd have ended up with a broken neck.'

Francie tossed back her hair impatiently.

'Don't give a damn what happens to Dada, do I? He can burn in hell as far as I'm concerned. It's Billy Parsons I'm thinking about. If the police get Dada, they get Billy as well. And I won't have it, see. Oh, I know you haven't got time for him, Josie, but he's been good to me, Billy has. I won't do the dirty on him.'

Francie showing some kind of principles? Josie couldn't believe it. Yet remembering Billy Parson's simple confession of love for her, Josie paused for thought and reluctantly changed her plans. She despised him but wouldn't be the one to do him any harm. He'd do that for himself one day.

Meanwhile, she'd watch her father carefully. If Reuben did try to move that woman into her mother's home, she would give him up to the police despite Francie's objections. Billy Parsons would have to take his chances.

She made up her mind that for the time being they'd make the best of their situation at Gwennie's. They'd been there just a week, but already she felt the tension between her mother-in-law and sister. It didn't help that they were sharing the bed, while Josie made do with the sofa. She knew it was an arrangement that didn't suit Gwennie at all, but she'd insisted that Francie have the bed due to her condition.

Now the three of them were in Gwennie's small living-room. Gwennie, with one arm comfortably across her ample chest and a freshly lit Woodbine poised between the fingers of her other hand, stared at their piles of clothes on the sofa. Josie regarded her anxiously, fearful her mother-in-law was already regretting taking them in.

'One wardrobe, I got, like,' she said, with a bemused expression on her face. 'Where we going to put it all, then?'

'I'll hang some things on the picture rail in the bedroom, if it's all right with you?' Josie suggested.

Gwennie drew deeply on the Woodbine and shrugged, not looking impressed with the idea.

'Going to be all right, it is, Gwen, I promise you,' Josie said, persuasively.

She prayed that it would be. Gwennie had taken them in quite readily that first night, giving them a sympathetic welcome when she heard what Reuben had done to them. She'd said nothing when she learned the reason for his wrath, but there had been disapproval in her glance and Francie was aware of it, too, Josie knew.

'Anyone would think you'd be glad of a bit of help with the rent,' Francie said tartly.

'Never needed no help with that,' Gwennie

bristled straight away, the cigarette in the corner of her mouth bobbing away furiously. 'Never been behind with my rent, never.'

'Well, we won't be here long, mind,' Francie said, glancing around the living-room disdainfully. 'Getting a place of our own, isn't it Josie?'

If she hadn't been feeling so angry and embarrassed, Josie could have laughed at her sister's superior expression, as though she'd come from a better home. Why wouldn't Francie understand how lucky they were that Gwennie had helped them?

Josie glared at her sister and put an arm around Gwennie's plump shoulders.

'Let's have a cuppa, Gwen, right, and an early night? We'll have to get back to work tomorrow, and I'm on the early shift as well, same as you.'

Gwennie trudged out to go down to the kitchen at basement level which she shared with the family upstairs, and Josie rounded on her sister angrily.

'Don't make life any easier, do you, Francie? Why can't you make the best of things like I do? If it wasn't for Gwennie, we might be sleeping on the sand under the Brymill arch.'

'Huh!' Francie swept the clothes to one side on the sofa and flopped down. 'Might be a bit cleaner than this place anyway. See the way she stubs out her fags in the tea dregs in her saucer? Makes my stomach heave, it does. And have you looked under the bed? Enough fluff to stuff a mattress.'

'Well, get your bum off that sofa, then, and clean it up,' Josie snapped. 'And stop grumbling. It wasn't often you did a hand's turn for Mama, anyway.'

Francie pouted.

'Don't want to stop by here, do I? She's a blooming nosy parker, that mother-in-law of yours. Been pawing through my things, she has. I won't stand for it. I hate sleeping with her as well. She snores.'

Francie sat forward and looked appealingly at Josie.

'Oh, let's push off from by here, mun, Josie. Get a place of our own, right?'

'And what are we going to use for money?'

Even as Josie asked the question she thought of her savings. She was reluctant to dip into them just to pay rent when they could share Gwennie's. She still clung on to her dream of setting up as a dressmaker, and was saving hard to buy another, better sewing-machine. The old one wouldn't last much longer.

She wouldn't be able to save anything, though, if she lost her job at the Ajax. That was why she and Francie had to get back to work the next day. The excuse of food-poisoning couldn't be stretched too far.

'How much longer do you think you'll be able to work, Francie?' Josie asked, hands on hips. 'It won't be long before I'm the only one bringing in any money. Things are going to be tight. Why don't you try to be practical for once, instead of being so selfish?'

Francie jumped to her feet.

'Look, I didn't ask you to help, remember? Billy still wants me, mind. You don't have to bother.'

'Oh, shut up, you silly little fathead!' Josie shouted at her, her patience snapping.

Why was she bothering when Francie seemed so unappreciative of all she was trying to do? She knew the answer to that. She'd made a solemn promise to herself that she'd take care of her sister no matter what happened, and felt bound by it.

Francie didn't have the same spirit or strength of character as herself. Getting mixed up with a married man, ending up pregnant, thrown out of her home ... She already had her feet on a slippery slope. Josie's one fear was that her sister would slide even lower. She hated to admit it to herself, but she knew it was possible that, unaided, Francie might end up on the streets.

Gwennie came in just then with the tea, squinting at them through the smoke from the cigarette dangling at the corner of her mouth.

'What's up then, kid?'

'It's all right, Gwen,' Josie said, swallowing her anger in an effort to restore the atmosphere to normal. 'Sisters disagreeing, you know.'

As she poured out their tea Josie felt sorry that she and Francie had brought upheaval into Gwennie's life. She understood her mother-in-law very well. For all her jollity and jokes while doing her shifts at the Ajax, Josie knew Gwennie worried and fretted about Stanley, as she did herself. It was a bond they shared. Gwennie might be a bit slap-dash and careless

163

in her ways, but she had a warm and generous heart. If Josie hadn't known better, she might suspect Francie was jealous of her closeness with Gwennie. It was something Francie would never be able to understand, she did know that.

They'd been a month at Gwennie's when it happened: the old sewing-machine finally gave up the ghost. Luckily Josie wasn't in the middle of making an ordered garment when the machine broke down, just a smock she was running up for Francie for later on.

'Well, that's that then, isn't it?'

Josie got up from the stool at the small kitchen table in Gwennie's living-room. She put both hands to the small of her back and stretched, groaning at the ache in her bones.

She felt so tired. She'd been to church that morning, something she hadn't done in a long time, and when she came home she'd set to cleaning Gwennie's two rooms, because it was obvious Francie wasn't going to do a hand's turn. She'd got on with her bit of sewing after tea even though she hadn't felt like it, and now the blinking sewing-machine had died on her.

'What you going to do now then, kid?' Gwennie asked, taking her attention off Vera Lynn on the wireless for a moment.

Her mother-in-law was sitting on the wooden chair in front of the small fire in the grate, a cigarette in her mouth, a packet of Woodbines at her elbow, and her stockinged feet on the fender.

'Try and get hold of another machine,' Josie

said, yawning and stretching again. 'I'll go to the post office tomorrow and draw something out. See if I can find a good second-hand machine.'

'Davies the Papers have got a card in their window, Josie,' Gwennie said. 'Saw it yesterday. Couldn't make out how much they wanted for the machine, mind. Didn't have me glasses, see.'

'Oh, thanks, Gwen. There's a bit of luck. I'll have a look tomorrow before I go into work. See if I can pick one up before the week is out.'

'It's not worth it,' Francie said, sitting on the sofa in her old dressing-gown, legs stretched out in front of her. She was busy applying spittle to her hair and rolling up the front and sides in dinky curlers.

'It's not like it was when we were with Dada,' she went on. 'You got most of your material from him, didn't you? What's the good of wasting money buying a sewing-machine when you can't get the stuff?'

'There's plenty of material about off coupons,' Josie said defensively.

'Oh, aye, old rubbish,' Francie said scathingly. 'I wouldn't want to be seen dead wearing that drab old stuff and neither will anybody else. You haven't had many orders lately, have you?'

Josie didn't answer but reached for her handbag behind the sofa. It was true. Her father had been her chief supplier. He always seemed to have a length of this or that which he was willing to sell to her for a couple of bob. The chance of getting hold of reasonably priced, well-made clothes without having to spend precious clothing coupons was what attracted most of her customers, she knew. Cramped though the conditions were in Victor Street, she'd done very well out of the arrangement. That was finished now.

But *she* wasn't! She wouldn't give up her dream just because she'd hit hard times. Things were bound to get better. One day the war would be over and life would get back to normal. She was determined to be ready for that. She and Stanley would have a good life; she'd set her heart on it.

'It's worth it to me,' she said, rummaging in her handbag for her Post Office savings book. 'You've got to speculate to accumulate, see, Francie. Haslem taught me how to make my own patterns, so I can make clothes up to my own designs and copy designs from magazines as well. Women will want that kind of thing after the war: something new, something extra special. We've all been doing without for too long.'

Francie pulled a face.

'Oh, listen to her by here. will you?'

'Go on, Josie love, tell us more, mun?' Gwennie said enthusiastically, turning down the volume on Vera Lynn. 'I could listen to you talk all night, kid.'

Josie laughed, pushing Francie's feet aside to sit down on the sofa.

'Oh, I've got plans, Gwennie, don't you worry. I've been thinking, me and Stanley will buy a house one day. Stanley, a property owner! Think of that, Gwen. No making do with rooms all our lives.'

'*Duw! Duw!*' Gwennie was impressed, but Francie blew a raspberry.

'Big talk. Where's the money coming from for all this mularkey?'

'From pattern- and dress-making, that's what,' Josie said quickly.

She opened her Post Office savings book, looking at the amount there with satisfaction. It was mounting up nicely. A sewing-machine would be a good investment, she was certain of it.

'Give us a look, then,' Francie said.

Before Josie could stop her, Francie snatched the book from her grasp, turning her back on Josie.

'Hey! Give that back, nosy parker!' Josie said, struggling to snatch the book away again, but Francie held her off, laughing.

'How much has the old miser got by here then? Let's see.'

'Hand it over, Francie, or I'll clock you a fourp'ny one. I'm warning you, mind.'

Still laughing, she held the book just out of Josie's reach and read aloud the sum of money totalled there. Abruptly, she stopped laughing and stared.

'All right, Francie,' Josie said. 'You've had your fun, now give me my savings book. That's private, that is.'

Francie was silent. She scrambled off the sofa and stood holding the book behind her back.

There was a look of dark fury on her face and Josie was immediately reminded of Reuben.

'You got all this money!' she said, with a rasp in her voice. 'You never said a word all this time.'

'It's none of your business,' Josie said, pushing herself up from the sofa. She held out her hand. 'Give it here, please, Francie.'

Her sister's mouth tightened, face turning red with anger.

'You bitch, Josie Jenkins!'

'*What?*' Josie's mouth fell open.

'Well, there's a way to talk, isn't it?' Gwennie burst out indignantly.

'Shut up, you fat old bag, you!' Francie rounded on her furiously. 'You'll keep your nose out of this if you know what's good for you.'

'Well!' Gwennie drew in a gasp. 'Would you believe it?'

'Fran!' Josie flared, staring at her sister in consternation. 'Don't speak to Gwennie like that. Apologise to her at once, will you?'

'I won't!' Francie stuck out her chin belligerently. 'She's always poking her nose in where she's not wanted. Spying on me all the time, she is. Worse than bloody Hitler.'

'Now that's enough,' Josie shouted at her sister. She turned to Gwennie, her tone placating. 'I'm awful sorry. I wouldn't blame you if you threw us out after that performance.'

Gwennie sniffed, clearly still offended.

They'd certainly be in a desperate fix if she told them to pack and go. Besides, Josie didn't want any quarrel to come between herself and her mother-in-law. They supported each other in their mutual anxiety for Stanley's safety. There was no one else she could share her fears with.

'What the hell's the matter with you, Francie?' she asked, struggling to control her anger. 'Have you gone daft or what?'

'Matter with me?' She was almost spluttering in fury. 'Preggers, that's what's the bloody matter with me! You could've given me the money to get rid of it and not missed it. You knew how desperate I was, and you never said a word, never offered a penny!'

'Wasn't going to give my sister money so she could kill herself, was I?' Josie said, trying to sound reasonable. 'Anyway, I'm dead set against abortion. And I lost a good friend because I tried to help you, don't forget that. You've cost me plenty already, mind.'

It was true. She'd lost Daisy's friendship because of Francie. She'd lost her family as well, and had done nothing wrong herself. If she had less spirit and determination she might consider it unfair, too heavy a price to pay.

'It always has to be you, doesn't it?' Francie snapped. 'Never mind about what I've lost. I could have married Billy Parsons, but no, you wouldn't let me have a bit of happiness. You want it all for yourself. Selfish to the core you are, Josie,' she said, flinging the savings book on to the floor. 'Selfish, and mean with it as well. There, take your bloody book and I hope it chokes you!'

Josie glared into the fury in her sister's eyes, meeting it with a rising anger of her own. She mustn't give way to it though, she told herself. She'd pledged herself to help Francie, and now she must see it through. Even so, her sister was pushing her too far.

'Now you look here, Francie,' she said, voice rising to a dangerous pitch. 'Don't you talk to me like that. And don't go blaming me for the mess you made of your life.'

She bent and scooped up her precious savings book, pushing it back into her handbag. This represented her future, hers and Stanley's. She'd worked hard for the money, and no one had the right to tell her what she should do with it, especially not her sister.

'If you've lost anything, it's your own doing. Stupid, that's what you are, Francie, getting yourself preggers by a married man. Why should Stanley and me give you our money, eh? Why should we have to pay for your blinking stupid mistakes?'

Francie's face whitened suddenly. She stood staring at Josie for a moment. When she spoke her voice was no more than a whisper.

'Because, maybe it's not only *my* mistake, see.'

Josie regarded her sister with a puzzled frown. 'What do you mean by that?'

Francie swallowed hard, but stayed silent.

'Tell me what you mean?'

Francie tossed back her hair, her composure returned.

'Had enough of this, I have. Going to bed.'

She marched out but paused in the doorway. She turned and looked at Josie with narrowed eyes, face set as hard as granite.

'I won't forget this, Josie and I'll never forgive you either. But you'll get paid back one day, mark my words, you and your precious Stanley. Huh! There's none so blind as them as won't see, they say. And it's true, isn't it?'

Chapter Ten

Mumbles, Swansea, 6 June 1944

'Has my pretty Birthday Girl got a kiss for Nanna, then?'

Daisy smiled as Edie eagerly took Valerie from her arms and carried her granddaughter into the big conservatory where Edie's three children were waiting for her, the two younger ones missing a day from school for the purpose. Immediately there was an excited argument between Amy and Florence, Edie's teenage daughters, as to whose lap Valerie should sit on first.

'Stop spoiling her, you two,' Daisy said good-naturedly. 'Otherwise she'll start thinking she's the centre of the universe.'

'Well, she is,' Florence said enthusiastically. 'Look at her. One year old and she's pretty enough to be in pictures. I like her Shirley Temple dress.'

Daisy sighed. The dress had been irresistible. She wouldn't think about the number of clothing coupons she'd had to use up to get it.

'Heard the smashing news this morning, Daisy?' Tommy asked. 'The invasion of Europe started this morning, somewhere in France. I said, didn't I, something was up with all those ships in the Bay?'

He was thirteen and enthusiastic about the progress the Allies were making in the war. Unhealthily interested, Edie always grumbled, but Daisy knew Tommy was just a typical teenage boy.

'Yes, I heard it,' she said, glancing at Edie's face, and hoping Tommy wouldn't go on about it.

'I'd planned for us to have tea on the front lawn,' she said. 'But wouldn't you just know it would rain on my granddaughter's first birthday? We'll have the conservatory to ourselves, though. I've made it off limits to guests for this afternoon.'

A fine drizzle, more like mist than rain, was masking the usually spectacular views across Swansea Bay.

'Bet our side was hoping for fine weather, too,' Tommy volunteered with the air of someone very much in the know. 'Hope we got it.'

'And I hope it won't be too wet for Mam-gu and Gramps to come up later on,' Daisy said hurriedly, trying to change the subject. 'It's ages since we've all been together. Where's William, by the way?'

'Crisis at the market garden or something,'

Edie said. 'It would happen today, wouldn't it?'

Daisy knew Edie was never happier than when she had her whole family around her. Daisy felt the same. She always loved it when there was a family gathering at *Tŷ Heulwen*, though of course it couldn't be complete without Gareth. They all missed him, Edie most of all.

'The announcer didn't say where we've landed,' Tommy went on, obviously determined not to be put off. 'But I bet you any money it's Normandy. Just think, right this minute our troops are fighting Jerry on the beaches. Wonder if our Gareth is in it?'

'Tommy, don't!' Edie's face turned white.

'Now stop it, Tommy, will you?' Amy warned, glaring at him. 'You're upsetting Mam.' She looked at Daisy. 'He's been on about the blooming invasion all day. I'll give him a clip across the ear in a minute.'

Daisy hid a smile. Amy was sixteen, outspoken, and thought herself grown up enough to throw her weight about where her younger brother was concerned.

'Jelly!' Valerie announced in a clear and determined voice. 'Jelly, Nanna. Jelly, now!'

The rain eased after they'd had their tea. Tommy went off out. Down to the foreshore, Daisy suspected, to establish his own beachhead. At the far end of the big conservatory Mam-gu, Gramps and the girls were amusing themselves listening to Valerie's rendition of 'The White Cliffs of Dover'. She hadn't yet mastered the

173

art of standing up unaided, but managed short toddles hanging on to Gramps's finger. She had plenty to say for herself, though. What a chatterbox!

Daisy was hoping for a quiet chat with her stepmother. She wanted some advice about Rhodri Lewis, and trusted Edie's judgement the most.

'Mam-gu had a batch of letters from Gareth yesterday,' Edie said quietly, as they sat on the window seat out of earshot of the others, looking out over a greyish sea.

She was holding her head low, Daisy noticed. She'd sensed her stepmother was upset the moment she'd arrived, and it wasn't all to do with Tommy's harping on the invasion, either. There was something else.

'It happens like that sometimes,' Daisy said reassuringly. 'Men are moved around a lot; letters get delayed.'

It was sad, she reflected, that Gareth had never written direct to Edie since he'd been called up in 1942. It was tragic that he couldn't find forgiveness in his heart for her, the woman who had taken him in from birth to save him from the shame of illegitimacy and the workhouse; the woman who'd loved him and cherished him as her own child. She was the only mother he'd ever known, yet when his natural mother had told him the truth, he had turned away from Edie, feeling he'd been cheated. Daisy loved Gareth like a real brother, but didn't know if she could forgive him for the pain he'd caused Edie these last two years.

She lifted brimming eyes to look at Daisy.

'I'm heartbroken, Daisy. In his last letter Gareth says he's determined to emigrate to Australia straight after the war. If he goes, I'll never see him again.'

Daisy put an arm around her shoulders and hugged her close.

'Oh, Mam, I'm sorry.' She put her lips against Edie's temple in a comforting kiss. 'But perhaps it's just as well, Mam. It'll give him time and space to sort out his feelings for you and his ... mother.'

Edie swallowed hard.

'When Mam-gu gets a letter from him, I let her read it out loud to me and we have a good cry together.' She choked back a little sob. 'Your father warned me when Gareth was born, when I was dead set on taking him in, that I might be making sorrow for myself. Wouldn't listen, would I?'

She gave a loud sniff, obviously trying to pull herself together.

'He was a wise man, your father. Perhaps I should have listened to him.'

Daisy gave her another squeeze. 'You wouldn't change anything, Mam, you know you wouldn't.'

Edie sniffed again.

'No, but it's a good thing we can't see what's in front of us, isn't it?'

Daisy felt she knew what was in front of her. Her mind was full of Rhodri Lewis these days, full of a new excitement. She was longing to talk to Edie about it, but hesitated. It seemed callous to talk of her own hoped-for happiness when her stepmother was feeling so low over Gareth.

They were silent for a moment. All that could be heard was Valerie's piping voice from the other end of the room demanding Gramps swing her around again, but Gramps was puffed out. And Tommy had come back. It was probably lonely on the beach with all his pals in school.

Daisy saw the look of love in Edie's eyes as she watched her younger son crawling on his hands and knees with Valerie on his back. Gareth would be missed but Tommy would be her stepmother's consolation.

Edie had recovered and there was a little more colour in her cheeks. She has plenty of courage and endurance, Daisy thought admiringly. She hoped she would have the same sort of courage if life treated her badly in the future.

'Do you see anything of Josie Jenkins these days?' Edie asked at last. Her tone was lighter, as though she was determined to put sadness behind her.

But for Daisy the question came out of the blue, and for a moment she felt flummoxed.

'Not for a long time,' she replied carefully.

She hadn't told Edie about the quarrel with Josie. It would mean explaining the reason and she couldn't do that. She felt too ashamed for her former friend.

'So you don't know Josie's father threw her out on the street, her and her sister, with just the clothes they stood up in?'

'Never! When was this?'

'Last summer. Josie's mother-in-law told me when I met her in town last week,' Edie said.

'I forgot to mention it before.'

Daisy stared out across the shrouded bay. It was almost a year since Josie had come to see her and they'd quarrelled so bitterly. Daisy suddenly felt partly responsible for Josie's predicament. She'd been no help at all to her in her trouble. Perhaps she'd over-reacted. She'd been outraged at what Josie had asked her to do, but it was such a long time ago now; her anger then only dimly remembered. In her heart she had long since forgiven her. Surely there was no need to let their quarrel drag on any longer?

'The sister's had a baby since,' Edie went on. 'February, I think. A little girl. Hadn't seen Gwennie for years. Oh, she's aged, mind, and she's not all that much older than I am. She used to work in the market like me when she was a girl. There's many a ham bakestone I've sold her of a dinnertime ...'

'Mam!' Daisy interrupted sharply. 'Never mind about going down Memory Lane now. Tell me what's happened to Josie?'

'Oh, she's doing all right, working hard apparently. She's dress-making on the side,' Edie said. 'And she's managed to get the sitting tenancy of the house in St Helen's Avenue.' Edie smiled with amusement. 'She's Gwennie's landlady now.'

Daisy continued to feel guilty. Josie's life had been in upheaval and she'd made no attempt to find out about it. She'd thought about Josie a lot over the intervening year. She'd been so angry with her at the time, but later on had felt nothing but regret for their quarrel. She regretted, too, the awful things she'd said about Josie's family. Josie would probably never forgive her.

Yet she ought to get in touch, make the effort. After all the things she'd said, it was her place to make the first move, wasn't it? But she'd have to think about it because it wouldn't be easy.

'I met Dr Lewis in the Dunns yesterday,' Edie said, changing the subject. 'He was asking after you.'

Daisy felt hot blood rush to her face and neck, all thoughts of Josie swept out of her mind.

'That was kind of him,' she said, because she couldn't think of anything else.

She tried to avert her face from Edie's sharp gaze, watching a new band of rain sweep inland from the sea. Yet behind the rain she thought she could see a brightening sky far out against the horizon.

'Daisy?' Edie's voice had a warmth to it. 'I believe you like him ... like him a lot? He strikes me as a very nice man, too.'

She let out a little laugh, turning her burning face towards her stepmother.

'Oh, Mam, I can't hide much from you, can I?'

Edie smiled. 'No, lovey. You wear your heart on your sleeve, like I do. We're a pair well met when it comes to showing our love. Tell me about Dr Lewis then?'

Daisy hesitated for a moment then let the words rush out, and it felt so good to confess her feelings to someone at last.

'Mam, I've fallen in love with him.' Daisy felt breathless now that she'd confessed. 'Such a lovely man, he is. So caring and compassionate. I can't explain how he makes me feel—just working with him or even meeting him casually on the street.'

Edie's face was beaming. 'Well, there's lovely.'

Daisy put fingers to her mouth, feeling she might burst into tears. She was sure about her love for Rhodri, but uncertain about other things.

'He's asked me to go with him to hear *The Messiah* at Tabernacle Chapel in Morriston next weekend,' she said at last. 'But I don't know what to do, Mam.'

'Don't be silly,' Edie said quickly. 'Of course you must go.

Daisy shifted uneasily in her seat.

'The thing is, Mam, it's not eighteen months since I lost Gerald. People in the village might think I'm fast. You know, taking up with somebody so soon after losing my husband. And I've got to think of Rhodri's reputation. There was an awful lot of gossip about him when he first came here. All nonsense, of course.'

'Listen, Daisy lovey, the most important thing in life is love, and don't let anyone tell you any different,' she said firmly. 'Love is the only way to find happiness believe me, and you deserve a bit of happiness, Daisy. We must all grab at love when it comes our way, and never mind what other people think.'

Daisy put out a hand to cover her step-mother's.

'Oh, Mam, there's a comfort you are. Always have been. God's gift to me, that's what you are.'

Daisy always thought Tabernacle Chapel, the most elaborate chapel in the whole of Wales, had the look and feel of a great cathedral, with its vast interior, steepled tower and the eight-sided spire that seemed to be pointing the way to Heaven. It dwarfed every other building in Morriston. She felt small and insignificant when she passed beneath the huge arched Corinthian columns, but today, sitting with Rhodri listening to the glorious music, letting the massed voices flow over her, she felt almost ten feet tall.

After the performance he gave her his arm as they came out of the tall doors of the chapel and descended the few steps to the pavement. He had parked his motor car a little way along the main road and they strolled towards it, arm in arm, in the warm evening air.

'What did you think of the performance then, Daisy?'

'Wonderful,' she said. 'Inspiring. I've never heard the work sung so well.'

Walking beside him, clinging to the strength of his arm, she felt she was treading on air. Just being with him, close to him, listening to his voice, was paradise. She'd never felt this way before, never. It was wonderful. Crazy, but she couldn't help thinking Rhodri was feeling something for her, too. A warmth had grown steadily between them these last months, a warmth that made her tingle from head to toe. Sometimes, when their glances met, it was difficult to turn her eyes away. Often she longed to open her arms to him, invite him into her embrace. What wild and wonderful thoughts she was having lately. If only he knew!

Rhodri took out his pocket watch and glanced at it.

'It's early yet. Let's not go back straight away. Shall we go for a spin?'

Daisy longed to snatch any extra minute with him. She didn't ever want the day to be over. She wanted it to go on and on and on, endlessly.

'Can you spare the petrol, though?'

'Pot on the petrol,' Rhodri said. 'Let's go down to Singleton Park. Or we could take a walk along the Promenade?'

They decided on Singleton Park where quite a few other people had the same idea, enjoying the summer air. They strolled past the Swiss Cottage, which was supposed to be a typical hunting lodge, where people were sitting listening to a Salvation Army brass band playing rousing hymns, and then on down to the pond to watch the ducks rooting amongst the water lilies. One could almost forget there was a war on.

'Let's get ourselves a seat,' Rhodri suggested.

They found one further away, where the music floated intermittently to them on the evening air. Rhodri took off his Homburg and put it on the seat next to him. They sat quietly for a moment, listening to the breeze fluttering the leaves on the trees—a breeze that brought them not only the sound of music but also children's laughter. A lovely sound, Daisy always thought. It made her feel that some day everything would be right again with the world.

Rhodri still held her arm tightly and after a moment grasped her other hand in his.

'Daisy, I've been planning to say something to you for ages. Now I'm tongue-tied. There's stupid, isn't it?'

'I don't know about that.' She laughed a little unsteadily. Her heart was fluttering like the leaves on the trees. What was he going to say? She was half afraid to hope. 'It's certainly unusual for you to be stuck for words.'

'Oh, so that's what you think of me, is it?'

'As a matter of fact,' Daisy gulped but the words seemed to spill out and she couldn't stop herself, 'I think a great deal of you, Rhodri. I ...' She stopped again, confused at her own boldness. 'I shouldn't have said that. You must think me awfully forward?'

Rhodri pressed her hand. His vivid blue eyes were shining as he looked into her face.

'Think you're wonderful, I do, Daisy, my dearest girl. I've grown more and more fond ... No! *Duw annwyl!* It's more than fond I am. Much more.'

He flung an arm around her shoulders and drew her close to him on the seat. Daisy's breath caught at the sudden, intimate contact; her shoulder against his chest, his face inches

182

from her. She could feel the warmth of him through the thin material of her dress. It made her feel light-headed and dizzy.

'Daisy, *cariad*, I'm crazy about you. Mad about you, I am. I can't get you out of my mind, day or night. I can't sleep. I'm off my food. I'm day-dreaming so much my patients are beginning to look at me sideways. What are you going to do about it?'

Daisy could hardly catch her breath for the pounding of her heart.

'What do you suggest, Doctor?'

'You could marry me?' he said, voice quivering a little.

Daisy leaned in a little closer to him, gazing into his face, taking in all the details of the features that she loved. The blue eyes that had a hopeful yet pleading look in them, the generous mouth, the lock of dark hair that had fallen over his forehead. She couldn't remember a moment in her life when she had felt happier.

'You know, Doctor, I believe I will marry you, because ...' Daisy smiled up into his face. 'Because I love you, Rhodri Lewis. Love you, love you, love you! Oh, there's a relief to say it to you at last. I can't wait to be your wife, my darling man, and I'll love you for the rest of my life, Rhodri.'

'Oh, my Daisy. My beautiful girl. Come here, give me a kiss.'

His lips were warm and tender, but he was trembling and Daisy understood what he was feeling for she felt exactly the same. She was committed to him and she trusted him. She wouldn't hold back with her love. She'd give it freely, for this love was meant to last for both their lifetimes, for ever.

Chapter Eleven

When the hooter sounded for the end of the early shift, Josie wiped a hand across her forehead, breathing a sigh of relief. Her head throbbed as if a herd of elephants was stampeding through it.

Too much broken sleep, that's what it was. No one could function properly when their sleep was continually disturbed. Little Rhiannon cried a lot in the small hours. Her crying never seemed to wake Francie who lay like a log in the bed. It was Josie, sleeping in the small back bedroom, who always made the effort to get up and tend the child.

She had decided it would be easier if Rhiannon slept with her in future. As she'd anticipated, Francie made no objection. She probably hadn't even noticed, and this indifference made Josie angry. Even though Rhiannon was only four months old, Francie was too quick to shrug off responsibility for her, too confident that her sister and Gwennie would take charge.

Not that Josie minded seeing to Rhiannon. She loved her baby niece as her own daughter, but it was the principle of the thing and couldn't

184

go on much longer. She'd have to have a word with her sister, she decided firmly.

Francie mustn't be allowed to get away with it, thought Josie as she put on her cotton edge-to-edge coat. They all had to pull their weight. Gwennie did her bit without complaint. If it wasn't for her mother-in-law keeping an eye on Rhiannon when Josie was in work, she didn't know what they'd do.

It was getting to the stage where she felt Francie couldn't be trusted to see to her own baby. Didn't she want Rhiannon at all? Josie wondered. If so, it was something she couldn't understand for the life of her. Of course Francie hadn't wanted to be saddled with a baby, but now Rhiannon was here, and such a lovely baby, too, how could her mother not love her?

Outside the gates of the factory, buses were just bringing in the three-till-eleven workers. Gwennie would be on one. Josie would take the same bus back.

She saw Gwennie hurrying towards her almost at a run, her thick legs encased in crumpled pale Lisle stockings, her great chest heaving under a tight cardigan that had only one button remaining on it.

'*Duw! Duw!* Oh, kiddo, I'm nearly passing out.' Gwennie lumbered up to her, face screwed up with effort. 'Let's sit down by here a minute, is it?'

They both sat on a low wall nearby.

'Oh, there's keen you're getting for work, then,' Josie said laughing. 'Can't wait to get yourself next to Islwyn Davies, is it?'

'Oh, aye. Have him for breakfast, I will.' Gwennie managed a wheezy laugh between panting for breath. 'No, kid. I wanted to see you before you went off. It's that bloody sister of yours, Josie.'

'Tsk! What's she done now?'

'She's a lazy little baggage, that's what she is,' Gwennie said in an aggrieved tone. 'Still in bed, she was, when I came to work. Rhiannon, the poor little mite, was crying her head off. Had to stop to change and feed her, I did. Nearly missed my flaming bus, as well.'

Josie raised her eyes to heaven and let out a heavy sigh of irritation. She was trying to be fair, trying to be understanding, and trying to be sensible, too. Nevertheless, she was getting fed up with Francie and her selfish attitude; fed up to the point of having it out with her once and for all.

'Have a word with her, I will, Gwennie,' Josie promised.

'She had somebody down in your living-room late last night,' Gwennie said, with a disapproving sniff. 'Heard 'em when I came in from work. A man it was, Josie. Heard him laughing, I did.'

Their living-room was on basement level and could be entered from the street by a door at the bottom of the front area steps. Both Josie and Francie used that entrance when coming in from work late at night, to save using the front door and disturbing Gwennie in her two rooms on the ground floor.

Being on the early shift this week Josie had

gone up to bed in decent time last night, taking little Rhiannon with her. She slept in the back bedroom on the first floor, so had heard nothing.

'You being the sitting tenant, Josie, her landlady, like,' Gwennie said, 'you ought to tell her, you know. Don't want our house getting a name, do we?'

Josie ground her teeth in silence. She'd thought it a golden opportunity when Gwennie's landlady, the sitting tenant in the house on St Helen's Avenue, had told them she was moving back to Carmarthen. Josie immediately applied for the tenancy, hardly daring to hope she'd get it, but she did and was thrilled. A place of her own, just what she'd always wanted.

The three of them and Rhiannon had the house to themselves, and there was bags of room for her dress-making scheme, too. Josie let Gwennie keep the two rooms on the ground floor which she'd occupied for years, much to Francie's annoyance. Josie turned the spacious attic bedroom into a workroom, and she and Francie had the two bedrooms and the basement living-room.

Yes, everything seemed rosy before Josie gradually began to realise that Francie had no intention of pitching in with her share of the expenses. During the months she was expecting, Josie had willingly footed the bills, telling herself it wouldn't be long before her sister was back at the Ajax earning good money again. Now four months had gone by since Rhiannon was born and Francie hadn't offered a penny piece, nor had she attempted to get her job back at the munitions factory.

For weeks Josie bottled up her disappointment and resentment but now things had come to a head. Francie's bringing an unknown man to their home secretly was the last straw. How often had it happened before? she wondered furiously.

'Thanks for telling me, Gwennie,' she said jaw tightening. 'Going to have things out with her, I am, good and proper.'

When Josie opened the door that led from the front area directly into their living-room she found Francie sitting painting her toe nails. Dirty cups and plates had been pushed under the sofa and left. The sight of them made Josie's anger swell up like a barrage balloon in her chest.

'What's this place, then?' she said, loudly. 'A pig sty?'

Francie looked up from her toe-painting, a faintly surprised expression on her face.

'What's the matter with you, then?'

Josie pulled a face, wiggling her head and mimicking her sister's voice. 'What's the matter with you, then?'

Francie shrugged, and went back to painting her toe nails.

Glaring furiously at her sister's bowed head, Josie took off her coat and headscarf and hung them up. Francie looked as though she didn't have a care or responsibility in the world. Push everything on to others who were daft enough to do it, that was her game. Well, enough was enough.

'Where's Rhiannon?'

'In Gwennie's bed.'

'Have you looked in on her recently?' Josie's lips felt stiff with her anger. 'Maybe your daughter needs another feed?'

Francie said nothing, concentrating on her toes, pretending she hadn't heard.

'Francie! Stop doing that, will you?' Josie shouted, standing with hands on hips. 'Listen, I've got a bone to pick with you. Fed up to the back teeth, I am.'

'Oh, heck! What's it now, Josie? You're always complaining about something or other.'

'Don't you care about your child or what?' she asked, conscious of a quiver in her voice. She tried to control it. Francie might think it weakness. 'Don't you love Rhiannon at all?'

Francie raised her head, pouting, looking faintly annoyed at being disturbed. 'Don't know what you're on about, do I?'

'You're neglecting your baby,' Josie said bluntly, though trying not to shout again. Losing her temper wouldn't help. 'You're leaving everything to me and Gwennie, and it's not right. It isn't fair, either. You've got to pull your flaming socks up, Francie, because I'm getting sick of it.'

'Oh, God, another lecture.'

'Hey! Come off it, now!' Josie warned loudly, lifting her chin aggressively and planting her hands on her hips again. 'Don't you be funny with me, Francie. Things are going to change round by here or there'll be trouble, big trouble.'

Francie gave a short laugh, twisting the top back on the nail-polish bottle.

'Oh, I'm quaking in my shoes, kid.' she said mockingly.

Josie clenched her teeth in fury. Francie was laughing at her, taking advantage, thinking she'd gone soft now that Rhiannon was with them. Maybe she had, a bit. She'd let her sister get away with murder these last months, but she couldn't let it go on much longer.

What could she do about it, though? She was longing to have a good old knock-down-drag-out fight with Francie, bring her to her senses. But she was afraid—afraid to disturb the balance of their lives. She didn't know what Francie might do. Josie knew it would break her heart if she lost Rhiannon now.

'You'd better be quaking, too,' she said, hearing the emptiness of her own threat. She wouldn't let Francie see her uncertainty, though, and must keep her temper in check.

'I mean it, Francie,' Josie went on. 'There's no free ride here, any more. Sister or no sister, you've got to pull your weight like the rest of us. Look at those dirty dishes under by there.' She pointed under the sofa. 'Get off your lazy bum and wash up, will you? You don't do a hand's turn, don't flick a duster even. I'm not having it any more, see?'

Francie picked up a newspaper and began fanning her toe nails with it, trying to make the varnish dry quicker. To Josie it was deliberate provocation.

'Now, look! I'm your landlady as well as your sister, mind,' she said, trying to quell the urge to raise her voice. 'I haven't had a ha'penny rent off you yet, and I have to pay for every damned household thing as well. It's about time you chipped in, isn't it?'

'How can I afford it on what I earn?' Francie said.

Josie gritted her teeth at her sister's obstinacy.

'If you went back to the Ajax, you'd be on good money again. Why waste your time in a tuppeny-ha'penny job serving behind a bar when you can do better, and help me out as well?'

'I'm not going back to the bloody munitions factory, and no one can make me now I'm a mother, so there!' Francie suddenly flared. 'It's taken months for my skin to come back to its proper colour. You might enjoy looking the colour of a copper pot, but I don't.'

'Mother!' Josie gave a high laugh of derision. 'That's rich, that is. Gwennie's more of a mother to Rhiannon than you are. You're unnatural, you are, Francie. More interested in painting your flaming toe nails than seeing to your own child.'

'Oh, shut up!' she said, getting up from the sofa and going towards the door. 'You're just jealous, you are. That's what this is all about.'

'Don't you dare say that!' Josie shouted after her, furious that Francie had hit a tender spot.

She did long for a child, Stanley's child, but didn't want to admit that envy even to herself. And she couldn't bear that Francie didn't seem to appreciate what she had, because despite everything, her sister was so lucky to have Rhiannon.

She followed Francie out into the passage, furious, too, that her sister had walked away from their argument when she hadn't finished all she wanted to say. She couldn't let her get away with it. If she didn't make a stand now, her sister would walk all over her.

Francie was just climbing the stairs that led to the front hallway.

'Hey, ignorant!' Josie said loudly. 'Don't walk away when I'm talking to you.'

Francie leaned over the banister, her expression stubborn and angry.

'I'm not going back to the bloody factory! I've told you once, haven't I?'

'And you don't bring any more men back here at night, either,' Josie flared, glaring up at her.

'What?'

'Oh, don't come the little innocent with me, will you?' Josie nodded knowingly at the changed expression on her sister's face. 'I know all about it. What are you playing at? Haven't you got yourself in enough trouble already?'

Francie tossed back her hair, chin jutting defiantly.

'Don't know what you're on about.'

Josie knew that look only too well.

'Yes, you do,' she said, lips thinning. 'Gwennie heard you last night. How long did you think you could get away with it?'

Francie looked furious.

'Tsk! I might have known she'd poke her nose in, the old bag.'

'Who was it?'

Francie ran the tip of her tongue over her lips. Josie knew that habit, too, knew it of old. She was either going to be evasive or tell an outright lie.

'An old friend.'

'Not Billy Parsons!'

'No.' Francie lifted a hand and looked at her freshly painted fingernails. 'As a matter of fact, his name was Hank.'

Josie's nostrils flared. 'An American soldier? Old friend be blowed! You brought an American soldier, a complete stranger, back here? What were you thinking of?'

Francie smirked. 'Oh, he wasn't a bit like a stranger. He was very friendly, as a matter of fact. Where do you think I got this nail polish, then?'

Josie was fuming. She knew plenty of girls who'd gone crackers over the American soldiers when they came to Swansea, with their posh uniforms, intriguing accents and tempting gifts. But there couldn't be a future for such relationships. She'd really thought Francie would have more sense and pride.

'You make me ashamed. Dada was right about you, wasn't he?' she said, flashing Francie a look of contempt. 'You *are* a slut.'

'Now, look here, you!' Francie said angrily, half turning to come down the stairs again, but obviously thinking better of it. 'It's none of your business what I do and who I see.'

'Excuse me!' Josie snapped. 'This is *my* house, and I won't have strange men traipsing back and forth at night. So you can pack that in as quick as you like, see.'

Francie pulled a face of disdain.

'Oh, mind now! Who the hell do you think you are, Josie Jenkins? I've a good mind to push off from by here. Me and the kid can soon find another place.'

Josie's heart thudded in sudden apprehension. She turned her back to walk into the living-room, not wanting Francie to guess at her feelings from her expression.

'Oh, aye!' she said loudly, though careful to control her voice. 'Rent free, is it, and maid service, like you got now? Don't make me laugh, Francie. You know which side your bread is buttered, don't you? But maybe you won't have to give notice. Maybe I'll throw you out. How would you like that?'

'Bitch!' was Francie's parting shot, shouted from the top of the basement stairs.

Josie stood for a few minutes in the kitchen feeling too angry to think straight. She'd not eaten since an early breakfast, but she couldn't eat anything just then, not feeling the way she did, and besides, there was Rhiannon to see to, poor neglected little Rhiannon. She must come first.

Josie went up to Gwennie's bedroom on the ground floor. Rhiannon was on the double bed, barricaded in with pillows. She waved her arms and kicked her legs excitedly under her blanket as Josie leaned over her, smiling.

'Hello, my little blossom.'

Josie lifted the child into her arms. Her heart ached at the thought of the hours the baby spent alone. She was safe and secure but it wasn't good for her, Josie was sure. She needed love and attention from her mother, like any other child.

'Come on, sugar plum,' Josie said. 'It's a nice warm bath and a clean nappy for you, then some din-dins, right?'

After her bath and clean clothes, Rhiannon chortled happily, blowing bubbles. Josie held her close, revelling in the fragrance of the child's freshly washed brown hair, the scent of babyness that made Josie ache with longing and tenderness for her.

Francie's daughter had none of her mother's pale colouring. The child's skin had a healthy glow. Josie looked at the rosebud mouth, the cheekily turned up nose, and the bright grey eyes whose gaze never left her face.

She needs me, Josie thought, a moment of revelation, and I need her.

As though reading her mind, Rhiannon curled a fist around Josie's thumb, holding on with surprising strength. Josie held her closer. How could Francie ignore such a beautiful little baby? It was shameful. She thought about her sister's threat of leaving. How would she bear it if Francie took the child away? She'd break her heart, Josie decided. She felt as bonded with Rhiannon as any mother would. She loved her much more than Francie ever could or indeed wanted to.

Josie made a resolution. She would be the mother to Rhiannon that Francie wasn't. Let her go if she wanted to. She wouldn't be missed. She was becoming more and more difficult, more of a hindrance than a help.

Over the last few months Josie had pictured how it would be if her sister did up and go, but leaving Rhiannon. She'd thought about it wistfully, though at the same time feeling it was wrong to covet her sister's child. Now she wasn't so sure. She'd done her level best for her sister, and what thanks did she get for it all? Not that thanks mattered. What mattered was Rhiannon. Francie didn't really want her child, didn't want the responsibility, and Josie did. That couldn't be wrong, could it?

What she'd like to do, Josie thought, was pack up her job at the Ajax to look after Rhiannon; concentrate on the dressmaking, instead. It had crossed Josie's mind to suggest the arrangement to her sister. Without her child, to whom she seemed indifferent, Francie could go where she pleased, do what she pleased.

But Josie hesitated to say anything. If Francie thought her sister was keen to take Rhiannon, she'd refuse out of spite. Josie knew her too well. Francie would have to be convinced that it was really worth her while to agree.

And in any case the idea of giving up the Ajax was impractical. She needed the money too much, especially now with Rhiannon needing things all the time. There was a limit to the dress-making work she could do while materials were still on coupons. Perhaps she wouldn't be able to do enough business to make ends meet? No, giving up her job was just a pipe-dream for now.

But her resolution to be a mother to Rhiannon still held. She'd manage it somehow.

She had just finished feeding Rhiannon when she heard someone knocking at the front door. With Rhiannon in her arms, she opened the front basement door, and stepping outside, looked up the area steps to see who it was. She was astonished to see Daisy Buckland standing at the front door with a child in a pushchair.

'Daisy!'

She looked down over the side of the steps.

'Hello, Josie.'

She looked uncertain of her welcome, but Josie was never more glad to see anyone—except Stanley, of course. Was Daisy here to make up? Josie hoped so with all her heart.

'I'll come up and let you in,' Josie said, hurrying inside.

They had parted with such acrimony that awful day just over a year ago, Josie thought, as she almost ran up the kitchen stairs, Rhiannon in her arms. She'd been full of regret for their quarrel since and now she couldn't even remember her anger. She'd thought about Daisy so much, and miraculously her friend was here.

'Leave the pushchair in the hallway,' Josie said eagerly. 'Our living-room is downstairs. Just going to make a cup of tea, I was.'

Daisy stood awkwardly in the centre of the living-room, holding Valerie. Josie smiled at her reassuringly.

'It is good to see you again, Daisy, and there's sorry I am we had a tiff.'

Daisy smiled back, a crooked little smile, somewhat shame-faced.

'It was more than a tiff, wasn't it? I said some awful things to you, Josie. I'm so sorry. I hope you've forgiven me?'

'Tsk! Don't be soft, will you Daisy?' she said, unable to suppress a grin. 'I was as bad as you. I should never have asked you to do it. Stupid of me, it was.'

Daisy looked at Rhiannon.

'And this is Francie's baby?'

'Yes, this is our little angel,' Josie said proudly. 'Rhiannon her name is. She'll be five months next week.'

'Oh, she's lovely, isn't she? Look at that little face. She is like an angel, too.'

Josie felt extraordinarily pleased and proud at Daisy's praise of Rhiannon. She could almost believe for the moment that she herself was the child's mother. Almost.

'Valerie's grown, my word!' said Josie, to exchange the compliment. 'She's a picture.'

'Don't be fooled,' Daisy said with a laugh. 'She's a little madam with a mind of her own, and talk about a chatterbox!'

Valerie looked from her mother's face to Josie.

'Valerie have biscuit?'

'And what do we say?' Daisy asked with mock sternness.

'Please?' she said.

'That's better.'

Daisy put Valerie down and the child immediately scrambled on to the sofa to wait for her treat.

'Come on!' Josie said, laughing. 'Sit yourself down by there as well, Daisy.' She held Rhiannon out to her friend. 'Perhaps you'll hold her while I get the tea? Then we can have a good old chat like we used to, and you can tell me all the news.'

Josie sat listening to her friend talk about her job as a midwife in the Mumbles, enjoying every moment of their companionship. It was like old times, the times she'd missed so much. She could hardly believe Daisy was here, and wanting to be friends again. It was just what she needed, someone she could confide in.

'Have you heard from Stanley lately?' Daisy asked, accepting a slice of Victoria sponge.

'A letter manages to get through now and then,' Josie said, 'But they're few and far between. Miss him so much, I do, Daisy. I've said endless prayers for him.'

'I pray for him, too,' said Daisy.

'Oh, there's kind of you, kid,' Josie said. 'After the way I behaved as well.'

Daisy put a hand on her arm and Josie eagerly covered it with her own, feeling a lump rise in her throat. She felt comforted that someone besides herself was praying for her Stanley.

'Let's not think any more about that silly quarrel,' Daisy suggested. 'Let's start again. I've missed you, Josie. I wonder ... will you be my matron of honour?'

Josie felt so astonished her jaw dropped.

'You're getting married?' she said at last. 'Oh, Daisy, there's wonderful! Of course I'll be your matron of honour. I'm so thrilled for you, kid. Who is he, then? And when is it going to be?'

She was amused to see Daisy's cheeks turn pink with pleasure.

'Next year. July. His name is Rhodri, Rhodri Lewis.' Daisy took Josie's hand and pressed it warmly. 'Oh, Josie, I'm so in love with him. He's wonderful. And he loves me, too. I never would've believed it could happen to me.'

Josie smiled at her, squeezing her hand in return.

'You deserve some happiness, Daisy. I'm so glad you've found someone. What does he do?'

'He's a doctor, a GP.'

'Ooh! There's posh!'

'Oh, go on, you!' Daisy laughed. 'And I've got another favour to ask you, Josie. Will you make my wedding dress?'

She clapped her hands together with excitement and pleasure.

'Love to, I would. Have you got a pattern or shall I make you one? We can design it together. It'll be unique.'

Daisy laughed again. It was such a happy sound that Josie felt her own spirits lighten considerably. Little Rhiannon, nestling in the crook of Daisy's arm, looked up into her face, round grey eyes shining as though she were sharing the joke, too.

'Oh, special treatment, is it?' Daisy said. 'Nice to have friends in high places.'

'Well, of course.' Josie grinned. 'Only the best for my very best friend. What about material? Have you seen something you like? And what about the clothing coupons? Will you have enough?'

'Lewis Lewis have some ecru figured silk, gorgeous!' Daisy said with enthusiasm. 'It's eighteen and eleven a yard, but worth every penny. Mind you, the number of coupons is ... well, astronomical, but Mam and Mam-gu are saving theirs for me.'

'You can have mine as well,' Josie offered generously.

After all, she wouldn't be needing anything new, not until Stanley came home. Who else was there to dress up for?

'What about a hat?'

Daisy looked starry-eyed for a moment.

'Oh, I think a big lacy hat, something really wonderful.'

'And I'll swathe it with the figured silk,' Josie said. 'Oh, Daisy, this *is* exciting. I've never made up anything with really expensive material. It'll be a masterpiece, leave it to me.'

'I know it will.' Daisy smiled happily. 'That's why I want you to make it. You're a genius when it comes to dressmaking. And I'm going to pay you for your workmanship this time, mind.'

'Oh, no you won't!' Josie said with mock indignation. 'You're my best friend.'

Josie stood with Rhiannon on the pavement waving until Daisy and the pushchair turned

201

the corner. Then she went back inside, feeling extremely pleased with the way the afternoon had turned out.

She and Daisy were back together, and there were exciting times ahead for them. Her head was already buzzing with ideas for her friend's wedding outfit. She'd start making some drawings after tea, just to give Daisy some idea of what she had in mind.

She felt surprised when her stomach started to rumble. And no wonder! She'd eaten nothing all day. Now, suddenly, she felt ravenous. Her mouth was watering for something tasty. A meat pie from Eynon's? Just the thing.

Josie put Rhiannon to lie on a folded blanket in her basket—a large cockle-woman's basket that Gwennie had bought for the purpose, which was very good of her, Josie thought. It was ideal for carrying the baby from room to room.

She picked up the basket by its stout curved handle.

'Come on, my little chicken,' she cooed to the baby. 'Your mammy can watch over you for a few minutes while I slip out.'

Josie went up the front bedroom, deliberately not bothering to knock. Francie was sitting before a mirror pinning the front of her hair into curls. A dress and a pair of new stockings were laid out on the bed.

'Here's Rhiannon. Keep an eye on her, right? Slipping up to Bryn-y-Mor Road, I am, to get some pies for tea. Do you want one, Francie?'

She spoke conversationally, as if their previous spat had not happened. It was the best way, she

202

always thought. It was no good letting things wrangle.

'Wasting your time,' Francie mumbled, a hair clip in her mouth. She took it out and stared at Josie in the mirror. 'They'll be closing in a minute. I can't hang about by here, mind. I'm going out. Meeting somebody.'

Josie swallowed back a sharp retort. Francie was right. She couldn't dictate to her sister about who she saw and where she went, and if she said anything now it would only lead to another quarrel.

'I'll catch them if I hurry,' she said, and left Francie to her preparations.

She made her way down to the kitchen. She kept an old tin tea caddy on the mantelpiece over the range. Gwennie's rent money and anything Josie might make from her dressmaking went in the tin. She normally waited a week or two until it was full before taking the contents to pay into her Post Office account.

She would have to do that soon, but for now the tin could spare her a few pennies for some pies, Josie decided. She'd get one for Gwennie, too. Her mother-in-law would appreciate something tasty when she came home from the factory.

As soon as she lifted the tin off the mantelpiece she knew something was wrong. This morning the tin had been heavy with silver and copper, but to her consternation it now rattled hollowly when she shook it. Taking off the lid, Josie saw a couple of half crowns and some pennies lying in the bottom.

She sat down heavily on a nearby chair. There had been almost four pounds in coins in the tin that morning. Now it was gone. She'd been robbed!

She felt sick at the thought. Who had taken the money? Had someone crept in through the front basement door? No, Francie had probably been sitting in the living-room all morning. She'd have seen anyone slipping in. Daisy and herself had been there all afternoon. How could it have happened, then?

In the silence Josie heard the front bedroom door slam and the sound of Francie's high heels on the linoleum at the top of the stairs. She felt as if every hair on her head was standing on end.

Francie!

Fired by a new wave of anger and resentment, she flung the tin box from her and bounded out of the kitchen, taking the stairs almost two at a time. This was it! The final straw.

When Josie reached the front hallway, Francie was already down the stairs. She stood on the bottom step pulling on some white lacy cotton gloves. She glanced up briefly—scornfully, Josie thought, fuming.

'Haven't you gone yet?' she asked, reaching up to adjust a tiny hat that was perched at a rakish angle on the side of her head. 'Eynon's will be closed by now.'

'Where is it?' Josie asked, though clenched teeth.

'What?'

'You know damned well what.' Josie reached

out a hand. 'Give me your handbag.'

Francie lifted her chin, pushing the bag securely under one arm.

'What for?'

'I want my money back, you little thief!'

'Hey! You watch it!' Francie tossed her head. 'I could have you up for saying things like that, mind. Defamation of character, that is.'

Josie ground her teeth in fury.

'How could you steal from your own sister? And I've been so good to you, Francie. Stood by you when you were in trouble, didn't I? Took care of you. Sacrificed. I don't expect thanks, but I do expect honesty.'

'I dunno what you're on about.' She waved a dismissive hand. 'Haven't got time to stand by here gabbing, have I? Miss my bus up to town, I will.'

Francie made to walk along the passage to the front door, but Josie stepped in her way.

'Oh, no you don't! My tin box is almost empty,' she said, holding herself in check with a struggle. She had the urge to snatch Francie's handbag from her, prove she was guilty by scattering the contents on the floor. 'You're the only one who could have taken the money. I worked hard for that. I want it back, now.'

Francie flicked back her hair, making the little hat wobble precariously.

'Look, if there's money missing, then that Gwennie took it. I told you, she's always poking about.'

Josie's mouth tightened in fury at Francie's

brazen attempt to pin the guilt on to someone else.

'Don't you try to throw the blame on her, you ungrateful bitch! We've carried you, Gwennie and me. And then you play a dirty trick like this.'

She knew Francie was hard, but hadn't realised just how unprincipled she was. If it weren't for the child, she'd tell her sister to sling her hook; get out now, and for good. Francie was trouble. Josie had helped out of sisterly loyalty and look what it had cost her already. Her family, her friend almost. It just wasn't worth it.

'You're no blinking good, you're not, Francie. You and Billy Parsons are a pair well met.'

Josie reached forward suddenly and snatched at the bag under Francie's arm. It was heavier than she'd anticipated. It slipped from her grasp and fell to the floor, bursting open. A shower of coins, silver and copper, scattered loudly over the linoleum.

Josie stared down at them for a moment then looked up at Francie's defiant face.

'Some of that's mine,' she said defensively.

'I know exactly how much was in my tin box.' snapped Josie.

She kneeled down and started to gather the money up. Now her suspicions were confirmed, she didn't know what she should do next. How could she ever trust Francie again? Could they go on living in the same house together? At that moment she felt helpless and hopeless. If it weren't for the love she had for Rhiannon, she might wish she'd never helped Francie at all. Maybe it would have been better for everyone if she *had* married Billy Parsons.

Josie was conscious of Francie just standing there staring at her bent head as she picked up the coins one by one.

'So, what are you going to do about it then?' she asked, sarcasm thick in her tone. 'Going to throw me and Rhiannon out on the street, is it?'

Josie looked up. 'You can push off whenever you like,' she said angrily. 'But Rhiannon stays. I wouldn't trust you to look after a cat. Go on, go and see if one of your fancy men can put you up—and put up with you, as well.'

Francie's smile was scornful and bitter.

'Oh, you'd like that wouldn't you, Josie? You're as jealous as hell. But I'm not budging from by here, see. You can throw me out if you like, but if I go, so does the kid.' She stepped past Josie's kneeling figure and made for the front door. 'Rhiannon is *my* baby, not yours. Though don't you wish!'

Chapter Twelve

Gwennie opened her eyes just a crack to squint at the clock. Half-past ten. Better get up. Reluctantly, she pushed the bedclothes off and slid her legs out of bed, curling her toes as they came in contact with the cool linoleum. She'd have to get a mat to put by there before the winter came. She stood up and stretched, then gave her abdomen a good old scratch.

Duw annwyl, she still felt tired. She'd be glad when this perishing week was over. Roll on Sunday. She smacked her lips a few times, grimacing at the sour taste in her mouth. The old cigs weren't doing her any good either. Never mind, a cup of tea should put her right.

She pulled on her old dressing-gown, ready to go down to the kitchen. It was lovely having the whole house to themselves. It would be nicer, though, if that Francie wasn't with them. There'd been some kind of a row yesterday, Gwennie thought. Josie had been awfully upset, but she hadn't said what it was all about. Gwennie thought she could give a good guess, though. Money.

Her hand tightened into a fist. Trouble-maker that Francie was. Trouble and strife to Josie, and, *Duw* help, the poor girl didn't deserve it. There's a way to treat a sister, isn't it, who has been as good as gold? Yes, it would be better for everybody, especially her daughter-in-law, if Francie would push off, Gwennie thought. But if Francie went, she'd take the baby too.

Gwennie's heart contracted at the thought. Little Rhiannon. Every time she looked at the baby's pixie face she was reminded of her own young daughter, lost to her from diphtheria years ago. They were as alike as two peas in a pod. They were so alike, it was unnatural. So alike that it had haunted her for months, not wanting to acknowledge what it might mean.

Gwennie shrugged her plump shoulders to throw off the ugly thought. Yes, it was nice to be able to wander about the house in the mornings in her comfy old robe without having to worry about bumping into other roomers in the kitchen or going out to the lavvie. And speaking of the lavvie ...

She was just pulling on her shoes to make the trek out to the back yard when there was a knock on the door. That would be Francie. Gwennie grimaced in annoyance. Now what did *she* want? It had to be her, because Josie had gone to work.

Gwennie opened the door and stood with it ajar, making it plain she didn't want her to come inside.

'What you want?'

Francie was standing there, all dolled up like a dog's dinner, looking down her nose, as usual, as though she had a bad smell under it, Gwennie thought. Stuck up piece of goods! Anyone who didn't know would think she came from a good home.

'Rhiannon's up in Josie's bedroom,' Francie said, gaze fixed on a spot just above Gwennie's head. Irritating habit, that.

'Have you changed and fed her, then? I hope you have, 'cos I got to go to work, mind,' Gwennie snapped.

Francie's eyes flashed.

'Course I have.'

'What you telling me for then?'

'I'm going out, aren't I?' Francie flicked

back her hair irritably. 'Though why I've got to explain myself to you, I dunno.'

'When you coming back?'

Francie pulled back her chin, giving Gwennie a haughty stare.

'That's my business, isn't it?'

'Well, I hope you're back before I go to work or else the poor kid'll be stuck in the house by here all by herself. That isn't right, that isn't. There might be a fire or something.'

'Don't talk so daft, will you?' Francie snapped. 'She'll be all right for an hour or two.'

Gwennie pursed her lips disdainfully.

'There's more to being a mother than giving birth, you know. Kids got to be looked after. You ought to be home by here instead of gallivanting about.'

'Blinking heck!' Francie looked furious. 'You can't expect me to hang about here all day. I'll go off my head.'

'Why don't you get a proper job, then?' Gwennie retorted quickly. 'A barmaid! And in Wind Street, as well. I'd be ashamed, I would.'

'You wouldn't get the chance of it, anyway,' Francie sneered. 'They want someone who looks like a woman, not a sack of potatoes.'

'Well!' Gwennie was too insulted to think of an answer.

She tried to slam the door but Francie put a hand against it, holding it open.

'There's something else,' she said. 'Josie asked me to collect your rent this morning.'

Gwennie opened the door wider, looking intently into Francie's bold stare.

'Pull the other one. It's got bells on it.'

'What?'

'You must think I'm as daft as a brush,' Gwennie snapped. 'I give my rent to Josie every Friday night, on the dot, and she knows it. She never asked you to collect it at all, you scheming little hussy.'

'Now, look here!' Francie was almost spluttering. 'Don't you talk to me like that. I could have you put out of here, mind. We could get twice the rent you're paying. These rooms are too good for you.'

Gwennie smiled narrowly.

'Well, it's lucky you're not my landlady then, isn't it? And don't talk of making trouble for me because if I wanted to I could make plenty for you.'

'Oh, yes? I don't think so.' Francie waggled her head, a sneering smile on her red lips.

'Well, I do,' Gwennie said, folding her arms across her chest. 'Like telling Josie the name of Rhiannon's father.'

The smile was wiped from Francie's face. The change was so sudden and comical that in other circumstances Gwennie would have had a good laugh. But she didn't feel like laughing now because Francie's reaction seemed to confirm she was on the right track.

An inner voice urged her to let the matter go before it was too late, before she discovered something she would regret knowing. But another voice drove her on. She had to know the truth. It was vitally important to her, if her guess were true.

211

Francie began to fidget with the string of beads around her neck, tugging at them and twisting them around her fingers.

'What you getting at?'

'I think I know who Rhiannon's father is,' Gwennie went on relentlessly. 'And he wasn't born a million miles from by here, either.'

Francie turned on her heel.

'I don't have to listen to this rubbish.'

Gwennie grabbed at her arm and hung on. Francie wasn't walking away from this. Gwennie had been waiting her chance for weeks to clear the air. She wouldn't let it go on any longer. She had to get Francie to tell the truth.

'We're going to have this out here and now,' she said determinedly. 'Or as soon as I see Josie, I'll tell her what I believe. And you know what that is, don't you?'

Francie lowered her head a little, glaring at Gwennie under her eyelashes, her face set hard as granite.

'You don't know what you're stirring up, you nosy old bag!'

'Tell me the truth. Is my Stanley Rhiannon's father?'

Francie stared at her, face impassive. The moment seemed to stretch forever as Gwennie waited.

Francie let out air noisily between her teeth as if she'd been holding her breath for a long time. Now she held her chin in the air, eyeing Gwennie down her nose with a supercilious look, almost triumphant Gwennie thought, and her heart sank.

'Yes, he is,' Francie said at last, an edge of spite in her tone. 'Now are you satisfied, Gwennie? Now do you feel better, eh? Rhiannon is Stan's bastard child. There's nice, isn't it? And you're her grandmother. How do you feel about *that?*'

Gwennie put fingers to her mouth in consternation, unable to utter a word, staring at Francie's mocking face.

She smiled disdainfully.

'And what are you going to do about it, then? Going to tell Josie, are you? Are you going to tell her that her precious husband slept with her own sister when he was on leave in May last year? And she thought she had him all to herself. That'll make her happy, won't it?'

'You dirty little bitch,' Gwennie said, in a voice almost strangled with emotion. She felt wretched now the truth was out, and guilty, like she'd done something wrong herself.

Francie tossed her head, arrogance in every line of her face. 'It takes two to tango, mind. I didn't get up the spout on my own.'

'You trapped him,' Gwennie said desperately. 'I know your sort all right. You led him on, and he's only a man after all.'

Francie smiled sweetly.

'Oh, there's touching, isn't it! You're making excuses for him. I wonder if Josie will do the same? I wouldn't be surprised if she told him to bugger off. You know what Josie's like, don't you? Shoot first and listen after.'

Gwennie turned away, holding back a sob. What would Josie do? She'd go mad. She'd

213

never forgive him. It would be the end of their marriage, Gwennie knew that for certain. Her daughter-in-law was a fiery one, sure enough. Francie was right there.

Gwennie bit at her thumb nail in agitation. What should she do? She loved Josie like her own daughter, and the girl had been so good to her, too. How could she destroy her by telling her the truth? And how could she destroy Stanley, her own son, ruin his marriage?

Despite what Francie said, Stanley loved Josie, worshipped the ground she walked on. He wouldn't deliberately hurt her.

And Josie adored him, that was the trouble. She'd put him on a pedestal for too long. Stanley was a good man, a loving son and husband, but he was no angel either. He was just a man, and sometimes irresponsible with it. Men could be very foolish on times, especially when tempted; their own worst enemy.

Gwennie reached her door and went inside. She wouldn't be able to go into work today. She was too upset. She needed time to think things through.

'I bet you wish you hadn't asked now,' Francie said from the hallway.

There was amusement in her voice. Gwennie knew immediately that the girl sensed her dilemma, and had probably already guessed what her decision would be. Gwennie turned slowly to look at her, face stiff with anger and misery.

'You're a bad lot, you are, Francie Randall, just like your old man,' she said quietly. 'The

214

Randalls have always been known for their bad blood. But you'll get your just desserts, mark my words. Don't forget, if Josie finds out about you and Stanley, she'll have your guts for garters, too. You'll be out on your arse quicker than you can say cheese.'

Francie's peal of laughter echoed in the hallway.

'That's what you think! Josie knows if I go, so does Rhiannon. And you ask her how she feels about Rhiannon. No, my sister won't risk parting with my baby. I'm safe as houses. You worry about your Stan. He's got everything to lose.'

Chapter Thirteen

June 1945

The Mumbles train swayed and rattled as it raced along the track that edged the bay; it was full of mums and kids with their buckets and spades, rolled-up towels, bags of jam sandwiches, bottles of pop, and Thermos flasks of tea.

On the upper deck Josie had to clutch at Rhiannon on her lap, hold a box between her feet, and at the same time try to hold on to the back of the wooden seat in front. The trouble with taking a seat upstairs, she reflected, was that the motion of the train was exaggerated. She wouldn't be surprised if she felt sick by the time they reached Oystermouth. She was lucky to get a seat at all, though. There'd been a long queue of mothers and children at Rutland Street terminus, even though school hadn't yet broken up.

Around her the noise of the kids was deafening. Everyone seemed bent on taking a trip to the Mumbles. And no wonder with the day so gloriously warm. The first real day of summer. You couldn't blame people for taking advantage of it, enjoying themselves. There was a lot to be joyful about, Josie reflected. The war was over—well, at least in Europe anyway. The first summer of peace was here.

'Sands, Auntie.' Rhiannon pointed through the window, her grey eyes bright and shining with excitement. She shook her head. 'Didn't bring bucket, Auntie.'

Rhiannon turned her gaze to the little boy sitting next to them. He was perched on the very edge of his seat, craning his neck to see the view, a large red sand bucket held tightly.

Rhiannon leaned forward suddenly and tried to grab it from him. He drew back startled, staring from her to Josie.

'Now, that's naughty, Rhiannon,' Josie scolded her niece. 'It's not yours, is it? We're not going to the sands today. We're going to see Auntie Daisy. And here's our stop.'

Holding Rhiannon and the box, Josie climbed carefully down the steep twisting metal stairs from the top deck, and was grateful when the conductor helped her get the pushchair out. After a minute or two the train, with its noisy cargo, moved off towards its destination at Mumbles Pier.

'Want to go sands,' Rhiannon announced defiantly, stretching her chubby neck to view the last of the disappearing train.

'Be good,' Josie said affably, as she strapped the child into the pushchair. 'And Auntie will buy you an ice-cream.'

She set off across Oystermouth Square and up Dunns Lane, carefully carrying the box containing Daisy's wedding dress by its string.

Today would see the final fitting. She'd worked so hard on the dress, not only on the sewing but also the designing, and Josie felt she could congratulate herself. It was a really beautiful creation, if she said so herself, and she could hardly wait to see her friend wear it on her big day. Just another three weeks to go, Josie reflected, and Daisy would get all she desired.

Her heart gave a little lurch. Her own big day would be when Stanley came home for good. He probably wouldn't be demobbed until next year but at least his war was over. There'd be no more action for him. He'd come through it unscathed. She had a lot to be thankful for when she came to think of it, despite not having a job.

But she didn't begrudge having to give up her job at the Ajax to a man who had come back home. It was only fair, after all, even though she'd miss the very good money. There were a lot of women in the same boat now, all chasing whatever jobs they could find. Poor old

Gwennie for one. Josie knew her mother-in-law hated having to go out cleaning for a quarter of what she'd been getting in the factory.

Things were tight for them, there was no getting away from it. Francie was contributing now, though reluctantly and irregularly. Josie had her dress-making, it was true, and that was keeping them afloat for the moment, but the one thing that preyed on her mind most was that there might come a time when they would not be able to keep the tenancy of the house on St Helen's Avenue. They were so comfortable there and it was so convenient, especially the way it gave her space to do her dress-making. If they had to give it up she didn't know what she'd do. Besides, she wanted Stanley to come back to a proper home.

In Woodville Road Josie stopped outside Daisy's and knocked at the door. Daisy was so excited about the dress being finished at last, and Josie looked forward to seeing her smile of greeting. Usually they did the fitting, then had a chat and a cup of tea while Valerie and Rhiannon played together.

When the door opened Josie was surprised to see Daisy's stepmother standing there instead of her friend.

'Oh, Josie.' Edie Philpots paused. Her expression was one of uncertainty, as though her caller were not welcome, and for some reason Josie felt a twinge of unease. Where was Daisy?

'You'd better come in, lovey,' Edie said, opening the door wider.

218

'Daisy *is* expecting me,' Josie said, feeling suddenly defensive and confused by the strange look on the older woman's face.

She manoeuvred the pushchair over the front step and into the narrow passage, half expecting, hoping, to see Daisy appear from the kitchen to welcome her.

'It's the final fitting for her dress today. She's not ill, is she?'

Edie still hesitated.

'No, not ill, lovey. Come into the front room a minute.'

Josie unstrapped Rhiannon from the pram then followed Edie into the front room, feeling a flood of relief on hearing that at least Daisy was not ill. It would be awful if the wedding had to be postponed now.

She put the box down on the sofa and undid the wrapping. With eager fingers she lifted out the dress and held it up. The material rustled and shimmered gorgeously. Looking at it, sometimes she could hardly believe it was her own creation.

Edie fingered the material then took it out of Josie's hands and held it, examining it closely.

'This is beautiful work, Josie,' she said. 'Really lovely.'

Josie felt warmed at the genuine admiration in her voice. It was nice when she was paid for dress-making, but even better when people appreciated and praised her workmanship. That was what made her hard work so worthwhile.

Edie looked at her with the same close

attention she'd given to the dress, obviously weighing her up.

'You've got a lot of talent, Josie, you know that, don't you? I think you'll go far.'

Josie felt a glow of pleasure rise into her face. She'd always admired Edie Philpots for her drive and energy. Daisy had told her how her stepmother had struggled up from nothing to build a successful business, and all by sheer willpower. Praise from Edie was well worth having.

'I can't wait for Daisy to wear it,' she said. 'Oh, it's going to be such a beautiful wedding, isn't it? And I'm so happy for her. She deserves it.'

Silently Edie folded the dress and placed it back in the box, securing the wrapping. Josie watched, frowning. What was going on?

'Isn't Daisy going to have a fitting, then?' she asked, puzzled. 'The big day is getting a bit close. I'll need time to make any alterations.'

Edie clasped her hands in front of her, as if cold. Her expression was grave as she looked at Josie.

'Something's happened, I'm afraid,' she said quietly. 'Daisy's had some news. It's hit her like a bombshell.'

Edie hesitated, and seemed to be having trouble speaking. Josie could see she was trying not to cry, though her eyes were now brimming. Josie felt her heart contract with dread. Whatever had happened, it was something awful, she could sense it.

'What is it, Mrs Philpots?'

Edie swallowed hard, obviously trying to pull herself together. She motioned to Josie to sit down. Pushing the box to one side, she sat on the edge of the sofa, leaning forward anxiously.

'Daisy was notified yesterday that her husband is still alive.' Edie said, in a low voice.

'*What?*' Josie blinked several times in astonishment. She couldn't believe what she was hearing.

'It's official,' Edie went on, and shook her head. 'It's been a terrible shock. She's upstairs now, packing a suitcase. She's going up to Yorkshire tomorrow.'

'Yorkshire?' Josie felt confused. None of this was making any sense. Daisy was a widow, had been for years. How could her husband suddenly be alive?

'Gerald's home is in Yorkshire,' Edie explained miserably. 'That's where he is, apparently. He's been in a prisoner-of-war camp all the time. No one knew. It's a shock to us all.'

'What about the wedding?' Josie asked, but already she knew the answer.

Edie put her fingers to her mouth to hide it but Josie could see her lips were trembling.

'There isn't going to be one.' Edie's voice was no more than a whisper now. 'She's not free, you see. She's already a married woman. Oh, Josie!' Her voice rose from a whisper to a wail. 'Daisy is so miserable. She loves Rhodri Lewis madly and she's breaking her heart.'

Josie sat for a moment, stunned by this turn

of events. Daisy wasn't free to marry the man she adored. What must she be feeling? She must be devastated.

'I'm so sorry, Mrs Philpots.'

That sounded inadequate, but Josie didn't know what else to say. She felt heart-sick for Daisy. To have this happen now, just weeks away from the ceremony. But better now, she reflected, than afterwards.

Edie sat silently with eyes downcast, and suddenly Josie felt uncomfortable. Her friend wouldn't want to see her now. She was in the way.

She stood up.

'I'd better go, then.'

Edie jumped up from her armchair.

'No, don't do that, lovey. Daisy needs someone to talk to, someone outside the family, someone she trusts. You're a young woman with plenty of common sense, Josie. You talk to her. Help her. She's so confused.'

Josie put a hand to her throat, uncertain of herself. How could she help? She had plenty of push, she knew that, but she wasn't brainy like Daisy. How could she advise her over something like this? It was well outside her experience. She couldn't even begin to understand what her friend was going through.

'Where is she?'

'Up in the front bedroom.' Edie clasped Josie's arm tightly. 'Make her see sense. I'm afraid she's going to ruin her life. She's got such a strong sense of duty, see, that's the trouble.'

Josie still hesitated, glancing at Rhiannon.

'You go up, lovey,' Edie urged. 'I'll look after the little one.' She bent towards the child. 'Would you like a cake, Rhiannon?'

Josie went hesitantly into the front bedroom, and found Daisy bending over a half-filled suitcase on the bed.

She straightened, turning towards her, and Josie almost cried out in dismay. Daisy's eyes usually so bright and alive, were darkly ringed. She'd been crying all night and all morning, by the look of it. Her usually clear complexion was blotchy and inflamed, and her upright figure bowed, weighed down with despair.

Josie's heart went out to her, deeply touched by her friend's obvious misery. She rushed across the room and clasped Daisy in an embrace.

'Oh, Daisy love, I'm so sorry this has happened.'

Josie didn't know if that was the right thing to say in the circumstances. She kissed her friend's cheek then stood with an arm around her, looking into her face, one she hardly recognised.

'Is there anything I can do, kid?'

'Josie, there's good of you to come,' Daisy murmured. 'There's nothing anyone can do.'

It was on the tip of Josie's tongue to remind her that she'd really come to do the fitting, but she quickly bit back the words. Daisy had forgotten why she was there, and now it didn't matter.

'There's sorry I am,' she said again.

Again her own words sounded empty, as though they were the wrong ones. Perhaps she *had* said the wrong thing; perhaps it wasn't sympathy Daisy wanted? She couldn't even speculate on how she herself would react in such a situation, Josie reflected, though an inner voice told her that love would decide for her. She believed in love deeply; love was everything. But perhaps Daisy didn't see things the same way?

Daisy was regarding her, her brief smile twisted and bitter.

'Anyone would think someone had died, the way we're talking,' she said. 'When actually someone has risen from the dead. I ought to be glad.'

She sat down heavily on the bed, hands in her lap, head bent. Josie moved swiftly to sit beside her, putting an arm around her friend's shoulders again, holding her tightly, feeling that somehow warm, physical contact might ease the despair she was suffering.

Josie could feel tremors shaking Daisy's body, and realised she must still be in shock.

'Of course you're glad he's alive, Daisy,' but Josie hesitated, wondering how her friend would take what she had to say next. 'You can't torture yourself and Rhodri like this. You and Rhodri belong together, anyone can see that. Gerald's not really your husband anymore, is he? I mean, not when you're in love with someone else. And in all innocence, too. These things happen in wartime.'

Daisy pulled a handkerchief from the sleeve

of her dress and dabbed at her eyes and nose.

'I feel so evil, so wicked, Josie,' she said, lifting her head to look out of the window at the warm sunshine. 'Crying and carrying on like this because my husband is alive. How many women would give all they possessed just to have their husbands come home to them? It makes me feel guilty to think about that.'

Looking at her friend, Josie wondered if she should go on speaking her mind. She couldn't help remembering their awful quarrel over Francie's pregnancy and how she'd regretted it in the months that followed. Daisy's friendship meant so much to her. She wouldn't want to jeopardise that again. Yet, at the same time, things needed to be said. Edie Philpots was right. It would be so easy for Daisy to make a bad mistake in the state she was in now. She needed help to think things through.

'Daisy, why ever didn't he write to let you know he was alive?' Josie said evenly. 'Peculiar that, isn't it? I mean, the Red Cross could've got a letter through during those two years, surely, and he must've been freed a few weeks ago now. Why hasn't he been in touch?'

Daisy turned to her.

'I thought about that all night, Josie.' She shook her head. 'Perhaps he regretted the marriage. Maybe he didn't want the responsibility of a child.' She turned her head and looked out of the window again. 'It was so brief, our time together. We hardly knew each other really. I'm ashamed to say I can't even remember what he looks like.' She turned to gaze at Josie again, shame-faced. 'Isn't that awful?'

'It's understandable, Daisy,' Josie said gently, putting a hand on her arm and giving it a reassuring squeeze. 'You're only human, after all, kid. You thought he was dead. You had to go on living, didn't you? Making a life, a new life, for you and Valerie. Your stepmother says Gerald's up in Yorkshire. Why didn't he come straight here to his wife and child, then?'

'He didn't know where we were.'

'Nonsense!' Josie said quickly, and with a touch of impatience. 'He could surely have found out from the Admiralty or the Red Cross. You've got to get this situation into perspective.'

Daisy turned to look at her, eyes brimming.

'Josie, I'm so confused and frightened. It's as if Gerald belongs to a different life, someone else's life, not mine. And yet, I am still his wife. I can't get away from that fact.'

'You're his wife in name only, Daisy, in name only.' Josie clasped Daisy's shoulders tighter.

Daisy bent her head.

'There's Valerie. I had his child, Josie, and I feel I owe him something. Loyalty, perhaps.'

'Daisy, listen, love,' Josie began. 'Gerald is a stranger now. You don't love him anymore; you hardly remember him. There's no shame or blame in that, under the circumstances.'

She was determined to go on and say it, even though it might not be what Daisy wanted to hear. She didn't want to upset her anymore than she was already, but it had to be faced.

'No one would blame you if you wanted a ... divorce.'

Daisy stood up quickly, staring aghast at her, shaking her head vehemently, and Josie's heart sank. Had she gone too far, presumed too much on their friendship? Would Daisy order her out of the house again?

'Don't be angry. I'm only trying to help you, kid.'

Daisy seemed to relax then, her shoulders slumping. She put a hand to her forehead as though it were aching.

'I'm not angry with you, Josie, just a little shocked at myself. I have to admit divorce was the first thought that crossed my mind yesterday. But I don't think I can do it. It's alien to me. I made my vows, and though it was on the hop, I didn't make them lightly. I'm not a woman who goes back on her word.'

Josie stood up quickly, thankful that she had not caused another rift between them.

'Of course you're not, kid. All I'm saying is, don't go rushing off. Think things through first. Don't go up to Yorkshire tomorrow. Wait a while. After all, you owe it to Rhodri, don't you?'

Daisy sank on to the bed again and burst into tears. Josie felt like crying too. She knew now, though, that if she were in Daisy's shoes the man she really loved would come first. Poor Rhodri. Was all his love for Daisy given in vain? Must it be sacrificed for long-forgotten vows?

Josie went downstairs feeling depressed and saddened. She wasn't doing any good here. Daisy must make up her own mind.

Edie had made a pot of tea and Josie thankfully accepted a cup. After a while Daisy came down, looking more composed, though just as washed out as earlier.

'You're both trying to help me, I appreciate that,' she said quietly. 'But I know what I have to do. Gerald is Valerie's father. It would be wrong to keep them apart. I must see him as soon as possible. I can't have this hanging over my head. I'm going to Yorkshire tomorrow and I'm taking Valerie with me.'

Edie tilted her head, her expression uncertain and troubled. 'Is that wise, lovey?'

'Yes, Mam.' Daisy looked determined. 'It's for the best, I know it is.'

She glanced at the box on the sofa, and her face turned pale.

'I shan't be needing that, Josie love. You keep the dress, sell it, get something out of it.'

She shook her head, appalled at the idea. Daisy's beautiful dress, sold? She couldn't bear the thought of that.

Daisy nodded her head, her expression resolute.

'You deserve it, Josie, for all the skill and hard work you've put into it. Anyway, I could never bear to look at it ever again. It would be too painful.'

With a heavy heart, Josie sympathised. It was only a dress, but to Daisy it represented the life she would never have with Rhodri; all the happiness that had slipped from her grasp. To Daisy it was no longer a thing of beauty, but an object of torment.

Chapter Fourteen

After slowly climbing up hills and racing down dales, the bus chugged its way into a small village of old grey stone, square-built houses, a village very like the last one where the bus had stopped. Even in the warmth of late-afternoon Daisy thought she could see an austerity and bleakness in the dark stone of the houses, so unlike the rows of tightly packed terraces back home.

'Scawsdale!' the bus driver called over his shoulder.

They'd arrived at last! Daisy was galvanised into action. She struggled up the aisle of the bus towards the door, a sleeping Valerie over one shoulder, a shopping bag over her arm, and almost dragging her bulging suitcase behind her with the other.

The young clergyman sitting in the front seat who had boarded the bus in York at the same time as herself, helped get the suitcase out on to the road.

'Will you be all right?' he asked with a smile.

'Yes, thanks,' Daisy nodded, smiling back

gamely. He touched his forehead in a salute and climbed back on board, and immediately the bus began to move off.

Daisy watched it go with growing apprehension. She was far from all right. She was hungry and near exhaustion; her legs ached, her head ached and her back was breaking. Her journey from early-morning seemed endless, first the train to York and then the bus to Scawsdale. And now what? How much further must she go?

She looked at her wrist watch. It was almost six. Everything would be closed. She looked around her. There was no one about to ask directions from. How could she find out where Gerald lived?

The village was laid out in a wide square, the doors opening straight off the road, with neither gardens nor pavements. She was standing on the edge of what must be the village green at the heart of the square. A small flock of sheep were nibbling quietly at the grass. In the centre of the green stood a tall wooden post. Daisy squinted at it. Could that be a gibbet? She shivered at the thought.

Opposite where she stood was a small general store and post office. She could see the 'Closed' sign hanging in the glass door. Further down was a pub. The sign outside said The Green Man, and with a sigh of relief Daisy saw the doors were open.

Inside, the cool air was a deliverance from the warmth that still clung to the June evening. She stood for a moment, blinded by the dimness.

When her eyes adjusted, she saw several tables spaced around the room between high-backed, dark wooden settles. Sitting on one next to the huge fireplace two elderly men smoked pipes. They turned their heads to regard her with silent curiosity.

There was no one behind the bar, and no sound to be heard. Daisy looked at the silent men and braced herself to speak.

'I'm looking for the Bucklands' farm. Can anyone direct me?'

They continued to stare at her for a moment then turned back to their pints as though she hadn't spoken.

Feeling suddenly helpless, she turned to the bar and almost jumped out of her skin as she saw that a stout man in a white apron now stood behind it watching her. She put her suitcase down and transferred Valerie to her other shoulder, reflecting that the sleeping child was getting heavier by the minute.

'The Bucklands,' she said again, trying to speak slowly and clearly, and willing her voice not to falter. Perhaps they were having trouble with her accent? 'I'm trying to find my husband, Gerald Buckland. He's recently been demobbed.'

The stout man came from behind the counter.

'Here, lass,' he said. 'Sit down before you fall down.'

He picked up her suitcase and, taking her by the elbow, led her to one of the settles. Daisy flopped down on the hard wooden seat with relief, Valerie on her lap, then looked up at the stout man hopefully, praying that he could help her because this was turning into a nightmare.

'Buckland, you say.' He scratched his head. 'Don't know of no Bucklands around here.' He turned to the pipe smokers. 'Jim? Know a family called Buckland?'

One of the men removed the pipe from his mouth to consider for a long moment.

'Used to be Bucklands over at Little Rixsby, other side of Aldholm Crag,' he said at last. 'Dead now, o' course. Don't know of no others. How about you, Jack?'

The other pipe-smoker shook his head, and having answered the landlord's question both men seemed to lose interest.

'His family lives around here somewhere,' Daisy said desperately. At least, this is the address the Admiralty gave me. What am I going to do?'

The landlord rubbed his apron unnecessarily over the table top.

'You could try Little Rixsby,' he suggested. 'You carry on down the road a piece then take the turning sign-posted Scaws Hill. Little Rixsby is about two or three miles further on ...'

'Dan Adams! Have you taken leave of your senses?'

Daisy was startled by the sudden intervention of a loud female voice but the landlord jumped nearly six feet in the air.

Daisy glanced towards the bar where a woman stood, hands on hips. She was short and round, and reminded Daisy of a barrel.

'Can't you see the lass is done up fit to drop?'

she said. 'You can run her over to Little Rixsby in the trap when she's had a cup of tea.'

An hour later Daisy sat in the trap beside Dan Adams, landlord of The Green Man. Valerie had dropped off to sleep on her lap after the hot tea and slices of home-made cake which had revived them both. She felt so much better now, so relieved to be coming to the end of her journey. Maude Adams, the landlord's wife, had the looks and manner of a virago but was really an angel in disguise. Daisy hadn't been able to thank her enough for her kindness.

She watched the rhythmic movement of the pony's hind quarters as it covered the distance along the moorland road at a sharp clip. Was her journey really coming to an end at last? Would she find Gerald? Perhaps this was another wild goose-chase.

A thought that had been on the edge of her consciousness crept in and she had to acknowledge it. What if she couldn't find him? She could go home and forget all about him, an inner voice said. No one would blame her. She'd get a quiet divorce as Josie suggested. Then she could marry her darling Rhodri.

Her heart faltered at the thought of Rhodri. For the last few days she'd been schooling herself not to think of him. Thoughts of him made her weak and indecisive, desperate sometimes. She couldn't let herself weaken now. Her head told her she must put Rhodri and his love to one side for sanity's sake, but her heart cried and cried.

Oh, God, why hadn't Gerald died? Why had he come back to ruin her life, spoil her happiness? The thought burst into her mind, catching her unawares. She felt appalled and deeply ashamed of herself. She swallowed hard on it, forcing it down, out of her mind.

She looked at the undulating moorland around them, realising they were climbing all the time. They were crossing over Aldholm Crag, Dan Adams had told her. This was high country, isolated, and windswept even in summer. Could she live in such a place? Would she and Valerie be able to survive the loneliness? One had to be born in such a place, she thought, to bear it. But she must keep her mind open, she decided; make no assumptions or judgements yet. She had not yet found Gerald. Everything depended on that. She wouldn't let herself think beyond that point.

They were going steeply downhill now, and Daisy could see what looked like a small farmstead in a shallow valley below. An old finger post at the roadside pronounced it to be Little Rixsby.

'This'll be the place.' Dan Adams nodded his head towards the farmstead below.

'Are you sure?' Daisy was uncertain.

It looked so small. Gerald had often spoken of his father's estate and of his father's 'men'. He had given her the idea of something much grander than this. She remembered it had made her feel nervous at the time, unworthy.

'This'll be the Buckland place Jim spoke of,' Dan Adams said. 'Nothing else around here for miles except some cottages lower in the valley. But ...'

Daisy glanced quickly at him, hearing the doubt in his voice despite his words.

'But I'll wait up by the gate until you're certain it's the right place,' he went on.

A million winged creatures seemed to be fluttering in her midriff as Daisy walked down the rutted road from the gate. The house was of the same dark grey stone as the village, square-built and unadorned. It didn't look much bigger close to than it had from higher up the mountain road. But what was now very evident was the unkempt condition of the place.

A small-holding, Dan Adams had called it when they arrived at the gate; a small-holding left to go to seed. But then the old man at the pub had said the Bucklands of this place had died. Yet someone was living here. Smoke was lifting thinly from the chimney.

Daisy stood at the door about to knock, but hesitated, glancing back over her shoulder at the man waiting in the trap. She was glad he was there. In fact she had the unreasonable urge to retrace her steps and go back with him to Scawsdale.

Instead she knocked at the plain dark blue wooden door which badly needed a new coat of paint. It seemed an age before she heard the latch being lifted, and the door opened, not wide, just enough for whoever was inside to peer around it at her.

It was a tall man with a thin, haggard face, from what she could see of it. He stayed partially behind the door as though shielding himself, his face half hidden.

'I'm looking for Gerald Buckland,' Daisy said, clutching a drowsy Valerie more tightly. Her heart was hammering away in her breast as though they were in some kind of mortal danger. Why was she being so foolish?

The man stared at her for a long moment in silence. Daisy shifted uneasily on her feet and darted a glance over her shoulder again at the trap. The man in the doorway followed her gaze, then drew back a little as he became aware of the trap and the man sitting patiently in it.

'Who are you?' he asked.

Daisy felt the breath leave her body with a rush as if someone had punched her in the stomach. Nothing about this man seemed familiar except his voice. She'd know that voice anywhere. It had been one of the most attractive things about him, and could charm the birds off the trees; even charm her into marrying him.

Daisy took a step forward, uncertain but determined not to weaken now. She felt she'd burned her bridges and there was no going back.

'Gerald? It's me, Daisy. Don't you recognise me?'

'Daisy?' His tone had changed. He sounded less suspicious and more uncertain.

'Yes, it's me.' She swallowed hard. 'And, look, this is Valerie, our daughter.'

Gerald's gazed flicked momentarily over Valerie before returning to Daisy's face.

'Why are you here?'

She tried to smile, but her facial muscles didn't seem to work properly. Her features felt stiff and distorted, more like stone than flesh and bone. 'Hadn't we better come in, Gerald?'

He opened the door a little wider to let them pass inside. Daisy picked up her suitcase and put it over the threshold. She paused in the doorway and turned, waving to Dan Adams in the trap, a prearranged signal that all was well.

As she watched him flick the reins across the pony's back she wondered if she were right. Was all well? It felt like entering the house of a total stranger.

Daisy carried Valerie inside the house and closed the door behind her. In front of her was a short passage with a door immediately on her left, which was probably the front parlour. Gerald had obviously retreated down the passage to a back room and Daisy followed uncertainly.

The room was large and very dated in its decoration and furnishing. A huge mantelpiece framed an old-fashioned range in which a small fire was burning. A large table stood to one side of the room, covered with a dark chenille cloth. There were one or two prints on the walls in old-fashioned frames, but there were no ornaments to be seen, no flowers, no sign of a woman's touch here.

Gerald was standing with his back to her, looking through the window which gave a view down along the valley behind the house. It looks like a picture postcard now, Daisy thought absently. Maybe it was because she had reached her destination at last.

'Why are you here, Daisy?' Gerald asked again.

She lowered Valerie into a deep-seated armchair nearby then reached up and took off her hat, fingering loosened hair back into the rolled style she found the most convenient and suitable for her profession. She'd worn her hair in a loose page-boy style when they'd married. Would he find her very much changed? she wondered.

'Why, Daisy?'

'I'm your wife, Gerald,' she said, trying to keep the tremor in her voice from being too obvious. 'Where else should I be?'

Her gaze ran over his back view as she spoke. He was so thin, painfully thin, and so stooped that his head seemed to be thrust forward a little.

She couldn't reconcile this image with the Gerald she'd known. He'd had so much life in him, so much vitality. She'd wondered when they married how she would ever keep up with him. Now he looked a shadow of the man he'd once been. He had suffered very much, that was obvious, and suddenly she was filled with pity and compassion. Poor Gerald.

'Why didn't you ever let me know you were alive, Gerald? There must have been some contact with the outside world during two years.'

She knew she was talking in ignorance. She couldn't possibly begin to understand what he'd suffered; what cruelty and deprivation he'd known. But if only she'd known he was alive, she would have saved herself so much pain. She would never have let herself fall in love with Rhodri.

A sob caught in her throat and she stifled it quickly. That wasn't true. She wouldn't have missed knowing Rhodri, knowing his love, for the world. She couldn't blame Gerald for something that must have been inevitable.

'Why didn't you come to me in Wales when you came back to this country, Gerald?' She glanced around the room, seeing no comfort or homeliness. 'There can't be anything here for you.'

'I didn't think you'd want to see this,' he said stiffly.

He turned slowly so that the light from the window fell on to the right side of his face. Daisy put up a hand quickly to cover her mouth but was unable to check a gasp of dismay and horror. She had seen terrible things in the London blitz, injuries and disfigurements, but those people had been strangers. It was different gazing at the damaged face of someone close, someone you had once believed you loved.

'Oh, Gerald!'

'A burning sea can do this to a man,' he said.

There was a terrible bitterness in his voice that made Daisy's heart ache with pity. But there was pity for herself, too, because there was nothing left of the Gerald she'd known. His voice, the last vestige of him, *was* changed, too. It was laced with bitterness and despair, and that was heartrending. She was married to a complete stranger.

As soon as the thought came into her head she knew it must make no difference. Gerald was Valerie's father, her husband, and he was in desperate straits.

The old Gerald had never really needed her. He'd been a free spirit, an independent force that carried all before him. She'd thought herself lucky, so lucky, to be carried along in his wake. Had he ever needed anyone then? she wondered. Now he needed her desperately.

Daisy felt a pain shoot through her, a searing pain. It was the pain of severing herself from Rhodri, once and for all. She mustn't think about him anymore. Now she must be a dutiful wife to Gerald. She must learn to love him again.

'Gerald, I'm so sorry.'

To match actions to her words she stepped quickly towards him, arms open to embrace him, but he turned aside abruptly to avoid the contact. Daisy pulled up short, uncertain. She felt keenly embarrassed for a moment by his rejection. But perhaps she was rushing things. It had been years. She couldn't expect him to take up where they left off, not yet anyway.

He went to the mantelpiece and took down a pipe, pressing a thumb into the bowl absently.

'How long do you intend to stay, Daisy?'

He sounded so distant and formal, and she let out a long breath, getting control of her voice.

'This isn't a flying visit, Gerald. I'm your

wife. You didn't come to me so I ... Valerie and I, we've come to you.'

He'd hardly glanced at Valerie, Daisy noticed. The child was dozing again, but once awake would be difficult to ignore. How would father and daughter get on? She still didn't know how he felt about children. She really didn't know anything about him at all. This house, for instance, was hardly what she'd been led to expect.

'I'd prefer to be in Wales, I admit,' Daisy said, lifting her chin. 'I've built up a very good practice in Swansea, that's where I'm living now ...' She hesitated, then corrected herself: 'Where I used to live. It was hard giving that up.'

He kept on fingering his pipe absently. Did he understand the implication of her words? she wondered. She regarded him with the beginnings of doubt in her mind. She had agonised over her decision to do the right thing by Gerald, to abide by her marriage, but perhaps he had other ideas? She hadn't considered that.

'You do want us to stay, don't you, Gerald?'

He looked up, startled at the question.

'That's hardly for me to decide,' he said. 'You've seen the place, seen me. Not a very attractive proposition, is it?'

Daisy felt a twinge of impatience.

'I didn't come looking for an attractive proposition, Gerald,' she said sharply. 'I came to preserve our marriage. I came because I thought you might be interested in seeing your own daughter, being with your family.'

Daisy hesitated, suddenly ashamed of herself. That wasn't the way one spoke to a man who'd been to Hell and back. Where was her professionalism now? Gerald was far from well, judging by his appearance. She looked directly into his eyes, and his gaze slid away from hers. She was uncertain about his mental state, too. Extreme suffering did terrible things to a man's mind. She had no right to be touchy, she told herself. She must be gentle and patient, help him through this crucial time.

'Gerald, Valerie and I are here to stay.' She paused, and then went on: 'If you want us, that is?'

He leaned on the mantelpiece and looked into the fire which was beginning to die. It needed more coal but the scuttle was empty, Daisy saw. How did he manage to live like this? How would she ever manage?

'Many people who are burned fear fire afterwards, but I don't.' He looked up at Daisy. 'Isn't that strange? I suppose I feel it has already done its worst to me. It can only kill me now. Besides ...' There was a strange faraway look in his eyes; his gazed fixed on another place, another time. 'There are far more terrible things that can happen to a man.'

'Gerald,' Daisy said quickly, uneasy at his strangeness, 'do you want us to stay?'

'Ask me again in a week,' he said.

Daisy came in from the kitchen later, wiping her hands. She'd made a meal as best she could. The stone-floored kitchen, though enormous,

242

was sparsely furnished with a table, a couple of wooden chairs, an old Welsh dresser and a china sink, but no cooking facilities. Its only redeeming features were a large window that looked out across the moors and a wondrously cold walk-in larder with marble slab shelves. Unfortunately, these were almost empty. What dismayed her more than anything was the lack of hot water. She would have to use the range in the living-room for everything, cooking as well as heating water. That seemed to be the worst inconvenience, even worse than the outside lavatory.

Daisy's heart sank when she realised this. How had Gerald's mother managed to cope? She must have been an extraordinary woman. Daisy thought of the warm little house she'd left behind in the Mumbles, and wished with all her heart she was there now.

'We're very short of food,' she said. 'Where do you get your supplies?'

Gerald lowered the book he was reading.

'I'm registered with the general store in Scawsdale. I arranged for a boy to come out once a week with my rations, but he didn't show up this week.'

'Why didn't you go and get them, then?'

His look suggested she was an imbecile even to suggest it.

'I'll have to go tomorrow,' she said, feeling vexed. 'Is there a bus passing this way?'

He smiled briefly, his facial muscles pulling grotesquely at the whitened scar tissue around his eye and mouth, and despite her pity and professionalism, Daisy felt a wave of revulsion, for which she was immediately very ashamed.

'Buses don't run to the back of beyond, Daisy. There's a push-bike in one of the outhouses. You can use that if you insist on going.'

The idea didn't appeal to her, remembering the steepness of Scaws Hill, but what choice did she have?

'We'd better root it out, then,' she said with a sigh of resignation. 'I shall want to set out early tomorrow.'

Daisy followed him into an outhouse, appalled at the neglect she saw around her. Everything was overgrown and rundown. It was obvious the place hadn't been worked for years. Tools and machinery were rusting as they stood against the outhouse walls.

He pointed to a large piece of machinery.

'That's the electricity generator,' he said.

She stood looking at it with her hands on her hips, appalled. It was in the same sad condition as everything else.

'Gerald, don't tell me this isn't working?'

He was wheeling an old push-bike from the back of the outhouse.

'No.' He sounded totally unconcerned. 'It's broken down, and I don't know the first thing about putting it right. I've got plenty of oil-lamps, though, and a decent store of paraffin.'

Oil-lamps! Daisy could have stamped her foot in anger. Now that was the last straw!

In a way she was relieved that Valerie remained sleepy and inactive for most of the evening, waking only briefly to have something to eat and drink. Daisy let her daughter remain on the sofa with a blanket over her for the time being. She was tired out herself, yet dreading bedtime.

They spent the evening sitting to either side of the fire in what was left of the daylight until it became too dark for Gerald to read, when he lit two lamps. Their glow softened the austerity of the room but offered very little comfort to Daisy. An old wireless set stood on a table at Gerald's elbow, but without the generator it was useless.

I'll go mad, she thought desperately, wanting to scream in the silence of the room, broken only by the loud ticking of the clock on the mantelpiece. How can I live like this? The generator would have to be fixed. At least they could have a little bit of music then, a little entertainment, could listen to the news. She'd speak to Dan Adams about it tomorrow. Maybe he'd know someone who could help.

She watched Gerald read, perfectly still, totally absorbed; shut away from the outside world. She couldn't remember Gerald, the old Gerald, sitting down to read. He wouldn't have been able to keep still long enough for one thing. Incarceration could change the habits of a lifetime, she supposed. In that terrible place he had built a wall around himself, an invisible wall. She had to find some way to break through, set him free.

'Gerald?'

'Hmmm?' He looked up absently, mind obviously elsewhere. It was unnerving. Had he forgotten she was there?

'How long have you lived in this house?'

'I was born here. So was my father.'

'You said he died in 1943. When did your mother die?'

'I don't know.'

'What?'

'She ran away when I was only six. We never heard from her again.'

He returned to his book and Daisy, silenced by this revelation, sat back and stared into the shadowy corners of the room.

Daisy's head fell forward and she woke with a jerk to find herself still sitting before the fire. The kettle was on the hob steaming away. Gerald came in with two white enamel mugs. 'I thought you might like some cocoa before retiring,' he said. 'You and the child can take my bed, then you'll know it's aired. I'll make a bed up in the back bedroom.'

For a moment Daisy was tempted to agree. It would be a relief to be on her own to think things through. But that would be a mistake. She had decided to honour her marriage vows and that couldn't be done by sleeping in separate bedrooms. The past must now be set aside for both of them. They must live as a normal married couple, as though nothing had separated them. The intimacy of a physical relationship would help break through that invisible wall, she was certain. Besides, she hadn't sacrificed her happiness for the sake of a sham marriage.

'We'll share a bed as we used to, Gerald.'

He was about to pour boiling water into the mugs but hesitated, glancing at her. His face paled a little with what she thought was reluctance. Was it disappointment she felt or relief that he was disinclined? Suddenly she was ashamed of her own mixed feelings. She had come fully prepared to renew their marriage, yet, at the same time, no longer loving him, she dreaded the prospect.

'How could you bear this face on the pillow next to you?' he asked, breaking into her thoughts.

That might have been amusing, Daisy reflected, if it weren't for the haunted look in his eyes.

'I'm your wife, for better, for worse, Gerald, remember?'

That sounded trite but it was true, wasn't it? She must face it. That was why she was here. Nothing else could have torn her away from Rhodri's love. She was still bound to Gerald, despite not loving him, and if they didn't share a bed together tonight, they never would.

'Daisy, you must be patient with me. For over two years I've been cooped up in a hell hole, a desperate man amongst hundreds of desperate men. I'm not free yet. Maybe I'll never be free.'

For a moment she was tempted to take the easy way, assure him that she didn't expect him to be everything a husband should be. She could spend her life taking care of him, a glorified nurse, but what kind of a life would that be for her? Without some kind of love she would wither and die.

Pulling herself together, she stood up quickly before he could discern her intention. She put her arms around his neck and kissed his face, deliberately kissing the damaged cheek.

She wasn't prepared for the sickening sensation of the crumpled skin and flesh under her lips, but steeled herself not to react. She would accept Gerald exactly as he was now, as he must accept her. There was no going back, either to what might have been with Rhodri or on her decision to do her duty by her husband. This was to be her life from now on.

Chapter Fifteen

Daisy woke early, surprised she'd slept so soundly in a strange bed. The space beside her was empty. Guiltily, she wondered how well Gerald had slept, having to share the bed with Valerie as well as herself. She'd get the bed in the back bedroom aired today. From now on Valerie must sleep there.

Poor kid! It would be hard on the child, Daisy knew. They had never slept apart from the day she was born almost. In her heart of hearts she wished it wasn't necessary, but it was. She'd given up Rhodri for the sake of her marriage vows. She had to try to find a way of reaching Gerald somehow. Living the life of a normal

248

married couple seemed the solution.

Daisy found no comfort in knowing that had she married Rhodri, Valerie's banishment to a room of her own would have been inevitable. Somehow she knew it would have been different then. Rhodri and Valerie were kindred spirits.

Where was the child anyway?

Concerned, Daisy scrambled out of bed, struggling into her dressing-gown. Then she saw her young daughter sitting on the floor in her nightie. She had pulled out the bottom drawer of the chest of drawers and was rifling through its contents.

'Valerie, leave that alone!'

'Play dress-up, Mammy.'

'Now stop it. That's not yours. There's naughty, you are, Valerie.'

Daisy stooped down and began to gather up the oddments of clothing and linen Valerie had scattered on the floor. When her fingers touched something cold and hard, she drew back her hand, alarmed. Gingerly, she lifted a crumpled shirt and stared with horror. Morning sunlight glinted menacingly off the blue-grey metal of a long gun barrel.

What on earth was this weapon doing in Gerald's bedroom? She found it shocking that anyone would have such a thing in the house.

Feeling decidedly shaken at the thought that Valerie might have found the gun and hurt herself badly, Daisy covered it again with the shirt, and grasping it by the barrel, held it away from her as though it were a deadly snake.

Where to put it out of Valerie's reach? The

only safe place was in a top drawer. Valerie was too small to reach that. Gerald must remove it to a safer place later.

Satisfied the weapon was secure for the moment, Daisy scooped her young daughter off the floor. Valerie screwed up her face and pouted as though about to grizzle at being frustrated in her explorations.

'Hey! Enough of that, my girl!'

Daisy surveyed the remaining mess with a sigh. She'd clear that up later. Right now she needed something to eat, but especially a cup of tea after her shock.

'Where's Nanna?' Valerie, obviously thinking better of her tantrum, asked as Daisy carried her downstairs.

Daisy was about to say 'At home' but bit back the words. This was Valerie's home now, and the sooner she got used to it the better. The sooner they both got used to it.

'In Swansea.'

'See her this afternoon, isn't it?' Valerie said, clapping her chubby hands. 'We go to the sands. Where's my bucket and spade, Mammy? Uncle Rhodri coming with us as well?'

Daisy's step faltered as a shaft of painful longing stabbed through her heart at the innocent question. What was she really doing here in this lonely house, with someone who was virtually a stranger, when the man she loved desperately was miles away, probably yearning for her too. It was cruel what she'd done to Rhodri, though God help her it wasn't her fault. She prayed that he would realise that and not think of her with bitterness.

Gerald had lit the fire and was already toasting the last of the bread. Daisy had noticed a box of Quaker oats in the larder. They must make do with that until she returned from the village. There was no milk, of course, but no shortage of water.

Valerie sat at the table, kicking her legs under her chair, spooning porridge into her mouth. She was watching Gerald's every move with curiosity, but no fear or revulsion, Daisy saw, and was relieved, marvelling at the way children accept people as they are.

When Daisy put on her hat, Valerie was at her side in a flash.

'Sands, Mammy?'

'No, chick. Mammy's going to the shops for rations.'

'I come too, Mammy.'

'No, it's too far,' Daisy said, glancing at Gerald when Valerie began to pout again. 'You stay here with your ... daddy. I won't be long. Be a good girl and I'll bring you a lollipop, right?'

Daisy wheeled the bicycle behind The Green Man, her small string bag of groceries slung over the handle-bars. It had been difficult riding a man's bike. She was dreading the journey back. Shanks's pony most of the way, probably.

When she knocked at the rear door she was relieved to see Maude Adams.

'Well, come on in, lass, you look done up already.' Maude's booming voice seemed to echo through the whole pub.

Daisy felt guilty about accepting a cup of tea. She ought to be getting back to Little Rixsby, she argued with herself, but felt justified when, after she'd explained their predicament with the generator, Maude said she knew a man who could fix it. She'd get him to call over to Little Rixsby.

'You found your husband, then?'

'Yes, thanks.'

'Funny we don't see him in the village?'

Daisy smiled faintly. 'He's not a well man. Been a prisoner-of-war, you know.'

'Ha!' Maude said, as though fully enlightened.

Maude Adams obviously wasn't the prying kind, Daisy saw, and was glad. She respected Gerald's need for privacy at the moment. There'd be plenty of time later to integrate him gradually into the life of the village.

When Daisy got up and said she must get back, Maude insisted Dan would run her back in the trap, bicycle and all. Daisy's protest was only feeble. She needed that lift. She doubted she could cope with Scaws Hill today.

'You planning to stay round here?' he asked.

Daisy nodded, not wanting to say too much. For the moment it seemed they must. And she had to earn a living, too. She doubted they could exist on Gerald's pension, and had no intention of merely existing.

'That bike is no damn' good for country like this,' he said, seeming to read her thoughts. 'Ought to get yourself a pony and trap, lass. I'll ask about, shall I?'

Daisy stood talking to Dan at the gate for a moment, telling him that she was a midwife by profession and was hoping to start a practice locally.

He shook his head in doubt.

'Folks around here rely on Ma Pickles over at Edgethorpe, and if there's real trouble a midwife comes out from Thirsk.'

Daisy put a hand to her face in consternation. 'All that way? There's no practice closer, then?'

Dan Adams shrugged.

'Population round here is sparse, and mostly older folk. Can't see as how you'll make a living, not in that respect anyway.'

Daisy thanked him for his kindness then pushed the bicycle down to the outhouse before going into the house. When she was almost at the door it opened and Valerie scrambled out over the step, running towards her on sturdy little legs.

Daisy was dismayed to see her daughter's face was blotchy from crying.

'Mammy! Mammy! I don't like that man!' she sobbed, and clutched desperately at Daisy's knees. 'I want to go home, Mammy. I want Nanna. I want Uncle Rhodri.'

'Mammy's here now. Don't cry, chick.'

Daisy picked her up and hurried into the house. What had been going on? She shouldn't have left Valerie, she knew, but what else could she have done? Was the child merely having a tantrum, or was there something really wrong?

The front parlour door was open, the first

time Daisy had seen it since she arrived. The room had the heavy odour of dust and musty air of a place shut off; the furnishings and curtains untouched for a long time.

Daisy walked into the parlour carrying the still sobbing Valerie. There were books strewn about the floor, probably taken from the shelves in an alcove near the old fireplace. Was that what her daughter had been up to?

Gerald was standing near the window. He turned as Daisy entered.

'What's going on, Gerald? Why is Valerie crying?'

Valerie lifted an arm and pointed an accusing finger at him.

'He smacked me, Mammy. Tell him to go 'way.'

'Gerald?'

His face looked flushed in the light from the window, the scarred half starkly white in contrast.

'Who was that man in the trap?' he asked. His voice was thick and tight, with an almost hysterical tremor in it.

'Dan Adams. Landlord of The Green Man.' Daisy felt confused for a moment, taken aback at the strangeness of his manner and voice. He looked almost feverish. 'Gerald, why is Valerie upset? What did you do to her? Did you smack her?'

'That's the second time that man's been here,' Gerald said, tautly, the expression in his eyes unreadable. He lifted a hand to touch his damaged cheek, his fingers shaking visibly.

254

'What does he want here, Daisy? What were you doing with him?'

'He gave me a lift from the village,' she answered, and shook her head, puzzled. 'Why are you so upset?'

Gerald took a step closer, features working as though he were gripped by some dreadful fear.

'I should never have let you go down to the village.'

'What are you talking about, Gerald. Of course I had to go.' With difficulty, Daisy checked a rising anger against his unreasonableness. He'd been in purgatory for two years. She had to remember that and make allowances. Yet she had no intention of letting him lay a finger on her child again. Their child, she reminded herself quickly.

'We have no food here, no electricity. Maude Adams says she'll find someone to fix the generator for us.'

'No! I'll have no one coming here.'

Gerald's eyes were wide with fear. Anyone would think she'd announced the arrival of the Devil, she reflected. Why was he behaving so strangely?

'You've been talking about me in the village, haven't you?'

His voice began to rise to a pitch too close to hysteria for Daisy's peace of mind. She shook her head emphatically, lowering Valerie to the floor. The child clung to her knees, sheltering behind her, watching Gerald warily, emitting an occasional sob, more for effect than anything else, Daisy realised.

'Valerie, go in the other room.'

Valerie pouted. 'Mammy, he's a naughty man. He smacked me. It hurted, Mammy.'

'Valerie, At once!'

She backed out of the door, glowering at Gerald, but Daisy could see he was totally unaware of the child. He was staring fixedly at herself, a wildness in his eyes that made her more uneasy.

'You've been gossiping,' he accused. 'You've been telling them what it's like being married to a disfigured monster. Making a laughing stock of me as my mother did to my father.' His voice rose even higher. 'I won't have it. Do you hear?'

'Gerald, please!'

Daisy was appalled at the state he was working himself into. She felt a disturbing coldness seep through her as she watched his agitated expression and the flickering light in his eyes. Gerald's scars were not only physical. His problems went a lot deeper than that, she knew.

'You're not to go to the village again,' he said. 'I forbid it.'

'Gerald.' Daisy's voice was soothing. She moved towards him slowly. 'I shan't do anything you don't want me to, but I'll have to fetch food. The shop won't be delivering anymore. It's too far out for the boy, so they told me.'

She reached him and put a hand on his shoulder, looking up into his face, holding on firmly when he tried to pull away from her. He was shaking so badly she wondered how he was able to stand up. She led him to an armchair, the hide dulled with a grey bloom from damp and neglect. He sank on to it, exhausted.

'Why don't you leave, Daisy?' His voice sounded feeble now. 'Go, and leave me alone here. I'm no good to you or anyone.'

She couldn't do that even if she wanted to, Daisy thought. Especially not now she realised the complete truth about him.

'Don't talk like that, Gerald.'

Raw pity for him rose up from her breast into her mouth. She thought she could taste tears in it and a sharp bitterness. She was trapped. She couldn't leave him, ever. She must take care of him. He needed her desperately, and for a moment she felt frightened by the depth of that need. Could she cope with it? Not here alone, she couldn't.

On top of all this came an awful longing, a yearning for home, for her old life. She had never felt such loneliness as this. She despised self-pity and tried to shake off the feeling, but it persisted. She missed the support of her family so much. And Rhodri, too. But she daren't think about Rhodri. Her situation was hard enough without torturing herself with memories of him.

'I'm not going anywhere, Gerald.' She forced the words out. 'Not without you.'

Valerie was shouting for her from the back room, but Daisy took no notice. The child had probably been misbehaving, that's why Gerald had smacked her. Yet it mustn't happen again.

If they must remain here, it would be very hard on Valerie. She'd miss the family, too. Daisy realised it would be equally hard on herself. Already she was missing village life, where she could step outside her door and exchange greetings with acquaintances, chat with passing friends. They were so utterly alone in this valley. She just wasn't used to the isolation. Could she stand it for any length of time? And there was the question of work.

Daisy gazed down on Gerald, slumped in the chair, eyes closed. He looked helpless and hopeless. Thirty-one years of age and already he seemed like an old man. He would never be able to earn a living for them and they'd never be able to manage on his pension. It was up to her.

Daisy looked around the room. How dismal it was with its dark green walls and black-painted floorboards. The heavy old-fashioned furniture seemed to be crowding them out.

The cottage where she had been born in the Gower had been primitive but it had never been dismal, especially not after Edie had married her father. She made their home into a cosy little heaven for them.

I'll never be able to do the same here, Daisy thought, feeling a cloud of depression settle on her. The Gower cottage had been filled with love. There was no love here, though; nothing but bitterness, fear and hopelessness.

They must get away somehow. She must persuade Gerald to leave. But did he love this place? she wondered. The only home he'd ever known, except for his years at sea. Now it was a bolt hole, a place in which to hide from the world, but did he love it? Out of necessity, he might have to leave it.

The more she thought about leaving Little Rixsby, the more she longed to. Yet the idea daunted her. How could she possibly make it happen?

In the days that followed Gerald returned to himself, or at least to the way he'd been when she'd arrived. But there was an increased tension of which Daisy was always aware. It didn't help that Valerie was fractious and badly behaved, stubborn and wilful. She showed nothing but open hostility towards Gerald, scowling and muttering under her breath. It might have been comical in a small child at any other time, at any other place, but now it set Daisy's teeth on edge, even though she understood the reason for it.

Valerie had not taken kindly to sleeping alone in the back bedroom, when she had always shared her mother's bed. Now she was ousted by this detested stranger. Difficult for a child to accept, Daisy knew. There had been the inevitable tantrums, and while her heart ached for the child's misery, and wished it wasn't necessary to put her through this ordeal, Daisy would not give in to her small daughter.

Gerald suggested that he and Valerie exchange places, but Daisy again resisted the temptation to compromise. If she were to regain a normal life for them, heal Gerald's damaged mind, she was sure it would be in the intimacy of the bedroom. She was convinced this was the only way finally to break through the wall that he had built around himself; the only way left to her for some kind of life for herself, now that her dream of being Rhodri's wife would never, ever come true.

But after a week of sleeping with him Daisy felt no closer to her husband. She'd hoped her warmth in the bed might have roused a response in him, but he remained resolutely on his side of the mattress.

One night when she had put out a hand tentatively to caress his shoulder and murmur his name, he'd shrugged her away.

Daisy had turned her face into her pillow and wept in silent despair. She didn't love Gerald now, but she had once. She might do so again, to some degree. She would never love him as she'd loved Rhodri. That kind of love couldn't happen twice. But she was young; she wanted a husband; she wanted a life. She'd given up Rhodri, but she hadn't given up living.

Later, she persuaded herself that she must give him time. If they could get away from this place he'd be a different man. He'd start taking an interest in things, in his family.

But it distressed her to see that Gerald ignored his daughter. She might not exist for all he seemed to care, and bitterly Daisy couldn't help comparing his attitude to Rhodri's. He and Valerie were so close. He had fussed over her like a doting father, and she adored him, insisting on including him in everything. They were so good for each other, a real family. Now the child was deprived of that love, as was Daisy herself.

She tried to comfort herself with the thought that it wasn't only his family Gerald ignored. He took little notice of anything except his books, which he kept in a bookcase in the parlour, now forbidden territory to Valerie.

Daisy half dreaded the need to return to the village the following week, but dire necessity would force her to, and she really wanted to, if only to hear the sound of a loving voice for she was determined to telephone her stepmother. She needed Edie's advice.

No one had called to fix the generator. While she missed and longed for contact with the outside world through the wireless, she wondered if it were worthwhile going to the expense of repairs. The idea of getting away, and the desire to, were growing ever stronger.

There was enough work around the house to keep her too busy to brood during the day: having to keep the copper boiler continuously heating on the fire, seeing to the oil lamps and the hundred and one extra jobs created by the lack of facilities. But in the interminable silent evenings she had nothing to while the hours away.

Daisy watched Gerald's still figure sitting in his chair and pondered, for the umpteenth time, on the depth of the change in him. In the old days he was so gregarious, constantly chattering, diving head first into any argument or discussion, having his say, giving his opinion. Never still. What terrible things had wrought this change? Daisy couldn't imagine it. By the beginning of the next week she felt she'd go mad.

'I need some money, Gerald. I'm going into Scawsdale to get the rations.'

They'd had their breakfast and Daisy was washing up. Valerie had gone outside to play. She'd waited until the child was out of earshot before she said anything. Gerald was sitting in front of the range fire, staring absently into it. Now he lifted his head, eyes suddenly fierce.

'I said, I forbid it.'

She swung around from the sink, suddenly angry.

'Don't be absurd, Gerald!' she cried sharply. 'Are we to starve just because of your groundless fears? You may want to hide yourself away, but must I cut myself off, too?'

The gauntness of his face was deepened by an expression of shock at her words, and Daisy was immediately repentant. She must try not to lose her temper with him, no matter how desperate she was becoming.

'I'm sorry, Gerald. I shouldn't have said that.' She wiped her hands on a towel. 'I'll use the bike again. I'll just get the rations.'

'Of course I don't want to cut you off from the outside. You and the child are free to leave any time, you know that. Go, if you must, but don't bring strangers here, Daisy.'

'I won't accept any lifts, not if you don't want me to. I also want to telephone my stepmother. She'll be worried about us. I haven't even written, have I?'

There was a performance from Valerie when she saw Daisy wheeling the bicycle out of the outhouse, and Daisy had to be firm with her, despite hating to. This was no life for Valerie, stuck out in the wilderness with no company but the two of them. It simply couldn't go on much longer.

The ride to the village was easy enough. Daisy wouldn't let herself think about the journey back. The steady pumping of the pedals helped her concentrate. She was free to go, Gerald had said, but that wasn't really true. How could she leave him now? It would be like leaving him to die. Because that was what would happen. If she and Valerie went, Gerald must come too. But how could it be managed?

Daisy found her hand was shaking as she held the telephone receiver to her ear, waiting for the voice of the operator. She felt several centuries passed before contact was finally made with the telephone exchange in Swansea. Then the operator was telling her to insert so many coins into the slot and press button A, and then, she heard her stepmother's voice.

'Daisy? Is that you, Daisy lovey?'

'Mam! Oh, Mam!'

Daisy swallowed hard against the lump in her throat that threatened to choke her. An aching longing for home swept through her, sharp and painful, and she thought she would burst into tears.

'Daisy! I knew it was you, lovey. I said to William, "That's our Daisy." How are you, my lovely girl? And how's my little Valerie?'

That loving voice! Daisy leaned against the side of the telephone box, feeling suddenly weak with relief as she listened to her beloved stepmother's voice, and the tell-tale tremor in it. Edie was on the verge of tears herself.

'Why didn't you write, Daisy lovey? I've been so worried about you both. Did you find Gerald? How is he?'

Daisy had to swallow again before answering.

'Yes, I found him. He's ... not very well. We're on a small-holding at a place called Little Rixsby ...'

Suddenly overcome, she couldn't speak another word for a moment.

'Daisy? Are you there?' Edie sounded alarmed.

She clapped a hand over her mouth to halt the flow of words and stem the tears that were burning the backs of her eyelids, but she couldn't hold back her misery any longer. Whenever she'd been in trouble all her life, whenever she'd needed comfort, Edie had been there with open, welcoming arms and tender words of sympathy. How she longed to be in that loving embrace now.

'Oh, Mam!' she wailed, unable to stop herself. 'It's an awful place, rundown and useless. Miles from the village. There's no electricity. I'm going out of my mind with loneliness. Valerie hates it. Oh, Mam, I wish I'd never come here ...'

'Daisy, come home at once!'

Edie's voice sounded stronger now. Daisy could picture her face, the widely set brown eyes, strong nose and generous mouth. Her jaw would be set with determination, ready to put everything to rights. And she probably could, too.

'It's not that easy, Mam,' Daisy said, miserably. 'Gerald's in a bad way mentally, I'm afraid. I can't desert him. But I can't stay in Yorkshire, either. I'm going to try to persuade him to sell up. I wonder, Mam ... I don't like to ask you, but I wonder if you could send me some money for our fares to Wales? I'll pay you back when I get home.'

'I'll do better, lovey. William and I will come and fetch you.'

'No, Mam don't do that.' Daisy was alarmed and yet elated at the suggestion. That was what she needed. Someone to come and take charge. But how would Gerald react to that? 'I'll manage somehow, Mam.'

'Daisy, now don't argue with me, there's a good girl,' Edie answered firmly. 'William and I will drive up to Yorkshire in the middle of next week. He'll find the petrol from somewhere. We'll bring you home, all of you.'

Daisy stood for a moment outside the telephone box, leaning against the side of it. She felt strange. The thought of Edie and William coming up to Yorkshire, taking charge, putting things right, filled her with excitement and new hope. At the same time her legs felt weak and her stomach churned at the thought of Gerald's reaction to the news. There'd be an awful scene and she didn't know what effect it would have on him. She wished she knew more about his mental state. Sometimes it seemed he was on a knife edge. She didn't want to do anything that might push him over. She ran her hand across her sweating forehead, feeling nausea at the thought.

'Are you all right, lass?'

Daisy looked up, startled to see Dan Adams staring at her closely, an expression of concern on his broad, weather-beaten face.

She straightened up, pulling herself together. What must he think of her? Village people were always curious about newcomers, but she must seem a very strange stranger indeed!

'Yes, I'm fine, thanks. Just a bit tired.'

He hesitated.

'I'll give you a lift back, shall I? I'll just be half a tick.'

'No!'

She recovered herself quickly, conscious of Dan's startled expression at her abrupt refusal. She'd sounded almost hysterical to her own ears.

'I mean, no thanks, Mr Adams. Don't want to be a nuisance, do I?'

He looked at her steadily for a moment, then nodded.

'Ah! Think I understand, lass. They say Mr Buckland likes to keep to himself.'

Daisy gave a non-committal half smile, then taking a firm grip of the handle-bars of the bicycle, began to push it on to the road.

'The generator,' Dan said, falling into step beside her. 'I've spoken to the chap Maude was telling you about. He's inundated with jobs, but he'll try to get out to your place one day next week.'

Daisy stopped suddenly.

'Oh, we shan't need him now,' she blurted, speaking on the spur of the moment, her mind filled with the prospect of going home. 'We'll be leaving Little Rixsby shortly, selling up. We're going home to Wales.'

Dan Adams raised his brows.

'Mr Buckland too?'

'Yes, of course.' Daisy tried a brave smile, loyalty to Gerald making her raise her chin. 'My husband never intended to work the smallholding, you know. He'll find plenty of work to suit him in Swansea, especially now the war is over for us.'

Pushing the bicycle up Scaws Hill, Daisy pondered on the wisdom of being so forthcoming with the landlord of The Green Man. No doubt her words would spread round the area in no time.

She'd been hasty and careless, which was unlike her, she knew. She was hardly behaving in a professional way. But the circumstances were exceptional, weren't they? she argued with herself. She was out of her depth here. Alone, in difficult circumstances, with a man she didn't know anymore; a man so changed he hardly seemed like the man she'd married. She didn't even know how he would react when she told him her step-parents were coming. It might seem she was defying his wishes. He would be angry, perhaps violent. She couldn't even guess.

Daisy stopped for a moment on the hill to catch her breath. How should she approach it? Suppose he took fright and ran off on to the moors? She couldn't risk that.

Perhaps she should say nothing until it happened? Fait accompli. Was that a sound decision, she wondered, or just cowardice?

And how would she get him to agree to leave Little Rixsby, to sell his family home? At the moment she had no idea.

Then there was his self-imposed isolation. Daisy continued to push the bicycle slowly up the hill, her heart heavy with dread and doubt. If he preferred near starvation rather than going into the village for food, how would she persuade him to travel all the way to Wales, to face life amongst strangers?

The new hope that had dawned for her at the sound of her stepmother's voice began to dissipate with every step she took nearer Little Rixsby. It was all useless and hopeless. She was trapped in a situation that was unbearable. And Daisy prayed, prayed for deliverance.

Chapter Sixteen

The road continued to fall away in front of the car, snaking down into the deeper valley below to disappear into the misty rain. William steered the Austin Eight on to the grass verge at the side of the road and applied the brake. To the left of them, below a steep incline, were a house and outbuildings. A long rutted track led down from the road. William regarded it dubiously. Despite the summer rain the ground looked hard and unyielding, the ruts threatening.

Edie glanced at him, her expression questioning.

'Aren't we going down, Will?'

He shook his head, taking off his spectacles and giving them a polish with his handkerchief.

'Not risking it, *cariad*. If we bust a suspension spring or damage the exhaust, where would we be? You can't get the parts, mun.'

Especially not in this Godforsaken hole, he almost added, but checked himself. Edie was upset enough already.

They sat for a moment, staring through the windscreen, not looking at the house.

'I'm dreading this, Will.'

She didn't have to tell him that. She'd been fidgeting all the way from York, where they'd spent the night. It had been a long drive out to Little Rixsby, and Edie had grown visibly more nervous with every mile.

William gave the lenses an extra little polish before putting his spectacles back on. He wasn't too happy himself at the prospect of meeting Daisy's husband under these circumstances, but it must be done. He couldn't bear to see Edie so worried and upset.

'Listen, Edie *cariad*. Leave this to me, right?'

Her expression looked hopeful for a moment before clouding over. She shook her head.

'Daisy is my responsibility, Will love. She's

terribly unhappy, I know she is, and it's breaking my heart.'

William grasped one of her hands as it trembled in her lap and pressed it reassuringly. He'd had plenty of time to think on their journey up from Swansea. An ex-prisoner-of-war would need careful handling. From what Edie had told him of her telephone call from Daisy, and from what he'd surmised, Gerald Buckland would be in a difficult frame of mind. Damaged, perhaps, both physically and mentally. If there were any persuading to do, it must be man to man. He felt this instinctively, would do it for Edie's sake, but didn't relish it.

'Edie love, for once, leave it to somebody else! If I were in Gerald's place, I'd rather talk to a man. There are things ... perhaps terrible experiences ... he'll want to get off his chest. He'll need a man to talk to, believe me. You concentrate on Daisy. She'll need all your strength and support.'

As they walked down the track under Edie's umbrella, William had the feeling that someone watched them. Daisy probably. No doubt she'd been looking out for them every day since she'd telephoned. They had almost reached the door when it opened and Daisy stood there, restraining Valerie from running out into the rain.

'Nanna! Bampa!' Valerie bobbed up and down like a doll on springs, her little face beaming. 'Nanna! Bampa!'

She lifted up her arms to Edie as they came over the threshold, and Edie gathered her up, kissing her. William gave Daisy a warm hug, shocked at her wan looks.

She was very pale and the skin around her eyes was smudged darkly. She appeared thinner, too, he noticed; a drained and defeated air about her. As she looked up at him, her eyes suddenly hopeful, William remembered the first time he ever saw her: that day, so long ago it seemed now, when he had helped move the recently widowed Edie from the Gower up to Swansea. For a child who had just lost her father, Daisy had acted so bravely that day. Now she looked at her wit's end.

There was a terrible irony here, he thought bleakly. A month ago Daisy had been happily looking forward to her wedding which was to have taken place this very week. William was ready to stand up for her, give her away to Rhodri Lewis. Now he had to stand up for her in an entirely different capacity.

He could make a good guess how she felt about losing Rhodri, though; the helplessness when someone loved is suddenly out of reach. He had felt the same, years ago, when he'd learned Edie was to marry another man, Daisy's father. Then emptiness and pain had almost killed him, but he had survived, as Daisy would survive somehow.

God had been good to him, though, because now Edie was finally his. At the moment there was no reason to suppose Daisy would be similarly blessed, and William looked at her with pity.

'I'm so glad you're both here, Will,' she

whispered, clinging to his hand for a moment. She turned to her stepmother, going into Edie's open arms with a sob. 'Oh, Mam!'

William was suddenly aware of someone else standing at the end of the passage; a tall man in shirt sleeves, lean and spare, and slightly stooped. He had a hand to his forehead, shielding the side of his face.

'Who are these people, Daisy? What are they doing in my house?'

'These are my parents, Gerald—Edie and William Philpots.' She turned to them. 'This is my husband, Gerald.'

William immediately walked forward, holding out a hand.

'Pleased to meet you, Gerald.'

In response, Gerald turned away abruptly and went into the back room. William glanced at Daisy over his shoulder, bemused.

This was going to be even more difficult than he had anticipated. Before he could persuade Gerald Buckland to leave this place, he had to weigh him up, decide on his line of argument. As an employer, William considered himself a good judge of men. He had to be. Something told him, though, that he'd need all his skills with Daisy's husband.

She was standing there looking very nervous. William could see her hands tremble as she held them clasped before her. Edie looked pale, too. The only one who had a happy smile was Valerie, clinging to Edie's hand.

'Courage!' William said to them in a low voice. 'We're here now, and we're not leaving until it's sorted out.' He nodded his head towards the back room. 'Lead the way, Daisy love.'

Gerald was standing with his back to the door, looking out of the window down into the valley, not that there was much to see today because of the misty rain.

'Gerald, my parents have come to see me. You can't object to my family, for goodness' sake!'

He didn't turn around.

'Why didn't you tell me they were coming? You must've known.'

'I ...'

'Did you prepare them for *this?*'

He swung round suddenly and William felt Edie flinch next to him, though, to give her credit, she made no sound. He remained apparently unmoved because he had been half expecting it from Gerald's mannerisms. The disfiguration wasn't all that ghastly. He knew it was the suddenness of its being revealed that had caused Edie's reaction.

'Daisy love,' William, said, as he started to remove his raincoat, 'any chance of a cup of tea? We're parched.'

Daisy looked ready to burst into tears again but obediently went into the kitchen. Gerald was gazing at them stonily, without even defiance in his eyes, and William's heart sank.

But he advanced on Gerald with determination, hand outstretched, counting on the man's innate good manners. Despite being a product of this humble hill farmstead, and the ravages of

273

his war experiences, Gerald still had the accent and bearing of a gentleman, intelligent and educated. He wouldn't refuse to shake hands again, not now he was over the initial shock of their intrusion.

There was no real hesitation. William, grasped Gerald's hand and shook it warmly, strongly, looking directly into the man's eyes. Gerald would want to size him up too. It was only natural. He'd not had Gerald's advantage of a good education, but he had proved himself in other ways, by his success in business and in life.

'I'm pleased to make your acquaintance at last, Gerald,' he said. 'I hope you're feeling a little fitter now you're home? It'll take time, mun.'

Gerald said nothing but regarded him with that stony gaze.

William turned to glance at Edie. She had removed her hat and coat but still stood, hesitating in the background, watching them, Valerie clinging to her hand.

'Come here, Edie *cariad*. Meet Daisy's husband properly.'

She bent to say something to the child, sending her off to the kitchen. Then she looked up, a smile on her lips, perhaps a shade too bright, and came forward to take Gerald's hand.

'How do you do, Gerald? I'm Daisy's stepmother, Edie, I expect she's told you about us both?'

She was gazing steadily at him, her smile not

wavering. William was proud of her, and for the first time since their arrival, felt hopeful.

'You'd better both sit down,' Gerald said. His tone sounded a little less hostile but not much.

The three of them sat in an awkward silence, except for the rattle of cups and saucers in the kitchen and Valerie's excited chatter.

Edie perched on the very edge of her chair and William wished she would relax. He was equally anxious to get to the point of their visit, but common sense made him realise it wasn't to be rushed. Let Gerald get used to their presence for the moment. A cup of tea and some idle chat might work wonders.

'How much land do you have here?' William asked, crossing his legs comfortably.

'What?' Gerald seemed to rouse himself from a reverie. 'Oh, not much, now. About ten acres left, I suppose. My father sold off most of the best pasture land before the war. It was once a thriving sheep farm. Best flocks in Yorkshire.' There was silence for a few moments. 'I never had much interest in the place, though. I wasn't cut out for the life, and he knew that.'

William glanced through the window. Hill farming. A bleak way to try to make a living, but it seemed to have paid enough for his father to afford his schooling, and save him from it.

If it seemed bleak to William now in rainy July, what would it be like living here in deepest winter? Not to Daisy's taste, nor Gerald's by the look of him. He was not here because he really wanted to be. It was just a bolt hole. Bolt hole or grave? There wasn't a great deal of difference, was there?

'You don't like Yorkshire?' Edie asked. 'Perhaps you'd prefer to be further south?'

William gave a little cough to clear his throat. Edie glanced at him, then lowered her eyes.

'I like Yorkshire,' Gerald said quietly. 'I'm a Yorkshire man after all. It's this particular piece of Yorkshire I hate.'

'Then why stay?' she said quickly.

Gerald stared at her without answering, then his gaze and fingers went to a book on the table beside him. He touched it lovingly, obviously itching to pick it up and read it there and then.

At that moment Daisy came in with a tray of tea. Valerie, skipping along behind her, went straight to Edie, trying to climb on to her lap.

'Nanna can't drink her tea and have you on her lap at the same time, Valerie,' said Daisy.

There was an edginess to her voice. William had never heard her use that tone before. This place, this situation, were doing her no good at all, nor Valerie neither.

'Come and sit on Bampa's knee,' he invited the child, and with an excited chuckle, Valerie scrambled up.

Daisy had made a plate of Spam sandwiches. They had missed a midday meal and William was thankful for the chance of something to eat.

As they ate and drank, Edie brought Daisy up to date on all the gossip from the village. Poor Daisy sat there eagerly lapping it all up. Watching her, William's heart went out to her. Loneliness. He knew about that; had had enough of it in the years before Edie.

Gerald was silent, making no attempt to join in the general chat, not really with them at all. He was receding, moving away into a world of his own, just waiting for the time when they would leave. William drained the last of his tea, knowing he would have to act soon.

When Daisy cleared away, William took out his pipe and tobacco. He was still a bit self-conscious about it, having only recently started to smoke a pipe.

'Do you mind, Gerald?' he asked, indicating the pipe.

Gerald shook his head, his gaze still stony, his face without any expression on the scarred side.

William lit up, puffing away. He flashed a meaningful look at Edie, who immediately announced her intention of helping Daisy in the kitchen.

When they were alone, William waited a few minutes, puffing away in the silence. It wasn't a companionable silence. There was an edge to it that scratched at the nerves. He wondered briefly what Gerald was like when Daisy had first met him, what had attracted her to him, and wished he'd had a chance to ask her.

'Gerald, this isn't a visit just to see Daisy,' William said carefully. 'We ... I came specifically to talk to you.'

Gerald looked up, and William saw he now had his complete attention.

'Why?'

William took the pipe out of his mouth and looked in the bowl. He pressed the tobacco down with his thumb nail.

'Daisy and Valerie can't stay here indefinitely, you know.'

'They can leave any time.'

'No, they can't, not without you, and you know it.'

'I didn't ask her to come here.'

'And you didn't tell her not to come, either,' William said, more sharply than he intended. 'What did you expect Daisy to do when she learned you were alive? Don't say abandon you, because you know her better than that.'

Gerald pushed himself out of his chair and stalked to look out of the window. His favourite stance, it would appear. What did he see out there? William wondered. Not comfort. He hated this land. Not inspiration. Only a poet would find inspiration in such a landscape, and Gerald was no poet. Or was he? Maybe that was part of his problem ...

William rose and walked over to stand beside him at the window.

'You need to get away from here, mun,' he said. 'Not only for Daisy and Valerie, but for your own sake.'

'What does it matter where I am?'

Gerald's voice was low and guttural, and William glanced at him, wondering if he were pushing too hard and too fast. But he had to go on now. He puffed his pipe for a few moments.

'It matters because you're a survivor, Gerald,' William said at last. 'You're alive and you have to go on living—doing your best.'

'Don't be so bloody patronising!'

He swung round and walked out of the room, down the passage. Startled and uncertain for a moment, William heard the front door slam hard and swore softly to himself. He'd been clumsy. Now it would be harder.

Daisy darted in from the kitchen, eyes wide.

'Was that Gerald going out?'

'Yes, in his shirt sleeves, too.' William knocked the dead tobacco from his pipe into the fireplace. 'Where's his coat? I'll go after him.'

Daisy rushed into the passage to fetch a raincoat, handing it to him as he went through the door. Her eyes were round as she stared at him, her expression one of dread.

'It's all right, Daisy love. I'll fetch him back.'

A breeze had sprung up since they had arrived. It made the fine rain billow and drive. William pulled up the collar of his raincoat, wishing he had thought to put on his trilby. The rain was like mist on his spectacles, and he had to keep wiping the back of his hand across them to see.

There was no sign of Gerald on the track up to the road. William hurried around to the back of the house where the ground fell away to the valley. There was a path of sorts and he hurried down it. He caught sight of Gerald some way below, strolling almost, as though certain no one would follow. The path appeared to peter out where he was and he was walking through bracken and heather on open moorland.

William hurried forward, cursing himself for misjudging the situation and not using more tact. Though maybe, he reflected, the bleak rainy moorland was just the place to persuade Gerald of the folly of remaining here.

The wet coarse grass was slippery under his feet, his hurrying strides making him slither dangerously in places. He was within ten feet of Gerald when he called the man's name. Gerald's reaction was astonishing.

He sprang to one side, turning as he did so, assuming a defensive crouch, arms raised in front of him to shield or defend himself. His eyes were alive now, lips pulled back from his teeth in a silent snarl.

William pulled up short.

'Gerald! It's me, mun. William. I've brought your coat.'

Gerald seemed to take a few moments to remember where he was. He straightened slowly, lowering his arms. William advanced cautiously, placing the raincoat over his shoulders.

Gerald said nothing, but turned abruptly to continue walking at a faster pace. Without hesitation, William followed, trying to get abreast of him.

'Gerald, let's get back to the house,' he said. 'You're soaked to the skin, mun. You'll catch your death.'

Gerald emitted a harsh laugh, but carried on walking downwards.

'Where are we going, then?'

'Anywhere. Nowhere. What does it matter?'

'This is no bloody good, Gerald,' William said, after a few minutes. Rain was driving onto his face, and he couldn't see where he was going. Water ran from his hair down under his collar.

'Go back then,' Gerald said. 'Leave me alone.'

William grabbed at his arm, jerking him to a standstill.

'Don't you *care* that you're worrying Daisy to death?' he asked, suddenly impatient. 'She's sacrificing a lot, you know. She's trying to make things up to you. Can't you see that? Can't you meet her halfway?'

'I didn't ask her to sacrifice anything for me. Why don't you take her home?' Gerald said harshly, pulling his arm away from William's grasp. 'Take her back where she belongs. Amongst the living, the free.'

'What the hell's the matter with you?' William asked, angrily. It was time for some straight talking, he decided. Tact obviously wasn't the answer here. 'You're talking as if you're still a prisoner. You're free, mun. Free to do anything, go anywhere. What's stopping you?'

There was bitterness in Gerald's eyes and voice.

'You've never been a prisoner. What do you know about losing your freedom?'

'Nothing, thank God,' William said soberly. 'But that's over now. You survived. Why punish Daisy? Give her back her life.'

Gerald abruptly strode off. William followed.

281

He didn't care if they walked from here to York, he wasn't going to let this man out of his sight.

'What's stopping you leaving this place?' he persisted, beginning to feel out of breath as Gerald's pace quickened. 'What is it? Pride or cowardice?'

Gerald stopped in his tracks, eyes glinting as he turned back to stare at William. A reaction at last.

'Well? You're still alive, but are you still a man?' William asked through gritted teeth.

He hated saying these things to one who had lived through Hell for years on end. Gerald was right. William had no idea what he had suffered, was still suffering by the look of him. He was still a prisoner. He needed to be rescued. Brutality had made him this way. Perhaps brutal words could bring him out of it?

'Do you have the guts to go on living, Gerald? Or are you just a lily-livered coward?'

Life flared in Gerald's eyes. His arm drew back suddenly, hand balling into a fist.

'Hit me if it makes you feel better,' William said, 'But wait until I take my glasses off.'

Gerald hesitated then turned abruptly, striding away through the glistening bracken down to the valley floor. Hoping for oblivion there? William thought. But had there been just the ghost of a smile?

'It took guts to survive that camp,' William shouted. 'It also takes guts to go on living. If you *can* find the courage to go on facing life, facing freedom, come back to the house now. If not ...'

William turned then and started to climb back, slithering and sliding on the sodden grass and heather. He almost went down once but saved himself. As he reached the path he glanced back. Gerald seemed a long way below. He was still moving, but slowly.

William watched for a moment. The figure seemed to stop, was still for a few moments, then was on the move again.

William let out a long sigh that was almost a sob. Gerald was climbing up. His own brutal words had worked. Gerald had decided to live.

Watching for a few minutes longer, William felt a little shiver go through him. But what of the future? What was in store for Daisy and Valerie now that Gerald had decided to return to the world? William couldn't rid himself of the presentiment that it would not be happiness.

Chapter Seventeen

The Mumbles, December 1945

It was crisp in the early mornings now, typical Christmas weather, Daisy thought idly. She wasn't looking forward to Christmas this year, not the way she usually did. Edie wanted them all to stay up at *Tŷ Heulwen* for Christmas Day and Boxing Day, and Valerie was talking of nothing else. But Gerald was refusing to go. She'd have to stay with him at Woodville Road, but she wouldn't deprive Valerie. There was a sense of joylessness in her heart at the thought of the Christmas she was likely to have, but she tried to ignore it.

She shivered as she let herself into the house. She'd walked briskly up to the surgery and back, but still didn't feel warm.

It wasn't only the weather that was chilling her, though. This feeling of coldness came from the inside, which was the worst kind of coldness, because it was with her day and night. It had been growing steadily worse since they'd returned from Yorkshire.

Each day was just that little more difficult to bear. It frightened her, too, because with the coldness came a numbness; all her feelings seemed to be dying. Was it true that people who lived together grew more and more alike? Daisy shivered again at the thought.

She took off her hat and coat and climbed the stairs, standing outside the back bedroom door for a moment, reluctant to enter. If only she could see a change in Gerald today. Some sign of interest, awareness of life outside himself. Some sign that he had ceased despairing; that he was willing to join the human race again. Because her husband had given up on living, must she do the same? Her heart cried out at the injustice of it.

Bracing herself, she went in to him. He was sitting up in bed reading, a woollen shawl around his shoulders against the cold. He was

284

always reading. Was it the only way he could exist, within the pages of someone else's life?

'How are you feeling now?' she asked. 'Chest any easier?'

He looked up from the book. 'You went out early.'

Daisy straightened the counterpane and fussed with the water jug on the side table.

'I've asked for Dr Hewson to call later to look at you,' she said quietly, knowing what his reaction would be.

'You had no right! I didn't ask for a doctor. I won't see him!'

'Gerald, please!'

Daisy put cold fingers to her temples. They were trembling. She'd noticed lately that her nerves were getting really ragged. Much more of this and she'd be ill herself, too ill to do her work, perhaps. Where would they be then?

'You need the doctor, Gerald. I could hear you coughing all night. I know you could hardly breathe. I was so worried.'

'My God! Can't a man have any privacy? That's why I moved into the back bedroom. Didn't I make myself clear, Daisy? I want no interference from anyone.'

'But, Gerald, I'm your ... wife.' Daisy couldn't help stumbling over the word. She didn't feel like a wife. She felt more like a trapped animal. 'It's my duty ...'

She couldn't go on speaking. That was what she was reduced to. Merely doing her duty, when what she really needed was to love and be loved. Duty was such an empty and lifeless thing.

Gerald didn't seem to notice her distress. He lived on a lonely island now, repelling all comers, even rescuers. Couldn't he understand she was trying her best to help, to make some kind of future? But was there any for them?

'It's bad enough having your grandmother back and forth all the time,' he said irritably. 'And that friend of yours—what's her name, Josie? I won't tolerate these people spying on me, treating me like a side-show.'

'That isn't true!' Daisy cried. 'I won't have you saying that. Mam-gu only wants to help, and I don't see Josie all that often.'

Whenever she came, Gerald disappeared into the bedroom without a word and stayed there until she had gone. Daisy was embarrassed by that behaviour. Surely he didn't expect her to give up her friends? She had seen much less of Josie over the last six months. Their days out together were very few and far between. Her stepmother was always willing to look after Valerie while she went out, but the difficulty now was Gerald. She couldn't leave him on his own, could she?

Josie said she didn't see why not. After all, he wasn't physically crippled. Daisy couldn't explain to her friend that she saw Gerald as a cripple, and it had nothing to do with his facial scars. It was always at the back of her mind that he might do something desperate. And while he was always demanding privacy, she was afraid to leave him alone for any length of time.

'When the doctor calls, you can tell him he's not wanted.'

Not willing to trust herself to answer, she hurried to the door.

'And keep that child away from me, please.' Gerald called after her. 'She gets on my nerves with her constant chatter.'

Daisy went downstairs and sat at the kitchen table, elbows on it, head in her hands.

Oh, God, let me have the strength to cope with it, she prayed earnestly. The last six months had been miserable. She hadn't been willing to admit that to herself until this moment. The only relief had been that Valerie was less fractious now that she was home and back in her mother's bed, though there was still ill-feeling between the child and her father. For some reason Gerald seemed to be turning completely against his own daughter. It didn't seem natural, but then, there was nothing natural about Gerald these days. It was an unnatural existence for all of them. How could a marriage survive in an atmosphere like this?

Sometimes she fancied he resented her too. Now and then she'd catch him looking at her, a glowering light in his eye, which made her uneasy. He hadn't forgiven her for helping to uproot him from Yorkshire. She wasn't sure, even now, how William had achieved it. Gerald behaved as though he'd been forced against his will. But as Josie had pointed out to her, what would have become of him if she'd left him there? He'd have died and he knows it, Josie said. And maybe, Daisy thought, that was what he resented. She had helped force him to go on living; no, not living, existing. Was he punishing her for it?

When Dr Hewson came she would have to explain. He was one of the older doctors in the village. A kind and compassionate man, he would not be offended. Perhaps he would advise her anyway. She had to talk to someone.

Valerie came down in her pyjamas for breakfast, fair hair tousled, cheeks glowing like pink velvet. She almost danced into the kitchenette, her old teddy bear clasped tightly to her chest. She was singing at the top of her voice, the high-pitched piping sound of the very young, tinny but penetrating. Daisy thought of Gerald's reaction, but had no intention of curbing the child's natural exuberance. Somehow she must find a way to please both of them.

'I sleep up Nanna's Christmas, isn't it, Mammy?'

Her grey eyes were bright and sparkling. She was talking incessantly about Christmas these days. It was hard to believe she'd be three years old in six months' time. The years were flying by.

Daisy felt a pain in her heart at the thought. They were flying by and they were wasted, too. She always planned on at least three children. Now that would never be.

'How many days till Christmas, Mammy?'

Valerie asked the same questions every morning. She clambered on to a chair at the table, waiting for her breakfast, a boiled egg and toast fingers, her teddy bear thrown carelessly on the floor.

'Fourteen,' Daisy answered, putting the food in front of her.

'What's Father Christmas bringing me, Mammy?'

'We'll have to wait and see.'

'I want a bike.'

'You're too young.'

'Shirley's got a bike,' Valerie said through a mouth of egg and toast.

'Shirley's older than you, and don't speak with your mouth full, Valerie.'

Shirley lived next door. She and Valerie were firm friends despite the difference in their ages. Shirley's parents were thinking of buying their own house in Fforestfach when they had saved enough for a deposit. Valerie would miss her very much when they left.

'It's a bath for you, my girl,' Daisy said. 'And keep quiet and out of Daddy's way today. He's not well.'

Valerie pouted, and regarded her mother from under puckered brows.

'I don't like this daddy. I want Uncle Rhodri.'

'Now, don't be silly, Valerie.' Daisy was shocked at the deep tone of rancour in her daughter's voice.

She'd thought she was doing the right thing, bringing father and daughter together. Now she wondered if there'd been more harm than good in it, especially for Valerie.

The child's look was sullen, the colour of her eyes darkened, so that for a split second it seemed to Daisy that those were Gerald's eyes glowering at her.

'Don't like him,' Valerie muttered. 'He better go 'way.'

When a knock came at the door about ten-thirty, Daisy went to answer it, rehearsing her excuse for Dr Hewson. But when she opened the door and saw who was standing there, she felt suddenly dizzy with shock and had to lean against the passage wall for support.

'Rhodri!'

'Hewson can't come,' he said, in a matter-of-fact tone, but there was an underlying tremor to it. 'He has an emergency.'

He stepped forward to come in, but instinctively Daisy held the door to, her mind whirling in confusion and pain at the sight of his beloved face. He mustn't come in, was her first thought. It was as though warning bells were ringing in her head, telling her that if he stepped over the threshold, she'd lose control of it all.

Although they met infrequently in the course of their work, their connection was always at a distance. Daisy made sure of that. They never had anything other than a professional conversation. It was a precaution she took because she knew she couldn't trust herself on any other level. It was weak, the barrier she had erected between them since she'd learned she was married, so weak that any pressure would break it down. She couldn't risk it, not only for herself but for Rhodri, too.

'Rhodri, I can't let you in.' She shook her

head emphatically. 'Don't you see? It wouldn't be right. Gerald is refusing to see a doctor anyway.'

He was regarding her with astonishment.

'Daisy, I'm here on a professional visit. Of course I must come in.'

He put a hand against the door and pushed it open despite her protest. Not very professional, she thought.

As he stepped over the threshold and into the passage, Daisy retreated, her heart spinning and somersaulting. Rhodri hadn't been in her home since before the telegram. Seeing him here was stirring up old memories, sharpening feelings, longings. She wondered if she could bear it.

'He won't see you,' she said desperately. 'Please go, Rhodri.'

His gaze was riveted on her face. Daisy started to tremble. It was as though he'd touched her. She turned hastily away and went into the living room. Rhodri followed.

'How are you, Daisy?' His voice was like a caress. 'You don't look well, *cariad*. I've been worried about you for weeks. You're not looking after yourself.'

She wished he wouldn't speak to her as though they were lovers. He was standing too close to her. She could almost feel the warmth of him in the small room. In rising panic Daisy clasped her hands together, twisting them in agitation. They were as cold as ice, yet her head felt hot and she was dizzy.

'Rhodri, please. You're making things difficult for me.'

'Daisy ...'

He took a step closer and she felt the panic inside herself. She moved quickly away, bending down for the coal scuttle and throwing a few pieces of coal on to the fire. The new coals settled into the red heart of the flames, sparks flinging themselves into space.

She stood with her back to him, waiting. Her heart ached, as if it were weeping. She was rejecting him when what she really wanted was to throw herself into his arms. But she mustn't think those thoughts.

'It's no good, Rhodri. Gerald's adamant. He refuses to see anyone.'

'Well, I want to see him,' Rhodri said, a harsh, jagged edge to his voice. 'I want to see the man who took you from me.'

Daisy whirled around, distress twisting within her like a knife at his words.

'Don't! It wasn't like that at all.'

'You chose him,' Rhodri accused.

Daisy's hand flew to her mouth to stifle a sob. They hadn't talked properly since the telegram came. That had been unfair to him. There were things he must have needed to say, still did, but they were things she didn't want to hear. Six months ago it would have taken very little to change her mind about standing by Gerald. Rhodri would have pleaded with her, and he was so persuasive. The truth was she couldn't have trusted herself not to give in. She loved Rhodri so deeply, needed him so much, but she'd thought she knew her duty. Perhaps if she'd known then what she knew now ...

'I didn't choose him over you,' Daisy said at last, shaking her head vehemently. 'There wasn't any choice, Rhodri. It was the war. It was fate. It was my duty.'

'Duty before love,' he said.

There was a bitterness in his voice which tore at her very soul. That wasn't like him at all. She'd never heard that tone in his voice before, never, not even when he spoke of his war experiences. Bitterness was alien to him, yet there it was, in his voice and in his eyes, and *she* had done this to him.

'Your sense of duty may be admirable, Daisy,' he went on. 'But it's broken my heart.'

Daisy covered her face with her hands. She couldn't bear to hear him say that. His heart was broken; her heart was broken, too, and it didn't help to realise that it was her own doing also. But what else could she have done in the circumstances? Turn her back on a husband recently returned from Hell?

She couldn't help herself; she burst into tears.

Rhodri's arm was around her in a moment.

'Daisy, my dearest ...'

At that moment there was an impatient knocking from above.

Daisy started guiltily, as though she'd been caught out in a compromising act, and stepped quickly away from him.

Breathlessly she said: 'Gerald needs me.'

'I'll go to him,' Rhodri said firmly, striding out into the passage.

'No!'

But he was already on the stairs and climbing them two at a time despite his limp.

In the passage Daisy stood with her back against the wall, listening as the bedroom door opened and closed. There was an exclamation from Gerald, and then his voice raised in protest. She could hear Rhodri's deeper, quieter tones, but couldn't hear what was being said.

Daisy walked slowly back into the living-room and sat down, feeling helpless. Somehow she felt guilty, too. Gerald would think she'd betrayed him, sending the doctor deliberately.

It seemed an age before Rhodri came down again. Daisy stood up as he came into the living room, his face composed so that she had no idea what he was thinking.

'His chest is slightly congested,' he said. 'Nothing to worry about. If you call at the surgery later, I'll have a bottle of linctus for him.'

'Thank you.' Daisy kept her eyes downcast. She felt subdued, ashamed that Gerald had caused a scene.

'About his mental state ...' Rhodri began. 'Daisy, I must tell you I think he'd be better off under professional care.'

She looked up, startled and horrified.

'An institution?'

When Rhodri nodded, Daisy shook her head. 'No. He'd hate that.'

'He needs proper treatment. He can be helped, I'm sure.'

Daisy frowned.

'What are you saying? You're talking as

though Gerald's unbalanced. He's suffered a lot ... he's just difficult, that's all. I can manage him. You're making it seem worse than it is, Rhodri.'

'There are signs, Daisy, that his trouble goes very deep. These signs can't be ignored. You need to think about it, not only for your own sake but for Valerie's too. And for Gerald himself.'

'Why are you saying this, Rhodri?' she asked sharply. 'Are you trying to frighten me so that I'll leave him and come back to you?'

Rhodri's nostrils flared, and Daisy wished she could bite back the words, knowing she'd gone too far. Rhodri would never stoop to that. He was too honourable. Whatever had made her say it?

She held out a hand to him. 'I'm sorry, Rhodri. Please forgive me. I'm not myself lately.'

When he made to grasp her outstretched hand she withdrew it sharply, turning her eyes away from the hurt expression on his face. She dare not risk any physical contact again. She didn't want to hurt him anymore, but it seemed she could do nothing else. She wished he would go and leave her alone.

'Daisy, we can't go on like this ...' Rhodri stepped forward suddenly and took hold of her arms. 'You can't dismiss what we mean to each other just because Fate, as you call it, dealt us an underhand blow.'

Daisy forced herself to step away, though she longed to be in his arms again. He made it all sound so easy, but it wasn't. Doing her duty was the hardest thing she'd ever had to do. If she wasn't prepared to abandon her marriage vows six months ago, she certainly wouldn't do so now, not when her husband needed her support more than ever.

And yet she knew she would love Rhodri, and only Rhodri, for the rest of her life. She felt tears prickle at the back of her eyes as she looked at him.

'What kind of a woman would I be if I deserted a sick husband? Don't you see, I can't do it? Gerald has no one but me.'

Rhodri shook his head.

'There's no future for you in this relationship; not for you or Valerie. Gerald isn't going to improve the way things are. It can only get worse.'

Confused and uncertain, she ran shaky fingers across her forehead. They were still cold. Would she ever feel warm again?

'Rhodri ...'

He stepped closer.

'I'm not willing to let you go, Daisy *cariad.*'

Looking up into his beloved face, she felt mesmerised. The expression in his eyes was so tender, so full of love, that it made her want to burst into tears again. With a deep sigh she felt herself sway forward, longing to surrender to the haven of his arms, to escape this awful coldness of her soul, to revive the feelings of love and security that seemed to have been draining away these last months. Duty and love. Why must there be a choice?

Someone knocking loudly on the front door broke the spell for her. She jerked back, realising how close she had come to surrender. Rhodri's expression was one of shock too, as though he'd been woken suddenly from a dream only to find the nightmare was real.

Her mind in a confused whirl, Daisy hurried into the passage to open the door to her rescuer. Whoever it was at the door had saved her from folly.

When Daisy opened the door Josie was standing there, smiling at her, Rhiannon in her pushchair.

''Morning, kid,' said Josie, grinning.

With a sense of relief, Daisy stepped aside as she manoeuvred the pushchair into the passage and sailed with it towards the living-room.

'Thought I'd call here first to do the last fitting on Valerie's dress before I go up to your mother's. Where is she, then?'

'Next door with Shirley,' Daisy said. She was conscious of sounding very breathless. She was always glad to see Josie, but this morning she was even more so.

When Josie reached the living-room she pulled up short at the sight of Rhodri standing patiently in front of the fireplace. Daisy was glad to see he'd put his overcoat on again. Josie glanced round at her, giving her a startled look.

'*Bore da*, Mrs Jenkins,' Rhodri said to her. 'How are you today?'

'Fine, thanks,' answered Josie, but her tone was subdued, as though she thought she was intruding.

Her friend was looking from one to the other, uncertainly, and Daisy wondered what was going on in her mind. Josie knew she and Rhodri had seen nothing of each other for the last six months. Daisy felt she must explain herself.

'Gerald's not well,' she hastened to say. 'Rhodri came to have a look at him.'

He picked up his hat and bag, ready to leave.

'I'll have that linctus ready for you then, Daisy.' he said, tone very professional now.

'Right.' She smiled stiffly. 'I'll pick it up sometime later.'

Rhodri walked past them into the passage.

'I'll let myself out. *Bore da* to you both.'

Nothing was said until they heard the front door close. Josie was regarding her curiously.

'Have I barged in on something?'

'Of course not. Whatever gave you that idea?'

'Because frankly, Daisy, you look lit up like a Christmas tree.'

She sank down heavily on the sofa, legs trembling too much to hold her up. She put her hand to her mouth as a sob threatened to erupt from her throat.

'Oh, Josie, I'm so miserable!'

Josie sat down beside her and immediately put an arm around her shoulders, squeezing her tightly.

'Oh, kid. I'm sorry.'

'It's the first time Rhodri and I have talked alone,' she said. 'He's so bitter now, Josie. I did that to him. I thought he'd accepted it but he hasn't. Our feelings are still there. You just can't turn off love, can you? Before you came I almost ...'

She couldn't go on speaking, and Josie patted her back in sympathy.

'Make a cuppa, shall I, Daisy? You look shaken.'

'I am. Rhodri wants me to put Gerald in an institution. He thinks it would be better for him.'

Jose nodded sagely. 'And it would be better for you too, Daisy. You're young, but you've got no life, have you? You can't go on like this, girl. You ought to think about it.'

Daisy sniffed.

'If it were your Stan, you'd stick by him, wouldn't you?'

'Yes, kid. But then, I'm not madly in love with somebody else.'

Later on Josie left to go up to *Tŷ Heulwen* to fit the dresses she was making for Edie's daughters Amy and Florence. Daisy walked part of the way with her on her way to the surgery to get the linctus.

When she returned she took the medicine up to Gerald.

'I don't want the bloody stuff,' he said morosely. 'Lewis is nothing more than a quack. I don't like him. Keep him away from me. You deliberately disobeyed me, Daisy, sending a stranger up to see me.'

She folded her arms across her breast to disguise the trembling of her hands.

'Dr Hewson couldn't come.'

'Has that woman gone yet? She chatters like a parrot.' His eyes narrowed. 'What were you two whispering about?'

'Josie and I weren't whispering,' Daisy said quickly. 'And you must've been on the landing to be able to hear us at all. You shouldn't get out of bed in the cold, not with your chest.'

'I might as well be up,' he said sullenly. 'For all the peace I get. She won't let me sleep. I can't concentrate to read. Must she be so noisy? Can't you control her?'

'Who are you talking about?'

'That child. Singing and shouting at the top of her voice.'

Daisy lifted her chin.

'This is Valerie's home, too, Gerald,' she said. She almost added that Valerie had been there first, but refrained. That remark would childish and pointless.

'Yes, I know,' he said heavily. 'But why must I be saddled with another man's child?'

'What?'

Daisy stared at him, astounded. She couldn't believe what he was saying.

'Gerald, don't say that! Valerie is *your* daughter. What on earth has got into you? You know she's your daughter.'

He looked up at her with that glowering gaze she was beginning to detest. She was trying to make allowances for the state of his mind but it was difficult and growing more and more so.

'I know nothing of the sort,' he said flatly. 'I'm away for two years and when I return you have a child. I knew nothing of it.'

Daisy put the bottle of linctus and the spoon down on the side table. Suddenly she realised the truth of Rhodri's words. Things could only get worse for Gerald. But she would have to weather it; talk him round.

'Why didn't you let me know you were alive, Gerald?'

His lips twisted.

'Would it have made any difference?' He gave a harsh laugh. 'It was going on all the time with the chaps around me. All they had were the memories of their wives and children. And all the time the women were betraying them! Time and time again I saw it happen to one man and then another. And that was even before I was taken prisoner.'

He flashed a look at her, sparking with animosity.

'I'm not a fool. Why should you be any different, Daisy?'

She put a hand to her throat, staring at him in dismay.

'Are you suggesting I was unfaithful to you?'

He laughed again, harsh and without humour.

'Are you saying you weren't? It was guilt, wasn't it, Daisy, the reason why you came searching for me, insisting on taking care of me although the sight of me must make you sick? I wonder if you'll run true to form and dump me when you've had enough of guilt?'

With a cry she hurried from the room, hurt and appalled at his words. She almost stumbled down the stairs, blinded by tears. What had she done?

She'd sacrificed a lifetime of happiness for herself and Rhodri out of a sense of pride: she would do her duty whatever the cost. She had betrayed Rhodri, trampled carelessly on his love. Oh, Rhodri! Remembering his tenderness, his kindness, the comfort of his arms, she couldn't hold back an anguished cry of pain. She needed him.

Sobbing uncontrollably, she realised that her hopes of mending her marriage were nothing more than a mirage. It had been doomed from the start. Everyone had seen it but herself. Why had she been so stubborn and arrogant, so misguided as to think she could do what others had failed to do?

Daisy lifted her head, looking into the glowing fire, thinking of Rhodri's earlier visit. She had almost surrendered to him, but even if she had it would have made no difference. It was too late. Gerald had no feelings for her, nor for anyone, not even himself. Her husband was a very sick man, and she was chained to him for ever.

Chapter Eighteen

Josie almost tripped over Rhiannon as the child squatted on the kitchen floor playing with her new doll.

'Rhiannon, chick, why don't you go and play

with your dolly and pram in the living-room while Auntie gets the dinner?' she suggested, smiling at Rhiannon's obvious enjoyment as she eagerly pushed her doll and pram out of the way.

It was going to be a good Christmas, Josie thought, the best they'd ever had. She wiped her hands, looking with satisfaction at the plump chicken on the kitchen table, waiting for its thyme and parsley stuffing. She had Edie Philpots to thank for that, and also for the Brussels sprouts out of the gardens of *Tŷ Heulwen*.

Feeling happier than she had for a long time, Josie set about preparing their dinner, singing along with the carols on the wireless in the living room.

Gwennie would be down soon to help with the vegetables. She didn't expect any help from Francie this morning. Her sister had come in very late last night and would probably lie in bed until everything was done. Oh, well, thought Josie, it is the season of good will to all men and sisters.

She didn't want anything to spoil this Christmas or the happy sense of anticipation she had. Rhiannon was old enough now to understand the excitement of the season, and the child's joy was infectious. After all, the future looked good, despite the fact that Josie didn't have a job yet. She was doing all right with the dress-making, and Gwennie had a permanent cleaning job at the Guildhall. Francie wasn't earning much as a barmaid—at least, she didn't contribute much—but never mind, they were holding their heads above water.

The most wonderful thing was that Stanley was coming home next month, home for good, and Josie was proud that he would be returning to their own place as she'd always wanted.

She was singing a verse of 'Good King Wenceslas' when Gwennie came into the kitchen, rubbing sleep from her eyes.

'Oh, you sound happy, then?' her mother-in-law said, reaching for the teapot.

'Of course I am!' laughed Josie. 'It's Christmas, the best yet, and next month Stan will be home. Oh, Gwennie, I'm so excited, I'm like a kid! I can hardly sleep at night. When he comes home for good everything will be all right from then on, you wait and see.'

Gwennie sat at the table, head bent over her cup.

'When Stan is here, what about Francie and Rhiannon? You'll want her to find a place of her own then, will you?'

Josie laughed again, astonished at the question.

'Good heavens, no! Plenty of room here for them. And you know Stan. He won't mind a bit of extra company.'

Gwennie said nothing, but drained her cup.

'Johnno will be round later,' Josie continued. 'I'm going to invite Mama and the kids over this afternoon. They can stay to tea. Give her a break, and it'll be a change for the kids. They've never had a really happy Christmas, poor little devils.'

'Good idea,' Gwennie agreed. 'Hey! I've got

a bottle of port. Do your mother a power of good to have a swig or two of that.'

Josie had just put the bird in the oven when Johnno came knocking at the basement entry door. As soon as he walked into the living-room, one look at his face told Josie there was something wrong. His eyes were red-rimmed and his cheeks stained with tears. He usually put on a brave face.

'Oh, Johnno love, what's the matter? Has Dada been beating you again? He hasn't hurt Mama, has he?'

Johnno shook his head.

'It's Mama, Josie. She's been taken to hospital.'

'What?' Josie's heart turned over in her breast.

'The doctor came round this morning.' Johnno swallowed hard. 'He said Mama had to go into hospital. An ambulance came for her and all. I don't know what's wrong with her, Josie. Nobody will tell me anything.'

'I must go to her. Where's my coat and scarf?' Josie tore off her apron and hurried towards the kitchen stairs. 'Gwennie! Look after the dinner for me. Come with me, Johnno love. We'll go round the hospital and find out.'

Her mind was in a whirl, Christmas and all her preparations forgotten. If Dada was responsible for this, she'd kill him. She should never have left her mother alone with him. She was to blame for this. She was too wrapped up in her own life, had neglected her mother. Josie felt a wash of guilt and despair sweep over her as she and her brother hurried towards Hospital Square.

The clerk at the Casualty desk couldn't or wouldn't tell her anything. Taut with impatience and fear, Josie hurried up the corridor to the Casualty waiting room, Johnno on her heels.

A tall, angular woman in a Nursing Sister's uniform regarded Josie's unseemly dash into her domain with a deep frown of irritation. Everyone knew Sister Dobson, scourge of Casualty. A dragon if ever there was one, everyone said. But right now Josie was in the mood for slaying dragons.

'My mother was admitted this morning,' she panted out 'Sophia Randall, Victor Street. I want to see her. I want to know what's wrong with her. I want ...'

'My dear.' Sister Dobson put a gentle hand on Josie's arm. There was no irritation on her sharp-featured face now, only deep compassion. 'Step into my office. The young man, too.'

Josie walked into the office on trembling legs, Johnno clutching her arm. Apprehension made it difficult to breathe properly. Whatever was wrong with Mama, it must be something very serious.

'Mrs Randall was brought in to Casualty this morning haemorrhaging very badly,' Sister Dobson said, motioning them both to sit down. 'She had a miscarriage.'

'*What?* But I didn't know she was expecting,' said Josie. 'She never told me.'

'I'm sorry to have to tell you, but Mrs Randall died half an hour ago.'

306

Josie stared at Sister Dobson, her hand covering her mouth. She shook her head. No, it couldn't be true. Mama couldn't be dead. Not now, not at Christmas time, when everything was coming right for them.

Mama! Oh, Mama! I love you and I let you die.

Josie's heart was bursting with anguish. She put an arm around Johnno sitting next to her, sobbing his heart out.

'It can't be, Sister. Not *my* mother!'

Sister Dobson held her head on one side, her eyes kind. Those who said she was a dragon clearly didn't know her.

'I'm sorry. This must be a shock. At present Mrs Randall is in the hospital mortuary. You understand, there must be a post-mortem? I'm sorry to talk about such matters at this time, but these things must be faced.'

Josie stood up, pulling Johnno with her.

'When ...'

Sister Dobson stood, too.

'The Almoner will let you know when you can make arrangements.'

Josie and Johnno walked slowly back to St Helen's Avenue, dragging their feet. There were few people about. Everyone was at home enjoying their Christmas morning as best they could with rationing. Josie's heart felt heavy. The joy she'd known earlier on was replaced now with grief and despair.

Warm, loving Mama was dead. Josie couldn't believe it. Mama, who had loved her children despite everything; who had struggled with a miserable life, always showing a smiling face for them.

Josie stopped in her tracks. She'd forgotten about her younger sister and brother. They would be frightened being left alone because Mama was always there at home for them. They'd break their hearts when they knew.

'What about Teresa and Dewi? Who's looking after them?'

'Kitty,' said Johnno

Josie frowned, not recognising the name.

'Who's Kitty?'

'Kitty O'Sullivan,' he said, rubbing his arms against the cold. 'She's living in our house now. Dada brought her home a couple of weeks ago.'

'*What?*'

'Kitty said it was best if Mama moved into the back bedroom on her own. Kitty and Dada had the front bedroom to themselves then. Mama was crying all the time, crying and praying.'

Despite the bitter coldness of the day, Josie could feel hot blood rise up in her neck and into her head. It made her feel dizzy and sick. She felt like a cauldron about to boil over.

'Why didn't you tell me?' she asked through clenched teeth. She took Johnno by the upper arms and shook him so violently that the flesh on his face quivered. 'I told you to keep an eye on Dada, didn't I? You should've come to me. Now look what's happened! Mama is dead.'

Johnno looked dismayed, then burst into tears.

'It wasn't my fault Mama died, Josie! Dada

said he'd knock my head off, and Kitty gave me two shillings.'

'You took money from her?' Josie was incensed.

'Kitty's not so bad, Josie, mun,' Johnno said, running to catch her up as she suddenly marched off. 'She slips me a bob now and then, and she won't let Dada hit any of us. Honest. And she made him send for the doctor when Mama was bad in the night.'

'He's gone too far this time,' Josie said tightly, hardly listening to what her brother was saying. 'He was warned what could happen if he put Mama in the family way again. He doesn't care about anyone but himself. Now he's taken her from us, and humiliated her first, bringing that fat old tart to the house! He'll pay for this as God is my witness. I'm going to give him up to the police, and her, too. I should've done it a long time ago.'

Josie let them in through the basement entry door. The chicken was almost done by the aroma from the kitchen, but she no longer had any interest in Christmas. She marched through the kitchen, past a startled Gwennie who was in the middle of basting the bird.

'How's your mother, kid?'

Josie didn't answer; she couldn't. She was too choked with grief and rage. The two feelings were fuelling each other and she felt on the verge of a screaming fit. She had to see Francie, tell her what had happened. They must go around to Victor Street together. Francie was lying in bed smoking a cigarette, an open magazine near at hand. She looked Josie up and down as she came into the room.

'What you got your coat on for? Bit late for church, isn't it?'

'Get up, Francie,' Josie said sombrely. 'Something's happened, something awful.'

'Oh, God, don't tell me you've burned the chicken? I was looking forward to that.'

'Get up, you lazy bitch!' Josie screamed at her, suddenly losing control. 'Mama is dead. She's lying on some cold mortuary slab while you're lolling about by here without a bloody care in the world. Get up or I'll drag you out of bed!'

Josie went out, slamming the door behind her. She felt sick and unsteady. She felt she was in some awful nightmare. Reuben had betrayed Mama in the worst way, cruelly, selfishly. Francie was exactly like him. No damn' good to anyone.

As she almost stumbled down the stairs, the bedroom door opened.

'What did you say about Mama?'

Francie's voice was almost a whisper. Josie turned slowly on the stairs to look up at her sister. With her white nightie and long pale hair she might pass for an angel, Josie thought, but it was only an illusion. Francie was no angel.

'Mama died this morning at the hospital. Another miscarriage,' Josie said, calmly now.

Francie leaned heavily against the door post, both hands covering her mouth. Her eyes, wide and round, stared down at Josie.

'Get dressed,' she went on. 'We've got to go

round to Victor Street now, fetch Teresa and Dewi back here.'

Francie started forward. 'What for?'

Her shocked expression at the news had suddenly been replaced with a stubborn lift of the chin.

'Because,' Josie said through tight lips, 'that flaming father of ours has only brought his floozy home, hasn't he? She's been living there a couple of weeks apparently. Put Mama in the spare bedroom, they did, while they carried on in the front. Can you imagine what she went through? The shame, the humiliation. I could kill him, I could. Oh, God, I wish I was a man. I'd beat him to death with my bare fists for what he did to Mama!'

'Talk sense, Josie,' Francie said. 'We can't do anything. He kicked us out, remember?'

'I don't care about that,' she flared. 'He's responsible for Mama dying. *He* killed her, the swine! I'm going to have him put away.'

Francie retreated into the bedroom, pushing the door almost closed. She peered through the narrow opening at Josie.

'I'm not going, and you can't make me. He nearly killed me before. I don't want anything to do with him. You can do as you like.'

With that she slammed the door shut.

Josie stood for a moment, fuming. But perhaps it was better she went on her own? Francie wouldn't be any good as an ally. Josie had managed on her own up to now, why should this time be any different?

For all her bravado, her steps faltered as she

311

neared the yard gates. She was frightened, she had to admit, but made herself move forward. If he laid a finger on her or even threatened her, she would call the police. She'd scream blue murder.

The front door was open as usual. Bracing herself, Josie stepped into the passage and walked resolutely through into the living-room. There was no one about, no sign of her father, which was a relief. She heard voices, children's voices, in the kitchen, and marched straight in.

Teresa and Dewi were alone, sitting at the table eating toffee apples. There was a bag of sweets on the table in front of each of them, but no sign of a meal being prepared, no evidence that this was Christmas Day.

They jumped up, smiling at the sight of her.

'Josie!' Teresa rushed at her, flinging her arms around her waist and hugging her tightly. 'Happy Christmas!'

'The ambulance came to our house, Josie,' Dewi said excitedly, taking hold of her hand. 'Took Mama to hospital.' He held out his other hand to show her a shilling nestling in his palm. 'Going to get her a Christmas present, I am. Kitty says we can go and see her this afternoon.'

Josie felt nonplussed for a moment, confused at their excitement and cheerfulness. She'd expected tears and misery. It was quite obvious they knew nothing of the tragedy.

'Kitty?'

'That's me, so it is,' a loud voice said behind

her, thick with an Irish brogue.

Josie swung round to see a woman standing in the kitchen doorway, wearing a shapeless flowered dress a size too small, the material straining across a huge abdomen. The dress looked in need of a good wash, too.

'Kitty O'Sullivan,' the woman went on. 'I bet you're Josie?'

Kitty O'Sullivan was about forty, Josie judged. She was enormously fat, almost as tall as Dada, and big-boned with it. She filled the doorway, her bulging hips almost touching the door posts to either side. Her short neck was hidden under many chins. She was wearing a hat, a man's trilby, with a little red feather pushed into the hat band. What disconcerted Josie most of all was the pleasant expression on her plump features.

Kitty waddled forward into the kitchen. The dress was sleeveless. Her exposed bulging arms reminded Josie of uncooked legs of pork. So this was the fat old tart from Port Tennant? She was grotesque! Josie could only stare at her, wondering how her father could possibly prefer this barrel of lard to beautiful Mama.

'Sit yourself down, then, why don't you?' Kitty said, pulling out a chair from the table. 'It'll be a hot cup of something you'll be wanting, I expect.'

Josie felt her throat tighten.

'Who are you to be offering me anything in my mother's home?' she demanded. 'My father had no right to bring you here. You'd better get out now.'

'Josie ...' Teresa was pulling at her sleeve.

'Now don't be working yourself into a lather,' Kitty said serenely. 'It'll do no good. Reub wants me to stay. It's helping with his totting I'll be from now on.'

'You've got a blasted cheek!' Josie snapped, head throbbing with fury. 'Making yourself at home in another woman's life. Shameless, that's what it is. Disgusting! You couldn't wait, could you? Couldn't wait for her to be ... gone.'

'Gone?' Kitty frowned. 'What's this you're saying?'

Josie bit her lip, tying to hold back a sob. She was shaking, not only with fury at this awful woman, but also with a debilitating grief.

Mama was dead. She would never see those loving eyes smile at her again; never feel those gentle hands ease her pain as she had as a child. And this woman was trying to take her place.

'She's gone ...' Josie glanced at the two children standing there, looking up into her face. She could see they were trying to understand why she and Kitty were quarrelling. 'Half an hour before we got to the hospital.'

'Oh, dear God!' Kitty crossed herself. 'I didn't know. No one's been round here to tell us. Reub doesn't know.'

'As if he cares!' Josie almost spat the words. 'He's hounded and terrorised her for years. She lived in fear of him. It's he that put her where she is now.'

Kitty shook her head.

'You're unfair, so you are. 'Tis true he's nasty in drink and too handy with his fists, but he's never laid a finger on her, not since I've been here.'

'Don't you understand, you stupid woman!' Josie shouted at her, incensed that Kitty should stand up for him. She wasn't even family. 'He was warned what would happen if she got preggers again, but he just didn't care!'

Kitty was silent. She waddled over to the sink, filled the kettle and put it on the gas burner, lighting a match with her thumb nail. Teresa and Dewi whooped with delight as though it were a magician's trick.

'See that Josie?' Dewi exclaimed. He was almost doubled over with laughter. 'Kitty can do all kinds of magic tricks, can't you, Kit?'

Holding back tears with great difficulty, Josie moved to put an arm around her brother and sister.

'Get your hats and coats on,' she said. 'And your pyjamas, too. You're both coming down to St Helen's Avenue to stay with me and Francie.'

'Whoopee! But we'll see Mama this afternoon, right?' Dewi asked.

Josie bit her lip.

'No, love. Mama is ... Mama can't see anybody today. Now go on, run and get your coats.'

'Leave them, why don't you?' Kitty said, as the children dashed off. 'Sure, there's no harm can come to them here.'

Josie lifted her chin, giving her what she hoped was a look of deep disdain and contempt.

'Leave those innocent children here with the

likes of you? No fear! I know what you are. Tell my father he's seen the last of them, too. He disowned my sister and me. Now we're disowning him. He can go to hell and rot there! Tell him that from me.'

Chapter Nineteen

January 1946

Josie lifted her head off the pillow, raising herself on one arm. Stanley was fast asleep. She gazed at him lovingly, still not able to believe he was really here, home at last, safe and sound. She longed to touch his sleeping face, but held back. He'd looked so tired last night, so worn out. It would take a while for him to settle back into normal life.

His face was leaner than she remembered, new lines etched in skin darkened by a foreign sun. He was much quieter than she remembered, too, but she put that down to his tiredness, war weariness. Perhaps his eyes were not as bright as they used to be, but he was still her very own Stanley, and she thanked God yet again that her husband had come home to her at last. From now on things would be all right.

Josie lay back again, staring at the ceiling. Was she being too optimistic? The dress-making was going well, and had been enough until her brothers and sister came to live with them. Now it was very different. Neither she nor Stanley had a job at present, and no prospects either. Stanley had been home just one week, and she was reluctant to broach the subject of work. He needed a long rest after what he'd been through, yet at the same time they couldn't afford to be idle with four extra mouths to feed.

Johnno was fifteen in a couple of months—time for him to find a job. He'd been talking about taking up totting, going round with a hand cart, but the thought horrified her. Johnno was not to go the way of her father—not that he was anything like him in nature. No, Johnno deserved better in life, something worthwhile and respectable, to be a man people would look up to, not despise.

Stanley opened his eyes, turned his head and smiled at her.

'Morning, love,' he said sleepily. 'There's gorgeous you look.'

'Oh, you!' Josie pulled a face, but was exceptionally pleased. It was lovely to wake up with your husband beside you instead of to a terrible, nagging fear for his safety.

He reached out a hand to touch her breast but the next instant the bed shuddered violently as Rhiannon leapt on to it, scrambling up between them. Stanley muffled a groan of impatience, Josie noticed, and turned over.

'Auntie! Auntie! When's Father Christmas coming again?'

'Not for a long, long time,' Josie replied, her gaze on the back of Stanley's head. This wasn't fair on him, was it? They had no privacy

317

anymore. Had his homecoming disappointed him? It made Josie's heart ache to think so.

'I want some more presents.'

'You'll have to wait for your birthday in a couple of weeks, then.'

Rhiannon caught hold of the headboard while at the same time bouncing up and down on the bed. It was like an earthquake and Stanley gave another groan, pulling the sheet up over his head.

'Come on.' Josie snatched at the child. 'Leave your Uncle Stan in peace. Go in with your mother while I make breakfast.'

Rhiannon pouted, clinging stubbornly to the headboard. 'Don't want to. She shouts at me all the time.'

'Behave then.'

Josie pushed the child in with Gwennie and Teresa before bringing Stanley a cup of tea. She sat with him on the bed drinking her own.

'Stan, I'm sorry, love.'

His grin was half-hearted. 'Have we got to have her sleeping in here with us? Why can't she go in with her mother?'

'Rhiannon has always been in with me, Stan. I'm ashamed to say this but Francie is a useless mother. She's got no interest in Rhiannon at all, and no patience either.'

The truth was, Josie knew, she'd been glad to take over the role of mother to the child. And the less Francie influenced Rhiannon, the better.

The thing that had worried her most since the war had ended was that Francie really would get together with the child's father and take Rhiannon away from her. But there had been no sign that he had been in touch, and with every passing month Josie felt the threat lessening.

Stanley looked down into his cup.

'I'd have thought Francie would have rooms of her own elsewhere by now. You've done enough for her. More than enough, so Mam told me. Why can't she get on with her own life instead of sponging on you?'

'Don't be daft, Stan love. I can't turf out my own sister, and her unmarried with a child.'

Josie looked at him keenly. This wasn't like her Stanley at all. She'd never thought of him as being resentful in any way, but since he'd been home she seemed to detect a veiled hostility between him and Francie, and was puzzled by it. Stanley had always been easy-going, willing to muck in. Had the war changed him that much?

'Rhiannon needs looking after properly. I'm sorry the house is so crowded, Stan, but with Mama dying so sudden, like ...'

Josie felt her lips tremble at the memory of her poor mother, and Stanley reached out a hand to touch her face.

'I know, kid. It can't be helped. It's just that we never seem to have a minute to ourselves nowadays. I thought about nothing else when I was away, longing to be with you, Josie.'

She jumped up from the bed, determined not to give way to unhappy thoughts.

'I'll try to keep Rhiannon from under your feet, Stan love. Maybe we can find a bigger place, though I don't know how we'll manage more rent.' She pushed her hair back from her face. 'Haven't heard anything about a job, Stan? Only things are getting tight, see, love. Four extra mouths to feed, like.'

Stanley finished his tea and swung his legs out of bed.

'Been down the Ajax yesterday, saw this foreman mate of mine. Not a sausage going, kid. Went up the steel works in Cwmbwrla, too. Nothing, nor any hope of anything.'

'What about the docks?'

Stanley gave a short laugh.

'Oh, come on, love. Dock work goes back three generations. If your granddad wasn't a docker, you've got no hope.'

Josie sank on to the bed again.

'Oh, Stan, I'm so worried. We've got to find something.'

He put his arms around her, hugging her close. 'Cheer up, kid. If the worst comes to the worst, I can always go round selling firewood, isn't it?'

'How's the job going then, Mam?'

'All right, son. Well, it's a dawdle, really, after the Ajax. Them Council offices don't get real dirty, see, Stan.'

Gwennie warmed a knife in hot water before blending their butter and margarine rations together in a basin to make them go further, the way Josie had shown her.

'Tsk! I'd have thought we'd be off rations by now, Stan, with the war over. How much longer, mun?'

'Going to be a while yet, I reckon,' he said, draining his teacup.

Gwennie thought he sounded dispirited. Her lips tightened. Well, he would be, wouldn't he? No job, and having to share a house with that bloody-minded Francie. Bent on making trouble, she was, you could see it in her face. Always making nasty remarks, especially in front of Josie. Worrying poor Stan to death, anyone could see that. It was a wonder Josie hadn't twigged it already. God help them all when that happened.

'Hey, Stan!' his mother said, in a lighter tone, trying to cheer him up. 'You should've seen your Josie's face the other day when that Kitty O'Sullivan called round here with the kids' ration books and clothes.'

Gwennie giggled, remembering how Josie's face had gone all red and puffed up when she saw that big fat woman standing on the doorstep. 'You could've knocked Josie down with a feather, she was that surprised. That Kitty can't be so bad after all, I told her. I mean, she needn't have bothered.'

Stanley didn't seem to be listening.

'Where's Josie gone?'

'Down the Mumbles to see her friend Daisy. She's taken Rhiannon with her.' Gwennie glanced at her son. 'Lovely little kid, isn't she, Stan? You can be proud of her, son, despite who her mother is.'

He looked up at her, his face dark with strain.

'Oh God, Mam I'm so ashamed, and so bloody sorry it happened.' He ran his fingers through his hair, and Gwennie could see they were trembling. 'What possessed me? What the hell was I thinking of? Me, with a lovely wife like Josie. It was madness, sheer bloody madness! I don't deserve her, I don't.'

Gwennie's face was grim.

'It was that Francie, coming round here when you were on leave that time, knowing Josie was in work. She did it deliberately: leading you on, tricking you. It's her fault, the slut!'

Stanley shook his head.

'Hold on, Mam I can't pile all the blame on Francie. Yes, she caught me at a weak moment—and I *was* weak, God help me! I can't forgive myself, though, Mam. I've done a terrible thing to Josie. And when I see the way Josie lavishes love on Rhiannon, all unsuspecting, it breaks my heart.'

Gwennie nodded. 'She's a real mother to that child. Heart of gold she's got.'

'I love her so much, Mam. I couldn't bear it if she left me. I'd ... I'd do away with myself, I would!'

'Don't talk like that, Stan love!' Gwennie put her hand to her mouth in distress at his words and expression. 'Josie won't find out if we're careful. It's that bloody Francie you've got to watch. She's a vindictive little bitch. How our Josie, who's so loving and kind, could have a sister like that, I don't know ...'

'Oh, aye, saintly bloody Josie,' Francie said loudly, flouncing into the kitchen. 'Anyone would think she was sprouting wings, to listen to you two.'

'You ungrateful little baggage!' spluttered Gwennie, suddenly enraged. 'Pulled you out of the gutter, didn't she, though?'

'And who put me there, then?' Francie snapped back, tossing her head. 'Your blinking Stanley, forcing himself on me, an innocent girl.'

He jumped to his feet, face whitening.

'That's not true, Francie, and you know it. I'm not trying to shift all the blame, but you were no innocent even then. You knew what you were doing, and like the bloody fool I was, I fell for it, hook, line and sinker.'

'You make me puke!' Francie curled her lip in scorn. 'You had your fun, now you're whingeing. You'll be right up the Swannee without a paddle when Josie finds out. I've a damn' good mind to tell her, too. It's time she knew the truth about her precious husband.'

Stanley's expression was grim.

'You're poison ivy, you are, Francie. I must have been off my flipping rocker—stark, raving mad—to be taken in by your tears. A proper little actress you are, pretending you were terrified of your bloody no-good father and had no one else to turn to. You're as bad as him any day. And when I see the way Josie loves little Rhiannon as if she were her own kid, it makes me sick to think we're all deceiving her.'

'Yes, Josie's worth twenty of you, she is,' Gwennie chipped in heatedly. 'You've got the Randalls' bad blood, you have. Rotten to the core.'

Francie looked furious.

'You'll be even sicker, Stanley Jenkins, when Josie hears *you* put me in the family way. All lovey-dovey with her, and seducing me as well? She'll never forgive you, Stanley boyo. She'll pack you in. You'll be out on your arse.'

'You evil little bitch, Francie!'

Stanley came round the table. Alarmed by the sudden savage look in his eyes, Gwennie caught at his arm, fearful that he was too worked up to know what he was doing. His face looked like parchment now, and she felt even more sorry for him.

'I won't be the only one, will I?' he said thickly. Gwennie clung on to his arm, feeling the tremors that were shaking his body. 'You'll be out on your ear, too. You've got it cushy here, Francie, letting Josie take all the responsibility, but you'd never survive on your own.'

She lifted her nose in the air.

'Who says I'd be on my own? Better men than you wouldn't mind keeping company with me.'

Stanley's look was disdainful. 'I believe you! Cheap as cheese, you are, Francie. I've only been home a week but I've seen the way you carry on, coming in all hours. And I'll tell you one thing: if Josie kicks you out of this house, you're not taking *my* daughter with you. You're not a fit mother for a cat.'

Francie looked so furious Gwennie could see spittle bubbling at the corners of her mouth. She was brimming with spite, eyes glassy with it. Had they both gone too far? Pushed her over the edge?

'Well!' Francie gasped out. 'We'll see who has the last laugh.' With that she turned on her heel and ran from the kitchen.

Gwennie gazed after her, biting her lip in consternation.

'Oh, Stan, we shouldn't have lost our tempers. She looks mad enough to do anything. She's going to make trouble, I know she is.'

He sat down heavily at the table, putting his elbows on it and his head in his hands.

'Mam, what am I going to do? It'll finish me if Josie and me part. I can't live without her. She's all I thought about when I was away, all that kept me going. This is a punishment, this is, for my wickedness towards her.'

His shoulders began to heave and Gwennie went to him, putting a comforting hand on his head, stroking his hair. She felt uncomfortable and disconcerted by his sudden tears. It didn't seem natural to see a grown man cry. But she felt like crying, too.

Stanley and Josie were such a happy couple, so much in love, anyone could see it.

Gwennie's lips tightened. That bloody Francie had seen it, and was jealous. She'd wanted to spoil their happiness, that's why she'd deliberately gone after Stanley. Well, it looked like she'd got her way. Josie was a lovely girl, and Gwennie loved her like her own daughter, but there was no getting away from it: when Josie was riled she was like a whirling dervish, striking out first and picking up the pieces later. But later would be too late for her Stanley. His happiness would be over.

Chapter Twenty

Josie gladly accepted Daisy's offer of a cup of tea and a piece of Victoria sponge. They sat in the kitchen while Valerie and Rhiannon played with Valerie's Mickey Mouse tricycle in the back yard. Josie watched them fondly through the window. They were good kids and such firm friends, too, young as they were. She'd never heard them squabbling yet.

It was good to have a real friend, thought Josie, especially when you were in trouble or needed a favour. It was always a pleasure to visit Daisy, but today she had a special reason for coming down to the Mumbles. She had to find a job somewhere and Daisy might be able to help.

'How's Gerald?' Josie asked, and was astonished to see Daisy's eyes immediately fill up with tears. She reached across the table to touch her friend's arm. 'Daisy love, what is it?'

Her lips were trembling so much that Josie saw she wasn't able to answer straight away. She had suspected for some time that Gerald was not getting any better, that things were

326

not as they should be. Obviously something had happened.

'Oh, Josie, the situation is unbearable. I don't think I can stand much more of it.' Daisy took a deep gulp, choking on her own words. 'I told you Valerie and her father don't get on? Well, now Gerald denies she's his daughter. Denies it! He accused me of being unfaithful. After all I've sacrificed ...'

Daisy burst into tears, laying her arms and head on the table. Josie jumped up immediately and went to her, putting an arm around her shoulders, hugging her tightly.

'Oh, kid, I'm so sorry. Is there anything I can do?'

Daisy lifted her head, sobbing.

'I don't see what anyone can do. I can't go on, Josie. I'm so lonely. I haven't told you before, but Gerald and I don't share a bed now.'

She looked up, and Josie thought she saw shame in her eyes along with tears.

'I tried, Josie, I really tried to put our marriage together again. I've made ... overtures ... but he won't ... can't ... oh! I don't know what it is. But it's like living with a complete stranger, a hostile stranger; like living with the dead. And now this insult! I know he's not himself, but this is too much to bear.'

Josie pulled up a chair and sat close to her friend. Daisy was falling to pieces right in front of her. Josie thought back to the time during the war when they'd first met. Daisy was her own woman then. She had been a young widow, or so she'd thought. She'd come to terms with life and was making the best of it. It had been wonderful to see her blossom again when she'd fallen in love with Rhodri Lewis. How quickly and tragically that happiness had been smashed.

'You don't have to bear it, Daisy love,' Josie said soothingly. 'Rhodri said, didn't he, that Gerald would be better off in an institution? Listen to him, mun. He knows what he's talking about.'

Daisy turned brimming eyes on her.

'I can't do it, Josie. Although he's upset me, denying Valerie, I feel such pity for him, what he's suffered, what he's still suffering.' She put the heel of her hand against her eyes to wipe away the tears that were streaming down her cheeks. 'Gerald has shut himself off from me, from all of us, but I can't shut him away in an institution and forget him. That's inhuman.'

'What does Edie think?'

Daisy looked startled.

'Mam knows nothing about it.'

'What?'

'I can't bring myself to tell her. She'd only ...'

'Do something about it?' Josie said quickly. 'Edie would get it sorted double-quick, I know hen You're afraid she'll do something drastic.'

Daisy nodded. 'I have to work it out myself. It's my problem, Josie.'

'Is it? What about Rhodri? My God, Daisy, you've only got to look at him to know how much he loves you, and I know you feel the same. How can you stay away from him?'

Daisy bit her lip, and began to trace patterns

with her nail on the table cloth.

'We have being seeing each other.' She looked at Josie, eyes widening. 'Oh, it's all completely innocent, Josie. He's been here a few times since he visited Gerald. We just talk. He's such a comfort to be with, just knowing he loves me, knowing that I'm not dead, too.'

'I'm glad, kid.'

Daisy swallowed, obviously trying to pull herself together. She pushed her fingers through her hair, and straightened the collar of her blouse.

'Rhodri's bought a house at the top of Newton,' she said, a little more calmly. 'Do you know, the poor darling suggested Valerie and I move in there with him?' She smiled weakly. 'I told him he'd be ruined, we both would. Can you imagine?'

Josie patted her friend's arm, feeling very sad for her. Her own problems were bad enough, but she didn't know the half of it. How would she cope in Daisy's shoes? She didn't have her friend's patience or tolerance. Josie wouldn't let anyone or anything come between her and Stanley. They'd never be parted.

'There must be some way out of this situation, kid,' she said. 'Why don't you ask Gerald what he wants? He may agree to go into a place.'

Daisy sighed. 'No. None of this is really his fault. I can't hurt him, although ... in a way I am.' She looked earnestly at Josie. 'It's all innocent with Rhodri at the moment, Josie, but I'm afraid one day our feelings for each other will be too much for us, and we'll do something we'll regret.'

'How can it be wrong when you love each other?' she said gently. 'You'd have been man and wife long ago if it hadn't been for Gerald coming back. You said yourself, he's like a dead man. You're young and alive, Daisy, my girl, and Rhodri loves you. Many women would give their right arm for a good man to love them the way he loves you. An arm, and a leg as well, kid!'

Daisy smiled. 'You wouldn't blame me then?'

'Blame you? I'd be cheering you on!'

'Oh, Josie, you are a tonic.' Daisy pushed herself up from the table. 'Have another cup of tea. You must be parched after listening to me moaning. How are things with you, anyway? Has Stanley found a job yet?'

Josie settled back on the kitchen chair with a sigh.

'No such luck, kiddo. I confess, I came down today to ask a favour. But, my goodness, my problems are nothing compared to yours!'

'Any favour I can do for you, Josie, I will gladly, you know that,' Daisy said.

Josie sat forward eagerly.

'I was wondering if there was a job going for me at Edie's guest house? I'll do anything. Scrub floors, make beds. I'm desperate for a job, kid. Stan can't find anything, and money's getting tight now I've got my brothers and sister with us.'

'Drink up,' Daisy said briskly. 'We'll go up now and see her.'

They walked up to *Tŷ Heulwen,* the two children in their pushchairs. When Daisy went upstairs to speak to Gerald before they left Woodville Road, Josie heard his complaining voice and couldn't help feeling angry on her friend's behalf. Perhaps it wasn't Gerald's fault, but he certainly wasn't helping in any way. Josie knew if she were in Daisy's shoes she'd speak her mind, show him just how she felt in no uncertain terms. Perhaps there was such a thing as being too patient and tolerant, too duty-bound?

Daisy let them in through the back door and into the big sweet-smelling kitchen of *Tŷ Heulwen.* Edie was at the table kneading dough vigorously.

'Tsk, Mam! Why do you wear yourself out making bread every day,' Daisy began, 'when you can get lovely bread from the Co-op baker delivered to the door?'

'I prefer my own, madam, if you don't mind,' Edie replied tartly. She looked keenly at Daisy. 'Your eyes look red. Have you been crying, lovey?'

Daisy turned to get Valerie out of her pushchair, mumbling something inaudible.

'Hello, Mrs Philpots,' Josie said quickly, to cover for her friend. 'There's a lovely smell of baking bread. You can't beat home-made, can you?'

Edie smiled. 'Ah! someone with a bit of sense.'

As soon as Valerie was unbuckled she ran to her grandmother, Rhiannon right behind her, watching, finger in her mouth, as Valerie clutched at Edie's skirt, tugging insistently.

'Nanna! Can I have a Welsh cake, please? And one for Rhia.'

'Please!' Rhiannon echoed, hopefully.

When the Welsh cakes were doled out, the children went to squat on stools in front of the range. Edie nodded towards the kettle.

'Make a cup of tea for both of you,' she said to Daisy.

'Thanks, but we've just had one. Listen, Mam, Josie is looking for work, any kind of work. She was wondering if you've something for her here?'

'I'm willing to do anything,' Josie said quickly. She realised she sounded over-eager, but couldn't help it. She was getting desperate, and it was no good pretending otherwise. 'Don't care what it is.'

Edie regarded her speculatively for a moment, then went to the sink to wash her hands. Josie waited patiently and hopefully. Maybe it was exaggerating to say this was her last hope, but in truth she had tried everywhere else. She would dearly love to work as an alteration hand in some good ladies' outfitters, but that was wishing for the moon. If Edie could fix her up with some job at the guest house, anything, she'd be so grateful.

'There may be something,' said Edie, wiping her hands carefully. 'I've been thinking about it for a while now. We can't talk here, though. Vera Pugh will be in shortly to start the lunches, and she's all ears. I don't want this to get about the village, not until it's settled anyway,' she added mysteriously. 'Let's go up to my living-room. We can talk in comfort there.'

In the quiet back living-room Josie sat on the very edge of the settee, wondering what Edie had in mind. Was her luck in after all? She couldn't afford to get her hopes up too high, though. As desperately as she wanted work, she had family responsibilities, too. Whatever work or hours Edie might suggest, Josie had to think of Rhiannon.

'Now, then,' Edie began. 'I've got a proposition for you, Josie. It's ambitious, but I think we can make a success of it. Of course, it all depends on you, and how you feel about it ...'

'Mam!' Daisy interrupted, sitting forward impatiently. 'For goodness' sake, stop being mysterious and get to the point. You're making Josie a bag of nerves. She doesn't know what's going on, and neither do I.'

'Right!' Edie nodded. 'Well, it's this, Josie. I've been watching you over the past few months. I'm really impressed with your dress-making skills. I thought it clever, brilliant even, the way you designed that dress for my Amy when she'd given you only a rough sketch of what she wanted. All the talent is going to waste, and it's such a shame.'

'Mam!'

'All right, I'm coming to it. I propose we set up in business together, Josie. A nice little made-to-measure outfitter's shop in the village. A partnership, of course.'

Josie felt her mouth drop open in astonishment. Did Edie say partnership? Edie wanted *her* for a partner? She couldn't believe what she was hearing. She must be mistaken. Josie could feel her hands begin to tremble in her lap. Please don't let it be a mistake.

'What? Me!'

'That's a smashing idea,' Daisy said. 'My word, Mam, you've got your head screwed on the right way, haven't you? A little gold mine it would be. What do you think, Josie?'

She swallowed hard. Daisy's words seemed to confirm she wasn't mistaken after all.

'I'm flabbergasted,' she said breathlessly.

She *was* astonished. Edie was offering her a partnership in a shop. She'd be her own boss. She could hardly catch her breath at the thought of the possibilities.

Then, suddenly, her elation and rising excitement crashed to earth. How could she be a partner with anyone when she had no money to put into the business? Disappointment was like a lump of ice in her stomach, cold yet burning at the same time. She'd been offered a wonderful prize only to have it snatched away the next minute.

Josie felt her shoulders sag as she gazed at Edie.

'It's a wonderful idea, Mrs Philpots. But,' she said quietly, 'I don't have any money for a partnership.'

'Oh, call me Edie, there's a good girl,' she said quickly. 'I've got all the money we'll need,' she went on. 'The only contribution I want from you, Josie, is your marvellous skill as a dress-maker and designer. We need each other, you see.'

Josie put a hand to her mouth. She had an urge to burst out laughing with joy and excitement again. She suddenly felt too overcome to say anything, could only smile and smile.

Edie nodded, showing she understood perfectly how Josie felt.

'Years ago, Josie, when I was down on my luck as you are now, a very wonderful woman gave me the same kind of chance as I'm giving you.' Edie, glanced at her stepdaughter. 'Daisy, you remember dear Dulcie Dewhurst, don't you?'

She nodded, smiling.

'Dulcie set me up as her partner in a café in town,' Edie went on. 'And I've never looked back. When she passed away, she left me this lovely house.'

Edie paused for a moment and Josie saw the older woman's eyes glistening with tears.

'I owe everything to her.'

And your own flair and determination, Mam,' Daisy said quickly, sliding an arm around her stepmother's shoulders for a moment. 'The café and this guest house are successful because of your sheer hard work.'

Edie lifted her chin, sniffing loudly, then laughed.

'Dulcie was a tower of strength, you know. It's silly but I miss her still, after all these years.'

'I don't think it's silly,' Josie said quietly. She was gazing at Edie, seeing her clearly, perhaps for the first time. She knew exactly what Edie meant. This Dulcie Dewhurst had been her salvation, as Edie would be Josie's. But would she come up to her benefactor's expectations?

'Do you really think I could do it, Edie?'

'If I didn't think so, Josie, I would never have suggested it. Now let's make plans ...' Edie sat forward eagerly, and with excitement beginning to bubble up inside her, Josie did the same. Was she dreaming this?

'I'll make some tea,' Daisy said, rising to her feet. 'Come on, girls,' she called to the two children, who were happily playing with their dolls on the rug in front of the fire. 'I think I know where there's an extra couple of Welsh cakes.'

'Now,' Edie said, 'to set your mind at rest I'll have my solicitor draw up the necessary documents next week. I've seen some premises that I think would be ideal for us on Newton Road. I've already made enquiries about them, but we must look at them together, just to be sure we agree.'

'I'll be guided by you,' Josie said, almost shyly. She wasn't all that certain what a partnership meant, what was expected of her.

Edie smiled.

'We're partners, Josie, equal partners. I value your opinion. You're a young woman with a lot of good sound commonsense.'

Josie felt her face glow with pleasure. Here was someone who took her seriously, who really valued her. That was a novelty. Stanley valued her, she knew that, but only as a good, loving wife. Now Edie, was showing her that she was more than that. It would take some getting used to, the idea that she and Edie Philpots, café owner and proprietor of a successful guest house, could be in any way equal. After all, she *was* only the daughter of a rag-and-bone man.

'You must advise me about the workshop,' Edie said, settling back against the cushions. 'The best situation for it and what equipment to buy. Then, of course, we must think about workroom staff. But I'll leave that to you, Josie. That's your sphere. You know the kind of people you'll want us to employ.'

Josie found she couldn't sit back and relax. Her heart was knocking against her ribs painfully. Was she getting into deep water here? Was it lapping over her head already? What on earth did *she* know about employing people? It began to dawn on her that this partnership meant taking on tremendous responsibility. What Edie proposed wouldn't come cheap. A great deal of her money would be at stake. Josie bit her lip. This was a chance to make all her dreams come true, but was she up to it? Would it all end in disaster?

'Edie, I'm not sure ...'

'I know what you're thinking,' Edie interrupted quickly. 'You're worried about travelling up from Swansea every day. I've got the answer. If you agree, that is?'

Josie shook her head, managing a weak smile. Travelling was the least of her worries.

'That's not what's bothering me ...'

Edie leaned forward again, her gaze eager.

'I'll take care of all the business side. You do what you do best, Josie: create good clothes for people who will appreciate them. The country's in a bad way now, but things are bound to improve. I'm sure in a few years there'll be plenty of money about, and this clothes rationing can't last for ever.'

'I don't want to let you down, Edie.'

Smiling, she reached out and put a hand on Josie's knee.

'I didn't get where I am today by misjudging people,' she said. 'Like you, I thought I'd never cope with the business side of things, especially after Dulcie died, but I did, and I discovered strengths I never knew I had. Trust me, Josie.'

She pressed her fingers against her mouth, not knowing whether she wanted to laugh or cry. She'd come looking for a job, any job, and next moment she was being offered a partnership. What would Stanley say? And the rest of the family? So many mouths to feed. This was a golden opportunity and really she couldn't afford to say no, could she?

Josie gathered up her courage and clung to it. 'It's a deal.'

Edie sat back again with a satisfied sigh.

'Good! Now, about accommodation. I have a nice little house in Church Road for you to rent. You wouldn't mind moving down from Swansea, would you?'

Josie cupped her chin thoughtfully. Move to the Mumbles? That would be wonderful, but was it practical?

'There are seven of us now—well, eight, counting my mother-in-law,' she said. 'I couldn't leave her on her own.'

'The Church Road house is too small, then,' Edie said, thinking hard. 'Wait! I have it. I've recently bought two more houses in Woodville Road.' She smiled. 'Property is still the ideal investment. One is next door to Daisy, and the other is only a few doors further up the road, next door to my mother. You could have both of them. I'm sure we can come to some arrangement about the rent. Come on, let's shake on it.'

Edie held out a hand and Josie, after a split second's hesitation, grasped it, shaking it solemnly, suddenly feeling overcome by it all.

'You're very good to me, Edie. I really don't know how to thank you. Especially for believing in me.'

Edie's grasp was firm, and her smile warm.

'Well, after all, Josie lovey, we're as good as family, aren't we?'

Chapter Twenty-One

Josie manoeuvred the pushchair over the threshold and into the comparative warmth of home. It had been a cold walk from the Mumbles train-stop on Oystermouth Road. Rhiannon had grizzled all the way, despite being tucked up in a rug. But Josie couldn't blame her. It was bitterly cold. She would be glad to see the back of January and February. Spring would be just around the corner then; spring and a new life for them all.

She was getting Rhiannon out of the pushchair when Francie came rushing down the stairs and stood posed on the bottom step, hand on the newel post as if posing for a photograph. Her expression was defiant; mouth tight, like a little prune. That expression usually spelt trouble.

'Josie, I've got something to say—something important to tell you.'

The next instant Stanley ran up from the kitchen, taking the stairs two at a time. Charging into the passage, he threw a dark glance at Francie.

'Josie! Listen, love ...'

Behind him Josie saw Gwennie struggling up the stairs, too, her big chest heaving from the exertion.

'Josie, don't listen to her, kid,' Gwennie said, her cheeks puffed out with panting. 'She's just a spiteful little bitch ...'

'Shut up, you fat old cow!' Francie screeched at her.

Instantly, there was bedlam, with the three of them all shouting at each other. To Josie it was an incoherent, senseless babble, and she wanted to clap her hands over her ears.

Francie was standing stiff and primed, like a cat about to spring into a fight. Gwennie was leaning against the passage wall, out of breath but gamely waving a fist at Francie. And Stanley ... Josie could only stare at him in astonishment.

Stanley had both his fists in the air about his head, face red, voice hoarse with rage.

Rhiannon had run to sit on the bottom stair, but when everyone started to shout she stared up at them, each in turn, then burst into tears. This was too much for Josie. They were spoiling her very special day, her grand surprise.

'Be quiet, Rhiannon, there's a good girl!' She turned on the others. 'and shut up as well, you bloody lot!'

'It's his fault, Josie.' Francie pointed an accusing finger at Stanley, almost squealing in fury. She came off the stair at a run, fetching up by Josie's side, grabbing at her arm. 'It's him!'

'Don't listen, love,' Stanley said.

Josie snatched her arm away, glaring round at them all. She had been cold but so happy coming home. Full of dreams and possibilities, plans and ideas. Their petty squabbling was spoiling everything.

This was her big day, the first day of the rest of her life. Nobody was going to ruin it for her. Whatever their problem was, it didn't matter a hoot compared to what she had to tell them.

'I turn my back for a minute and you're at each other's throats. Well, I don't want to hear about it, right? Got that? I'm sick of you bickering all the time.'

'But Josie ...' Francie was grabbing at her shoulder. 'I'm trying to tell you something you ought to know, mun. Really important, it is.'

'Important?' snapped Josie, shrugging her off. She picked up Rhiannon, who was still snivelling, and moved away towards the stairs to go down to the basement living-room. 'There's only one thing important in this house at the moment, Francie, and that's trying to earn a living. While all of you have been wasting time arguing here, I've been out, finding us a future.'

They all followed her downstairs. With Rhiannon in her arms she turned to face them as they crowded into the room.

'You can all start packing up as soon as you like because the weekend after next we're moving to the Mumbles, lock, stock and barrel.'

It delighted Josie to see them look flabbergasted, and in the stunned silence that followed her words they just stared at her. Stanley was the first to find his voice, and sounded bemused.

'We're what, love?'

'What the flipping heck are you talking about, Josie?' Francie scowled.

Josie put Rhiannon on her feet. The child ran off to play, her sunny disposition restored now that the shouting had stopped. Josie felt gleeful, her earlier irritation with her family evaporated. They'd be even more astonished to hear the rest of her news. She couldn't wait to see their faces when she told them about the partnership.

'You'd better sit down, all of you,' she said, and couldn't help grinning from ear to ear like the Cheshire Cat. '*I've* got something to tell *you*. And this *is* important.'

Gwennie was the only one who sat down, though, probably glad to get the weight off her feet. Stanley's eyes were as round as saucers as he gazed at Josie, but Francie's eyes narrowed, perhaps already guessing they had reached a turning point in their lives and feeling jealous because it wasn't her triumph.

'I'm going into business down the Mumbles,' Josie said airily, enjoying the sensation she must be causing. 'I'm going into partnership with Edie Philpots.'

The reaction was not what she'd expected.

'But she keeps a guest house,' Francie said, frowning furiously. 'What are you going to do down there, then? Make the beds, empty the slops?'

'Wash you ears out, Francie!' Josie snapped, disappointed at not being swamped in congratulations. 'I said a partnership. We're opening a made-to-measure outfitters in the village. We'll have a workroom, and it's my job to pick the staff.' She couldn't help lifting her chin a little higher. 'I'm going to be an employer.'

'Oh, my God!' Francie turned away and flopped into a chair. 'Are you going barmy or what? You haven't got a ha'penny to scratch your bum with, let alone go into partnership.'

'I don't need capital, clever clogs,' Josie flashed back. 'Edie's providing that. I provide the skill and flair for designing and making clothes.' She felt her features stiffen up like cardboard, seeing the smirk on her sister's face. 'Edie believes in me anyway!' she went on loudly.

Stanley came forward to put his arms around her.

'I believe in you too, kid. It's just a bit of a surprise, that's all.' He kissed her on the temple. 'Congratulations, love. I always knew you had it

343

in you, though. I always said, didn't I, Mam?'

'Oh, listen to him!' Francie's lip curled in disgust. 'Buttering you up now, he is. Smarmy bugger.'

'Now don't start again, Francie!' Josie warned angrily. She might have known her sister would try to throw cold water over everything, just for spite.

Francie stood up, hands on hips.

'Partnership, my foot! I think it's a lot of blooming nonsense. Who the heck do you think you are, Josie?'

She ground her teeth in vexation, taking a few steps forward to confront her sister.

'I'll tell you who I am,' she said furiously. 'I'm the one who's doing everything she can to get us out of the mess we're in. My savings ... you know the ones I mean, don't you, Francie? The ones you wanted to *borrow*, like? Well, they're almost gone now, after having to pay for Mama's funeral when Dada washed his hands of it. We're more or less broke, and that means you're going to go hungry.'

Francie pouted.

'What are you on about? I'm not going hungry. I'm working.'

'Looking tarty behind a bar? I don't call that work,' Josie sneered. 'Why don't you try getting a proper job with a decent wage? You've been scrounging off me and Gwennie for ages. I only put up with it because of Rhiannon.'

'Oh, yes, Rhiannon.' Francie looked past Josie to sweep a glance at the others.

'Now don't start arguing again, Francie,' Josie

344

warned quickly. 'Unlike you, I'm determined to make something of myself. I don't want to be remembered as the rag-and-bone man's daughter. I'm going to achieve something worthwhile, and Edie Philpots has given me the chance. Nobody's going to spoil it for me. Nobody! Got that?'

'Josie, love.' Stanley came to her, putting an arm around her waist, pulling her close to him. 'I don't want to hold you back, kid, nor Mam neither. I think this shop thing is wonderful. And you deserve it too. I'm going to try hard to get a job, honest. But what's all this about moving to the Mumbles?'

Feeling mollified, she reached up and planted a kiss on his cheek, ignoring the sound of a raspberry being blown by Francie.

'We said we needed a bigger place, didn't we, now Johnno and the kids are with us?' she said. 'We're going to rent two houses from Edie in Woodville Road. It'll be ideal. I'll be close to the new shop, and the Mumbles is a lovely place to live. Think of it! Living at the seaside.'

'We were almost doing that in Victor Street,' Francie remarked scathingly. 'What about my job? I'm not giving it up. I like being a tarty barmaid.'

Josie waved a dismissive hand.

'There are plenty of buses and the Mumbles train. You'll manage.'

'Oh, will I? Well, I've got news for you, Lady Muck,' Francie said, lifting her nose in defiance. 'I'm not moving from by here. You lot can do as you like, but me and Rhiannon are staying.'

'Now wait a bloody minute!' Stanley said furiously to her. 'That child isn't going anywhere with you. I warned you, didn't I, Francie?'

His face was turning red with fury, and Josie was touched by his jumping in to protect her feelings. Stanley already realised how much she loved Rhiannon, as if she were Josie's child. He knew she'd break her heart if Francie took the child away.

She was angry with her sister too, but what she realised and Stanley obviously didn't, was that it was more bravado on her sister's part than anything else. Josie had never been more convinced that Francie had no real interest in Rhiannon. She'd proved that over and over since the child had been born. The last thing her sister wanted was to be saddled with her just when she was beginning to have herself such a good time. No, Francie was bluffing, trying to put a spoke in the wheel, anything to spoil things. Mam had been right about her, she was eaten up with envy. Well, thought Josie, for once she was going to call her bluff.

'Hold on a minute, Stan,' she said, reasonably and calmly. 'If Francie wants to stick by here, pay the rent on this place and look after Rhiannon as well, that's up to her, isn't it?'

'You bet it is,' Francie sniffed, but Josie thought her cheeks had paled a little.

'I think you're right, Fran,' Josie went on. 'Rhiannon is your daughter, after all. You've got a right.'

Stanley looked agitated. 'Josie love ...'

'No, Stan, it's the best thing, and I'll get

346

over it, don't you worry. After all, I'm going to be very busy from now on, setting up my business. I won't have a lot of time for looking after somebody else's child. It's time Francie took responsibility. Gwennie and I have been carrying her for too long.'

Francie had her thumb in her mouth now, biting the nail. Her eyes darted. She was doing quite a lot of quick thinking now her bluff had been called, and Josie was happy to see her squirm; happy to push her further into a corner.

'Ever since Rhiannon was born, Francie hasn't had a moment's trouble. Coming and going any time she wanted; staying out until all hours. I don't think she's changed a nappy more than half a dozen times. Have you, Fran?'

Francie's mouth closed up into that prune shape again.

'You think you're very funny, don't you, Josie?'

'Oh, I don't think it's funny, Fran.' She looked at her sister wide-eyed. 'I think you're very brave, taking on the responsibility all alone. You up by here and us down the Mumbles—all of us, because Gwennie's coming, too. Aren't you, Gwen?'

'Oh, yes, kid!' Gwennie was beaming now.

She had been very quiet since Josie had announced their move, probably thinking she was going to be left behind. Josie had no intention of letting that happen. She'd always liked her mother-in-law, and since they'd been living together and sharing responsibility for

347

Rhiannon, Josie had grown to love the older woman. She might be a bit slap-dash, but Gwennie had a good and generous heart, like Mama.

Josie shook her head sadly.

'Yes, it's going to be tough, Francie kid. There won't be a lot of time for enjoyment. Queuing for the rations, doing the washing, cooking, cleaning, taking care of Rhiannon ... Mind, you'll have to find somebody to look after her when you're in work in the evenings. Perhaps one of the neighbours will do it for a couple of bob? I hope you can afford it. Still, you'll manage, won't you?'

'She'll blinking well have to,' Gwennie said cheerfully.

Francie compressed her lips so hard they almost disappeared.

'You're all against me, but you'll be sorry, I promise you!'

Spraying them all with a look of fury, Francie turned on her heel and dashed out of the room.

That settled that, Josie thought, with some satisfaction. She'd be surprised if there was anymore talk of Francie staying on.

She became aware that Stanley was watching her with wonder on his face, and hid a smile. She'd surprised him. She'd surprised herself.

'Well, I'd better get on with the kids' tea,' she said to no one in particular. 'They'll be home from school in a minute. I wonder if Johnno has found any work?'

She felt exceptionally pleased with the way

the day had gone. Since Edie's offer she felt more confident, more sure of herself. She wasn't just a rag-and-bone man's daughter after all. She was much more than that, and she was going to prove it.

Chapter Twenty-Two

February 1946

When Gwennie stepped off the Mumbles train at Oystermouth station she thought the icy gale blowing in from the sea would knock her off her feet before freezing her into a solid block.

The wind was whipping up from the sea, and she could feel cold spray on her face—cold enough to burn like acid. Even the air tasted salty. She couldn't see the water in the late-evening darkness, but she could hear the waves dashing against the promenade wall. She thought she could smell snow. Thank God it was Friday. Day off tomorrow. And it was Rhiannon's birthday.

Head bent against the wind, she clutched her parcel closer to her as she crossed Oystermouth Square and made her way up the Dunns towards Woodville Road. It wouldn't do to lose Rhiannon's birthday present, especially when she'd splashed out most of her wage packet on it: a beautiful doll in a red velvet dress. Rhiannon would love it. She could hardly believe the child would be two years old tomorrow. Where had the time flown?

Gwennie gave an inner sigh. She would give anything to be able to tell people she had a lovely little granddaughter. She'd love to show her off, boast about her at work as other women did about their grandchildren.

Gwennie turned the corner into Woodville Road. Of course, if that time ever came it would mean Stanley was in deep trouble. How relieved he'd been when Josie decided that Francie would live in the rented house further up the street with Teresa and the two boys.

Of course, Francie pretended it didn't suit her, grumbling all the time about being parted from Rhiannon. But it was just the ticket for her really. Gwennie could read her like a book. Francie could come and go all hours. Those Randall kids wouldn't be any the wiser. As long as she didn't start bringing blokes back with her. That's what Josie worried about, she had told Gwennie. Still, the kids were much happier now than they had ever been in Victor Street.

Stanley didn't look so drawn and worried since they'd moved down the Mumbles, either. He would be happier still, though, if only he could find work. But at least with Francie out of the way there were no arguments or fights. He could relax a bit.

Gwennie let herself into the house, going quietly into the front room to hide the parcel behind the sofa. After taking off her coat and head scarf, she went into the living-room, hoping Stanley had a cup of tea ready for her.

She could do with one, she still felt that cold.

He was sitting in the armchair in front of the grate, eyes closed, legs outstretched, gently snoring. Rhiannon was sitting on the mat at his feet, playing with a wooden horse on wheels.

'Gwennie! Look, Gwennie.' Rhiannon held the toy out for her inspection, little face beaming. 'Look what Val gave me. She said I could keep it.'

'There's lovely, chick,' Gwennie answered absently, looking at the grate with irritation. The fire had dwindled to almost nothing because Stanley hadn't bothered to put on any coal. Just when she wanted a bit of warmth, too.

'Stan!' She kicked at his foot.

He almost jumped out of the chair.

'Oh, Mam, it's you, is it? I thought it was that blinking Francie again.'

'What's the matter with you, Stan, mun? Put a bit of coal on, will you? And use that newspaper by there to draw it up. Let's have a bit of comfort, shall we? I'm perished. Did the kids come in for their tea?'

Stan picked up the coal scuttle, threw a few lumps on the fire.

'No. Now Josie's so busy with the shop, Edie's mother Margaret says she'll go in and get their tea every day as she's only next door. The kids are over the moon, especially Dewi. She makes a big fuss of him.'

'*Duw!* There's good of her,' Gwennie said. 'Especially as that old leg of hers is playing her up. And where's our Josie?'

'Came home, had her tea. Now she's gone

back up Newton Road with Edie Philpots. There's a lot of scrubbing to do or something, before they can start fitting it out.'

He held the newspaper against the grate opening, letting the draught draw up the flames.

'I dunno, Mam, there seems an awful lot of work involved with this partnership. I hope Josie hasn't taken on too much.'

'She's landed, mun. Her dream is coming true,' Gwennie assured him as she went in to the kitchenette to put the kettle on the gas ring. 'Francie's been in, has she? What did *she* want, then?'

Stanley came after her, leaning a shoulder against the door frame.

'Came in pretending to be worried about Rhiannon. Says I'm trying to turn the child against her.' He ran his fingers through his hair. 'She only came in to have a go at me, though, reminding me she's got me over a barrel. Says I owe her something, and she can make it hot for me with Josie any time she likes.'

Gwennie ground her teeth in fury as she poured boiling water into the teapot.

'Little blackmailer!' she said, reaching for the tea cosy. 'She'll come to a bad end, she will, mark my words.'

For two pins she'd go up the road and give that Francie a piece of her mind. But Francie had gone to work long since, and it wouldn't have done any good anyway. Probably only make things worse.

'Come on, Stan love,' she said. 'Sit down by here and have a cup of tea.'

Stanley sat with his elbows on the table, hands clasped tightly together.

'Mam, I've been thinking. Why don't I make a clean breast of it to Josie? You know, before Francie can say anything. I don't think I can go on like this much longer.'

Gwennie sat down at the table, biting her bottom lip in vexation. She knew how he was feeling. Sometimes she longed for the truth to come out, too. It would get Francie off their backs once and for all, and Gwennie could openly acknowledge Rhiannon as her grandchild. On the other hand, there was every likelihood that the truth would destroy Stanley's marriage. Josie had many virtues, but forgiveness wasn't one of them.

'Steady on, Stan love,' she said carefully. 'Josie is wound up with excitement about the shop at the moment. You know they plan to open in the summer. I think it's a bad time to tell her something like this. Very bad. Leave it a bit longer. You'll find a job soon, I'm sure. You'll be out of Francie's way, then.'

He looked grim.

'I've a feeling that's just what she's waiting for. She knows I haven't two ha'pennies to rub together at the moment. She's just waiting her chance.'

Gwennie put a hand on his shoulder.

'Stan love, don't do anything hasty. You'll regret it, I know you will.'

He gave a wry smile.

'Too late, Mam. I already did something hasty two years and nine months ago tomorrow.

353

And there's nothing in the world I regret more.'

Josie was washing the breakfast dishes at the sink in the kitchenette. She smiled as she watched Rhiannon playing outside with her friends Valerie and Shirley. Cold as March was, they were happy strutting up and down the back yard in their Welsh costumes: plaid shawls and tall hats made out of shiny black cardboard.

Stanley glanced over her shoulder as he helped wipe the dishes.

'You'd think they'd have had enough of that yesterday,' he said. 'Looks like St David's Day is going to last well into next week.'

'Bless them!' Josie said, with a laugh.

She laughed a lot lately, she realised, and it was a funny thing because, apart from being her own boss now, there wasn't much to laugh about. There were still eight mouths to feed and the rent on two houses to find each week, though she was sure Edie wouldn't press her if things got too bad.

And what with the Government cutting down on the rations last month, and money being so tight with Stanley not working and no income coming in from her partnership with Edie, things were pretty grim. Life was far from funny at the moment, yet she had never felt happier.

She was busier, too, than she'd ever been before. The premises on Newton Road were ideal, yet there was a lot of work needed to make the shop ready for business in the summer as they had planned. When she wasn't helping to get the place ship-shape, she was interviewing workroom staff—a nerve-racking job, she found. And she still had to find time for the usual dress-making jobs, their only source of money except for Gwennie's contribution to the housekeeping.

'Once we reach the first days of March,' Josie said cheerfully, 'I always feel spring has arrived.'

'Don't feel like it,' Stanley said gloomily. 'I had to break the ice in the lav again this morning.'

'You're a pessimist,' Josie said, giving him a dig in the ribs with her elbow.

'It's hard not to be when you're out of work.'

She turned to him, reaching up to frame his face in her wet hands.

'My poor old love,' she said sympathetically. 'Something will turn up, I know it will.'

Someone knocking on the front door interrupted their kissing.

Josie wiped her wet hands quickly.

'I'll go, Gwen,' she called to her mother-in-law, sitting in the living-room listening to the wireless.

She opened the door to find Edie's husband standing there.

'Good morning, Mrs Jenkins.'

'Mr Philpots!' Josie exclaimed in surprise. 'I'm meeting Edie later up the shop. Is something wrong? Is she ill?'

William Philpots removed his trilby, smiling.

'No, no, nothing like that.'

He had a nice smile, Josie noticed not for the first time, with an open and pleasant face, and soft brown eyes behind horn-rimmed spectacles.

'Oh, come in, come in,' she urged, stepping back quickly. 'There's rude you'll think I am, keeping you standing on the doorstep like this.'

William stepped into the passage and Josie led the way into the living-room. He nodded to Gwennie, who was hastily running a comb through her hair.

'My mother-in-law, Mrs Gwennie Jenkins,' Josie introduced them. 'This is Mr Philpots, Gwen. Edie's husband.'

Gwennie was all smiles, eyes bright with curiosity.

Josie indicated William should take a seat, then sat down herself. After a moment's hesitation he sat on a straight chair at the side near the door.

'I've come to talk to you about your brother, Mrs Jenkins. The older one.'

'Johnno?' Josie was startled, a hand going to her throat. Where was Stanley? Was he going to stick in the kitchenette all morning? 'What's he done, Mr Philpots?'

'Quite a lot,' William said, smiling still. 'According to my mother-in-law.'

'Mrs Bayliss?'

'Johnno's been making himself very useful to her, apparently,' William went on. 'Chopping wood, fetching coal, running messages. She

356

thinks he deserves a job, and she's asked me to look into it.'

'A job?' Josie felt her jaw drop open with astonishment.

'I have a builder's merchant's business in Swansea,' William said, 'and I'm looking for a boy to work in the stores there. Mind you, I'll have to talk to him first, of course, to judge if he's suitable.'

Josie swallowed hard against her rising excitement.

'I understand, Mr Philpots.'

'Is he about?'

'He lives at the other house we rent,' she explained.

Gwennie bobbed up from her chair.

'I'll go and fetch him,' she volunteered quickly, and Josie was grateful to her.

'This is very good of you, Mr Philpots,' she said, when Gwennie had gone. 'Johnno's a good boy. Sensible. And he's very quick on the uptake.'

She could hear the eagerness in her own voice and felt embarrassed for a moment, then realised she was being foolish. Edie knew very well how desperate they were for money. There was nothing shameful in that. Perhaps a year from now things would be very different for them.

Stanley decided to come out of the kitchenette then and Josie quickly introduced him to William Philpots, who got up from his chair immediately to shake hands.

There was an anxious expression on Stanley's

face and Josie knew he had been eavesdropping in the kitchenette.

'You wouldn't have a job for me, would you, Mr Philpots?' he asked. 'I can turn my hand to just about anything.'

'There's sorry I am, Mr Jenkins.' William looked crestfallen and apologetic. 'I'm obliged to keep any openings for demobbed men who worked for us before the war. They're entitled to their old jobs back, you see. What I'm offering Johnno is only a trainee's job, a boy's pay not a man's.'

Stanley's shoulders sagged, and Josie felt so sorry for him. It just wasn't fair, was it? Stanley's previous employer had gone to the wall a year or two after the war had started. There was nothing for *him* to come back to.

'I'll keep my eyes and ears open, though,' William said cheerfully. 'Don't get down-hearted.'

Josie saw Stanley's face cloud over and reached out to touch his arm, fearful that he would say something hasty to William. Somehow Stanley had changed since he'd come home from the army. She hardly ever saw that sunny, happy-go-lucky expression on his face anymore. Sometimes he looked as though he had a great weight on his mind. Well, of course, he had, she told herself. He was the head of a big family. He must feel the responsibility, especially as he wasn't able to provide for them. Any good man would feel weighed down by that. She prayed he would find work soon. She didn't want to see him lose his self-respect.

At that moment Johnno came charging in, his gaze sweeping round to land hopefully on William.

'Here's Johnno now, Mr Philpots,' Josie said, relieved that the awkward moment with Stanley had passed.

William shook Johnno's hand. Josie liked that. William had respect for people, and she felt he was a man of his word. He said he'd look out for something for Stanley, and she felt he would.

William and Johnno went into the front room, closing the door behind them. Gwennie flopped down into the chair again.

'Make us a cuppa, our Stan,' she said, a hand on her large bosom, 'I'm puffed out.'

'Don't get downhearted, my arse!' Stanley sounded scathing, and Josie was shocked at the bitterness in his voice. 'That's easy for him to say, isn't it? He didn't even go to the bloody war!'

'Now don't get bitter, Stan,' Josie said quickly. 'It's not his fault you're out of work. He didn't go into the Forces because he was in a restricted occupation, working nearly sixteen hours a day, helping to keep our food supplies going. And when he wasn't doing that, he was up in Swansea fire-watching. He was burned by an incendiary bomb. Edie told me all about it.'

Without another word Stanley stalked off to the kitchenette to make Gwennie's tea. Josie exchanged a meaningful look with her mother-in-law.

'Don't be too hard on him, Josie love,' Gwennie pleaded, her eyes glistening. 'He hasn't been home from the army two months yet. He'll settle down soon.'

Johnno came out of the front room, his eyes shining, William right behind him.

'Josie, I start work on Monday!' Johnno announced gleefully grinning from ear to ear. He was looking so happy, and proud too.

Josie clapped her hands together with delight. She was proud of him. She thought of all the knocking about he had suffered at Dada's hands. He'd come through it and kept his self-respect. He hadn't gone off the rails like a good many boys might have done. Like herself, Johnno had backbone and determination. He had a future now, and she knew he would do well.

'Oh, thanks, Mr Philpots. Johnno's a good boy. You won't be sorry.'

She put her arm around her brother's shoulders, giving him a hug, and his young face flushed immediately. Things were changing for them, she knew it. Now if only Stanley could find something ...

William stood with his hat in his hand, looking around.

'Is Mr Jenkins here?'

Stanley came in from the kitchenette carrying a cup of tea for his mother.

'Ah! Mr Jenkins,' William began. 'I've just remembered. The manager of the bus company in Swansea is a pal of mine. He was telling me the other day he's looking for a couple of men to work as conductors. Would you be interested?'

Stanley almost dropped the cup of tea. His mother managed to grab it from him just in time, spilling most of it in the saucer.

'I certainly would,' he said eagerly. He already stood a little straighter, Josie thought. 'When can I see him?'

'I'll have a word with him,' William said, putting on his trilby ready to leave. 'I'll let you know.'

The following week Josie said cheerio to Edie in the shop before slipping home to make a midday meal for Stanley and the kids. Margaret Bayliss, Edie's mother, was laid up with phlebitis and wasn't able to do her usual good deed for them.

Josie felt like singing as she walked briskly up Newton Road and turned left towards home. Edie had given her a message from William: Stanley was to go up to Swansea the following morning for an interview at the bus company's offices. There was a vacancy for a conductor on the Mumbles train, and William had put in a word for him. She could hardly wait to get home to tell him.

She really had a lot to sing about, too, she reflected, as she hurried up Woodville Road. The store room was fitted with racks and shelves to take the bolts of material. The workroom was now ready to receive the equipment which was expected to arrive the following day; tables on which to lay out fabric and cut patterns, and new sewing-machines.

The area where they would receive their customers was something very novel for a shop, Josie thought. It had been Edie's idea to have individual tables scattered around where customers could examine cloth and choose patterns, instead of at traditional counters. Edie had spared no expense and was as enthusiastic as Josie herself. The future looked so exciting sometimes she felt it must be a dream, even though her aching muscles told her otherwise.

Things *were* coming right for them, she knew it. Johnno was thrilled with his new job. He liked his new mates, he had told them enthusiastically after his first day, and he liked the job. He was going to work hard, he said then one day Mr Philpots might make him manager.

Josie approved of his ambition and was moved by his eagerness to make a success of his life. Secretly she had dreaded he might turn out like Dada. But Johnno had dreams, like herself. It was good to have dreams, however improbable. Sometimes they came true. Her dream was coming true anyway, and when Stanley had that job with the bus company, which in her heart she just knew he would get, everything would be perfect.

When she got home she saw Gwennie had just arrived before her from shopping in town. Dewi was playing with a football in the back yard, but Teresa wasn't home from school yet, and there was no sign of Stanley, either. Josie was disappointed. She was bursting to tell him about the job. Now it must wait until later.

Her mother-in-law had dumped her shopping basket on the kitchen table and was just struggling out of her coat and head scarf.

'Josie kid!' Gwennie said, as soon as she set

eyes on her. 'You'll never believe what I heard up in Swansea?'

Josie was just about to take off her own coat but paused when Gwennie went on: 'It's your blinking father!'

'What?' Josie was startled, feeling a chill across her shoulder blades. Had Dada heard about her new venture? Maybe he was thinking he could cash in in some way?

Gwennie folded her arms across her chest, her head on one side.

'He's gone and got married again to that fat Kitty Whatsit. And your poor mother not three months in her grave. Tsk! Oh, there's disgusting, isn't it?'

Josie felt her jaw tighten painfully. She had been trying to take Francie's advice and forget their father. But she would never forgive him for what he'd done to Mama; the misery he'd made for her and the children, for all of them.

So he'd married that fat tart? More fool him! Yet she hated the thought that he might be happy. He didn't deserve to be. He deserved to roast in Hell!

She felt a burning sensation in her chest and knew it for that old familiar companion of her former life, the fire of revenge.

'I'll put a spoke in his wheel,' she said hoarsely, between gritted teeth. 'Give him up to the police. I've been saying that for a long time, but now I will do it. They're asking for information about black marketeers. I saw it in the paper. Dada is one of the worst there is. I'll have him behind bars, him *and* his fancy piece.'

'Hold on, kid,' Gwennie sniffed, putting a hand to her plump chin thoughtfully. 'Listen, you're in business now. You can't afford to get yourself mixed up in anything like that. It'll be in the papers, and mud sticks, don't it? I know your father is a proper old devil and deserves what's coming to him, but let somebody else do it, right?'

Josie sat down at the table, her chin in her hand. Perhaps Gwennie was right, and Francie, too. Josie had a lot to lose now, and couldn't let everything slip through her fingers for the sake of taking revenge on someone who wasn't worth a light. What would Edie say if the story got in the papers just when they were about to open the shop? With clothes rationing tighter than ever, getting the business started wasn't going to be easy anyway. Scandal would make things worse for all of them.

Josie stood up, putting a hand on Gwennie's arm affectionately.

'Thanks, Gwennie. It's a good thing one of us has some common sense. I could have done something then which I might've bitterly regretted later.'

Gwennie ran the tip of her tongue over her lips, her glance sliding away.

'Hope you'll remember that, kid, when ... if there's trouble in the future.'

'Such as?' Josie asked, putting on her headscarf again.

Gwennie shrugged, looking uncomfortable, Josie thought vaguely, her mind on rushing round to tell Francie the news about Dada.

'I dunno, do I?' her mother-in-law mumbled, and went into the kitchenette to put the kettle on.

'Start a bit of food, will you, Gwen?' Josie shouted as she hurried to the front door. 'Stan and Teresa will be here in a minute, I hope. I've got to see Francie.'

She let herself into the house a few doors away. Francie was sitting painting her nails, the tip of her tongue protruding as she carefully applied the colour. Teresa perched on the arm of the chair, watching enviously, Josie thought. The air was pungent with the smell of cheap perfume. Where was she getting this nail varnish and perfume? Josie was afraid to ask. It would only start another row.

'Teresa, go and have your meal,' she said. 'Gwennie is cooking it now.'

'I want to stay by here, mun,' the girl said sulkily. 'Francie's going to paint my nails in a minute.'

'Oh, no, she's not,' Josie said firmly. 'You can't go back to school this afternoon with painted nails. Miss Ferguson would send you home again. Now go down to Gwennie, like I told you.'

'You're not my mother!' Teresa shouted defiantly. 'You can't tell me what to do.'

Josie compressed her lips with irritation. Teresa was at an impressionable age. She was only twelve, but already Josie was noticing a change in her physically. Her periods had started the month before, and young breasts already thrust under her gym-slip. She was growing up fast. Josie was beginning to realise that Francie was a bad influence on the girl. She would have to do something about that.

'Do you want a flip across the head, Teresa?'

'Oh, for God's sake, leave the kid alone, Josie,' Francie chipped in irritably. 'Why don't you get back to your blinking shop? Stop interfering by here, will you?'

Josie lifted her chin.

'I came to give you a piece of news about Dada.'

'Huh! Not interested.'

Josie was fuming. 'Not interested in anything, are you, except tarting yourself up? I don't know why you bother. That pub you work in is nothing but a dump. All the customers are either drunks or crooks.'

Francie stuck her nose in the air and gave Josie a superior smile.

'For your information, I don't work in Swansea anymore.'

'What?'

'I've got a nice little job as barmaid in a hotel in Oystermouth. Classy place it is, too. The customers obviously like my phizog, because they tip well.' She gave Josie a mocking glance. 'You're not the only one who can improve herself, mind!'

'You're a sly one, Francie,' Josie said. 'You never said a word.'

'None of your business, is it? Anyway, what's this news about Dada? I can see your bum is on fire to tell me.'

Josie took a deep breath to control herself.

She wasn't going to get into a slanging match with Francie. It just wasn't worth it. Especially not with Teresa looking on.

'Dada's married that Kitty O'Sullivan. He's hardly been a widower three months. Shows how much he cared about Mama. What do you think we ought to do?'

Francie shrugged and went on painting her nails, totally unmoved. The only one interested was Teresa.

'Dada married Kitty?' She jumped off the arm of the chair. 'Did they have a party? I wish I'd been there.'

Josie was impatient. 'Oh, don't talk so foolish, Teresa,' she snapped. What short memories her sisters had. Had they forgotten poor Mama so soon, forgotten what she had suffered?

'Hey!' Teresa exclaimed. 'That means Kitty is our stepmother.'

Without stopping to think Josie lashed out, catching the girl a stinging slap across the face.

'Don't you ever say that again,' she warned savagely. 'Never mention her and Mama in the same breath. That woman is nothing to us, and neither is Dada, now.'

Teresa burst into tears immediately and rushed from the room, sobbing. Josie heard the front door slam behind her.

'Proud of yourself, are you?' Francie asked. There was a fixed sneer on her face. 'You carry on about what a brute Dada is, but you're just as bad, Josie. You always hit out first and think after. Teresa didn't mean any harm. She's been

367

telling me about Kitty O'Sullivan. The woman doesn't sound so bad to me.'

Josie blinked back the sting of tears, unwilling to show any weakness in front of Francie. But she was right for once. Josie had been sterner with Teresa than was necessary, and she resolved to make it up to her younger sister later. She was worried about Teresa. The girl needed a firm hand before it was too late, but Josie had gone too far this time, reacted too harshly.

It wasn't true that she was like Dada, though. She knew she was inclined to fly off the handle when her temper got the better of her, and sometimes acted impetuously and was sorry later. But she *wasn't* like Dada.

She felt responsible for them all and it was a load on her shoulders, always with her. Sometimes she acted rashly, but it was because she cared so much, felt so much. She couldn't forget what they had left behind them and didn't want any of them to slip back.

'*I* haven't forgotten what our lives were like before we got away from Victor Street,' Josie said, struggling for self-control at the memory of her mother's bruised and battered face. 'And the miserable existence Mama had, too. I'm not going to let Teresa grow up like you, Francie. Look at the mess you've made of your life!'

Her sister stood up, expression one of fury.

'Oh, you're so high and bloody mighty, aren't you? Full of snooty ideas now you're a so-called partner. Think you're rubbing shoulders with the *crachach.* But you're riding for a fall, let me tell you, Josie. You can get as swanky as you like, but underneath you're only the rag-and-bone man's daughter, and you'll always be that.'

Chapter Twenty-Three

June 1946

'It's very good of you, Josie, putting up with a houseful of kids,' Daisy said, cutting another thin slice of bread. 'And on your day off as well.'

'Glad to do it,' she replied, as she divided the next sandwich into four equal pieces, then divided the pieces again. It was a real job, making bread go round these days. Drat the new rationing! The war had been over for nearly a year, yet food rationing and restrictions were getting tighter all the time. It really was hard to bear, especially today when they were trying to give the kids a treat.

'Perhaps you can do the same for me sometime?' Josie went on.

Daisy looked up, her expression dark.

'I hope I'll never have to, Josie love. I feel terrible that Valerie can't have her birthday party in her own home, but Gerald won't hear of it. I mean, what sort of father ...' She bit her lip. 'I'm sorry, Josie, you don't want to hear me grumbling. And I shouldn't anyway.'

'Go on, kid.' She put a hand on her friend's shoulder. 'Have a good grumble. Get it off your chest, mun. It'll do you no end of good.'

'No,' Daisy said with a weak smile. 'I'm going to forget it this afternoon and enjoy myself with the kids. Thank goodness there'll only be six of them, though.'

'What, only six?' Josie pretended to look disappointed, and was pleased when her friend laughed. She hadn't heard that infectious laugh in a long time.

Daisy wasn't looking well these days. She used to hold herself so straight, head held high, Josie remembered. Now it seemed her shoulders sagged under a great weight. Which, of course, was true, Josie thought. There was no doubt in her mind that Gerald was a tyrant in his way, even though he hardly ever left his bedroom. Daisy had no life at all.

They must have one of their days out together, she decided firmly. Maybe Stanley could sit with Gerald for an hour or two when his shifts permitted? He seemed to be the only outsider Gerald could tolerate.

'Oh, by the way, I've got some bananas for the kids,' Daisy told her.

'Bananas!' Josie squealed, staring. 'Where from?'

'I was in town yesterday, saw a queue outside Chitzoy's. Well, of course, I joined it. I nearly fell over when I realised I'd been queuing for bananas. They only let me have four. Never mind. We'll cut them in half. I'm longing to see our Valerie's face when she sees her first banana.'

'Or we could slice them up with milk. Might go further.'

Daisy looked doubtful. 'Better go easy on the milk,' she said. 'The milkmen might go on strike again like they did last week.'

Josie made a face. 'You're right, kid. Tsk! Everything's going to pot.'

The party was a great success, Josie thought, despite the wafer-thin sandwiches. There was dandelion and burdock pop, jelly and blancmange, and Daisy's grandmother had donated a tin of pears. After the first shocked curiosity the bananas went down well, except in the case of Rhiannon, where it went down and came up again straight away. What a waste! Josie had been longing to taste a bit of banana herself.

After tea the children played hide and seek, but spent most of the time rushing round the rooms screaming at the top of their voices. Josie and Daisy brought two kitchen chairs and sat out in the backyard, getting a bit of sunshine.

Josie sat with her face turned to the sun, legs outstretched, skirt raised to her thighs, totally relaxed. She was very conscious of Daisy sitting alongside, tense and fidgety, and felt sad for her friend.

How things had changed for them, as though their lives had reversed! Josie was so happy at the moment. Stanley had been working on the Mumbles train for nearly four months, and privately she thought he looked quite dashing in his conductor's uniform with his peaked cap, his ticket machine over one shoulder and his number badge clipped to his waistcoat.

Johnno had settled into his job well, and according to him was William Philpots's right hand man. Now Francie was living under a different roof there weren't the incessant rows in the home there used to be, and that was a relief.

And the best tonic of all was the shop. They had started trading the previous week. The rush of customers had astonished Josie. She'd told Edie she was terrified it wouldn't last, but her partner had smiled that calm smile of hers and assured her they were on their way to success.

'Oh, I forgot to tell you, Daisy,' Josie began. 'Mrs Price-Pugh came in the shop yesterday. She brought a photograph of Rita Hayworth wearing a fabulous red dress and said she wanted us to make one exactly like it for her.' She laughed, remembering. 'Edie pointed out it would take yards and yards of material and the coupons would be a problem. Do you know what? She opened her handbag and it was stuffed, literally stuffed, with clothing coupons! Edie nearly had a fit.'

Josie laughed again, but Daisy's smile was weak. There's something on her mind, Josie decided. She wants to talk about it but can't. Keep up the chatter, thought Josie, then maybe her friend would find the courage.

'They were talking about free milk and school dinners on the wireless again last night,' she said. 'I hope they do it, don't you? Wouldn't it be handy if the kids could have dinner in school? Especially our two, when they start.'

'Yes,' Daisy said, but Josie could see she was hardly listening.

'Looks like this National Health Service is going ahead, though,' Josie persisted. 'How will it affect you professionally then, Daisy?'

Daisy turned to her, her expression troubled.

'Josie, listen, I've got to talk to you.' She turned away, her shoulders stiff and tense. 'Oh, I don't know what you'll think of me,' she went on miserably. 'I wouldn't blame you if you didn't want to know me anymore.'

Josie sat up quickly and put a hand on her arm.

'Come on, Daisy love. We've been friends a long time and been through a lot together, as well. You can tell me anything. Nothing will change between us. Come on, girl, get it off your chest.'

Daisy turned to face her again and grasped her hand, holding on tightly.

'I've been so miserable, especially since we came home from Yorkshire,' she began. 'And what happened at Christmas was the last straw, when Gerald denied Valerie was his and accused me of being unfaithful. Oh, Josie, I nearly broke my heart over that. I was never unfaithful in the true sense. Rhodri and I had never ...'

'Daisy, I'm so sorry.' Josie didn't know what else to say. Her friend didn't deserve this fate. If only Daisy could bring herself to leave Gerald. It was the only way. But Josie checked her tongue. She couldn't advise her and be sure she was saying the right thing. Daisy's situation was so complicated.

There were tears in her eyes.

'Josie, do you remember the day you called on me and Rhodri was there? He came by chance. We hadn't seen each other outside of work for months and months. He was so understanding, tried to make me face up to what was really happening.'

'He loves you, Daisy.'

'Yes, I know.' Her voice broke into a sob, but she managed to get control of herself again quickly, Josie saw, and realised her friend had guts and determination.

'After Rhodri had gone, Gerald and I had an awful row. He accused me of carrying on when he was away, as though I were a common ...' Her voice broke. 'He wouldn't listen to reason.'

Tears started to glisten at the corners of her eyes. Daisy pulled a handkerchief from the puffed sleeve of her dress and blew her nose determinedly. She looked a lot like Valerie when she did that, Josie thought, young and vulnerable.

'Rhodri had just bought that house at the top of Newton,' she went on. 'I waited until I knew he'd be home from surgery. I went up to see him. I know I shouldn't have, but I *needed* him. Just to talk to, you know.'

Daisy compressed her lips hard for a moment, and Josie realised she was fighting back more tears. She tightened her grasp on her friend's hand, encouraging her.

374

'Go on, Daisy love?'

'He was wonderfully understanding. He gave me some medicine to soothe my nerves. We talked for ages. He was very patient. After all I've put him through.'

'None of it was your fault, Daisy kid,' Josie assured her.

It had taken great courage to put aside the man she loved to preserve her marriage, or try to, she thought. How could Daisy have known it was a lost cause; that she'd sacrifice not only her happiness, but that of Valerie and Rhodri? And for nothing, for a husband who was past help.

'Perhaps not, but now I've put Rhodri's professional reputation at risk. You see, I've been visiting him regularly for counselling. I knew what could happen between us, but I made myself believe I had more control.' Daisy bowed her head, little sobs escaping her. 'I was selfish, Josie, thinking more about my own feelings that Rhodri's.'

'You're only human, Daisy love.'

She looked up, eyes wide and swimming with tears.

'It was friendship I was looking for, Josie, I swear it. But how could I expect Rhodri to cope with that? It was friendship at first, but now ... now we are lovers. We couldn't help ourselves.'

Daisy burst into tears then, and Josie got off her chair to put an arm around her friend's shoulders, giving her a reassuring hug.

'Daisy love, don't upset yourself like this.'

Josie wasn't surprised. She'd suspected as much for weeks.

'You're the only person I've told, Josie,' Daisy said, dabbing at her eyes with a handkerchief. 'I couldn't tell Edie. She loves me, but she wouldn't understand this. She'd say it was wrong and immoral. Oh, Josie, I can't give him up a second time. I can't!'

Surely Daisy would consider divorce now? Josie thought, hugging her friend tighter. Divorce rates were rising. She'd read that in some newspaper only the other week. Thousands of couples were divorcing due to pressures put on marriages by war. No, there wasn't such stigma attached to divorce as there used to be. Of course, that didn't make it right, Josie brooded, but it was a sign of the times, and Daisy's marriage was just another casualty of war.

'Of course you can't give him up,' Josie said. 'Not with the way you two feel about each other.' She paused for a moment, wondering if she should say what was on her mind. 'Daisy, you really ought to think about divorcing Gerald now.'

Daisy straightened up, looking dismayed.

'Josie, I can't do it. I've already betrayed him. I can't abandon him as well. What would he do? Where would he go? He's so alone.'

'But, Daisy love, what about Rhodri? What about Valerie? You and Rhodri belong together. And besides, you can't go on living this awful life.'

Daisy swallowed hard.

'I think I must, Josie. I can't bring myself to do anything else. If Gerald were to accuse me of being unfaithful today, I wouldn't be able to look him in the eye. Do you blame me for being weak? Do you think less of me?'

'How can I think less of you for loving so deeply, Daisy?' Josie said, sad that her friend was suffering so very much, and all in the name of duty. 'How can I blame you for being human?'

Daisy shook her head despondently.

'Rhodri is so dedicated to his profession. The scandal will ruin him if it gets out about us. He vows he'll never give me up, though.' She clutched at Josie's hand again. 'Oh, I've made such a mess of everything, haven't I? I've spoilt everything for Rhodri and Valerie. I've ruined all our lives.'

Chapter Twenty-Four

December 1946

'Roll on Christmas,' Edie said, closing the order book with a snap. 'I can't wait to put my feet up.'

'Phew! I know what you mean.' Josie flopped into a chair near Edie's desk. 'Talk about busy! Where do they find the clothing coupons? That's what I'd like to know.'

Thank goodness it was half-day closing, she thought. The workroom staff had gone and so had the two young shop assistants. Even with the staff they had, there was plenty for the partners to do, enough to send them trotting off home each night tired out.

Edie occupied herself with the book-keeping, dealing with suppliers and sometimes greeting customers, while Josie spent most of her time in the workroom at her drawing-board working on designs.

Often, though, she would chat to a customer about a special order.

Really, it was all wonderful, she reflected, and they shouldn't grumble at being busy. Philpots and Jenkins, Outfitters, had been an outstanding success since it had opened in the summer. Edie had predicted it would be a good investment, but even she was surprised at the volume of business they had done over the last six months, Josie realised. They were gaining a reputation for quality and style. The order book was full and Josie looked forward to the coming New Year with pleasurable anticipation.

'Well, come on,' Edie said, putting the books in the desk drawer and reaching for her coat and hat. 'Let's not waste our free afternoon.'

The day was crisp and cold but not uncomfortably so. Josie paused in the doorway of the shop, watching as Edie locked up the premises securely. She was just about to say goodbye to her when the sound of her name bellowed in the street made her turn, startled and confused.

'Josie! Hoy, Josie!'

She stared, the hot blood of embarrassment rushing painfully to her neck and cheeks as she realised who was calling her. Plodding up Newton Road, and now drawing level with them, was a horse and cart, all too familiar to her. Perched high up on the seat were two figures.

'Ah, Josie, 'tis a sight for sore eyes you are, girl,' the fat woman said.

Kitty O'Sullivan, or Randall as she was now sat on the cart seat like a great elephant, Josie mused, feeling her face going stiff with shame.

Kitty still wore her man's trilby with the little red feather. It looked as though she hadn't taken it off since the day Josie had last set eyes on her, the day Sophia had died, a year ago this Christmas.

Kitty was wearing a coat today against the chill air. It had a moth-eaten fur collar and no buttons on it, Josie noticed. Though that hardly mattered really, since it was too small to meet around her enormous belly.

'Who on earth is that?' Edie asked.

Conscious of her partner's open-mouthed stare at the spectacle, Josie was tempted to say she didn't know, but was really too mortified to say anything.

Kitty waved gleefully, as though they'd never had words and were the best of pals.

'How are the kids, Josie? Me favourites, so they are. I'll call in and see them, so I will.'

Josie winced at the very thought.

'Isn't that Reuben Randall on the cart, too?' Edie said, glancing in astonishment at Josie. 'Isn't that your father?'

Josie wished the earth would crack open and swallow her up.

Edie was still staring from one to the other, obviously bewildered by the sight of this strange couple and Josie's silence.

'Yes, that's my father,' she said quietly at last. 'Used to be my father anyway.'

Although Kitty waved and shouted, Reuben made no effort to halt the horse's progress up the road, and the horse kept plodding on. Reuben looked neither to left nor right, nor showed in any way he knew Josie was there.

Piqued at his disregard in spite of herself, she stared hard at him. Then, with a little shock, she became aware of a change in him. His shoulders seemed more bent and rounded than before. His face was paler, too, and thinner than she remembered. He looked totally miserable, Josie realised, and seemed hardly at all the man he once was. So changed was he, she wondered if she would have recognised him in a crowded street.

Bewildered herself now, her glance darted again to Kitty. She was still waving, but her other hand, an enormous one, was clamped on Reuben's shoulder, in a way that was both proprietorial and domineering. Josie stared at the rather comical tableau they made, and realised with a jolt that there *was* such a thing as justice after all.

'But who is that enormous woman?' Edie asked, and Josie knew she was holding back laughter, and couldn't blame her.

'Nemesis.' Josie recovered enough to smile

herself as the cart passed on its way up the road. 'In other words, Kitty, my father's new wife, my ... stepmother.'

When Stanley came home from work, Josie told him and Gwennie about her extraordinary encounter with Kitty and Reuben. She'd thought about her father most of the afternoon. She couldn't get over the way he had changed, all within the space of a year. Perhaps he had been ill? Though she couldn't imagine Reuben in ill-health. He had always appeared robust, as strong as an ox. But was it more a change in spirits than any physical change? she wondered, as a picture of Kitty, waving cheerfully, came into her mind's eye again.

After tea, Teresa and Dewi called in to see Rhiannon, but Josie suspected it was really to talk about the coming Christmas and perhaps get a clue as to what presents they could expect.

Josie had been regretting her previous harshness towards her young sister, and was determined to make it up to her. Last Christmas had been a very sad one. This year was Stanley's first Christmas home since leaving the army. They were better off than ever before what with his wages and her salary from the shop. She could afford to be a little extravagant, the dratted rationing permitting of course, and hope she could make it a Christmas to remember for them all.

'Bet you can't guess who I saw today?' Josie said to Teresa and Dewi, as she sat darning Stanley's socks.

'Father Christmas?' Dewi asked hopefully. He was sitting on the settee, elbows on knees, chin in his hands. He looked the picture of health and happiness since moving to the Mumbles, Josie thought, and realised she hadn't seen him cry since leaving Victor Street.

'Kitty,' she said. 'On the cart with Dada, totting up Newton.'

Teresa sat forward, eyes alert, abandoning the cat's cradle she was making out of a piece of string. She didn't speak.

'Did she say anything?' Dewi asked excitedly. 'Did she ask about me?'

'Well, she said she'd call in to see you both.'

'Whoopee!' he yelled. 'She'll do some tricks for us, I expect. I like the one with the disappearing sixpence. It always turns up in my pocket, and she lets me keep it.'

'Josie?' Teresa was looking at her doubtfully.

'Well, it's all right, I suppose,' she said, anticipating Teresa's question. 'She can come if she wants to.'

Teresa lowered her head, regarding Josie through her eyelashes.

'I thought you didn't like her?' There was puzzlement in her voice, and a challenge, too, Josie decided. 'You said I wasn't to mention her name again.'

Josie moistened her lips.

'I didn't say that exactly, Teresa love?'

'Yes, you did. Near enough, anyway. What's made you change your mind, then?' the girl persisted.

'Comeuppance.'

'What?'

Stanley laughed. He was sitting in the armchair in front of the fireplace, reading the evening paper. Teresa frowned, glancing at him suspiciously.

'What's so funny?'

'Maybe I misjudged her,' Josie went on quickly. 'I could see today that she's brought a change to Dada's life—probably a change for the better, I don't know.'

'So you like her now, then?'

'Hold on now, Teresa love,' Josie said hastily. 'I'm not saying I want Kitty for a pal.'

'Oh, Heaven forbid!' Stanley said, mimicking her, and she threw a sock at him, trying to stifle laughter herself. She didn't want the children to think she was making fun, even if perhaps she was.

Why Teresa and Dewi were so taken with that blowsy and grotesque woman, Josie couldn't understand for the life of her, but they were and she must consider their feelings now they were getting older.

'What I'm saying is, if Kitty wants to call in to see you and Dewi, she can ... once in a while.'

A very long while, Josie added, under her breath.

'Can we go up to Victor Street to see her and Dada?' Teresa asked.

Josie hesitated, considering. She had said Dada would never see his children again, and had meant it at the time. She'd said it in a moment of great pain and grief. He had treated them all so badly, he really didn't deserve to see them.

An image of Reuben's bent shoulders and miserable expression came to mind. She was surprised how strong the image was, as though she had seen him only a moment ago. She couldn't bring herself to feel sorry for him, but the sight of him today would stay with her for a long time.

Perhaps it would be a good thing for the children to see him, too. Yes, they could go if they wanted to, she decided. She would never go herself, though.

Josie and Gwennie bustled about the kitchenette Christmas morning, getting the dinner ready. A workmate of Stanley's kept chickens in his back garden to sell off at Christmas.

They had bought two, which were now roasting away deliciously.

With her family busy and noisy around her Josie felt she'd never been happier, but thought sadly of Daisy next door, and the miserable Christmas she must be having. Valerie was spending Christmas up at Edie's but Daisy wasn't able to go because of Gerald. She would be missing Valerie now. Christmas wasn't Christmas without children around.

She must be ever so lonely, Josie thought, loving Rhodri and not able to be with him. Gerald was no company at all, only a horrible reminder of the happiness she had lost.

After Christmas dinner was over and everything cleared away, Josie went next door and knocked on the kitchen window. Daisy opened the back door almost immediately. She's been crying, Josie thought, and suddenly the glitter of this Christmas faded for her.

'Daisy love, come next door for a while,' she coaxed. 'Just an hour or two. Come on. Come and have a drop of Gwennie's port wine.'

Daisy hesitated, glancing back into the passage.

'I'd love to come in, Josie,' she said, and wetted her lips nervously. 'I don't know about leaving Gerald ...'

'Stan will sit with him, if you like?' Josie volunteered, without stopping to think whether Stanley would object. 'To give you a break, like.'

'No,' Daisy said quickly. She shook her head. 'I don't want to spoil Stanley's Christmas.'

'Do come in, Daisy,' Josie coaxed. 'I mean, Gerald is on his own when you're working, isn't he? He can't object to your having an hour or two of relaxation. After all, it is Christmas Day.'

Daisy smiled rather sadly, Josie thought.

'There's kind you are, Josie. You've got a houseful already.'

'Oh, plenty of room for one more, especially as she's my best friend. Go on, kid, get your coat. Tell Gerald you won't be long, and if he'd like a glass of port, too, Stan will bring one in.'

During the course of the afternoon, sitting companionably in front of the living-room fire with Josie and Gwennie, Daisy was doing her best to be cheerful, Josie could see. But every so often she would look pensively into the fire, her mind far away, deep sadness in her eyes. Thinking of Rhodri all alone in that big house of his, Josie surmised, and wishing she were with him.

Sometimes Daisy would glance at her, lips parting, as though wanting to say something but prevented because of Gwennie's presence. Josie remembered Valerie's birthday party last June. Daisy had behaved much the same then. She had something on her mind again, Josie decided. She must get her on her own for a few minutes.

'Oh, listen, Daisy love, I nearly forgot,' Josie said. 'A customer of ours ordered a dress for her daughter, round about Valerie's age, she is. She paid the coupons, but her husband wouldn't let her buy it.' Josie wrinkled her nose in disgust. 'Said it was too expensive. Listen, I wonder if you'd like it for Valerie?'

'But can't you sell it on?' Daisy asked.

'It's very pretty,' Josie said evasively. 'It'd suit her down to the ground. It's upstairs. Come up a minute.'

In the bedroom Josie laid the dress on the bed for Daisy to have a good look at it. She watched her friend finger the material absently, and knew her mind wasn't on the dress at all.

Josie sat on the bed and drew her friend down beside her.

'Daisy love, what's the matter? You've been crying, I can see that. Is it Gerald? What's wrong?'

Daisy sat still, head bent, hands restless in her lap.

'I don't know how to tell you, Josie. Something's happened and I don't know what to do.'

'Maybe we can sort if out together? You can tell me anything, Daisy, you know that.'

Daisy turned glistening eyes towards her.

'I know now how Francie felt when she was in trouble,' she said quietly, and Josie couldn't prevent a sharp intake of breath.

'You're going to have a baby? Oh, Daisy love!'

She nodded.

'I'm two months gone. Oh, Josie, what have I come to? I'm a married woman expecting another man's child. I can hardly believe this is happening to me!'

Josie grasped her friend's hand as it lay in her lap and pressed it reassuringly. Yet, at the same time, her heart contracted with the sharp pain of yearning. Envy, deep purple envy, engulfed her for a moment, and her earlier pleasure at having her family around her at Christmas disappeared like early-morning mist.

Why was it that she, who longed so fervently for a child, was disappointed, while other women found falling for a baby nothing but a burden? If only she had their chance! If only God would be good to her and give her a child of her own.

With difficulty, Josie pushed aside her envious thoughts. God was good to her. Her life was coming right now. How could she be so ungrateful? What sort of friend was she anyway, being so jealous when Daisy needed her support and friendship?

Josie did think it ironic that Daisy should think she and Francie had something in common. Daisy was the best mother a child could have. Whatever happened, she would love and cherish this child, not least because it was Rhodri's. She was distressed now but she would never be indifferent to her child as Francie was.

'Does Rhodri know yet?' Josie asked, ignoring the ache in her own breast.

When Daisy shook her head, she went on: 'You should tell him. He ought to know, Daisy.'

'I'm afraid to, Josie,' she said. 'He'll insist I leave Gerald. We'd quarrel over it, I know we would.' She bit down on her lip hard, visibly straining not to burst into tears. 'After the holiday I'm going to tell Rhodri it's over between us. I can't see him anymore.'

'Can you really bring yourself to do that, Daisy?'

She nodded miserably.

'I must do it. It was my fault we fell into this relationship in the first place. I was weak. It wouldn't be right for us to go on now. And besides, I don't want him to find out. He'll expect too much.'

Josie had been so envious a moment ago. Now she realised she was glad she wasn't in Daisy's shoes. The only comfort Daisy had in her life was Rhodri and now she had to give him up. It was cruel and unfair. But how would Rhodri take this decision?

Josie didn't know him very well. To her he was just the panel doctor who called when the kids were sick. Since Daisy had told her about their relationship last June, Josie had studied him more carefully whenever he visited the house. There was something about his bearing, the look in his eyes, which expressed a deep sensitivity, even passion. He wouldn't take Daisy's decision at all meekly, Josie was sure of that.

'What about Rhodri's feelings, Daisy? He'll be so hurt,' Josie asked quietly.

'I know!' She bent her head, covering her face with her hands. 'Oh, why did this have to happen? Why must we all be so unhappy?'

'Maybe you should leave Gerald instead of giving up Rhodri?' Josie suggested after a moment's thought. 'If you must make a choice, choose Rhodri. Choose love, Daisy.'

'No, I wouldn't leave Gerald.' Daisy jerked up her head, tone emphatic. 'It would turn into a scandal in no time in a small village like this. Rhodri's career would be in tatters. I won't let that happen.'

Josie nodded, sighing deeply. Daisy was of the same mind as last June, she could see that by the firm line of her friend's jaw, set with determination even in her deepest misery. Daisy was suffering now but inside she was strong and resilient, so different from Francie.

'There's one good thing anyway,' Josie said, sighing. 'No one can possibly know the child isn't Gerald's.' She hesitated. 'Except, perhaps, Edie? She knows the way things are between you and Gerald, doesn't she?'

Daisy nodded again.

'She knows about Gerald but she doesn't know about Rhodri. I know what she'd say. She'd think it was disgusting, disgraceful, "carrying on" when I'm married. She'd say I should have more restraint and self-respect.' She shook her head again. 'I'm not going to tell her, Josie. She wouldn't understand.'

Josie was dubious about this decision. Over the last six months she had begun to know Edie very well, and liked and respected her a good deal. In Josie's opinion it wouldn't be too long before Edie guessed the truth anyway. Josie felt her friend was wrong in not attempting to get her stepmother's support at this time. Edie might surprise her. But she kept these thoughts to herself.

'What about Gerald? He's bound to suspect in time. I mean, when it becomes obvious. Have you considered what he might do?'

Daisy bit her lower lip in consternation.

'I think about nothing else. He's so unpredictable.'

'Daisy.' Josie said hesitantly, 'I know I shouldn't poke my nose in, but my Stan really believes Gerald belongs in an institution. He says he's seen men similarly affected through their war experiences, and being put in one of those places was invariably the answer, for a while at least. They either come out of it or they don't. Gerald isn't getting any better, is he? Be honest with yourself now, Daisy love.'

'I can't, I won't do it to him,' she said

in agitation, getting to her feet. 'He's been betrayed enough. He feels betrayed that William somehow persuaded him to come to Wales. He resents it, I know he does. And maybe he's right. There's nothing here for him.'

'Is there anything for him anywhere in his present state of mind, Daisy?' That sounded brutal, but Josie couldn't help saying it.

'I don't know,' she said miserably. 'All I do know is, I've betrayed him again.' She turned to Josie, obviously distressed. 'I feel I ought to tell him about Rhodri and me, even though it's over, and about the baby. Confess it all and be done with it, because all this hole-in-the-wall business is driving me mad.'

Appalled at the idea, Josie got to her feet and grasped her arm. She felt she wanted to give her friend a good shake.

'Oh, Daisy, don't do that, for heaven's sake! What good would it do? You'd only make things worse between you. Gerald would be more resentful than ever.'

'But what am I to do?'

Josie put her arms around her friend and gave her a hug. Poor Daisy. Life had been so unfair to her. Josie felt guilty then because she had everything and Daisy nothing but misery and unhappiness.

Josie had carried a pocketful of daydreams around with her for such a long time, and now they were all coming true. She had Stanley, she had a successful business. There was more money in her purse these days than she'd ever seen before, and she had her family around her.

She had always believed in going out to meet trouble head on, but in Daisy's case her friend was convinced that would be a disaster.

She hugged her friend again, and patted her back in an effort to comfort her.

'Daisy love, sit tight and say nothing because once you've confessed to Gerald, there's no going back.'

Chapter Twenty-Five

Rhodri would be waiting for her as he always was, meeting her in the hallway; eyes eager, arms open. That unruly lock of hair falling over his eyes, making him look like a little boy sometimes. She would step into his arms and he'd kiss her. Being in his loving arms was always like stepping out of the darkness into sunshine—the sunshine of his love.

His love had sustained her for so many months. Now she must turn away from it, turn away from him. It was breaking her heart to do it, but it was only right. She knew it was. She tried to check a rising surge of guilt, knowing this separation would hurt him badly again. Rhodri would understand, though. He had to.

Daisy's step faltered as she approached his house in the leafy road near the park. Guilty still, she thought of him waiting there for her, eagerly, all unsuspecting. He would be hurt, of course he would. He'd invent all kinds of reasons why they should go on seeing each other. But in the end he must see it was for the best.

She wouldn't tell him the complete truth, not about the baby. If he knew about that he would do something drastic; force her into a decision she wasn't ready to make. When would she be ready? she asked herself.

Daisy used the key he had given her. She didn't like using it but it was better than standing around outside the house. There was always a chance someone would see her and wonder what she was doing there in the middle of the day. Midday was the only time they could meet, unless Rhodri had an emergency. Often they went hungry rather than waste precious time when they could be together in Rhodri's bed, loving each other. And it felt so right, that was the thing. With his lips, his hands, on her, she always had a feeling of coming home; being with him was her rightful place, where she belonged. Now all that must end.

Oh, God! Now she would be out in the wilderness again without him, in the dark and the cold; the cold that penetrated to her very soul and shrivelled her up.

As soon as she opened the door he appeared in the hall in shirt sleeves.

'Daisy *cariad!* You're late. I thought you weren't coming. It seems like a year since I've seen you. How are you, love? How was your Christmas? I missed you like mad.'

He came forward smiling, arms open to

embrace her. But Daisy made a big thing of struggling out of her coat, twisting away to hang it on the hall-stand.

'Christmas was so-so, you know?' she said, taking her time about hanging up her coat. She didn't take off her midwife's cap, though. By leaving it on she wanted him to guess that this was not one of their usual meetings, prepare him for what she had come to say.

He stood so close to her, she could smell the body scent of him. It filled her nostrils, and despite her resolve not to be affected by his presence, she felt herself begin to quiver.

Please let me be able to do this, she prayed earnestly. Because, despite all the pain it would cause them both, it was the right thing to do, the proper thing.

With a tremendous effort she controlled her unsteady legs and the shaking of her hands, standing stiffly, waiting for him to move away.

He must sense her coolness, she told herself. Usually they were in each other's arms by now, and Daisy would be tingling at the thought of the pleasure that lay ahead of them in the next hour. Now she dreaded the next few minutes, because she must tell him straight away. She dare not delay for too long. She might weaken.

'Is something wrong, Daisy *cariad?*'

Daisy rubbed at her arms.

'It's cold. Can we go into the sitting-room?'

He hesitated for a moment, looking at her keenly, and for once she found she could not meet his gaze. To what had she been reduced?

Deception bred deception, it was true. She had betrayed and deceived Gerald. Was she doing the same thing to Rhodri?

Without a word he walked into the sitting-room and Daisy followed, sitting down near the fire, holding out her hands to the warmth. Despite the coldness of her hands, her lips felt hot and dry as she ran her tongue over them. How should she start to tell him the end had come for them?

'Where did you spend Christmas, Rhodri? Not here all by yourself?'

He was standing looking down at her, the eagerness gone from his eyes now, replaced by puzzlement. How could she expect him to guess?

'No. I went up to my parents in Merthyr.'

Daisy nodded. He had told her all about his boyhood in Merthyr Tydfil, and his struggle and determination to lift himself out of that kind of life. He had never wanted to be a miner like his father. He had always wanted to be a doctor. She mustn't be the one to destroy that.

'I met a friend from college days,' he went on. 'He's in general practice in Merthyr. His partner is retiring in a couple of months and he's looking for another doctor to replace him.' Rhodri laughed. 'He asked me if I'd consider it.'

Daisy's heart contracted. He was going away. She would never see him again. She felt panic for a moment and dismay. What would she do if he went away? But a calm inner voice told her that was the best thing that could happen now. Once they stopped seeing each other, life would be impossible if they had to meet professionally almost every day. She wouldn't be able to stand that.

'Are you going to take it, Rhodri?'

He laughed, puzzled.

'Of course not. Why would I go back up to the Rhondda when all I ever want is right here? I couldn't leave you, Daisy *cariad.*'

She turned her gaze to the flickering fire, remembering the morning he had called to see Gerald, and the way she had felt then; longing for him, yearning. And she had succumbed. Now she had to give it all up.

'I think you should.'

'What?'

'I think it would be better if we never saw each other again.'

'*What?*'

She glanced at him through lowered lashes, half afraid of what she would see in his eyes. Puzzlement lay over his face like a mask. She swallowed hard, gathering her courage to say the words that were as sharp and painful as tacks in her mouth.

'Rhodri, listen! We can't go on this way. I think people are beginning to whisper.' She didn't know whether that was true or not, but it was likely. 'You have your career to think of. So have I. It isn't as though it can lead anywhere.'

'Of course it can,' he said, pushing back the lock of hair impatiently. 'All you have to do is leave Gerald.'

Daisy bit her lip. 'We've been through all

that. Why won't you see that I can't just desert him?'

'Daisy *cariad*, what are we arguing about? Why these doubts all of a sudden? What happened over Christmas? Is it Gerald?'

He had so many questions, Daisy thought, and none that she wanted to answer.

'That's just it, Rhodri. I have no doubts any longer. We've got to end it, here and now.'

'Why?' He was half-smiling, disbelief plain on his face. 'Daisy you're not making any sense. How can you even think of it?'

She closed her eyes, trying to steady the thumping of her heart and the rising panic fluttering in her midriff. She wasn't handling this very well. He expected an explanation and she couldn't give him one, not really, not without revealing the truth.

'Because, Rhodri, I realise now it's the right thing to do.'

'The right thing?' His voice was suddenly louder, and she detected an edge of irritation. 'You mean, as opposed to the wrong thing. You think it's wrong for us to love each other? You didn't think that when I asked you to marry me.'

'I thought I was free then,' she said to defend herself. She stood up. Why couldn't he understand? 'I'm not free now. Our coming together was ...'

'A mistake?'

There was bitterness in his voice. It was reflected in the vividness of his blue eyes. They were cold now, steely.

Daisy wanted to cry out: Don't look at me like that. It's not my fault. Instead she shook her head, putting one knuckle to her mouth to prevent a sob escaping.

'I didn't mean that, Rhodri,' she said at last. 'I meant it was a weakness, on my part.'

He held his head on one side.

'You mean I was an interlude.' Anger flickered in his eyes like blue fire. 'Something to take your mind off poor deranged Gerald?'

'Oh, Rhodri!'

'You don't love me, do you?' He was staring at her, his expression one of surprise. 'What a prize fool I turned out to be. Did you ever love me? My God, Daisy! I'd never have believed I could doubt *you.*'

'Rhodri! Don't say that!' She couldn't bear the thought that they were quarrelling. She had never felt so miserable in her life before. 'I do love you! Don't you see, that's why I've decided we should stop?'

'You've decided, just like that? And you expect me to accept it, don't you? Perhaps you wish we'd never even met?'

'I do love you! I do!' she cried out. She felt her heart was about to splinter into a million pieces with the pain. 'I've always loved you. I'll never love anyone else.'

He stared at her for a moment, then shook his head sadly.

'You don't know how empty those words sound to me, Daisy. If you love me, how can you give me up? I'll never give *you* up.'

'Do you think this is easy for me?' she blurted

out, driven by a surge of anger at his words. 'Do you think I *want* to be on my own again, with no one and nothing in my life?'

'You've got Gerald,' he said, between gritted teeth. 'Once again you've chosen him over me. I don't know what love means to you, Daisy, but to me it means total commitment: body, mind and soul. Do you love Gerald?'

'*No!*' Daisy exclaimed. Tears were beginning to blur her vision. 'But I'm tied to him. Not only legally, but morally too. I can't abandon him, anymore than I could abandon Valerie. Please, Rhodri, don't turn from me like this. It has to be over between us, but don't let's part in bitterness.'

'Then tell me you didn't mean it?' he said earnestly. 'Tell me it was just a moment of panic ... uncertainty? I love you, Daisy. I don't want us to be apart. I want to care for you. You *and* Valerie. I feel about her as I would my own child, you know that. And Valerie loves me too, I know she does.'

'Don't! Don't!' Daisy cried out. 'Why won't you understand? We can't go on as we were. I can't stand this hole-in-corner way I'm living, terrified someone will find out. My livelihood is at stake, and so is yours, Rhodri. We'll both end up with nothing. Then we'll start to blame each other. I'm trying to protect us both. I'm hating every minute of it, but it has to be.'

She could bear no more of this torture. Turning on her heel, she darted to the door and out into the hall.

'Daisy! Wait!' He came hurrying after her.

She snatched her coat from the stand and threw it over her arm. She wouldn't stay another moment even to put it on despite the coldness outside. She fumbled in her coat pocket for the key he'd given her and flung it on to the hall table. She opened the front door then paused for a moment, looking at his stricken face as he stood motionless in the hall, staring at her.

'I didn't want it to end like this, Rhodri. Perhaps I have made a mess of my explanation, but there is one thing I know: love isn't selfish. I think you're being selfish in not understanding my position. You're not even trying to understand, and I thought I knew you so well.' She shook her head, the draught from the open door chilling the tears in her eyes. 'We have no more to say to each other. Except ...' She wanted to tell him again she loved him, but instead she said: 'Goodbye, Rhodri. Have a good life in Merthyr Tydfil.'

Chapter Twenty-Six

March 1947

There weren't many people in church this morning, Daisy noticed. Who could blame them really under the circumstances? The weather had been bad since early February. Conditions were still appalling, with apparently little or no hope of its ending soon. The roads and pavements

400

were treacherous, piled with snow and ice. Daisy couldn't remember a worse winter, especially with the chronic fuel shortage.

Old people suffered most, she reflected, thinking about her own grandparents. Life was hard enough for them already with food rationing being cut back further all the time.

Unable to suppress a shiver at the coldness in the church, Daisy wondered if she would ever be warm again. Resolutely, though, she stood, pulling Valerie to her feet, as the organ sounded the opening chords of the second hymn of the Sunday morning service.

Valerie had been fidgeting since the service began, noisily kicking off her wellingtons; wriggling on the pew and staring around at the congregation. Daisy had been forced to gently bring her to order more than once already. She understood. At three and a half, Valerie was really much too young to appreciate the solemnity of the service, but Daisy felt her daughter should be brought up to understand the importance of faith, and it was never too soon for a child to learn that.

But Valerie was especially restless today, and Daisy knew her young mind was on the party at *Tŷ Heulwen* that afternoon. It was to celebrate Edie's forty-fourth birthday, and was also a send-off party for Daisy's stepbrother, Gareth, who was emigrating to Australia tomorrow.

The party was especially important to Edie because this was the first time Gareth had agreed to meet her since 1942. Edie had been praying constantly for this reconciliation, Daisy knew. She really felt sorry for her stepmother, because the day she was reunited with her beloved son, she would have to part with him again. But at least now the parting promised to be a loving one.

Daisy felt a catch in her throat as she remembered her parting with Rhodri before the New Year; a parting so full of acrimony, it was painful to remember it. They had said such hurtful things to each other—things she was bitterly sorry for now. Often over the past months she had regretted her decision to end their relationship, but in saner moments knew she'd been right, no matter how hollow her life was now.

Valerie missed Rhodri, too. She had been asking for him constantly, demanding to know why she wasn't allowed to see him. They had got on so well together, almost like father and daughter. Every time Valerie mentioned his name Daisy felt like bursting into tears. Their separation was so cruel, and it didn't help to accept that she alone was responsible.

She hadn't set eyes on him since December last, but Edie said she'd heard in the shop that he had moved back to the Rhondda and was now practising in Merthyr Tydfil.

Daisy's heart had ached for long hours at the news. Now he was out of reach and out of her life for ever. Her common sense told her it was just as well, because she would never stop loving him, wanting him.

The hymn ended, bringing Daisy back to reality. She sat down again, but Valerie, standing on tip-toe, was having a good gawk at the people in the back pews.

'There's Uncle Rhodri!'

'Hush!' Daisy whispered urgently, disbelieving but suddenly petrified. She wanted to turn around and look, too, but her neck felt as stiff as a rod. She dared not look.

'But, Mammy, Uncle Rhodri's sitting at the back. Can I go sit by him?'

'No, keep quiet, Valerie,' Daisy hissed. 'Sit down, or ... or I'll smack you.'

A vain threat, and Valerie knew it, Daisy realised. Valerie flopped on to the pew but stood up again immediately, raising a hand to wave tentatively, mitten dangling from the cord threaded up her sleeve.

'Valerie! I won't tell you again.'

'But, Mammy ...'

Was Rhodri really there, sitting at the back, watching her? Or was it only Valerie's vivid imagination? How could he be here when he was in Merthyr Tydfil? The bad snowstorms of the last two months had brought Swansea and the Mumbles almost to a standstill. The Rhondda must be practically inaccessible. How could he have got through? It was impossible.

Although she kept telling herself that it was impossible, the rest of the service was meaningless for Daisy. Valerie kept turning around to look behind her while Daisy sat rigidly, afraid to turn her head to left or right. She wished her stepmother was with her, then she wouldn't feel so helpless. They usually came to church together, but today Edie

403

was too busy preparing for the family gathering. Everything had to be perfect for Gareth's return to the fold.

If only she hadn't come to church herself this morning! She should have had more sense because of the weather. But every Sunday morning she came to church, rain or shine, and had felt it a weakness to let a little snow stop her. Besides, she wanted to come to worship, to renew her spirit. That was the way she felt. She needed this time in church to give her the strength to face what was in front of her in life. Oh, if only she'd let it go this once.

She began to dread the end of the service when everyone would start leaving the church. People usually stood around in groups outside, chatting to friends before dispersing; today it was far too cold for that. Daisy usually stopped to chat, too, but today wanted to find a quick and easy exit, avoiding everyone, including the supposedly imaginary Rhodri.

Was he really there? Was he? Had he braved the ice and snow just to come to her? No, Rhodri had more sense than to take such risks.

From the corner of her eye Daisy saw Valerie turn around again and lift a hand. Could he really be there? Her heart thumped at the prospect, yet at the same time she quaked with panic. Would he approach her when the service was over? What would she say to him? What could she say?

When the final prayers came, Daisy sat with

eyes tightly closed and head bent. Even when the prayer was over she remained that way for moments longer, until Valerie shook her arm.

'Come on, Mammy. We'll miss Uncle Rhodri in a minute.'

Daisy found the courage then to turn and look towards the back pews, her glance taking in the few people making their way to the door. There was no sign of Rhodri, of course, and the thumping of her heart began to ease. It had been Valerie's imagination after all.

A strange feeling stole over Daisy as she walked out of the church; an all-over achy feeling as though she was in for a bout of 'flu. It wasn't due to the cold weather, she was sure, but wasn't certain whether it was relief or disappointment.

Outside, a deathly white blanket covered everything; snow drifts piled against the churchyard walls and the church itself, something Daisy had never seen before. This winter they'd remember for a long time, she thought. Overhead the clouds were heavy and grey with the promise of yet more snow. A cutting wind blew in from the sea, promising blizzards when the snow did come.

Daisy quickly fastened up Valerie's fur bonnet, tied the scarf more tightly under her chin and pulled on her mittens.

'Don't dawdle,' Daisy said, clutching at her daughter's hand and walking as quickly as she dared towards the church gates. 'Let's get home.' She felt the cold strike up through the soles of her shoes. 'I promised Nanna I'd help her with the party preparations.'

Valerie pulled back, resisting.

'But, Mammy. Let's say hello to Uncle Rhodri. He's over by there, look.'

'Now don't start that nonsense again,' Daisy said desperately.

She had the urge to run but resisted it, telling herself not to be such an idiot. People would think she was mad, trying to run on the icy path. But her steps were hurried just the same. As they passed through the gates she saw Rhodri standing right in front of them, waiting, the collar of his overcoat pulled up around his ears, looking very much the way he had the first day she had set eyes on him. He wasn't smiling, though, as he had on that day.

Astonished, Daisy stopped so suddenly that the woman walking behind bumped into her.

'So sorry, dear!'

Daisy didn't even hear. She was staring at Rhodri, her mind a complete blank.

'Uncle Rhodri!' Valerie made a dash for him, and he lifted her up on one arm.

'Hello, my lovely girl,' he said, kissing Valerie's cheek, but his gaze was on Daisy. 'Your face is cold, my little chick.'

'Uncle Rhodri, we're going to have a party,' Valerie said excitedly, her arm around his neck. 'Nanna's birthday today.' She held her head to one side. 'Would you like to come? I'll ask Nanna, shall I?' Valerie looked at her mother. 'Uncle Rhodri's coming to our party, Mammy.'

Daisy suddenly found she was holding her

breath and let out a long uneven sigh. Her breath seemed to hang in the air like a frozen cloud between them.

'I thought you were in Merthyr Tydfil,' she said, realising how dry her mouth was. 'How on earth did you get here?'

'I drove down. Started out early yesterday,' he said. 'Didn't get here until late last night. I'm staying with the Hewsons.'

Daisy felt a chill go through her, thinking of his driving on those treacherous mountain roads. They must be wellnigh impassable.

'You must be mad to attempt it,' she said. He could have been killed. Her heart turned over at the thought.

His smile was wry.

'The going *was* rougher than I imagined—a nightmare, in fact. But I'm here.'

Daisy swallowed hard.

'I thought I'd never see you again.'

'Did you?'

He was still angry with her, she sensed. If he was, why had he bothered to come in such appalling weather? Why seek her out like this? Did he want a repeat of their angry exchange? Well, if he did he was out of luck.

Daisy lifted her chin.

'Yes, I did. Why did you come?'

Rhodri glanced about.

'We can't discuss it on the road like this. Besides, it's too damned cold.' He put Valerie on her feet but still held her hand. 'Let's go up to my house,' he suggested. 'It's not sold yet. I still have the key. We could get a fire

407

going. I've a few pieces of coal left.'

Daisy swallowed. Coal. A decent fire. With the scarcity of fuel all through this awful winter, like everyone else she'd been trying to make do with cinders to get some kind of fire going in the house, but cinders were no substitute. She couldn't remember the last time they had had a decent fire, so the urge to do as he asked was overwhelming, but she resisted, commonsense telling her it would be an unwise move, coal or no coal.

Her feelings for him were just as strong as ever, and she knew they would always be there, but their relationship was over. They had nothing more to say to each other.

Besides, Valerie would certainly blab about a visit to Uncle Rhodri's house. The child might mention it in front of Gerald, and Daisy wouldn't be able to explain it away.

'I can't,' she said, trying to steady her voice. 'I have things to do. We're on our way home. I have a busy day ahead.' She held out a hand to her daughter. 'Come along, Valerie, please.'

'Oh, Mammyah! I want to go to Uncle Rhodri's. I haven't been there before.'

Daisy felt her nerves fraying, and with it her temper.

'You're asking for a smack, my girl,' she said, more harshly than she intended.

'Daisy! For God's sake!' Rhodri was staring at her. 'Don't take it out on the child. All right, if you insist on going home, I'll walk with you.'

She stared.

'But ...'

'We're going to talk, Daisy, whether you like it or not,' he said, and leading Valerie by the hand, began to walk along the pavement. 'I haven't come all this way, risking my neck in the snow and ice, for nothing.'

Reluctantly, she fell into step beside him, all too conscious of his presence. She glanced about them nervously. People must be wondering.

'You still haven't said why you came?'

'I had a telephone call from your stepmother,' he said.

'*What?*' Daisy stared at him, stopping in her tracks so suddenly she slithered, almost losing her balance. 'Why?'

Rhodri stopped, too, and turned his head to look at her. His mouth was a tight line and his blue eyes were as cold as the ice and snow under her feet.

'She had some news for me. Something she thought I ought to know.' His gaze sharpened. 'Why didn't *you* tell me you were pregnant, Daisy? Did you decide it was none of my business?'

Her mouth dropped open with astonishment. 'I never told her. How did she know?'

'So it's true, then?' he said. 'Why didn't you tell me?'

Daisy was silent for a moment. She was thinking of Josie. Had her friend betrayed her confidence to Edie? No, she wouldn't believe that.

'I had my reasons, Rhodri,' she said. 'How did she find out? Did she say?'

'Edie's no fool. She guessed,' he said flatly.

'As she guessed I'm the father. She knows it couldn't be Gerald.'

Daisy walked on, shaken. She had taken so much trouble to hide it, not only from Edie but from Gerald, too. But her stepmother was more astute than she'd realised. She had never dreamed that Edie had guessed about Rhodri, too.

'So, now you know,' Daisy said, lifting her chin. 'Everyone will think Gerald is the father. Now that we're not seeing each other, no one will suspect you so it needn't concern you at all.'

'Needn't concern me?' She heard him draw in an angry breath. 'Damn it, Daisy. I had every right to know. You're carrying my child!'

She moistened her lips.

'I'm going to have twins, so they tell me.'

Rhodri stopped to turn and stare at her. He looked taken aback for a moment, then she thought he looked pleased, despite his anger.

'Well! This changes things, doesn't it?' he said. There was an edge of determination in his voice that made her uneasy. She knew what was coming next. 'There's no question now that you must leave Gerald and come to Merthyr Tydfil with me,' he went on. 'We'll marry as soon as your divorce is through.'

'Divorce!' Daisy said loudly, then looked around quickly. Had anyone overheard her remark? 'Are you mad? The scandal would ruin both our careers. I've told you before. Why won't you accept it?'

'Daisy, be realistic.' His jaw tightened at the

shocked and angry expression on her face that she knew she couldn't hide. 'It isn't so much of a scandal these days. The divorce rate has shot up since the war ended. I've read in the papers that there are thousands of cases awaiting a hearing. People don't think so much of it these days, and it's quicker since last summer when they changed the divorce laws.'

Daisy's mouth tightened. 'Other people may take it lightly, Rhodri, but I don't. Easy divorce makes marriage meaningless so far as I can see.'

He took a deep, noisy breath.

'I didn't struggle down from the Rhondda, risking life and limb, to argue ethics with you, Daisy. Those children will be ... are, even now ... my responsibility. They're *my* children, Daisy. Mine as much as yours. And I demand ...'

'Demand! How dare you?' Daisy almost stamped her foot in outrage.

'Mammy!' Valerie's face was screwed up as though she were about to cry. She was glancing from Daisy to Rhodri, not understanding their anger.

'Now see what you've done,' Daisy said to Rhodri, somewhat unreasonably. 'You have no rights whatsoever. As a matter of fact, I've made enquiries.'

'You did what?'

'There was always the chance you would find out. I knew what your argument would be,' she said firmly, though her legs were trembling so much she didn't know how she was still standing. 'I'm not prepared to leave Gerald,

411

not prepared to get a divorce. I'm sorry, Rhodri. You don't know how sorry.'

'Now, wait one damn' minute!' he said. He looked about to explode.

They were almost at the turning for Woodville Road. Daisy tugged at Valerie's hand and began walking rapidly. She heard Rhodri swear behind as she walked away as swiftly as the icy pavement would allow, and felt the hairs on the back of her neck rise. She had never heard him swear before.

Chapter Twenty-Seven

Stepping over the threshold of her home, Daisy was still shaking from her new quarrel with Rhodri. He had upset her for the day. She didn't know how she was going to cope with the family party later. It was difficult to keep smiling when your heart was breaking, she reflected sadly.

She shivered as she stood in the passage, helping Valerie out of her coat and wellingtons. It wasn't much warmer indoors than outside these days. Rhodri might have offered her the coal, she thought tetchily.

She had to put him out of her mind, she decided, because it was no good going over it all in her head like an endless gramophone record. She must put her past behind her, no matter how painful that was. Her life would be difficult enough from now on without torturing herself with memories of their love. She and Rhodri were finished, and her heart must learn to live with that.

She would have to face Gerald soon. She'd made up her mind only this morning to tell him everything. She wouldn't let herself dwell too much on his reaction. He'd be angry, of course he would. He could leave her, but he couldn't throw her out of the house. She was the tenant. And besides, she knew her stepmother wouldn't stand for it.

She recalled the names he had called her on a previous occasion and the insults he'd subjected her to. His reaction couldn't be worse than that, and she would steel herself against it. Yes, she had betrayed him, but it wasn't entirely her fault. He would have to take some of the blame. She was satisfied in her own mind that she *had* tried to rekindle their marriage; had tried and failed.

And when she told him the truth? He would go or he would stay; she would abide by any decision he made. As for herself, she was prepared to go on as before for his sake. After all, she had made all the sacrifices so far, and no doubt would go on making them. Her heart was already broken after giving up Rhodri. What could hurt her now?

Shrugging out of her coat, she put it with her hat on the newel post at the bottom of the stairs to take them upstairs later. She had better get on with preparing their lunch. They had used their meat ration earlier in the week so there wasn't much. She had plenty of vegetables, thanks to

William, and had managed to charm the butcher into selling her some sausages. Hardly a feast, but never mind.

She was surprised to find Gerald sitting in the living-room and to see that he had actually banked up the fire with more cinders. It gave off a feeble warmth: one had to sit almost on top of it to feel the benefit. Daisy thought about Rhodri's coal again with bitterness.

Gerald looked up as she came in.

'William called with a cauliflower,' he said.

'That was good of him. Is that why you're up?'

'Not entirely. I thought I'd clear the yard of snow later. That slippery patch in front of the lavatory is dangerous.'

Daisy was startled, staring at him keenly. This was the first time he had shown any interest in doing anything around the house. Her spirits lifted a little.

'Good idea,' she said steadily. 'I'll get on with lunch.'

She went into the kitchen, eager now to light the gas in the oven ready to make roast potatoes. Valerie was standing by with her teddy bear, watching her every move.

Gerald came and stood in the doorway.

'William brought me some tobacco and a pipe,' he said, almost smiling. 'He's still trying to convert me. I might try it. Couldn't find the matches.' He put the pipe in his mouth experimentally.

'Top shelf,' said Daisy. 'Out of the way of busy fingers.'

She stretched up, straining, to take the matchbox down from the highest shelf.

'Ooh, Mammy!' Valerie exclaimed, loudly. 'Your tummy is getting fat.'

There was total silence in the room for what seemed to Daisy like aeons. Then her grip on the matchbox faltered and it fell, bouncing on top of the cooker to fall behind it with a rattle of matches. She turned her glance towards Gerald, suddenly apprehensive.

He was staring at her in a strange way, as though he had never really seen her properly before. There was a faint look of surprise in his eyes. He took the pipe out of his mouth.

'Daisy?'

She moistened her lips, attempting a rueful smile.

'I'll get that old walking stick and hook the box out,' she said. 'Lunch won't be long.'

'Daisy?'

'What?' She swallowed against the apprehension.

'Are you pregnant?'

She caught her lower lip with her teeth before answering. It shouldn't happen this way. She'd wanted to prepare him first. But now there was nothing for it but to admit it.

She looked him squarely in the eye. His face had whitened as he waited for her to reply, and his eyes, previously almost blank, were now glittering. She saw that it wasn't going to be easy. There was going to be a showdown.

'Valerie,' she said sharply, 'go in the front room and play with Teddy.'

She pouted.

'It's cold, Mammy.'

'Valerie! Do as I say. Now!'

Valerie stamped off, muttering protests, but Daisy was hardly aware, her attention completely on Gerald. She swallowed hard before taking a deep breath and answering: 'Yes, Gerald, I am pregnant.'

'I should have noticed it myself,' he said tightly. He put a hand on the door frame as though supporting himself, hanging on like grim death, knuckles white. 'Just as I was beginning to hope that you *were* different ... You whore!'

'Gerald, please!' Daisy was appalled. She had forgiven but not forgotten the last time he'd called her names when she was entirely innocent; insulted her, denying his own daughter. She had excused him because of his mental state. Now, even though she had deceived him since, it was too much to bear. He himself had driven her into Rhodri's arms.

'Bloody women!' He turned abruptly into the living-room. 'You're all the same. You can't be trusted. Sluts, all of you!'

Daisy rushed after him.

'Don't speak to me like that!'

'What did you expect me to say, Daisy?' He stood in front of the fireplace, shoulders stooped, thrusting his head forward aggressively. 'You betrayed me! What did you expect me to do? Ignore it? Did you think I'd just meekly accept it? Live with another man's bastard? Would any husband?'

'Husband!' Daisy exclaimed hotly, moved to

anger herself. 'You've not been a husband to me, Gerald, since the war years. And how can I betray a man who won't even acknowledge I'm alive?'

His lip curled.

'You don't expect me to believe you came looking for me in Yorkshire because of love?'

'No, not love, Gerald. Something perhaps even more demanding: duty. Honouring my marriage vows.' She hesitated to mention pity.

'Duty, honour!' He gave a laugh that was dry with bitterness. 'I know what women are like. I learned young. Even my own mother ...'

Daisy remembered the bleakness of that hill farm on the moors. The isolation and the loneliness. That farmhouse had never known love within its walls. She had sensed that from the moment she'd stepped over the threshold.

'No one can live without love,' she said. 'No one should have to.'

'Do you think I'm a fool, Daisy?'

'I would never have married you if I thought that.'

'Why *did* you marry me?'

'I ...' Daisy hesitated. She'd been asking herself the same question since she'd received the telegram telling her Gerald was alive, knowing she would have to sacrifice Rhodri, sacrifice love, and yes, even life.

'That question is unfair.' Suddenly she felt intense anger. It burned in her throat. 'Why did *you* marry *me*, Gerald, if you didn't trust me? Because the war was on? Because life was uncertain; because it was the fashion; because all our friends were rushing to tie the knot themselves?'

'That's all in the past, Daisy.' He waved a hand dismissively, as though he hadn't brought up the subject himself 'It's the here and now that concerns me. You standing there brazenly, telling me you're pregnant by another man. Who is he?'

Daisy took a deep breath, trying to control her anger. It wouldn't do any good to quarrel with him. And she had to keep remembering he really wasn't himself. This man wasn't the Gerald she'd married. Why did she feel the burden of duty towards him so heavy on her shoulders? Because he was lost, like a lost child. And she wouldn't abandon a child.

'I lived the life of a widow for two years, Gerald. Then I met someone. I was about to marry again when I learned you were alive,' she said, trying to steady her voice. 'But I gave him up for you, because you are my husband. I gave up the man I loved so very deeply ...' Her voice faltered. 'A love like that can't be put aside in a moment, if ever. Life and love don't work like that.'

'So much for your feelings for me! Who is he?'

'You were dead!' She choked back a sob. 'I thought you were dead. I had a right to go on living, didn't I?'

'So, this man you love.' There was bitterness and rancour in his voice. 'You couldn't wait to get back to his bed at the first opportunity?'

'That's not true! It wasn't like that.'

'So you say. Do you expect me to believe that, Daisy, after what you've done? Duty, honour ... You didn't have the decency to stand by me!'

'Oh, I stood by you, Gerald,' she cried out. 'Putting up with your strange moods, your petty suspicions. I even put up with your insult in denying Valerie was your child. I could have left you in Yorkshire. I could've divorced you. No one would have blamed me.'

His lips drew back in a sneer.

'Why didn't you?'

She swallowed. 'You need me, Gerald.'

For some reason that seemed to make him angrier. A pulse beat wildly in his temple.

'I need you like a bullet in the guts!'

'My God, Gerald, you say that to me after all I've given up for you? Have you no feelings left at all? I was terribly lonely and you obviously didn't want me.'

'That's no bloody excuse. Tell me his name, you slut!'

Daisy steeled herself not to react to the names he called her. He wasn't himself. He was angry, she understood that. Soon he would calm down. She prayed he would.

'There's no need for you to know that now,' she said as calmly as she could, yet she could hear the tremor of desperation in her own voice. 'I've told him it's over. Besides, he's left the area. I'll never see him again.'

Gerald's eyes narrowed.

'Valerie's always talking about Rhodri Lewis. And he's left the village, so your grandmother told me. It's that bloody doctor, isn't it?'

Daisy put a hand to her throat, suddenly alarmed. Normally so dull and expressionless, Gerald's eyes were almost glowing with rage.

'Well, he's not getting away with it, Daisy. I'm going to report him to the Medical Association for gross misconduct. I'll see the swine is struck off.'

'Gerald, listen to me! Please. Rhodri isn't to blame. I went to him. You didn't want me and I needed him. I was dying of loneliness, Gerald. If you want to blame anyone, blame me.'

She reached out a hand to him, but he shrank away.

'It's no good pleading for your lover, Daisy,' he rasped. 'It's too late. You should have thought of the consequences of acting like a whore.'

'You can call me any name you like, Gerald. It makes no difference. Rhodri and I love each other. He wanted me to go with him, but I wouldn't abandon you.' She lifted her hands in a pleading gesture. 'He hasn't taken me from you. I'm still your wife.'

'You're no wife of mine,' Gerald snarled at her. He reminded her of a cornered animal. 'Do you think I'll have anything to do with a slut like you? You disgust me!'

'At least I'm alive! Not dead like you.' Daisy's anger flared again. 'I've got feelings. I need love. I tried to make it work for us again. You wouldn't even meet me halfway. You just wanted to die, didn't you? Just die. And perhaps you wanted me to die with you. Well, I won't!'

She felt her patience snap suddenly, like an elastic band. She felt it in her head and in her heart. Rhodri was right. She should have listened to him. Gerald was going to make trouble, terrible trouble. The very thing she had tried to avoid.

She stared at him, all her pent-up feelings bursting like the waters of a breached dam. Resentment, bitterness, grief for her lost love. She could hate Gerald now, for the pain of loss he had caused her to suffer; for bringing her to this; for not being dead.

'God! I wish I'd never met you. I wish you *were* dead, Gerald!' she blazed at him, clenching her fists so tightly in her anger and frustration that her fingernails dug into her palms. 'I wish you *had* died in that camp.'

Staring at her, he suddenly went still, so still Daisy was startled. He looked as though he had turned to stone. Not a muscle in his face moved, and his eyes, which a moment before had blazed red hot rage at her, were glazed over and dead-looking.

Daisy swallowed apprehensively, filled with intense remorse for her cruel words.

'Gerald?'

He turned abruptly and without a word left the room. She heard his feet drumming up the stairs, his bedroom door slam.

She sank down on to the settee. She felt drained, as if all the life had been sucked out of her. The room began to spin. With one hand she clutched protectively at her abdomen, at the same time hanging on to the arm of the settee with the other, fearing she was about to fall to the floor.

What had made her say such terrible things? Conscience told her that these dark thoughts had probably been in the deepest recesses of her mind from the beginning. But that was no excuse, she chastised herself. She had been unfeeling and brutal, and he'd had his fill of brutality. She didn't love Gerald now, but she did care about what happened to him.

Hadn't she already proved this by denying Rhodri and cleaving to her husband?

Daisy put her hands to her forehead, feeling how hot and flustered she was. Should she go on making the Sunday lunch as though nothing had happened, or should she go up to her stepmother's for an hour or two until they had both simmered down?

Valerie came into the room, still clutching her teddy bear, and clambered on to the settee. Her lips were pursed disapprovingly.

'He was shouting at you, Mammy. He's a naughty man. I'll tell Nanna about him.'

Daisy hugged her daughter to her. Poor Valerie. She put her lips against the child's silky hair, breathing in the scent of it. This situation was hardly a happy one for Valerie in her early years. It couldn't be doing her any good, living in this unnatural household.

In being determined to honour her marriage vows, had Daisy been wrong all along? Had it done more harm than good for all of them? She knew one thing for sure: it had broken her heart, and almost her spirit.

'Come on, chick,' she said, wearily. 'Mammy's got to get on with the lunch.'

As she got up from the settee she heard Gerald coming down the stairs. Daisy gave a heavy sigh. Was the row going to start all over again? Maybe she and Valerie should go up to *Tŷ Heulwen* now? But she would apologise to him first. What she had said was unforgivable.

When he came into the room, Daisy opened her mouth to speak the words of contrition but instead was struck dumb at the sight of him, and began to tremble with fear.

Gerald was holding a gun in his hand, pointing it straight at her. She stared at it transfixed in horror, recognising it as the one she'd seen in the chest of drawers in Yorkshire. Her teeth were chattering in fear, but she managed to cry out: 'Gerald! What in God's name are you doing with that thing?'

'What I should have done a long time ago.' He smiled strangely, eyes alive again, glittering in a way that struck abject terror into her heart. 'Don't worry, Daisy, you won't feel lonely or neglected anymore. And your poor bastard children will never grow up to be ashamed of their mother.'

'Gerald! What ... what are you going to do?'

'You're wishing I was dead. Well, I'm going to oblige you. But I won't be going alone. You intended to abandon me, just as my mother did. I'll not let you go, Daisy. Neither you nor Valerie. You won't run away like my mother did. She didn't give a damn about me either. She betrayed my father and me. Left us. But that won't happen to me again.'

'Stop it, Gerald!' Daisy cried out, terrified at his words. 'You don't know what you're saying.'

Rhodri had warned her about Gerald's condition. Why in God's name hadn't she listened? Why had she been so stubborn? Now it was too late. She had pushed him right over the edge. Her pride and stubbornness had put herself and her children in jeopardy. She must talk him round.

'I'm not running away, Gerald. I wouldn't leave you. I'm your wife. Put the gun down, please! You're frightening us. Stop this craziness before it's too late.'

'I'm not crazy. I've just come to my senses. I shall leave a note explaining how Rhodri Lewis tried to steal my family. You can thank *him* for this, Daisy. He's the one that destroyed us.'

His eyes were open wide, pupils dilated with a feverish gleam in them. It flashed through Daisy's mind that he was under the influence of some kind of drug. His face was flushed, the scar tissue standing out ghastly white in comparison.

Terror was making her throat close up, and her mouth was so dry with fear she could hardly speak. If he was under the influence of a drug, he was beyond reason, beyond mercy. She drew Valerie closer to her, pushing the child behind her. They must try to get away.

She darted a glance towards the kitchenette and the back door. Was it open? Unlocked? She couldn't remember. She prayed that it was. She swallowed painfully, feeling her chest heave with the effort of breathing and speaking.

'Gerald, listen to me. You don't really want to do this,' she said, playing for time while taking small tentative steps towards the kitchenette, pulling Valerie along behind her. 'I'm not leaving you. I've sent Rhodri away. He's out of our lives. We're a family now, as you say. Your family, Gerald. We've got years ahead of us. And I'll make it up to you, I promise. Only put the gun down, please.'

'I'm in control again,' he said, as though she hadn't spoken. 'It feels good; it feels right. I've been a prisoner too long.'

'Then let's enjoy your freedom, Gerald,' Daisy said quickly, edging closer to the door.

A few more steps and she would be in the kitchenette. Her mind raced ahead. She must get into the yard somehow and then the back lane. She would take refuge in Josie's house.

'We'll leave the Mumbles, Gerald.' She was afraid to take her eyes off him for a second, afraid even to blink. 'I know you hated being uprooted, coming here. We'll go somewhere else. Anywhere you like. Back to Yorkshire.'

'You searched me out in Yorkshire.' There was a peevish tone in his voice, as if that was the root of all his resentment. 'I didn't ask you to come. You thought there was money, didn't you?'

'Money?' Daisy was hardly listening to what he was saying now. She was near the doorway. She scooped Valerie up, balancing her on one hip, still trying to shield her. She felt the muscles in her legs tense up, felt the adrenaline flowing. Any moment now she would make a dash for it. She breathed in deeply, counting the seconds ticking away; for all she knew, the last seconds of their lives.

'We're young,' she said, trying to sound as convincing as she could. 'We have so much to live for. There's no need for any of us to die yet, Gerald.' She began trembling again, suddenly terrified that her legs would fail her at the last minute. 'Valerie and I don't have to die here and now. Neither do you.'

'It makes no difference where you die, Daisy,' he said thickly. 'The hell is in living.' He lifted the gun. 'You don't deserve to live anyway, you whore!'

With a turn of speed that astonished her, Daisy wheeled round and was through the doorway. Her free hand fumbled at the latch and as it opened under her hand, she let out a cry of thankfulness at the miracle.

She heard Gerald shout her name in fury as she raced out into the yard. He was coming after her! The winter air hit her like the cold blast of death itself. She gasped at the pain of it. She'd forgotten the frozen snow in the yard! She began to slither on the icy surface, nearly losing her balance, legs not moving fast enough for her terrified mind. She was almost at the gate.

Oh, God! Don't let her fall now!

Daisy felt her shoulders and back tingle as she ran with Valerie clutched close in her arms. Gerald was coming after them! Every second she expected to feel a bullet thudding into her flesh.

She was through the gate into the back lane. 'Josie! Stanley!'

Her scream turned into a dry croak in the cold air. Was Gerald gaining on her? She feared to look behind her in case she lost her footing on the treacherous ground.

The Jenkinses' gate was closed! There'd be no time to open it before Gerald came into the lane with the gun.

Oh, God! Help!

'Josie!' The scream ripped from her throat this time, loud and piercing. 'Stanley! Help me, somebody!'

As she reached his gate Stanley ran into the yard in his shirt sleeves. 'Daisy! What the hell's the matter?'

'Gerald's got a gun!' she screeched, slithering the last few steps in her haste. 'Quick, Stanley, help us!'

He had the gate open in a second, and with an arm around her waist, dragged her across the yard to where Josie was standing on the doorstep, eyes wide with fright, knuckles pressed against her mouth.

Stanley slammed shut the back door behind them, and shot the bolt. As she passed over their threshold, Daisy felt ready to collapse and frantically held Valerie out to Josie, who grasped the child safely in her arms.

Daisy staggered, legs trembling so much they were unable to bear her weight any longer.

'Let her sit down, love,' Stanley said, putting

an arm around Daisy again and supporting her weight. 'She looks all in.'

Daisy collapsed on to a kitchen chair while Stanley fetched her a glass of water. It was icy cold and stung her throat.

'Daisy, what happened?' asked Josie, bouncing Valerie on her arm as the child began to grizzle with fright. Daisy could see her friend looked bewildered and fearful.

Daisy put a hand to her throat, panting, unable to speak a word for a moment.

'Gerald has a gun,' she gasped at last. 'He says he's going to kill us. He's out there now somewhere, waiting!'

Stanley glanced through the kitchen window into the yard.

'There's no sign of him,' he said, turning to look at her. 'Take it easy, kid. It's all over now.'

Daisy looked up at him, struck by his calm tone. He didn't believe her.

'He was going to shoot us!' she cried out desperately. 'I didn't imagine that, Stanley. He found out I'm pregnant. He went wild. Called me all kind of names. I said some awful things to him ...'

She put a hand to her mouth, stifling a sob. It was all her fault. She should have held her tongue. Now everything had fallen to pieces.

Stanley reached for his coat behind the door.

'Perhaps I'd better go and have a word with him?'

'No!' Daisy almost screamed. 'He's got a

gun. He's gone mad. He could do anything, anything!'

Stanley put on his coat.

'He's a bit worked up, that's all. He's probably calmed down by ...'

The sound of a report, loud and shocking, rang out, cutting through Stanley's reassurances and reverberating in the cold air outside. Daisy had never heard such a sound before, but by the haunted look that immediately appeared on Stanley's face, she knew instinctively it was a gun being fired.

The silence after the report seemed thicker, denser than before. Everyone was motionless for a moment as though turned to stone; Daisy with a glass of water to her lips, Stanley with his coat half on his shoulders. He was the first one to move, struggling into the coat, in haste now.

'I'll go and see.'

'No!' Josie reached out a free hand to him frantically. 'Don't, Stan. He's dangerous.'

'I think the danger is all over now, love,' he said in a subdued voice.

He unbolted the door and went out. Daisy could hear his feet crunching on the frozen snow for a moment and then the silence again. Josie sat down, cuddling Valerie on her lap. Neither spoke, and Daisy was afraid even to look at her friend, afraid of what she would see in her face.

It seemed a lifetime before she heard Stanley's boots on the snow again. He came into the room bringing a blast of icy air with him. He didn't have his coat on now. His face was white, as white as the snow on the roofs of the houses across the lane. He looked sick, too, Daisy thought; sick and haunted.

'Daisy love ...' He swallowed hard. 'Gerald's lying in the back yard. He's ... he's dead.'

'Oh, my God! Gerald!' She jumped to her feet. 'I must go to him. I'm a nurse. There must be something I can do!'

'No!' Stanley said forcefully, taking her arm to restrain her. 'You don't want to see him, kid, believe me. Listen, I'll go and get a bobby.'

'Then get a doctor!' cried Daisy. 'We must do something for him.'

Stanley shook his head.

'There's nothing a doctor can do for him, believe me,' he said vehemently. He strode towards the passage, calling over his shoulder: 'Keep Daisy by here, Josie love. She mustn't go next door. Make her some tea.'

Daisy allowed herself to be led to the settee and sank down on to it, Valerie close beside her.

Gerald was dead! Somehow the words didn't seem to make sense. The gun had fired. Was it an accident? Or had he ...

Daisy wanted to scream at the thought. Gerald had killed himself! He had committed suicide, and *she* was to blame. She had driven him to it. She had wished him dead and had told him so to his face. She remembered his words: 'You're wishing I was dead. Well, I'm going to oblige you.'

Josie was standing in front of her with a cup of tea.

'Drink this, Daisy love, it'll make you feel better.'

'Oh, Josie!' she wailed. 'I can never feel better. It's my fault! I might as well have pulled the trigger myself. I killed him. I told him I wished he was dead, and now he is. Oh, God! What have I done?'

Josie quickly put the cup of tea down on the floor and got on to her knees in front of Daisy, taking hold of her hand and squeezing tight.

'No, Daisy, don't say that. It's not your fault. Gerald wasn't a well man. He was ... well, strange, wasn't he? Oh, Daisy, I'm so sorry!'

She clutched at Josie's hand, holding on tightly, May God forgive me, thought Daisy, for the terrible thing I've done to Gerald. She hoped God would forgive her, because she didn't know whether she would ever be able to forgive herself.

Chapter Twenty-Eight

April 1947

Swansea Bay was shrouded in a fine misty rain, like seaspray, which sparkled through the bright early-April sunshine. Daisy sat, chin in hand, thoughtfully gazing out over the sea from the conservatory of *Tŷ Heulwen*.

These last few weeks had been the worst in her life, she thought sadly; worse than anything she had felt in the London blitz during the war. She had seen some terrible tragedies then, and had been moved to weep many times, but always as an observer. Tragedy had not touched her personally until now. Not even her father's death when she was still a child had caused this much pain. It was the pain of guilt, Daisy knew; always the hardest to bear.

And she was exhausted. The inquest had been a nightmare. All through the hearing she'd had a great urge to blurt out to the coroner that *she* was responsible for Gerald's suicide. She longed to confess all, unburden herself, assuage her guilt so she could go on living with some kind of peace of mind. But of course she didn't. How could she do that to Rhodri, to Edie, to her own children?

The temptation was to dwell on what might have been, but this could be dangerous; worse than that, fatal. She was alive and carrying the future lives of her children, Rhodri's children. She had to go on pulling the pieces together somehow.

Daisy glanced up as Edie came in with a cup of tea.

'Here you are, lovey,' her stepmother said, too cheerfully, Daisy thought. 'This'll buck you up.'

'I've been thinking, Mam,' she said, as she accepted the tea. 'I'll never be able to go back to Woodville Road. I couldn't face it.'

'You and Valerie can stay with me as long as you like, you know that.'

'I do, Mam,' she said, giving Edie's hand an

affectionate pat. 'But you know me. I like a place of my own.'

Edie sighed, taking a seat next to her.

'Well, there's a cottage at the top of Newton you could rent. I'm having it done up. The work will be finished in a few weeks, so the builders tell me.'

'Oh, Mam! Thank you!' Daisy exclaimed, with an enthusiasm she really didn't feel.

She ought to be more grateful, she knew. Her stepmother was so good to her, and Daisy didn't know how to explain that her repugnance towards her former home in Woodville Road, and her growing unease, were just part of a larger picture. She needed to get away altogether, make a fresh start elsewhere; escape the place of her unhappiness and go where she could erase painful memories and regain her life.

She hadn't been down in the village since the tragedy, unable to face the curious glances, the murmured comments. She'd always loved the Mumbles; loved living amongst its people. Now she felt like an outsider. There was her work, too. Could she go back to nursing in this place, as though nothing had happened? She didn't believe she could.

'I don't think you should be moving in on your own, though,' said Edie. 'Wait until after the babies are born.'

'I can't hang around here for four months, Mam.'

She *had* to get away! Already she was beginning to feel stifled. Not by Edie's love and support, but by her own loss of freedom. She felt herself a prisoner of circumstances now.

'Why don't you go away for a while?' Edie said, as though reading her thoughts. 'You could go up to Bath for a few months. Stay with my cousin Mabel.'

'I'm a stranger to her.' Daisy was dubious. 'I don't like to impose.'

'Nonsense!' Edie brushed aside her doubts. 'She'll love having you there. I'll write to her this afternoon.'

'Mrs Buckland?'

Daisy looked up to see Barbara, Edie's young receptionist, standing hesitantly in the doorway.

'What is it, Babs?' Edie asked.

'Dr Lewis is downstairs, asking to see Mrs Buckland.'

'Oh, no!' Daisy caught at Edie's hand. 'I don't want to see him, Mam.'

Edie hesitated for just a split second. 'Babs, ask Dr Lewis to wait a moment, will you please?'

'I can't face him,' Daisy said desperately when Barbara had gone. 'We quarrelled bitterly last time I saw him. We've nothing more to say to each other.'

Edie held her head to one side, looking keenly at her, and Daisy recognised the set of her stepmother's mouth.

'That quarrel happened before Gerald's ... passing. Things are different now. You're a free woman, Daisy.'

'Free! That's the last thing I am.'

'What happened wasn't your fault.'

'Yes, it was, Mam, and we both know it.'

Edie flicked one hand impatiently.

'The balance of Gerald's mind was disturbed, that's what the coroner ruled. You heard the evidence. It was on his mind to do away with himself from the start. Daisy, you can't spend the rest of your life blaming yourself.'

'I betrayed him when he needed me most. I can't forgive myself for that.'

'Daisy! Be sensible!' Edie's mouth was a thin line. It was rare for her to show anger. 'Gerald is beyond help now. But you still have your unborn children to consider, as well as Rhodri. He is their father and deserves consideration. Don't try to punish yourself by denying his love.'

'Mam! You make me sound selfish.'

Edie's features relaxed and she smiled, reaching out to take Daisy's hand.

'Selfish? No, not you, Daisy lovey. But don't you see? You're back now where you were before that telegram came. You're free and you're in love.' She hesitated. 'I have to say it, Daisy. Gerald was never the right one for you. I felt that as soon as I met him. And I don't mean because of his condition. You married in haste, lovey. It would never have worked.'

Daisy squeezed her stepmother's hand. Edie wasn't telling her anything she didn't already know. In the early years of her marriage to Gerald, when Valerie was on the way, she had wondered and worried about the future. She could never picture Gerald in Civvy Street. She'd always dreaded that the war years were his 'finest hour', and that after the war he'd never be able to settle to anything, a fish out of water.

'Don't make another mistake, Daisy. Rhodri loves you very much.'

'I know.'

'Right!' Edie said, rising. 'I'll ask him to come up, shall I?'

Daisy nodded, smiling. What would she do without Edie's common sense and good counsel?

'Yes, I'm ready to see him now. I've got some apologising to do.'

When Rhodri came into the room Daisy stood up immediately, her pulses racing and her heart thudding at the sight of him. She hadn't known what to expect, half hoping that he would greet her with open arms, make things easy for her. But he came into the room unsmiling, looking at her warily, Daisy thought, her spirits dropping.

'How are you?' he asked quietly. 'How are you bearing up?'

Daisy moistened her lips, chastened by his subdued manner but touched by the deep concern in his voice.

'I'm well, thank you.'

She sat down and Rhodri took a chair nearby. She thought he didn't look very well himself. He seemed tired, his face drawn. She felt a pang of guilt. She had brought him to this.

He leaned forward, resting his elbows on his knees, hands clasped together.

'Daisy, our last two meetings were ... well, let's face it, acrimonious to say the least.'

'I'm sorry,' she said quickly.

'So am I.' His eyes filled with compassion.

436

'And I'm sorry for what happened to Gerald. I was jealous of him, I admit it, but I never wished him harm. You know that, don't you, Daisy?'

She sat forward eagerly. 'Of course, Rhodri. If anyone's to blame, I am.'

He sat up straight. 'No, you must never think that. It was inevitable, believe me.' He waved a hand as though to finish with the subject of Gerald. 'That's over, done with. Now we, you and I, must put things right.'

Daisy fiddled with the collar of her dress. 'I don't understand.'

'Yes, you do, Daisy.' He was gazing at her earnestly. 'We must do what we always intended to do. Get married. The sooner the better.'

'Rhodri!' Daisy was staggered. 'My husband was buried only a week ago.' She was astounded by what seemed like insensitivity to her period of mourning. 'How can you suggest that?'

'How can you hesitate, Daisy?' he countered quickly. 'You told me you loved me. You're carrying my children. July is only four months off. I don't want them born out of wedlock. This is vitally important to me, Daisy. Do you understand?'

'Yes, but ...'

'Daisy, *do* you love me?'

She felt her heart swell with her feelings for him. She had never stopped loving him, yearning for him, even when she believed they would never see each other again.

'You know I do Rhodri.'

She could see the pain in his face and knew

he, too, had suffered over the last twenty-three months. She had no right to hurt him more. She wondered why she resisted him now. Was it pride? Or was it shame?

'And I love you, *cariad*, deeply,' he said. 'Let there be no more barriers between us, for pity's sake.'

'But what will people say ...'

Rhodri brought his fist down on his knee.

'To Hell with people, Daisy!' He ran trembling fingers through his hair. A little more calmly, he said: 'It's you and me and our children that matter now. Look, your stepmother has just told me you're going to Bath for a few months' rest. That's ideal. I strongly recommend it. I'll get a special licence. We'll be married there, then go straight to Merthyr. I'm renting a house there. It's very comfortable. It's got a big garden. Valerie will love it, and so will you.'

Despite her lingering uncertainty, Daisy felt excitement bubble up. If only it could be so! Rhodri's wife. She had dreamed about it for so long. But they must avoid any hint of a scandal at all costs. A mother of three children, her career as a midwife was over, but she still worried about the impact on his.

'Rhodri, I don't want to damage your reputation. How will it look if you suddenly turn up in Merthyr Tydfil with a pregnant wife?'

He smiled broadly and Daisy revelled in it. He looked more his old self.

'Very natural,' he said. 'I've already told them I'm married, and that my wife's expecting.'

'Rhodri!' she stared. She didn't know whether

to be angry or not. 'That was taking a lot for granted, wasn't it?'

'No, not really,' he said, gaze softening as he looked at her. 'We love each other. I'm more of a husband to you than Gerald ever was. *I'm* your real husband; your only husband.'

Looking into his eyes, seeing the warmth of love and compassion in them, Daisy felt her heart bursting with love for him, an overwhelming love. She hadn't been happy, she realised, since that day in 1945 when the telegram arrived. And even later, when she and Rhodri had come together again out of desperation and loneliness as well as their love, happiness had eluded her. Then their love had been tinged by deceit, giving it a bitter-sweet quality. Could she be happy again? Would she dare grasp at another chance?

His loving eyes were pleading with her and Daisy smiled, holding out her hand to him. It was true. He was her only husband. She could never love any other man the way she loved Rhodri. And now, carrying the unborn twins, the bond between them was stronger than ever before.

'I'll come home to have my babies, mind,' she said. She wanted her family around her when the time came.

He stood up, smiling and holding on to her hand, drawing her to him. She went into his arms as though they had never been parted. Daisy felt the months rolling away as his warm lips met hers. She remembered the happiness she had felt the first time their banns had been called in church, proclaiming to the world their love for each other.

There was nothing to fear for them now. They belonged to each other; destined to be together the rest of their lives.

Daisy reluctantly relinquished his embrace, and looked up into his face, aglow with love.

'Oh, Rhodri! I love you so very much.'

Chapter Twenty-Nine

May 1947

Josie looked up from the fashion magazine she was studying to where Stanley was sitting in his armchair before the fireplace, even though there was no fire lit. And there wouldn't be a fire, either, not until September. With the continuing fuel crisis the Government had banned gas and coal fires, even if you could get the coal.

Josie sighed. It just wasn't the same, sitting in front of an empty grate. Oh, well! What couldn't be cured had to be endured.

It was nice, though, just the two of them for once, she reflected, fire or no fire. Rhiannon was in bed already, and everyone else was out. Such moments alone with Stanley, quietly companionable, meant a great deal to her.

She glanced down at the illustrations in the magazine again.

'I thought I'd make Gwennie a costume for

her birthday.' she said. 'I've got some coupons saved.'

He lowered the *Evening Post* and glanced at her, smiling his approval.

'Mam would love that, kid. There's good of you to think about it.'

'Well, she's been good to us, hasn't she?' Josie pointed to the page. 'There's a style by here that would just suit her. I can copy that. Don't you mention a word, mind, Stan. I want it to be a surprise.'

'You'd better put that book away, then,' he said, turning a page of the newspaper. 'She and Teresa will be back from the pictures soon.' He glanced at the clock on the mantelpiece. 'It's gone seven. You should call Dewi in. Tell him to go home now, and get ready for bed.'

Josie made a face. 'Let him stay out a bit longer, Stan. At least until Teresa comes home. He doesn't like being in that house on his own, not since ...' She jerked her head towards next door, where Daisy had once lived. 'You know.'

Stanley's mouth stretched into a hard line.

'Where the hell has Francie got to anyway? How long has she been missing now? Four days?'

'Three, Stan. Don't make it worse than it is.' Josie put a finger to her lips. 'I'm worried about her, though.'

'Well, don't be!' he said bitterly. 'She's with some bloke somewhere.'

'I know! That's what I mean. I hope she's not bringing more trouble home.'

He glanced up. 'Rhiannon's no trouble,' he said sharply.

'Of course not! I didn't mean that, Stan. You know I love that kid like she was my own. I can't imagine life without her.'

It was true. For all the unhappiness Francie's pregnancy had caused in the beginning, Rhiannon was a vital part of Josie's life now. She loved the child deeply, more than she could express, even to Stanley. Her life had been enriched by Rhiannon. She knew Gwennie and Stanley felt the same by the way they spoiled the kid rotten. Josie smiled, picturing Rhiannon's little face. She was a beautiful child, with a lovely nature.

'And you're a good mother to her, too,' Stanley said. 'Thank God she's got you. That Francie's bloody useless.'

Time to change the subject, Josie thought. If it wasn't Francie running Stanley down, then it was Stanley complaining about Francie. She couldn't listen tonight, she was tired already.

'Oh! By the way, Stan,' she said quickly. 'Edie gave me some news today about Daisy.'

She hadn't meant to tell him Daisy's secret yet, but it might take his mind off Francie's shortcomings and save herself from earache. She knew he would keep the secret if she asked him.

'Daisy and Rhodri Lewis were married by special licence in Bath last week. They're up in Merthyr Tydfil now.'

'Bit soon, isn't it, after ...'

'Tsk!' She frowned at him. 'Don't be so

old-fashioned, Stan. Daisy deserves a bit of happiness after what she's been through. Do you know, it's nearly three months since that awful day. Mind you, I don't blame her for not coming back next door, not after ... But I do miss her so much, Stan. She's the best friend I ever had.'

'Well, you've got me, Josie love.'

She thought he was looking a bit crestfallen, and with a laugh she got up and went to sit on his lap, linking her arms around his neck and giving him a quick kiss.

'My big handsome husband! Don't tell me your nose is out of joint, then?'

He grinned at her, squeezing her tightly against him.

'Wait until I get you upstairs, my girl.'

Josie laughed, resting her head against his.

'Daisy will come back home to have her babies,' she said thoughtfully. 'And I'm looking forward to that. But, oh, Stan, when are we going to have a baby of our own? Is it me or what? Perhaps I ought to go and see the doctor?'

He kissed her cheek gently. 'It'll happen, kid. Don't worry about it. There's plenty of time. And, besides, let's try and get a bit saved first. You've got as much as you can manage now, what with this house and the shop.'

Josie sighed. Stanley was right, of course. They were rushed off their feet at the shop, especially now materials were a little more plentiful, even if clothing coupons were still necessary and looked likely to be for a long time yet.

Just the same, almost all the young women she knew were in the family way, and she ached, simply ached, for a child of her own.

'And you've got Rhiannon, love.'

'Yes.' Josie sighed again. 'I've got her.'

But Rhiannon wasn't *really* hers. Josie couldn't forget the little girl belonged to Francie, and God only knew who her father was. Josie wanted Stanley's child, their child. Most of her other dreams were coming true. When she carried Stanley's child, her happiness, her life, would be complete.

Josie jumped up from his lap as she heard the front door open and footsteps in the passage. It must be Gwennie and Teresa. She hurriedly pushed the fashion magazine under a cushion.

She looked up as the living-room door opened, and felt her jaw drop in astonishment. Francie stood there, posing, one hand on her hip, the other resting on the door post.

She was dressed up to the nines in a blue linen two-piece under a white thigh-length swing coat. A frothy little veiled hat was perched on her head at a rakish angle. Her make-up must have been applied with a trowel, Josie thought, mouth tightening at the sight.

'Francie! Where've you been? We've been worried sick.'

'Oh, yeah!' Francie looked sceptical, one side of her scarlet mouth slanting in a sneer. 'I'll bet!'

'Where were you?'

444

She sniffed. 'London, if you must know. Getting married.'

'*What?*'

Josie heard Stanley gasp with astonishment, and couldn't help gasping herself. She was conscious then of someone else standing in the passage behind her sister.

'You what?'

Francie pulled in her chin, looking down her nose.

'You're not the only one that can get a bloke, mind.' She looked over her shoulder at her half-hidden companion. 'Come in by here, darling, and meet the family.'

The man with Francie stepped into the room and Josie stared in shock.

Billy Parsons! She hardly recognised him. He was looking very prosperous. His face had filled out a little and his skin didn't look so sallow, but he still had that little moustache. He still reminded her of Hitler. Dressed to kill he was, too, she noticed. He wore an expensive-looking belted camel-hair coat, and a smart brown trilby. His tie-pin glittered in the electric light, and Josie stared. Diamonds?

'You married *him?* Have you gone barmy?' she cried out, unable to hide the dismay in her voice. 'You want your head read, Francie.'

'Hello, Mrs Jenkins, Mr Jenkins.' Billy nodded amicably, obviously determined to ignore Josie's attitude.

She glanced at Stanley, wondering what his response would be. He was standing, too, staring silently at Francie and her new husband. Josie didn't know whether it was just the light catching his face but he looked pale and there was a grim cast to his mouth.

'Hey! You watch what you're saying,' Francie said loudly. 'Billy's my husband now, part of our family. And he's taking good care of me, see.'

Part of their family! Josie turned her startled gaze back to her sister again, appalled that Francie had actually married this little twerp. Her sister knew Josie couldn't abide him, and to bring him here to their home ... a known criminal! She could feel her anger mount. It was too much.

'Wait a blooming minute!' she said. 'If you two think you're going to move in up the street, think again. I'm paying the rent on both houses, and you haven't contributed much, Francie. You've got a damned cheek if you think you and ... Mr Parsons are going to live off me.'

Francie curled her lip, looking down her nose again scornfully.

'Huh! Catch us living round by here! Billy and me got a lovely flat in London. Real posh, it is, isn't it, Billy?'

Josie felt deflated for a moment. 'That's all right then, as long as we know.'

'Plenty of opportunity up the Smoke, see, Mrs Jenkins,' he said. 'Got a barrow, I have, in Petticoat Lane. Doing all right, too.'

'Get a load of that, will you?' Francie held up her left hand to exhibit her ring finger. As well as her shiny new wedding band there was also a solitaire diamond ring, the size of the stone making Josie stare. 'Won't get many of those to the pound, right?'

Josie pursed her lips, trying not to look impressed. Money wasn't everything, and Francie was likely to find that out in the future. Billy Parsons was trouble, she knew it. He thought he was so smart and clever because he hadn't been caught yet, but it was only a matter of time.

For a moment she felt sad for her sister. There was misery and hardship ahead of her, Josie could feel it in her bones. Francie would rue the day she married Billy Parsons. But what was the good? She wouldn't be told.

'Where are you staying, then?'

'We're going back to London tonight.' Billy jerked his thumb towards the front door. 'Got the car outside.'

Stanley stepped forward.

'What have you come here for?' There was a tremor in his voice and Josie glanced up at him, wondering why he seemed so tense and upset.

Francie lifted her chin, staring at him arrogantly.

'Rhiannon, my baby. Where is she?'

Josie caught her breath, and put a hand to her throat in sudden dread. Rhiannon?

'What's all this to do with Rhiannon?' she asked, mouth drying with fear at the answer.

'Well, she is my child, Josie,' Francie said defiantly, but she was glaring at Stanley. 'I'll be living in London from now on. You didn't think I was going to leave her by here for ever, did you?'

Josie put her hand to her mouth to prevent a sob.

'But you can't take Rhiannon from me ... us now, Francie. We love that kid and she loves us. My God! She hardly knows you. You've never wanted to be a mother to her before. Why start now?'

Francie's features hardened.

'I *am* her mother. I've got every right to take her any time I want to. She's coming to live with me and Billy. He's her step-dad now, and can give her anything she wants.'

Josie felt dread suddenly turn to burning rage.

'What Rhiannon wants is someone who will love her and take care of her,' she shouted, clenching one fist and waving it under Francie's nose. 'You, Francie? You're not fit to mother our cat, and I've known you too long to hope you'll ever change! You're nothing more than a selfish little tart. Yes, tart, Billy Parsons! As if you didn't know.'

'Hey! You can't talk to me like that,' Francie shouted back. She turned to her husband. 'Don't just stand there, Billy. Say something, for God's sake! I'm being insulted by here.'

But he was silent, looking apprehensively at Stanley whose face was as dark as a thunder cloud. A muscle was working in his jaw. Josie knew the signs. Billy Parsons was likely to get thumped if he interfered, and he knew it, if he had any sense.

Encouraged, she folded her arms across her chest, chin up aggressively, legs standing firm.

'You're not taking our Rhiannon anywhere, so forget it.'

'I'll have the police on you,' Francie yelled at her furiously, face turning red under her make-up. 'I'll have you prosecuted.' She pointed a finger at Stanley. 'And that bugger will go to prison for raping me.'

'*What!*' Stanley and Josie shouted the word at the same time.

'Hey, kiddo! Steady on, mun!' Billy grasped at Francie's arm, but incensed she shrugged him off.

'You bitch!' Josie said through clenched teeth. 'You scheming little bitch. You're trying to start trouble between Stan and me now. That's wicked, that is. You've got the Devil in you, Francie, just like Dada.'

Stanley lifted an arm suddenly, making Billy jump back, startled.

'Get out!' Stanley thundered, waving his arm threateningly. 'The pair of you. Get out, and don't show your faces round here again. Got that, Parsons? I'll knock your bloody head off your shoulders if you bring that lying bitch to my home again.'

Billy hurriedly moved to leave, but Francie stood her ground. Her eyes were flashing like blue diamonds, and Josie could see her sister was almost beside herself with rage.

'Don't kid yourself, Stanley Jenkins. You're not getting away with it so easy.' She turned to Josie. 'Your precious husband! Butter wouldn't melt in his mouth, is it? Well, let me tell you something for nothing. Your husband is the father of my baby. Yes, *he's* Rhiannon's father. Why do you think he's getting so worked up?'

Josie stared at her open-mouthed. She knew Francie would stoop to just about anything, but this deliberate attempt to destroy her happiness, to push a wedge between herself and Stanley, was beyond belief.

'May God forgive you for that awful lie, Francie,' she said in a subdued voice. 'Because I don't think I can.'

There were footsteps in the passage and Gwennie and Teresa came into the room, staring at the visitors. Francie ignored them. There was a deep scowl on her face, and her boiling rage made her skin look blotchy under her make-up.

'Stanley is Rhiannon's father, I'm telling you,' she shouted, hands on hips, leaning forward aggressively. 'If he didn't rape me, he certainly seduced me. Me, an innocent girl!'

'Innocent girl, my arse!' exploded Gwennie. 'You were a proper little tart, even then. You did it on purpose ... threw yourself at him. He told me all about it ...'

She stopped, staring in dismay at Josie. There was silence for a moment then Francie's features lit up with triumph. Josie was dumbfounded. She opened her mouth to say something, ask for a denial from Stanley, but couldn't speak. The room felt very hot all of a sudden, and she clawed at the collar of her dress. Was the world spinning round extra fast, or was it her?

'It wasn't *his* fault, kid, honest,' Gwennie rushed on, turning a dull red around the gills. 'He was tricked, wasn't you, Stan love?'

Stanley was staring at Josie, his face as white as new snow.

'Listen, *cariad*, it's not the way you think. You've got to let me explain ...'

'You mean, it's true?' Josie's voice was just a dry whisper.

It was true! She could hardly believe it. She'd been betrayed by the one she loved most in the world. How could he do that to her? A dull ache started in the region of her heart and was growing sharper every second. It would engulf her soon, she knew it would.

Stanley and Francie together! Images were going round and round in her head. She wanted to blot them out, but couldn't.

'You and my own sister? You and her ... together?'

She still couldn't believe it; didn't want to believe it, even now, but the look in his face was telling her she must.

'It was an ... accident,' Stanley said. His hands were clasped together in front of him, knuckles white. He looks as though he's praying, she thought vaguely.

'An accident!' Francie hooted with laughter. 'That's the first time I've heard it called that.'

Josie turned towards her, jaw set. A moment ago she'd been burning up. Now she suddenly felt cold. Rage was flowing through her body like icy water in her veins. She felt as though her heart had frozen over and was still. It felt like the end of everything.

'You slut, Francie! You worthless piece of putrid rubbish!' she said through gritted teeth.

'And to think I helped you when you were in trouble. Worked my fingers to the bone for you. Saved you from Dada.'

The iciness was right through her now. She felt numbed. It was getting into her brain. She wanted to scream at the pain of it. Betrayal. She'd never realised it could feel like this; like death itself.

'Oh, God! I wish I'd let him push you down the stairs that night. I wish you were dead, you bitch! But I'll swing for you yet.'

Bedside herself with anguish and hurt, she snatched up the poker from the hearth, and raising it above her head, rushed at Francie, a scream of rage ripping from her throat.

Francie screamed, too.

'Keep her away from me! Don't let her get me! She's mad!'

Next thing Josie knew, a powerful arm gripped her from behind, swinging her round, and the poker was wrenched from her hand.

'Josie, for God's sake, no!' Stanley was shouting in her ear. He still had his arm around her and she wriggled free.

'Don't you touch me!' she panted, backing away from him. 'Don't you ever come near me again.'

'Josie, for pity's sake! You've got to listen to me.'

He took a step towards her but she turned away quickly, clasping her arms around herself, feeling the coldness of her flesh. It was like a nightmare. They were all staring at her as though she were mad.

Perhaps she was, because she had never felt so wretched before in her life. Not even when Stanley had been sent overseas and she'd thought she'd never see him again; not even when Dada had thrown her out into the dark night with nothing.

Those had been bad times, but they didn't compare to this. Everything she'd ever worked for, everything she'd ever dreamed of, was for Stanley and her, for their love and future. It hurt beyond words to know that this perfect love she'd always believed they had was nothing more than an empty illusion. How could she have been so wrong? How could she have fooled herself so thoroughly?

Francie was standing by the door, hiding behind Billy's shoulder. She was watching Josie warily. She found she couldn't bear to look at her sister now. Felt sick at the images that tortured her imagination.

'Mr Parsons,' she began, trying to control her voice, though it seemed as brittle as ice, and she felt it would break any minute. 'Get that creature you married out of my sight. Tell her never to come back here again. Because if she does, I will kill her, and that's a promise.'

Billy began to push Francie towards the passage, stifling anything she was trying to say.

'Wait!' Josie said. She stared at him for a minute. 'I've never liked you, Mr Parsons, never trusted you. You're a pathetic little crook, and will probably spend most of your life in prison. But today,' she shook her head solemnly, 'I feel sorry for you, because you married *her* and you'll curse the day you did, believe me.'

They went without another word, and then there was silence in the room. Josie could feel it as though it were tangible. She felt now it had always been there, but she had never noticed it before.

'Josie kiddo ...' Gwennie began hesitantly. She was almost wringing her hands.

'Don't speak to me,' Josie snapped. 'You knew all along, didn't you, and you never said a word?'

'Josie love, listen ...'

'I loved you, Gwennie,' she interrupted sharply. 'Like I'd love a mother, and you deceived me.'

Josie kept her gaze deliberately turned away from Stanley. She couldn't bear to look at him either. It was all finished, all done with. There was nothing else for her here.

'You can tell your son I'm finished with him. I don't want anything to do with him or you.'

'What about Rhiannon then, Josie?' Gwennie sounded choked, and tears were streaming down her cheeks. Josie regarded her unmoved. The coldness had taken all feeling away. There was just emptiness, and she was glad of it. She couldn't have stood that pain much longer. It was better to be dead than to suffer.

'Rhiannon belongs to Stanley. She's his responsibility now. She's nothing to do with me. I don't want her.'

She didn't know whether she could ever bear to look at the child again, now she knew who the father was. It would be too painful to bear. She didn't want to think about Rhiannon anymore.

Josie looked at her younger sister who had been standing at the door to the kitchenette, silent, with a bewildered look in her young eyes.

'Teresa love, go and get some clothes packed for you and Dewi. I'm leaving this house, and you two are coming with me.'

'I don't want to go with you, Josie.' Teresa went and stood near Gwennie, taking hold of the older woman's hand. Her eyes were glistening, and she looked frightened. 'I'm staying by here with Gwennie. Dewi won't want to go either.'

Josie felt her shoulders droop. She was alone. She could understand Teresa's fright, though. Josie's attack on Francie must have seemed like the act of a madwoman, but she didn't regret it. Whatever bad luck Francie had coming to her, she deserved it.

'All right, Teresa love, that's your decision,' she said. She felt calm now, calm and cold and distant. 'I'm sorry, though.'

With her head held high, she marched out into the passage without another word or glance.

'Josie!' Stanley's cry was full of pain, but in her frozen state Josie wasn't touched by it. She didn't trust that show of feeling anymore. It was all false. He had betrayed her. He was no longer her husband.

She had almost finished packing when someone tapped at the bedroom door and Johnno came into the room. His young face was white and strained. There was a look of disbelief in his eyes.

'Josie, this is daft, you leaving like this. Where will you go?'

'Come with me, Johnno love,' she said eagerly. She realised she had never been alone before. She didn't know where she would go, but she could not stay here.

He looked down at the floor, shaking his head.

'I got no quarrel with Stan or Gwennie,' he said. 'And I've got my job to think of, too. Don't go, Josie. Don't make this mistake.'

She bit her lip, trying not to burst into tears. It would only embarrass him.

'The mistake I made was trusting Stan. Oh, Johnno! What a fool I've been. I put him on a pedestal. I thought I'd found a man who was different from Dada; someone with principles; someone who really loved me. And all the time he was carrying on with my sister!'

'No!' Johnno said, shaking his head emphatically. 'That's not true. Stan swears to me it isn't.'

Josie sniffed miserably. 'And you believe him? How do I know there weren't other women before or since?' She shook her head. 'No, it's finished, Johnno. Over. I'll never trust him again.'

Chapter Thirty

'Goodnight then, Josie lovey.'

Edie stood in the doorway of the workshop, pulling on the cardigan of her twinset.

Dreading to see her partner go, leaving her to the loneliness of another night alone, Josie looked up from the design she was trying to work on, attempting a smile but knowing she was failing.

'Goodnight, Edie.'

Would she ever smile or laugh again, Josie wondered, now that her world had shattered? She felt as though she was cast adrift at sea, the waters threatening to close over her head at any moment. She had tried to conceal her misery as best she could. It wasn't fair on Edie and her other colleagues to bring her troubles into the workplace.

Edie took a couple of steps back into the room.

'Josie, why don't you come and stay up at *Tŷ Heulwen?* At least until you can sort out something better than this.' She waved a hand. 'That room upstairs is very cramped, and it doesn't do any good living over your work.'

Josie shook her head sadly.

'Thanks, Edie, you're very kind. But my work is all I have left now. I need to work. I need to bury myself in it.'

'Yes, bury is the operative word, Josie!' Edie said forcefully, shaking her head. 'You're on your own too much these days. You need company. I don't like to see you in such misery.'

Josie, unable to answer, compressed her lips and mastered the swell of tears that seemed to lodge in her throat. There was no hiding her heartache from Edie. She was too shrewd.

She regarded Josie for a moment.

'Well, lovey,' she went on, 'if you change your mind, come straight up. Don't stand on ceremony, will you?'

Josie found her voice at last. 'I thought *Tŷ Heulwen* was already filling up with holiday-makers?'

'Yes, we're booked solid until the end of September,' Edie agreed. She looked pleased at the prospect of a busy summer. 'But there's always a place for you, Josie.'

'Thanks, Edie, you're a real friend.'

And she certainly needed a friend now, she reflected, with her life turned upside down. She missed Daisy so much at a time like this; the comfort of talking it through with her. But in the absence of Daisy, Edie had been supportive and sympathetic.

'Well, I'd better go,' she said, giving Josie one last speculative look. 'Will you be all right?'

'Yes, of course,' she answered, swallowing hard, lifting a hand as Edie left.

But she was far from all right. She'd never felt so wretched, miserable and lonely in all her life before. No matter which way she twisted and turned there was nothing left, nothing to look forward to, nothing to hang on to except her work, and she had thrown herself into that head first since she'd left Woodville Road. Maybe she was overdoing it but she dared not stop, not for a moment. It was the only way to fight off the black despair just lying beyond the edges of her mind. It would engulf her in a moment if she wasn't vigilant. And she could do without self-pity.

Josie laid down her pencil and rose reluctantly from the chair. She did feel tired. If only she could sleep. Even Edie, all-seeing as she was, didn't know that Josie often spent the small hours in the workroom, trying to escape her own sleeplessness. She had wept so much that first week alone, grieving for what she had lost; the sense of loss as sharp as if someone had died. Now she was all cried out. But although her eyes were dry, the heartache of Stanley's betrayal was still there, burning continually.

Josie glanced about her. There was nothing for it but to go upstairs now. She could delay it no longer. Going into the shop to lock up, she reached to pull the blind down over the door as a woman and child passed by outside, hand in hand.

Josie's heart turned over as she stared at them. The child was so like Rhiannon; the same little pixie face, the same dancing walk as though she had wings on her heels.

Josie pulled down the blind quickly to hide the sight. Everywhere she looked, she thought she saw Rhiannon; in the shop, in the street. At first she'd thought the sight would only remind her of what Stanley and Francie had done, but after a week alone, thinking, remembering, she realised it wasn't true. Rhiannon was as much a victim of their treachery as Josie herself. She had deserted the child without a word. That had been very wrong, and now she bitterly regretted it. She should have brought Rhiannon here with her. She was the only mother the child had known. They belonged together. Now it was too late.

Josie leaned against the locked door, feeling sharp regret mingle with the longing deep inside her. She would never have guessed how much she could miss Rhiannon, and the child was missing her too, she had no doubt.

Josie felt a swell of bitterness as well. She was separated from the child she loved because of Stanley. He had not only robbed her of her future, but of Rhiannon, too. How she longed to be nursing her now. She could almost feel Rhiannon's sleepy little head on her shoulder; the warmth of her arms around her neck; the scent of her hair. All that had been taken from her. She could never forgive for that, either.

Josie went upstairs to the room where she lived and slept. Edie had loaned her a wireless set. She turned it on now simply to break the neverending silence, and set about preparing something to eat.

Despite her resentment, she couldn't help wondering how they were getting on without her at Woodville Street. She took no satisfaction from believing things must be difficult for

Stanley. She knew he paid the rent on both houses now, because Edie had told her, and that must be stretching his wage as far as it would go.

Sometimes she couldn't believe she had just left them, walked out without a second thought. She didn't know why she felt guilty about it. After all, she was the injured party. She'd had plenty of second thoughts since, sitting alone in this room, night after night. What disappointed her greatly was that neither Teresa nor Johnno had been to see her. She longed to see them because she missed the warmth of her family around her, and they could have given her news of Rhiannon.

After eating, Josie turned off the wireless. The music was either too happy or too sad. She couldn't stand either, nor bear to listen to programmes she usually enjoyed with Stanley. They shared a similar sense of humour and laughed at the same kinds of things. Now everything made her want to cry only no tears would come, just eyes burning, burning.

The silence was no better. Should she go down to the workshop again? Edie's warning made her hesitate. Although it was early Josie reluctantly went to her bed, to lie sleepless, plagued by memories. She couldn't even spend the empty hours of darkness making plans. Before one could plan, one needed to have a future. Stanley had been her future; Stanley and the children they would have. Firmly, she pushed down any feelings of missing him. She wouldn't let herself miss him. He had made no attempt to contact her since she'd walked out. She was glad, she told herself. She much preferred to think of him only with bitterness and anger, now. As far as she could see, there was nothing ahead of her.

Teresa called to see her the next day after school. Josie took her eagerly upstairs to her room. The girl looked around, wrinkling her nose.

'Poky, isn't it?'

'It suits me,' Josie answered shortly. 'Have you had your tea?'

'No. I'll be going in a minute to have it. Listen, Josie, when are you coming back home? Haven't you stopped sulking yet?'

'Sulking!' she compressed her lips. 'Who's been saying that?'

'That's the way it looks to me and Johnno,' Teresa replied. 'He says you're making too much of it. Poor old Stanley doesn't know whether he's coming or going, mun.'

'Poor old Stanley, my backside!' Josie exploded. 'What about me? I'm the one who's been cheated, deceived—and with my twin sister, too.' She shook her head. 'You're too young to understand.'

Teresa looked annoyed. 'Of course I understand. I'm thirteen. I'm not a child! But it happened ages ago, didn't it? It's not as though he's been carrying on or anything. And he's awful cut up because you've left home.'

Josie drew in her chin, pursing her lips in contempt. 'So he should be!'

462

Teresa flung her satchel on the floor at the side of the only armchair then flopped down into it, folding her long skinny legs up underneath her.

'Well, I don't see why you had to leave home, Josie. After all, Mama didn't leave Dada, did she? She stuck it out. And he was beating her, as well.'

Josie put hands on hips, taking a defiant stance.

'I'm not Mama. She had nowhere to go anyway, and nothing to live on. She didn't have any choice but I do. I've got my own business to support me. I'm independent.' And lonely, too, she thought, but that was neither here nor there. 'I won't put up with bad treatment from any man. I don't care who he is.'

'Oh, come on now, Josie!' Teresa said. 'Stanley is a lamb. He never knocked you about. He's a good bloke, mun. Just because he made a little mistake ...'

'Dry up, Teresa!' Josie snapped, shaking her head, suddenly impatient. 'I don't know why you're on his side. You don't know anything about real life. It's not like the pictures, mind. I'll talk to you when you're a bit older, my girl.'

She glared up at Josie.

'Francie always said you were a hard case. I can see now she's right.'

Josie's mouth dropped open.

'Huh! That's a good one coming from her, isn't it? The brazen bit! She couldn't get a decent bloke of her own, so she tried to grab mine. I should've sent her packing ages ago.'

'What? And Rhiannon as well?' Teresa asked disbelievingly. 'Poor little kid doesn't stop crying for you. Gwennie and Stan are at their wit's end with her.'

That was too much for Josie. She put a hand to her mouth to stifle a sob. Rhiannon! The little darling was grieving, thinking she'd been abandoned which of course she had.

Josie bit her thumb nail anxiously, worried about the effect on Rhiannon. This crying and grieving would do her no good at all. She felt like wringing her hands. What could she do about it now? Oh, it just wasn't fair!

Teresa scrambled off the chair, slinging her school satchel over her shoulder, preparing to go. Josie could feel loneliness closing in again.

'Have a bit of tea, Teresa, mun?' she said coaxingly.

She shook her head.

'I'm going to the pictures with Gwennie tonight, so I can't stay. I only came to tell you that Stan's had a letter from Francie. She says she's going to have the police on him for taking her child from her.'

'Hah!' Josie laughed derisively. 'She's bluffing! She wouldn't dare talk to the police, not now she's married to that little crook Billy Parsons. If the police start poking around his business deals, he'll be in clink before you can say Jam. No, Stan doesn't have to worry about the police getting involved.'

'Well, he's taking it seriously anyway,' Teresa said. 'I heard him tell Gwennie he's going to see about adopting Rhiannon. Says he'll take Francie to court to prove she's an unfit mother.'

Josie was silent. All that would take money, and he didn't have it. Francie had all the rights on her side. She could come and take Rhiannon away any time she wanted, if she and Billy felt brave enough to face Stanley.

Josie lifted her chin, watching her younger sister closely.

'Did Stan send you here to tell me that?'

'No. I just thought you might be interested in what's going on.'

'Well, I'm not! Stanley's made his bed. Now he can lie on it.'

Alone, she thought, like me.

'Got any message for him?'

'No, I haven't! And don't you go telling him anything about me, either. What I do or say is none of his business anymore. I'm doing extremely well on my own. I like it, as a matter of fact.'

Josie was to recall her words a couple of weeks later. She rose late after a restless night, feeling like nothing on earth. That was one of the worst aspects of living alone, she reflected. When you were ill there was no one to help or complain to.

Josie clutched at her stomach as she came out of her bedroom, feeling nausea rise like a tidal wave. The lavatory was on the ground floor at the back of the workroom, and she almost didn't get there in time. She knelt on the floor, with her head hanging over the pan, wondering what she had eaten that had upset her so much.

She didn't feel quite herself all day and made an excuse when Edie asked her why she was so pale.

'Bit of food-poisoning, I expect,' she said, recalling the time she had made that same excuse for Francie's morning sickness. Why did she have to remember that now? she asked herself irritably.

When she was sick again the following morning, it dawned on her that she, too, was suffering morning sickness, and she was stunned by the thought. Could it really be true that she was going to have a baby? She had missed her last period, but had put that down to the stress of discovering Stanley's treachery, and her leaving home.

She would have to see the doctor to confirm it, but in her heart she knew it was true. She was going to have Stanley's baby! She felt breathless at the idea and elated. What she had dreamed of since marrying him was coming true at last.

Then, suddenly, through the elation, she felt a great sadness. This should be a joyous occasion, and she did feel joyous, but now she couldn't share her happiness with Stanley. They should be celebrating together, but instead she was here, alone and miserable.

One thought made her thankful. Stanley had betrayed her, yet her marriage to him had not been in vain after all. Through him she was to have a child of her own at last.

Josie decided to keep her news to herself for

the moment. She wouldn't even tell Edie, at least not until it was confirmed. She must go on as before, working as hard as she could, and she must make plans now.

She hugged herself, not feeling so lonely anymore. She had a new future to look forward to now. She'd have a child to bring up, and she would do it alone. She wasn't afraid.

One Saturday morning a few weeks later Josie stepped out of Taylor's the Grocer on to the pavement, recounting the change in her hand and not looking where she was going, when she collided with someone just coming around the corner.

'Oh, sorry!' she said, squinting up into the sunshine.

'Josie!'

Stanley! She almost jumped out of her skin to see him standing there staring at her; embarrassment rising up into her cheeks. Before she had a chance to say anything, Rhiannon flung herself at her.

'Auntie Josie!' She clutched Josie around her thighs, almost knocking her off her feet. 'Auntie Josie! You've come back! You've come back!'

Overcome by the sound of the child's ecstatic cries, and despite her own embarrassment at meeting Stanley like this, she scooped Rhiannon up into her arms, kissing her beaming little face.

'Hello, my lovely girl. How are you, my little chick?'

'It's good to see you, Josie,' Stanley said

quietly, standing by watching them. 'You're looking a bit pale, love. Are you all right?'

Josie buried her face in the child's hair.

'Yes, I'm fine,' she mumbled. Why did she feel embarrassed? *She* hadn't done anything wrong.

She ventured a glance at him. He didn't look all that well himself, she saw, trying not to show she was observing him. He appeared tired, worn out. There were dark circles under his eyes, and he'd not taken much trouble shaving.

Was he eating properly? she wondered. Gwennie wasn't much of a cook, and the notion of regular mealtimes was foreign to her.

Stanley would be missing Josie's good home-cooked meals, and, if truth be told, she reflected, she missed making them for him. There didn't seem any point in cooking for one, though now she was pregnant, she must look after herself, of course.

Should she tell him about the baby? The doctor had confirmed it over a week ago, and she longed to tell someone in her family. But he might take it the wrong way, and think she was angling to come back to him. Fat chance!

Josie was distracted from these thoughts when Rhiannon put her arms around her neck, looking earnestly into her face. The child's eyes were so like Stanley's, it made Josie want to cry.

'We have some ice-cream now then we all go home, right, Auntie Josie?' she said, planting a wet kiss on Josie's cheek.

Feeling trapped, she darted a glance along the street in sudden agitation. Rhiannon was

468

clinging to her as though she would never let go. It was going to be difficult to tear herself away, thought Josie, feeling panic start low down in her stomach.

'I don't know, chick. Auntie's getting the rations and ...'

'You can spare the kid five minutes, can't you, Josie, mun?' Stanley asked quickly. 'Look at her!'

Josie flashed him a look of irritation. She didn't need to be told the state the child was in, but it was no good raising Rhiannon's hopes.

His return look was challenging, and he held her gaze as though as innocent as the day was long. She knew what he was up to. He was trying to back her into a corner; make it difficult for her to refuse to be in his company. It would be better if she walked away now. Better for all three of them.

Even as the thought came, her arms tightened around the child. How many times over the last weeks had she wished to see and hold Rhiannon? Being parted from her was like being parted from her own child. Who else had cared about bringing up Rhiannon but herself?

'Well, perhaps five minutes,' she said carefully. 'Just for the ice-cream.'

They went into the ice-cream parlour on Dunn's Corner, taking a table overlooking the bus terminus and, beyond it, the sea. Rhiannon dragged her chair nearer to Josie's, scrambling up and sitting close, reaching out a chubby hand to touch Josie's now and again, as though reassuring herself that her beloved auntie was really there.

'What would you like, Josie? Cup of tea?' Stanley asked, reaching into his back pocket for money.

'Nothing, thank you,' she answered stiffly. 'This isn't a social occasion, Stanley. I'm only here because of ...' She glanced at Rhiannon.

Without a word he went to the counter and brought back a small dish of ice-cream for Rhiannon and a cup of tea for himself.

'Thought I'd have heard from you by now,' he said, spooning sugar into his cup.

She raised her brows, looking down her nose at him.

'Why?'

'Thought you might be wondering how we're getting on, like. I'm thinking about you all the time, Josie. Remembering, regretting ...'

She said nothing but glanced quickly out of the window to watch passengers step off a bus that had just pulled in. There were kids with buckets and spades, and mothers with rolled-up towels and sandwiches in carrier bags.

She remembered a similar scene the day Daisy had given away her wedding dress in despair. It seemed so long ago now. She'd never dreamed she would be despairing herself one day. Did Stanley think he was the only one with memories, the only one who had regrets?

'There's glad I am we bumped into each other,' he went on. His voice had an urgent ring to it now, and Josie guessed what he was going to say next. 'There's something I wanted to tell you. It's important. I'm going to adopt Rhiannon, or at least try to.'

'I know,' she said shortly. 'Teresa told me.'

He nodded. 'You understand then what I want? What it means for us?'

'*Us?*' Josie was nettled. She frowned, shaking her head. 'There's no *us*, Stanley. Not anymore. You destroyed that, you and Francie.'

What was she doing? she thought wildly, sitting here with Stanley as if he'd never betrayed her, as if they were still a happy family.

He bowed his head for a moment. When he looked up his face was tight and strained. He must be suffering, too, thought Josie. She hoped he was, after all he'd done to her. Was that vindictive? she wondered. If it was, she couldn't help it. The pain and heartache she'd suffered over the past month were still strong. It was only knowing she was having a baby of her own that made them bearable now.

'I can't accept we're finished, Josie, after all we meant to each other.'

'Well, that couldn't have been a lot, could it?' she snapped. 'Not on your part anyway.'

'You haven't given me a chance to talk to you, have you? If only you'd let me explain.'

'Huh!' Josie pulled in her chin, voice edged with derision. 'I don't want an explanation, thanks! I don't want it explained how you and Francie made a fool of me. What are you trying to do?' Her voice rose in pitch, and heads turned in their direction. 'Rub my nose in it?'

Stanley glanced round uneasily at the other customers, his mouth tightening.

'All right!' he said. 'Forget about us ...'

'I will ... don't worry!'

'Look, I don't want to argue with you. All I'm concerned about now is Rhiannon.' He lowered his voice. 'I don't want that scheming bitch Francie to have her. I'm going to do everything I can to stop it. Can you imagine what the kid's life would be like?'

'That scheming bitch is the mother of your child,' Josie said through clenched teeth. 'Don't forget that when you're piling it all on her.'

He was acting as though Francie had injured him in some way, when the truth was that both of them had stolen *her* life, even before she was aware of it. It still made her angry to think of all those years she'd lived in ignorance of the truth.

He stared.

'Oh, you're taking Francie's side now then, are you?'

'No! I hate her,' Josie hissed at him. 'And I wasn't joking when I said I'd kill her if she came back here.'

She had wanted to kill them both at the time, so enraged had she been, before the pain set in, before she finally realised she had lost everything.

But with her baby, she now had a new start and a new future, while Stanley still milled around in the debris of their old life. All he had was Rhiannon, and perhaps he wouldn't be able to hold on to her long either. But that thought gave her no satisfaction. She loved Rhiannon and wanted a good life for her. The girl's best chance was with Stanley, and in that respect she wished him well, for Rhiannon's sake.

'Josie, I need your help.'

He pushed his cup and saucer aside to lean closer to her across the table. The familiar scent of him made all kinds of memories thrust themselves into her consciousness. Suddenly she felt hot and suffocated, recalling how they had been together, how she had trusted and loved him. He'd said he couldn't believe it was over for them. At this moment she could hardly believe it herself.

'I'll have the fight of my life proving your sister is an unfit mother,' he went on, obviously unaware of her confusion, for which she was thankful. 'I'll stand no chance if it gets out I'm separated from you, Josie. Regulations are strict on adoption, and I'm desperate.'

He reached out and put a hand on hers as it rested on the table top.

'Will you come back home to live with me?'

'What?' She stared at him in astonishment, her momentary confusion evaporating in the face of his audacity.

'The Adoption Society will laugh in my face, and so will the Courts, if I can't present myself as a happily married man.'

Josie snatched her hand away. Pushing back

her chair, she stood up abruptly.

'You've got the cheek of hell, Stanley Jenkins!'

He rose, too.

'For Rhiannon, not for me. I don't expect anything for myself, but for the child. You've got to help me.'

'You're despicable!' Josie said through clenched teeth. 'Using your own daughter as leverage. Moral blackmail, that's what it is. You know I love Rhiannon, and you're trying to use it against me.'

'It isn't like that. You're angry and hurt, Josie, I realise that, and you don't know how sorry I am ...'

'You're sorry! Oh, well, thanks a lot!' She was livid. 'What am I supposed to say? "That's all right, Stanley, all is forgiven"?'

Her legs were shaking and she was beginning to feel nauseated again. She glanced towards the door. She had to get out into the fresh air, away from him and the memories that continued to tumble around her.

Rhiannon grabbed at her skirt.

'We go home now, isn't it, Auntie Josie?'

Josie swallowed the lump in her throat as she looked down at the little pixie face, the innocent eyes so like her father's. Why was life so unfair? Why did she have to hurt the child? She shook her head.

'Not today, chick. Auntie will see you again, right?'

She tried to release her skirt, but Rhiannon clung like a limpet. 'No! No! Auntie, I come with you! I come with you!'

The child's screams tore right through Josie's heart.

'Look what you've done!' she was shouting at Stanley above Rhiannon's crying, trying to pull free, desperate to get outside. People sitting at nearby tables were staring at them.

Stanley bent and scooped up a protesting Rhiannon, holding her tightly against his chest while she, tears rolling down her plump cheeks, strained forward, one arm outstretched.

'Auntie!'

Stanley was white-faced.

'Josie, for heaven's sake! You can't leave us like this. What in God's name do I have to do?'

Josie stood for a brief moment, trembling like a reed in the wind, staring helplessly at the two people she loved most in the world.

She had at last to concede the truth she had been denying for weeks. She still loved Stanley. That was *her* torment. She loved him, but she would never trust him again. She longed for what had once been; their love, which she'd thought was the truest love ever. Yes, she wanted him still, but her pride wouldn't allow it. She'd been humiliated, and her sense of justice wouldn't allow it. She was sorry to the depths of her heart that little Rhiannon had to suffer for it, but she could never go back to him. Never.

Chapter Thirty-One

July 1947

'What do you think of my twin sons, then?' Daisy asked from the bed.

Josie was at the window looking out over the sweep of Swansea Bay and the sea sparkling in the warm sunshine, thinking that normally she and Rhiannon would be heading off to Bracelet Bay on a day like this. Rhiannon would be happy making sand castles and poking about in the rock pools while Josie scoured the beach for pretty shells and coloured pebbles, before they settled down for their picnic of Spam sandwiches and red pop.

In Josie's head she could still hear the child's screams and cries as she had hurried away from the ice-cream parlour. She couldn't stop thinking about it, feeling guilty, as though she'd committed some barbaric crime. Perhaps she had. The feeling of hope and new beginning that had come to her when she knew she was going to have a baby had tarnished somewhat since that awful Saturday.

'Josie?'

She spun around, startled, staring at her friend sitting up in bed, wearing a fluffy pink bed-jacket.

'Oh, Daisy! I'm sorry. I was far away.'

'I can see that,' Daisy said with a smile. 'And I'm sorry, too, Josie, about the way things have turned out for you.' She shook her head. 'I can hardly believe it of Stanley.'

'Me too,' Josie answered forlornly, walking over to the two cribs side by side near the bed. She looked down at the sleeping babies: button noses, rosebud mouths and dark silky hair.

'They're beautiful—adorable, Daisy. Ten days old and they're already as handsome as their father,' she said, looking up at her friend with a broad smile despite her own sad thoughts. 'Rhodri must be so proud.'

'I won't tell him you said that,' Daisy said. 'He'll get a big head.'

'I can hardly wait for my own baby to be born,' Josie said wistfully. 'I'm throwing myself into my work at the shop, but it still isn't enough to stifle the pain.'

'You need your family back, Josie, my girl.'

Josie sat down on the side of the bed.

'What family? It's all gone, kid, like it never was.'

Daisy put her head on one side, giving her a slanted look.

'That's not true and you know it.'

'Daisy, you don't know what it's like.' Josie lifted her chin defiantly. 'When the man you love, trusted, does the dirty on you.'

Daisy lowered her head, examining her thumb nail.

'No, I don't know what that's like, but I know how it feels when you're parted from the man you love desperately.' She looked up. 'Listen,

Josie, we're friends, right? And friends can talk straight to each other, can't they, without it damaging their friendship?'

'Of course,' Josie agreed. 'A friendship worth having is one that will last a lifetime.'

'I couldn't agree more,' said Daisy, settling herself more comfortably against her pillows. 'That's why I'm going to talk to you now like a Dutch uncle.'

'A what?' Josie couldn't help smiling at the serious expression on her friend's face. Childbirth obviously agreed with Daisy. Her skin glowed and her eyes sparkled.

'Frank advice, that's what you need, Josie,' she said firmly. 'Someone to drill some sense into you. I've been through a bad patch myself, a very dark time, but thanks to Rhodri I've come through it. I'm so happy now, being his wife. I might have stayed in the dark, too, if he hadn't talked to me straight; showed me the right thing to do. I'm going to do the same for you.'

Josie reached out a hand to touch Daisy's arm.

'You're a lovely girl, and you've been a good friend, but not even you can work miracles.'

She didn't even know whether she wanted a miracle to happen. That Saturday, bumping into Stanley so unexpectedly, had confused her about her feelings for him. She had imagined she would hate him from now on, expected to hate him after what he'd done, but had found, seeing him again, being with him, that her feelings were unchanged. She was angry with him, and hurt, but she didn't hate him. She loved him still.

Oh, it was all so hopeless!

Daisy sniffed.

'Well, we'll see, won't we? Let's talk about Rhiannon first. No, don't make a face like that, Josie! I know I'm touching a raw spot. You've given that child a lot of love and care. But you did something else as well. You took responsibility for her when she was born. You elected to be a substitute mother.'

Josie shrugged. 'I didn't have much choice, did I?'

'Well, I don't know about that.' Daisy pursed her lips thoughtfully. 'I mean, you didn't *have* to. You could've turned your back; let Francie get on with it as best she could. Instead you *took* responsibility. You can't turn that off now just because it doesn't suit you anymore.'

Josie lifted her chin. 'You're being unfair, Daisy! What happened wasn't my fault.'

'Don't get shirty now, Josie, just because I've hit the nail on the head,' Daisy said with a smile. 'Remember, I'm your Dutch uncle? What you're doing to Rhiannon is wrong. It's not fair on the child, and I'm sure you see that, knowing you.'

Josie nodded, looking down at her hands in her lap and sighing.

'Yes, I do.'

Daisy smiled.

'And it can't go on, can it? It's your duty, the duty you chose willingly, to go on caring for Rhiannon.'

Josie lifted both shoulders, spreading her hands helplessly.

479

'What can I do about it? I can't see Stanley calmly handing her over to me, just like that. especially now he's made up his mind to adopt her.'

Daisy sighed. 'He doesn't stand a chance, the way things are.'

Josie sighed. Daisy was trying to help, she knew that, but she was only going over things Josie already knew were true, deep in her heart. She knew her treatment of Rhiannon was shabby. She didn't need anyone to tell her that. There was a solution, she knew, but she couldn't accept it. It would be like condoning what Stanley had done.

'The next thing to talk about, Josie, is your baby,' Daisy went on. 'It's no picnic bringing up a child on your own. I know. You'll have to think carefully before you decide to deprive your child of its father. Stanley has rights, too, mind, and whatever he's done, he's still your child's father.'

Josie took a deep breath, outraged.

'Whose side are you on anyway?'

Daisy laughed.

'Yours, of course. I'm your best friend, aren't I?'

'I'm beginning to wonder,' Josie said gloomily, pulling a face.

'Are you going to divorce Stanley?'

Josie was startled by the blunt question, startled and suddenly uneasy. Divorce had not entered her mind. She was a bit shocked at Daisy's mentioning it.

'Divorce is rather drastic, isn't it?'

'So is leaving your husband,' her friend countered. 'Josie, you're young yet. How old are you? Twenty-six?' When she nodded, Daisy went on: 'Are you going to live without love for the rest of your life?'

Josie felt her unease grow. This was something else she hadn't thought about. She could only deal with the here and now: the heartache she still felt so bitterly, and the hurt. It would take a long time to get over that, if she ever did.

Daisy talked about switching off responsibility and duty, but you couldn't switch off love at will. It lingered on, and either survived or died. It was much too soon to know what would happen to her feelings for Stanley. At the moment her love for him was burning brightly, yes, as bright as it ever had, if the truth be told. How did she deal with that?

'Josie, be careful!' Daisy warned. 'Don't wreck your life for the sake of wounded pride.'

'Pride?' Josie stared at her friend. 'There's a bit more than that at stake here, Daisy,' she said forcefully. 'I've been wronged. I know that sounds old-fashioned but it's true. My love and trust were thrown back in my face. He hurt me, Daisy, badly!'

She reached forward to take Josie's hand, squeezing it encouragingly.

'I know he did, Josie love, but can't you be magnanimous, for your own sake as well as his?' Daisy wrinkled her nose, her tone cajoling. 'Can't you be a little forgiving? Not only to Stanley but yourself as well. Forgiveness is the reward of love, Josie. And you do still love Stan.'

Josie pulled her hand away.

'I don't think I can forgive or forget.'

She felt unreasonably annoyed. What was Daisy getting at, talking about pride when her heart was broken? It was true what people said. If you haven't been through a traumatic experience, you can't understand what it's like for someone else. Daisy had had a bad time of it with Gerald, Josie knew, but the man she really loved had been true to her. She hadn't had that kind of pain to deal with.

'Why do I need forgiveness, anyway? I haven't done anything wrong, Daisy.'

'Oh, Josie, of course not. I didn't mean that,' she said quickly. 'This separation is distressing for you. It's as though you're punishing yourself as well as Stanley and Rhiannon, and your own child, too. If you deny Stanley his child, sharing in its growing up, you're denying the child as well. Do you have the right to do that, Josie?'

She stood up abruptly, clasping her hands tightly together.

'I don't want to talk about it anymore, Daisy. I need more time to think, more time to get over what's happened. I'm still all mixed up.'

'All right, Josie love,' Daisy said. 'This is hard on you, I know. You've been very patient with me.'

Josie reached for her handbag and cardigan lying across the foot of the bed. Her head ached now, and she felt very tense; the muscles in her midriff were strung tight like piano strings. She needed time alone to think.

'I'm determined to get up tomorrow,' Daisy said lightly. 'Despite Mam saying I should stay in bed another ten days. I don't believe in this long lying-in after childbirth. Will you be in to see me again? I'll be staying at *Tŷ Heulwen* another month yet before going back to Merthyr.'

'Yes, of course I'll be calling again. You're my best friend. But no more Dutch uncle stuff, Daisy, please?'

'All right!'

Daisy caught her bottom lip between her teeth and, looking at her, Josie wondered what she was going to say next. It was something she wouldn't like, she was sure of it. Daisy was determined to get everything off her chest by the look of it. But all this frankness was making Josie feel uncomfortable and confused. Daisy was raking up things she didn't want to face, at least not yet.

'Josie, there's something else I have to say. Stanley's a good man despite this mistake ...'

'Mistake!' Josie's nostrils flared.

Why did everyone persist in calling Stanley's betrayal a mistake? First Teresa and now Daisy! Friend or no friend, she had no right to make little of it. Stanley was a good man, Josie didn't deny it. But she realised now that he was weaker than she in many ways. He'd always been pleasure-loving, she'd known that, though she'd noticed a change in him since he came home from the Forces. He was more serious than he used to be. No one could live through a war and not be changed. For all that, he couldn't be excused for what she still saw as treachery.

'Yes, mistake!' Daisy went on forcefully. 'Stanley is not a womaniser, Josie. You know that deep in your heart, don't you? And he *is* a good man. He doesn't beat you like your father beat your mother ...'

'Daisy, don't bring that up!'

She lifted her hands in apology.

'I'm only trying to make you see what you've got in him. He's been a good husband to you over these last years, and a good father to Rhiannon. You can't deny it, Josie.'

She bit her lip, saying nothing.

'He knows he's done wrong by you, as you put it. Do you think he isn't suffering now as you are?'

Josie shrugged into her cardigan, still silent. If he was suffering, he'd brought it on himself, hadn't he? She recalled the strained look on his face the day she'd bumped into him. Was he suffering because of her or was he just worried about Rhiannon?

'His adopting Rhiannon,' Daisy said, as though reading her thoughts, 'depends entirely on you, Josie. You know that, don't you? You're in a position of great power now—I know that sounds awfully cynical but it's true. He needs you desperately. You could go back to him on your own terms.'

'Go back!' Josie stared, pushing her handbag under one arm, ready to leave. 'There's not much chance of that.'

'Well, think about it,' Daisy persisted, straightening the counterpane unnecessarily. 'Think carefully, because your future, Stanley's future, Rhiannon's future and the future of your own baby, are in your hands alone.' She shook her head. 'That's an awful responsibility, Josie.'

'Daisy, you're getting me all confused ...'

Her friend sighed. 'I'm sorry. I know you'll do the right thing, Josie, because, most important of all, you still love Stanley. Can you really consider living without him for the rest of your life?'

The late afternoon was so sparkling clear that from the top of Newton Road, Josie could see right across the sweep of Swansea Bay to the far side, and the town of Port Talbot. She could see some of the town's industrial structures clearly. She wished she could view her future as clearly; see what she ought to do.

Daisy had brought up many problems she hadn't wanted to face yet, or hadn't even considered. She was concerned for Rhiannon. The thought that Francie might get hold of the child, influence her, yes, even corrupt her, made her blood boil. She still got angry whenever she thought of her sister. That had been quite frequently until she'd learned of her own pregnancy.

Josie reached the chemist's shop on the corner, a third of the way down the road, and paused, undecided. She could carry on down Newton Road to her shop, now closed for half-day, and spend the rest of the day in her lonely room, or she could take this short cut to Woodville Road. To do what?

She didn't quite know, but found her feet were leading her towards Woodville Road, seemingly of their own volition. Daisy's candid advice had unsettled her, making her question all that she had done since learning the truth. Was it really her own dented pride that was giving her so much pain? If so, it wasn't fair that Rhiannon should suffer. There was a lot left unsaid between Stanley and herself. Perhaps now was the time to sort it out?

Josie clutched her handbag tighter under her arm. What happened next was entirely up to her, as Daisy had pointed out. She was determined to be strong and in control, despite her feelings for Stanley.

Her legs felt shaky as she stood outside what used to be her own front door, and she was breathing hard, as though she'd been hurrying. She had to wait only a minute or two before her knock was answered.

Stanley stood there staring at her, his face going chalky white.

'Josie!' He seemed astounded to see her. 'You're the last person I expected to see.'

He continued to stand on the doorstep, staring.

'Well, aren't you going to ask me in, Stan?'

'Oh! *Duw! Duw!*' He jumped aside to allow her to pass. 'What's the matter with me? Come in, come in.'

Josie carefully moved past him and walked

down the passage to the living-room. The house seemed very quiet. She hadn't known what shift Stanley was working, and so hadn't been sure anyone would be home. She was glad she'd caught him because she doubted whether she'd have had the courage to call again.

'Where's Rhiannon and Gwennie?'

'They've gone down the beach for an hour or two, to take Rhiannon's mind off ...' He paused uncertainly then went on: 'Mam was on early turn today.'

Josie gave the room a quick all-round glance. The mats obviously hadn't been lifted for a week or two if not more, and there wasn't much shine on the linoleum. A glimpse into the kitchenette showed dirty dishes piled in the sink. How quickly everything went to pot if no one cared.

She ran a finger along the top of the sideboard, more of a reflex action then anything else. As she looked at the dust and fluff on the finger of her pink cotton glove, Stanley gave a little cough.

'Mam doesn't get a lot of time to do much housework, Josie, what with her job and looking after Rhiannon.'

'Oh, really? But then, housework was never one of her strong points, as I recall,' she said, brows raised defiantly.

Now she was being catty, and knew it. But she didn't care. There were a lot of feelings she had to get out of her system, and resentment against her mother-in-law, whom she had always trusted implicitly, was one of them.

With a hesitant half-smile, Stanley quickly

moved some newspapers off the sofa.

'Sit down a minute, love ... I mean, Josie. Would you like a cup of tea?'

She sat of the very edge of the sofa, feeling awkward and out of place. It was ironic, wasn't it, being asked to sit down like a visitor in one's own home? Then a little voice in her head, which sounded remarkably like Daisy's reminded her that it was *not* her home any longer, by her own choosing. She was a visitor and should act like one.

'No, thank you, Stanley. I shan't be here that long.'

'Oh!' He sounded disappointed but sat down in an armchair opposite her. He still wore his working trousers; had obviously been on the early shift today. His hair was tousled as though she'd roused him from a doze in the chair. He looked tired. Perhaps he wasn't sleeping well alone at night. She sympathised with that. You missed the comforting warmth of someone else in the bed beside you; the reassurance you were not alone in the world.

'Why have you called then, Josie?' he asked, leaning forward with his elbows on his knees and his hands clasped tightly together.

She wetted her lips, not really knowing how to start. She didn't want him to think she was weakening and giving in. She was in control now and intended to make sure she stayed that way. Whatever happened in the future, she'd make sure it was what she wanted. She'd been too accommodating in the past, too trusting. She had so much love to give, and had let it blind

488

her to weakness in Stanley and deviousness in others. But no more!

He looked at her closely, waiting for her to speak. When she continued to hesitate, he asked: 'Is it about Rhiannon?'

'Yes,' she answered almost eagerly, glad of the opening he'd given her. 'It isn't true that I don't want to see her. In fact ...' Josie hesitated for just a second. 'I think it best if she comes to live with me. I am her aunt, after all.'

'And I'm her father, damn it!' he said. 'Listen, Josie. You can forget that as quick as you like.' He prodded his chest with one finger. 'Nobody brings up *my* kid but me.'

Josie tossed her head, annoyed and somewhat surprised at the sudden gleam in his eye and his sharp tone. She'd expected him to be repentant and eager to please her.

'Well, I wouldn't count on that, Stan. Legally, I don't think your position is very good.'

'Do you think I don't know that! It's going round and round in my head, morning, noon and night. But I'm not letting Francie have her. I know she's your sister and all, Josie, but she's no bloody good.'

'She's no sister of mine,' Josie said darkly.

'I'm glad you feel like that, because my idea is that we fight this together, as a couple. I know I'm on shaky ground as I'm only Rhiannon's natural father. Although Reuben is next-of-kin, after her mother, you are the one Rhiannon loves the most. If we can get the courts to declare Francie unfit, they might well appoint you Rhiannon's guardian or something.'

'This is all speculation, Stan. And it sounds expensive, too.'

'I know that, mun.' He ran his fingers through his hair. 'But we might manage it if we were together, pooling resources.'

Josie was nettled. He was going too far.

'You mean, you want me to pay for your little bit of fun?'

Stanley frowned at her, face clouded darkly. His expression was one of exasperation, as though she were being petty and childish. 'We're talking about *my* daughter here, Josie, and your niece,' he said. 'Look! When Mam wrote to me to say I was the father of Francie's child, I was scared stiff that it would separate us. As time went by I realised you had no inkling of the truth and I got used to the idea of being a father. When I came home and saw how beautiful my daughter is, I was so proud of her. It was breaking my heart that I couldn't tell her I was her dad.'

Josie tightened her mouth.

'You could have told *me* when you came home.'

'No, I couldn't Josie. And it wouldn't have done any good. You'd have left me anyway. We were happy together, weren't we? I wanted it all, you and Rhiannon.'

She flashed him an angry glance.

'You sound as though you're glad it happened. And you expect me to help you! You've got a damned cheek, Stanley.'

'Oh, God, Josie! You're not going to let your

stupid jealousy ruin Rhiannon's life, are you, for pity's sake?'

'Jealousy!' she exploded, jumping to her feet.

But she sat down again immediately. She was going to have it out with him now. Something had been on her mind for months, keeping her awake at night; something Francie had said.

'If I am jealous, Stanley Jenkins, you've given me cause to be. Listen! When Francie told me she was pregnant, she also said that the father of her child was married but he'd told her he loved *her* and was going to leave his wife after the war.' Josie lifted her chin and looked down her nose at him. 'Now, Stanley! What have you got to say about that? Do you deny telling Francie you loved her?'

'Of course I deny it, woman!' he stormed. 'It's all lies! How can you believe anything Francie says, knowing what a devious little bitch she is? And if you'd let me explain at the beginning what happened, we wouldn't be arguing now.' He grimaced mockingly. 'But, no, not you. You've got everything off pat. You know it all.'

'I *know* what happened, Stan,' she cried, panicking that she was losing control after all. He wasn't supposed to react like this. According to Daisy, he was supposed to be putty in her hands.

'Rhiannon's proof of what happened,' she went on lamely. 'I'm a big girl now. I don't need it explained to me how my husband deceived me so spare me the details.'

'Shut up, Josie!' Stanley roared. 'Shut up, for

God's sake!' He brought his fist down on the table top with a crash, making the fancy glass bowl at the centre wobble alarmingly.

Josie nearly jumped out of her skin at the violence of the gesture. She stared at him open-mouthed. For a fleeting moment she was reminded of her father. But she wouldn't be like Mama, taking it all helplessly. She would fight back—when she got over her surprise.

'Why don't you try listening for a change!' Stanley shouted again, eyes flashing and face turning red with anger. 'You're always mouthing off, threatening this and that, throwing your weight about when anyone annoys you. Just like your bloody father. You're so clever, Josie, with your own business and all, but you don't know everything.' His lip curled. 'You *think* you do, but you don't.'

She stood up, furious, mouth pinched, nose in the air in righteous indignation.

'I don't have to listen to this in my own home.'

'Sit down, woman!' He pointed at the chair. 'I said, sit.'

Confused, Josie flopped back on to the chair, staring at him. This wasn't going right at all. Stanley had never spoken to her like that before. And she didn't like it. Not one bit!

'Now, for starters,' he said through gritted teeth, 'this is my home, not yours. I pay the rent, and my name is on the rent book. Yes, that's right, Josie. *I'm* the tenant now.'

'You ... you had no right ...' She felt out of her depth, and was beginning to wish she'd never come to see him.

'I have every right, Josie. You pushed off, remember, and left me flat.' He shook his head, looking gravely at her. 'Poor little Rhiannon. Near broke her heart, poor kid.'

Josie felt a pang of remorse, not the first to strike her heart. She bitterly regretted abandoning her niece, but she was here to put that right, wasn't she?

She opened her mouth to speak, but Stanley forestalled her.

'Keep quiet! I'm doing the talking now, Josie. Next point is, I don't like people thinking me a liar, especially my wife.'

Josie tossed her head. 'I don't know what you mean.'

'I could see it in your eyes the day Francie told you the truth, and again the other Saturday when we bumped into each other. You've got it into that stubborn noddle of yours that I was up to no good all along. And you're thinking maybe there were others at home, too. Well, you're wrong, Josie, dead wrong. I was never unfaithful to you, except on one occasion, and then I was ... tricked.'

Josie tossed her head haughtily.

'Oh, come off it, Stanley! I wasn't born yesterday, mind.'

He pointed a finger at her, his mouth a hard line.

'Now, you're going to keep quiet and listen to me for once. I'm going to explain how it happened. All right, I'll tell you what. When I've explained, I'll leave it to you to judge me.'

He got up from the table suddenly.

'Do you want a cup of tea, Josie?'

'No, I don't!' she flashed at him. 'I want to get this charade over and done with. How do you think I feel, sitting here listening to this?'

Stanley sat down again, reluctantly.

'All right. Do you remember that leave I had in May 1943, just before I went to North Africa?'

Josie nodded. Looking back now she felt that week was the last time she had been really happy until Stanley was demobbed. They were so in love then, and she was so sure of him.

'Yes, of course I remember, Stan,' she said gently. She would never forget that time as long as she lived.

'On the Friday of that week, after you'd gone to work, Francie came round to see you.' He bowed his head and seemed to have difficulty swallowing for a moment. Recovering, he went on: 'Reuben had been knocking your mother about, she said. And he'd had a go at her, too. She had a nasty weal across her face. She was crying and very upset, shaking like a leaf. I wanted to make her a cup of tea, but she said she was too upset to drink it.'

He looked up at Josie. She could see his eyes were glistening now.

'She looked so pitiful, and I was thinking, that could have been you, kid. She said she had no one to turn to. Her sister had a husband, she said, but she had nobody, nobody at all. Oh, Josie, I felt so sorry for her. I put my arms around her, just to give her a bit of a hug, like

494

a brother would, not meaning anything more. Next minute she was clinging to me; frantic she was, kissing me, begging me to love her. I ... I was confused. I got mixed up ... between her and you ... and the next thing ...'

He buried his face in his hands. Josie could only stare at him in silence. She felt numb all over, as on the day Francie had revealed the truth. Numb and disbelieving. Did he really think a few words of explanation would put everything right; that they would kiss and make up?

'I'm so sorry, Josie love,' he said at last. 'If only I could go back in time, have a second chance to live that day all over again, change everything ... but I can't.' He looked up. 'And I wouldn't be without Rhiannon now for the world. So it wasn't all bad, was it?'

But Josie found she couldn't meet his eye. If he were lying she'd know it in a minute, and she didn't want to know, didn't want to be certain.

'Afterwards,' he went on, in a low voice that trembled on every breath, 'I was so ashamed, remorseful ...' He paused, the tone of his voice changing to become louder and a shade cooler.

'But sorry isn't enough, is it, kid?' he said. 'I can see that in your face now, the way you're avoiding looking at me. You've still got doubts.'

Josie looked down at her hands in her lap, gulping back tears, unable to reply. After a brief and embarrassing silence, he said, with unmistakable bitterness in his voice: 'Afterwards Francie acted like, well, like I'd made some commitment to her. Started to talk wild. I felt so wretched at what I'd done to you, Josie, I couldn't bear to listen to her. I told her to go, push off. Perhaps I was too harsh. She turned nasty; said she'd tell you I'd raped her. I was frightened then, I can tell you. I told her if she'd keep quiet, I'd give her money when I got hold of some. Played right into her hands, didn't I? She calmed down then and left, and I thought that was the end of it. Bloody hell! Was I wrong!'

Josie remained still, unable to speak. Stanley got up from his chair after a while and went out into the kitchenette. Josie heard him filling the kettle with water, striking a match, and the small soft explosion of the gas burner igniting. Then it was very quiet, with just the clock on the mantelpiece ticking away their lives.

It would be just like Francie to take advantage that way, Josie thought. Mama always said she was jealous of me; jealous because I had Stanley. Was his explanation plausible? She didn't know. She couldn't view it objectively. The question was, should she give him the benefit of the doubt? And would it make any difference to them if she did? Their relationship had changed, she realised, changed for ever, no matter what the truth was. Her husband had slept with her sister, and nothing could ever be the same again.

Not unless they started a new relationship from scratch, a little voice in her head told her. A relationship based on what? she asked the voice, but here was no answer. She didn't even know whether either of them was capable of sustaining it. Any relationship depended on trust, and trust was something that had to develop in its own time. Would her heart ever trust him again?

But there was Rhiannon to think of, her conscience reminded her. To make amends there, she must help Stanley keep her with him. Letting Rhiannon go to Francie, especially to a household run by the likes of Billy Parsons, didn't bear thinking about.

She couldn't forgive Stanley or forget, not yet anyway, perhaps never, but she must compromise, meet him halfway, for the sake of her own child. He didn't know he was to be a father again.

Josie rose and went into the kitchenette. Stanley was arranging cups and saucers on a tray, with a small plate of biscuits. She tried not to see the dirty dishes piled on the draining board, though her hands itched to get at them.

'I'll help you, Stan.'

'It's all right. I can manage, kid.'

'No I mean, help you keep Rhiannon.'

He almost dropped the tray, but saved it in time.

'You mean, you'll move back here?' His eyes were shining and his hands shook as they held the tray.

Josie looked away. She had to put him straight as to her terms.

'Yes, but not as your wife. It'll be separate bedrooms, Stan, or nothing. Your mother must move up to the other house. There's plenty of room there for her.'

'Oh, kid! Don't you believe me?' It was a cry of despair.

He looked crestfallen and his shoulders drooped. 'After all the years we've known each other, been together, if you don't know me by now, you never will.'

Josie bit her lip, struggling not to be moved by his distress.

'That's just it, Stan, isn't it? I only *thought* I knew you. Maybe you don't even know yourself. When you were away in the war you never doubted me, did you? But I had chances, Stan, lots of them.' She shook her head. 'I was lonely, you don't know how lonely, but I would never, never be unfaithful to you, because I love ... loved you so deeply, so completely.'

She wouldn't let love or sympathy blind her like that again. She'd be a sentimental fool, wouldn't she, if she did? Stanley might really be as remorseful as he said he was, but it was he who had spoiled their lives. She would have to be a saint to forgive and forget just like that, and Josie was no saint.

'Anyway,' she said briskly, fighting back tears, 'that's neither here nor there now, is it?' She straightened her spine in an effort to stand proud and strong and not give way to the pity for him that was stealing through her heart in spite of her resolve. 'We've got to go forward from this moment. Try to make a life as best we can under the circumstances. Things will never be the way they were. That's impossible. You'll have to face that.'

Stanley put the tray on top of the cooker, then leaned on it with both hands. Josie regarded his bent head, again feeling sympathy and love in her heart, but quelling them mercilessly.

'There is one thing, though, Stan, that you might be glad to know. You're going to be a father again.'

He turned his head slowly to look at her, an expression of astonishment wiping the distress from his face and making his eyes gleam.

'Oh, Josie love! Oh, *Duw!* That's wonderful news. I can't believe it, mun. Wait until Mam hears this. Our own baby. Hey! Maybe it'll be a boy. A son!'

He moved quickly, as though to embrace her, but Josie turned away. She didn't know whether she could bear his touch or what her reaction would be. Loneliness had been unbearable of late. She didn't want to make any silly mistakes, not this time.

'Josie!' His tone was urgent. 'I love you. I do, kid, and you know I do. I miss you so much. I'm so lonely, I long for you. Please don't punish me anymore. Please! I'm breaking my heart over us. I can't get over it. I'll never get over it.'

She turned sad eyes on him. 'How do you think I feel, Stan?'

'Give me another chance, kid, especially now you're going to have our baby.' He took a few steps towards her but Josie turned aside again, afraid of her own feelings.

'I'll make it up to you, I promise,' Stanley went on eagerly. 'I'll work hard, day and night, if you like, just so long as we can be a family again.'

More composed, she turned to face him.

'Not yet, Stan. It's too much to ask now. I don't know if I can. It's too soon after ... I don't know what the future holds for us.'

'All right, love, I understand,' he said quickly, but his eyes were shining. 'Oh, kid, I'm over the moon about this new baby. It'll heal us, I know it will.'

Maybe it would. She was glad that he was so thrilled anyway. Now he knew, she could tell everyone else, enjoy their congratulations and the prospect of being a mother.

'Can I kiss you, Josie?'

She swallowed hard.

'On the cheek, perhaps.'

His kiss on her cheek lingered. It was electrifying, and she felt her heart beat faster. She stepped away quickly into the living-room.

'I must go now, Stan.'

'Oh, must you? What about your tea, love?'

'I'll move in next Monday. Is that all right with you?'

'That's fine by me.' His voice was gruff, as though roughened by tears.

She kept her eyes averted.

'Remember, Stan, the baby makes no difference,' she said quickly. 'We're not back together, not like before.' She pushed her handbag under her arm. 'I'll find my own way out. Have your tea. And ... get those dishes washed!'

Chapter Thirty-Two

Josie flopped into the armchair in front of the empty fireplace, and again picked up the sock she was darning.

Stanley looked up from marking his pools coupon.

'What was it this time?'

'She said there was a bear under the bed.'

'Ah, love her! She's only making sure you're still here, Josie.'

'I know.' Josie kept her head bent over her darning.

Rhiannon had been wound up all day, running around the place like a clockwork toy, getting under Josie's feet as she'd moved her few things back in and given the house a thorough clean.

She'd thought she'd never get the child to bed. Three times she'd been out on the landing already, calling Josie on one excuse or another. It was only natural. It would be some time before she would get her confidence back.

Josie knew how she felt. She could hardly use the needle properly this evening, her hands were so shaky. It was really silly, feeling nervous and awkward just because she was alone here with Stanley on her first night back.

'Ouch!' Josie let out a yell as the needle stuck into her finger, drawing blood.

Stanley was on his feet in a flash, bending

over her solicitously. 'What's wrong, love? Oh, here! Let me have a look at it.'

Josie pulled her wounded finger away from his grasp.

'It's nothing, Stan. Go and sit down.'

She felt really stupid at the fuss he was making. She'd had the freedom of the house all day, and it had felt good. Since Stanley had come home from work, she could hardly move without his wanting to know if she was all right or if he could do anything for her. It would have been comical if it wasn't so embarrassing.

He sat down again opposite her but seemed to have lost interest in his football coupon. They sat in silence as Josie continued with her darning, though she felt his eyes on her all the time. At last he said: 'I can hardly believe you're here with me, kid.'

His voice sounded husky, full of emotion, and Josie didn't want him to say anymore.

'Switch on the wireless, Stan,' she said lightly, though her heart was pounding. '*ITMA* will be on in a minute. We don't want to miss that, do we?'

Stanley flashed her a grin as he got up to switch on the set.

'Like old times, kid.'

'*It's That Man Again!*' the announcer yelled at them through the loud-speaker.

Josie settled back to listen to the comedy half-hour. She chuckled at Mrs Mop, and the Diver, and when that familiar and comically sinister voice said: "This is Funf speaking", Josie couldn't help letting out a peal of laughter, forgetting everything for the moment, thinking Tommy Handley had never been funnier.

'It's good to hear you laugh again, Josie,' Stanley said. 'This house was a grave without you. Welcome home, my lovely girl.'

'Thank you.' Josie smiled, swallowing down a lump in her throat. 'It does feel good to be back.' She hesitated for a brief moment. 'I've been lonely, too, Stan.'

'Oh, Josie love!'

She swallowed hard again, and trying to regain her composure and appear unmoved, tossed her hair back carelessly.

'Make some tea, Stan, will you, please?'

'Anything for you, kid.'

He stood up, striding towards the kitchenette.

'Oh, and Stan?'

'Yes, love?'

Josie turned in her chair to look at him, smiling.

'Thank you so much for my baby.'

'Our baby, love.'

'Yes, Stan. Our baby.'

She held her breath for a moment, her heart beating fast as they looked at each other, looked right into each other's eyes, frankly, openly. The tears, the pain, the hurt, seemed to slip away. Josie felt as though years had slipped away, too.

It was remarkable how strong true love really was, she reflected. It clung on even when there was little hope. She knew then nothing could kill her deep feelings for Stanley. She'd go on loving him always, in spite of everything in the past.

Perhaps their troubles were behind them now? A new baby. A new start. They could make it happen.

'Come on, Stan!' she pretended to scold, her voice more than a little breathless at the depth of her feelings. 'Where's that tea, then? I'm parched.'

'It's coming up on the lift, love!' he said cheerfully, and marched into the kitchenette, whistling the catchy tune Billy Cotton's band was playing on the wireless.

Josie found herself humming along, too, and was startled. Anyone might think she was happy at this moment! Well, happier than she'd been for months. She was back in her own home with her family.

She thought about Gwennie. She'd be thrilled about the baby. Tomorrow, Josie decided, she'd call in before her mother-in-law went to work. She'd give Gwennie the glad news, and make up with her. She wanted them to be friends again. It was only right. After all, Gwennie hadn't done anything except try to protect her son and granddaughter. Josie really couldn't blame her for that, and she was fond of her really. She was a good old stick, and loyalty was hard to come by.

Josie thought of Francie then, disloyal and treacherous, and gritted her teeth. She would *never* forgive her, and Francie would never be part of Josie's family again. There'd never been real sisterly love between them, and now they were bitter enemies; their only link Rhiannon.

Stanley was determined to keep her, and so

was Josie. She'd fight Francie tooth and nail in the highest courts in the land, if need be. She had the money to do it now, and her heart was still fired up with a lust for revenge. Rhiannon was hers and Stanley's. They'd never part with her. Never. They both loved her too much.

Would she forgive him one day? Josie listened to the voice in her heart that told her she would, because their mutual love for Rhiannon and their own child would heal all wounds.

She leaned back in the chair, thinking of Daisy's words: 'Forgiveness is the reward of love.' She was a good friend and wiser than she knew.

Forgiveness is the reward of love. Josie smiled to herself. How true that was.

This Large Print Book for the Partially sighted, who cannot read normal print, is published under the auspices of

THE ULVERSCROFT FOUNDATION

Other MAGNA General Fiction Titles In Large Print

FRANCES ANNE BOND
Return Of The Swallow

JUDY GARDINER
All On A Summer's Day

IRIS GOWER
The Sins Of Eden

HELENE MANSFIELD
Some Women Dream

ELISABETH McNEILL
The Shanghai Emerald

ELIZABETH MURPHY
To Give And To Take

JUDITH SAXTON
This Royal Breed